WINTER GARDEN

Kristin Hannah is an award-winning international number one bestseller with over 15 million copies of her books sold worldwide. The blockbusters *The Nightingale* and *The Great Alone* were named Goodreads Best Historical Novel for 2015 and 2018. Shortly to be made into a major movie, *The Nightingale* won the coveted People's Choice Award for Best Fiction and *Firefly Lane* was screened on Netflix in 2021. Kristin is a lawyer-turned-writer and is the mother of one son. She and her husband live in the Pacific Northwest near Seattle.

Also by Kristin Hannah

The Four Winds

The Great Alone

Fly Away

Home Front

Night Road

Winter Garden

True Colors

Firefly Lane

Magic Hour

Comfort & Joy

The Things We Do for Love

Between Sisters

Distant Shores

Summer Island

Angel Falls

On Mystic Lake

Home Again

Waiting for the Moon

When Lightning Strikes

If You Believe

Once in Every Life

The Enchantment

A Handful of Heaven

WINTER GARDEN

Kristin Hannah

PAN BOOKS

First published 2010 by St Martin's Press, New York

First published in the UK 2014 by Macmillan

This edition first published 2022 by Pan Books
an imprint of Pan Macmillan
The Smithson, 6 Briset Street, London EC1M 5NR
EU representative: Macmillan Publishers Ireland Ltd, 1st Floor,
The Liffey Trust Centre, 117–126 Sheriff Street Upper,
Dublin 1, D01 YC43
Associated companies throughout the world
www.panmacmillan.com

ISBN 978-1-5290-8957-8

1 3 5 7 9 8 6 4 2

A CIP catalogue record for this book is available from the British Library.

Typeset by Palimpsest Book Production Ltd, Falkirk, Stirlingshire
Printed and bound by CPI Group (UK) Ltd, Croydon, CR0 4YY

To my husband, Benjamin, as always;

to my mother—I wish I had listened to more of your life stories when I had the chance;

to my dad and Debbie—thanks for the trip of a lifetime and memories that will last even longer; and

to my beloved Tucker—I am so proud of you.
Your adventure is just beginning.

Not, not mine: it's somebody else's wound.
I could never have borne it. So take the thing
that happened, hide it, stick it in the ground.
Whisk the lamps away . . .
Night.

—Anna Akhmatova, from *Poems of Akhmatova*,
translated by Stanley Kunitz, with Max Hayward

Prologue

1972

On the banks of the mighty Columbia River, in this icy season when every breath became visible, the orchard called Belye Nochi was quiet. Dormant apple trees stretched as far as the eye could see, their sturdy roots coiled deep in the cold, fertile soil. As temperatures plummeted and color drained from land and sky, the whitened landscape caused a kind of winter blindness; one day became indistinguishable from the next. Everything froze, turned fragile.

Nowhere was the quiet more noticeable than in Meredith Whitson's own house. At twelve, she had already discovered the empty spaces that gathered between people. She longed for her family to be like those she saw on television, where everything looked perfect and everyone got along. No one, not even her beloved father, understood how alone she often felt within these four walls, how invisible.

But tomorrow night, all of that would change.

She had come up with a brilliant plan. She had written a play based on one of her mother's fairy tales, and she would present it at the annual Christmas party. It was exactly the kind of thing that would happen on an episode of *The Partridge Family.*

"How come I can't be the star?" Nina whined. It was at least the tenth time she'd asked this question since Meredith had finished the script.

Meredith turned around in her chair and looked down at her nine-year-old sister, who was crouched on the wooden floor of their bedroom, painting a mint-green castle on an old bedsheet.

Meredith bit her lower lip, trying not to frown. The castle was too messy; not right at all. "Do we have to talk about this again, Nina?"

"But *why* can't I be the peasant girl who marries the prince?"

"You know why. Jeff is playing the prince and he's thirteen. You'd look silly next to him."

Nina put her paintbrush in the empty soup can and sat back on her heels. With her short black hair, bright green eyes, and pale skin, she looked like a perfect little pixie. "Can I be the peasant girl next year?"

"You bet." Meredith grinned. She loved the idea that she might be creating a family tradition. All of her friends had traditions, but not the Whitsons; they had always been different. There was no stream of relatives who came to their house on holidays, no turkey on Thanksgiving or ham on Easter, no prayers that were always said. Heck, they didn't even know for sure how old their mom was.

It was because Mom was Russian, and alone in this country. Or at least that was what Dad said. Mom didn't say much of anything about herself.

A knock at the door surprised Meredith. She looked up just as Jeff Cooper and her father came into the room.

Meredith felt like one of those long, floppy balloons being slowly filled with air, taking on a new form with each breath, and in this case the breath was Jeffrey Cooper. They'd been best friends since fourth grade, but lately it felt different to be around him. Exciting. Sometimes, when he looked at her, she could barely breathe. "You're right on time for rehearsal."

He gave her one of his heart-stopping smiles. "Just don't tell Joey and the guys. They'd give me a ton of crap for this."

"About rehearsal," her dad said, stepping forward. He was still in his work clothes, a brown leisure suit with orange topstitching. Surprisingly, there was no smile lurking beneath his bushy black mustache or in his eyes. He held out the script. "This is the play you're doing?"

Meredith rose from the chair. "Do you think she'll like it?"

Nina stood up. Her heart-shaped face was uncharacteristically solemn. "Will she?"

The three of them looked at one another over the expanse of the Picasso-style green castle and the costumes laid out across the bed. The truth they passed among themselves, in looks alone, was that Anya Whitson was a cold woman; any warmth she had was directed at her husband. Precious little of it reached her daughters. When they were younger, Dad had tried to pretend it was otherwise, to redirect their attention like a magician, mesmerizing them with the brightness of his affection, but as with all illusions, the truth ultimately appeared behind it.

So they all knew what Meredith was asking.

"I don't know, Meredoodle," Dad said, reaching into his pocket for his cigarettes. "Your mother's stories—"

"I love it when she tells them," Meredith said.

"It's the only time she really talks to us," Nina added.

Dad lit a cigarette and stared at them through a swirl of gray smoke, his brown eyes narrowed. "Yeah," he said, exhaling. "It's just . . ."

Meredith moved toward him, careful not to step on the painting. She understood his hesitation; none of them ever really knew what would set Mom off, but this time Meredith was sure she had the answer. If there was one thing her mother loved, it was this fairy tale about a reckless peasant girl who dared to fall in love with a prince. "It only takes ten minutes, Dad. I timed it. Everyone will love it."

"Okay, then," he said finally.

She felt a swell of pride and hope. For once she wouldn't spend the party in some shadowy corner of the living room reading, or in the kitchen washing dishes. Instead, she would be the center of her mother's attention. This play would prove that Meredith had listened to every precious word Mom had ever said, even those few that were spoken softly, in the dark, at story time.

For the next hour, Meredith directed her actors through the play, although really only Jeff needed help. She and Nina had heard this fairy tale for years.

Later, when the rehearsal was over and everyone had gone their separate ways, Meredith kept working. She made a sign that read ONE NIGHT ONLY: A GRAND PLAY FOR THE HOLIDAY and listed their three names. She touched up the painted backdrop (it was impossible to fix entirely; Nina always colored outside of the lines), and then positioned it in the living room. When the set was ready, she added sequins to the tulle ballet-skirt-turned-princess-gown that she would wear at the end. It was nearly two in the morning by the time she went to bed, and even then she was so excited that it took a long time for her to fall asleep.

The next day seemed to pass slowly, but finally, at six o'clock, the guests began to arrive. It was not a big crowd, just the usual people: men and women who worked for the orchard and their families, a few neighbors, and Dad's only living relative, his sister, Dora.

Meredith sat at the top of the stairs, staring down at the entryway below. She couldn't help tapping her foot on the step, wondering when she could make her move.

Just as she was about to stand up, she heard a clanging, rattling sound.

Oh, no. She shot to her feet and rushed down the stairs, but it was too late.

Nina was in the kitchen, banging a pot with a metal spoon and yelling out, "Showtime!" No one knew how to steal the limelight like Nina.

There was a smattering of laughter as the guests made their way from the kitchen to the living room, where the painting of the castle hung from an aluminum movie screen set up beside the massive fireplace. To the right was a large Christmas tree, decorated with drugstore lights and ornaments Nina and Meredith had made over the years. In front of the painting was their "stage": a small wooden bridge that rested on the hardwood floor and a streetlamp made from cardboard, with a flashlight duct-taped to the top.

Meredith dimmed the lights in the room, turned on the flashlight, and then ducked behind the painted backdrop. Nina and Jeff were already there, in their costumes.

There was only a little privacy back here. If she leaned sideways, she could see several of the guests, and they could see her, but still it felt separate. When the room quieted, Meredith took a deep breath and began the narration she'd composed so painstakingly: "Her name is Vera, and she is a poor peasant girl, a nobody. She lives in a magical realm called the Snow Kingdom, but her beloved world is dying. An evil has come to this land; it rolls across the cobblestone streets in black carriages sent by a dark, evil knight who wants to destroy it all."

Meredith made her entrance, taking care not to trip over her long, layered skirts as she took the stage. She looked out over the guests and saw her mother in the back of the room, alone somehow even in this crowd, her beautiful face blurred by cigarette smoke. For once, she was looking directly at Meredith.

"Come, sister," Meredith said loudly, moving toward the streetlamp. "We shall not let this cold stop us."

Nina stepped out from behind the curtain. Dressed in a ratty nightgown with a kerchief covering her hair, she wrung her hands together and looked up at Meredith. "Do you think it is the Black Knight?" she yelled, drawing a laugh from the crowd. "Is his bad magic making it so cold?"

"No. No. I am chilled at the loss of our father. When will he return?" Meredith pressed the back of her hand to her forehead and sighed dramatically. "The carriages are everywhere these days. The Black Knight is gaining power . . . people are turning to smoke before our eyes. . . ."

"Look," Nina said, pointing toward the painted castle. "It is the prince. . . ." She managed to sound reverent.

Jeff moved into place on their little stage. In his blue sport coat and jeans, with a cheap gold crown on his wheat-blond hair, he looked so handsome that for a moment Meredith couldn't remember her lines. She knew he was embarrassed and uncomfortable—the red in his cheeks made that obvious—but still he was here, proving what a good friend he was. And he was smiling at her as if she really were a princess.

He held out a pair of silk roses. "I have two roses for you," he said to Meredith, his voice cracking.

She touched his hand, but before she could say her line there was a loud crash.

Meredith turned, saw her mother standing in the center of the crowd, motionless, her face pale, her blue eyes blazing. Blood dripped from her hand. She'd broken her cocktail glass, and even from here Meredith could see a shard sticking out of her mother's palm.

"Enough," her mother said sharply. "This is hardly entertainment for a party."

The guests didn't know what to do; some stood up, others remained seated. The room went quiet.

Dad made his way to Mom. He put his arm around her and pulled her close. Or he tried to; she wouldn't bend, not even for him.

"I never should have told you those ridiculous fairy tales," Mom said, her Russian accent sharp with anger. "I forgot how romantic and empty-headed girls can be."

Meredith was so humiliated she couldn't move.

She saw her father guide her mother into the kitchen, where he probably took her straight to the sink and began cleaning up her hand. The guests left as if this were the *Titanic* and they were rushing for lifeboats stationed just beyond the front door.

Only Jeff looked at Meredith, and she could see how embarrassed he was for her. He started toward her, still holding the two roses. "Meredith—"

She pushed past him and ran out of the room. At the end of the hall, in a shadowy corner, she skidded to a stop and stood there, breathing hard, her eyes burning with tears. She could hear her dad's voice coming from the kitchen; he was trying to soothe his angry wife. A minute later a door clicked shut, and she knew that Jeff had gone home.

"What did you do?" Nina asked quietly, coming up beside her.

"Who knows?" Meredith said, wiping her eyes. "She's such a bitch."

"That's a bad word."

Meredith heard the trembling in Nina's voice and knew how hard her sister was trying not to cry. She reached down and held her hand.

"What do we do? Should we say we're sorry?"

Meredith couldn't help thinking about the last time she'd made her mother mad and told her she was sorry. "She won't care. Trust me."

"So what do we do?"

Meredith tried to feel as mature as she had this morning, but her confidence was gone. She knew what would happen: Dad would calm Mom down and then he'd come up to their room and make them laugh and hold them in his big, strong arms and tell them that Mom really loved them. By the time he was done with the jokes and the stories, Meredith would want desperately to believe it. Again. "I know what I'm going to do," she said, moving through the entryway toward the kitchen, until she could see Mom's side—just her slim black velvet dress and her pale arm, and her white, white hair. "I'm never going to listen to one of her stupid fairy tales again."

We don't know how to say goodbye:
we wander on, shoulder to shoulder.
Already the sun is going down;
you're moody. I am your shadow.

—Anna Akhmatova, from *Poems of Akhmatova*,
translated by Stanley Kunitz, with Max Hayward

One

2000

Was this what forty looked like? Really? In the past year Meredith had gone from Miss to Ma'am. Just like that, with no transition. Even worse, her skin had begun to lose its elasticity. There were tiny pleats in places that used to be smooth. Her neck was fuller, there was no doubt about it. She hadn't gone gray yet; that was the one saving grace. Her chestnut-colored hair, cut in a no-nonsense shoulder-length bob, was still full and shiny. But her eyes gave her away. She looked tired. And not only at six in the morning.

She turned away from the mirror and stripped out of her old T-shirt and into a pair of black sweats, anklet socks, and a long-sleeved black shirt. Pulling her hair into a stumpy ponytail, she left the bathroom and walked into her darkened bedroom, where the soft strains of her husband's snoring made her almost want to crawl back into bed. In the old days, she would have done just that, would have snuggled up against him.

Leaving the room, she clicked the door shut behind her and headed down the hallway toward the stairs.

In the pale glow of a pair of long-outdated night-lights, she passed the closed doors of her children's bedrooms. Not that they were children anymore. Jillian was nineteen now, a sophomore at UCLA who dreamed of being a doctor, and Maddy—Meredith's baby—was eighteen and a freshman at Vanderbilt. Without them, this house—and Meredith's life—felt emptier and quieter than she'd expected. For nearly twenty years, she had devoted herself to being the kind of mother she hadn't had, and it had worked. She and her daughters had become the best of friends. Their absence left her feeling adrift, a little purposeless. She knew it was silly. It wasn't as if she didn't have plenty to do. She just missed the girls; that was all.

She kept moving. Lately that seemed to be the best way to handle things.

Downstairs, she stopped in the living room just long enough to plug in the Christmas tree lights. In the mudroom, the dogs leaped up at her, yapping and wagging their tails.

"Luke, Leia, no jumping," she scolded the huskies, scratching their ears as she led them to the back door. When she opened it, cold air rushed in. Snow had fallen again last night, and though it was still dark on this mid-December morning, she could make out the pale pearlescence of road and field. Her breath turned into vapory plumes.

By the time they were all outside and on their way, it was 6:10 and the sky was a deep purplish gray.

Right on time.

Meredith ran slowly at first, acclimating herself to the cold. As she did every weekday morning, she ran along the gravel road that led from her house, down past her parents' house, and out to the old single-lane road that ended about a mile up the hill. From there, she followed the loop out to the golf course and back. Four miles exactly. It was a routine she rarely missed; she had no choice, really. Everything about Meredith was big by nature. She was tall, with broad shoulders, curvy hips, and big feet. Even her features seemed just a little too much for her pale, oval face—she had a big Julia Roberts–type mouth, huge brown eyes, full eyebrows, and thick hair. Only constant exercise, a vigilant diet, good hair products, and an industrial-sized pair of tweezers could keep her looking good.

As she turned back onto her road, the rising sun illuminated the mountains, turned their snowcapped peaks lavender and pink.

On either side of her, thousands of bare, spindly apple trees showed through the snow like brown stitches on white fabric. This fertile cleft of land had belonged to their family for fifty years, and there, in the center of it all, tall and proud, was the home in which she'd grown up. Belye Nochi. Even in the half-light it looked ridiculously out of place and ostentatious.

Meredith kept running up the hill, faster and faster, until she could barely breathe and there was a stitch in her side.

She came to a stop at her own front porch as the valley filled with bright golden light. She fed the dogs and then hurried upstairs. She was just going into the bathroom as Jeff was coming out. Wearing only a towel, with his graying blond hair still dripping wet, he turned sideways to let her pass, and she did the same. Neither one of them spoke.

By 7:20, she was drying her hair, and by 7:30—right on time—she was dressed for work in a pair of black jeans and a fitted green blouse. A little eyeliner, some blush and mascara, a coat of lipstick, and she was ready to go.

Downstairs, she found Jeff at the kitchen table, sitting in his regular chair, reading *The New York Times*. The dogs were asleep at his feet.

She went to the coffeepot and poured herself a cup. "You need a refill?"

"I'm good," he said without looking up.

Meredith stirred soy milk into her coffee, watching the color change. It occurred to her that she and Jeff only talked at a distance lately, like strangers—or disillusioned partners—and only about work or the kids. She tried idly to remember the last time they'd made love, and couldn't.

Maybe that was normal. Certainly it was. When you'd been married as long as they had, there were bound to be quiet times. Still, it saddened her sometimes to remember how passionate they used to be. She'd been fourteen on their first date (they'd gone to see *Young Frankenstein*; it was still one of their favorites), and to be honest, that was the last time she'd ever really looked at another guy. It was strange when she thought about that now; she didn't consider herself a romantic woman, but she'd fallen in love practically at first sight. He'd been a part of her for as long as she could remember.

They'd married early—too early, really—and she'd followed him to college in Seattle, working nights and weekends in smoky bars to pay tuition. She'd been happy in their cramped, tiny U District apartment. Then, when they were seniors, she'd gotten pregnant. It had terrified her at first. She'd worried that she was like her mother, and that parenthood wouldn't be a good thing. But she discovered, to her profound relief, that she was the complete opposite of her own mother. Perhaps her youth had helped in that. God knew Mom had not been young when Meredith was born.

Jeff shook his head. It was a minute gesture, barely even a movement, but she saw it. She had always been attuned to him, and lately their mutual disappointments seemed to create sound, like a high-pitched whistle that only she could hear.

"What?" she said.

"Nothing."

"You didn't shake your head over nothing. What's the matter?"

"I just asked you something."

"I didn't hear you. Ask me again."

"It doesn't matter."

"Fine." She took her coffee and headed toward the dining room.

It was something she'd done a hundred times, and yet just then, as she passed under the old-fashioned ceiling light with its useless bit of plastic mistletoe, her view changed.

She saw herself as if from a distance: a forty-year-old woman, holding a cup of coffee, looking at two empty places at the table, and at the husband who was still here, and for a split second she wondered what other life that woman could have lived. What if she hadn't come home to run the orchard and raise her children? What if she hadn't gotten married so young? What kind of woman could she have become?

And then it was gone like a soap bubble, and she was back where she belonged.

"Will you be home for dinner?"

"Aren't I always?"

"Seven o'clock," she said.

"By all means," he said, turning the page. "Let's set a time."

Meredith was at her desk by eight o'clock. As usual, she was the first to arrive and went about the cubicle-divided space on the warehouse's second floor flipping on lights. She passed by her dad's office—empty now—pausing only long enough to glance at the plaques by his door. Thirteen times he'd been voted Grower of the Year and his advice was still sought out by competitors on a regular basis. It didn't matter that he only occasionally came into the office, or that he'd been semi-retired for ten years. He was still the face of the Belye Nochi orchard, the man who had pioneered Golden Delicious apples in the early sixties, Granny Smiths in the seventies, and championed the Braeburn and Fuji in the nineties. His designs for cold storage had revolutionized the business and helped make it possible to export the very best apples to world markets.

She had had a part to play in the company's growth and success, to be sure. Under her leadership, the cold storage warehouse had been expanded and a big part of their business was now storing fruit for other growers. She'd turned the old roadside apple stand into a gift shop that sold hundreds of locally made craft items, specialty foods, and Belye Nochi memorabilia. At this time of year—the holidays—when trainloads of tourists arrived in Leavenworth for the world-famous tree-lighting ceremony, more than a few found their way to the gift shop.

The first thing she did was pick up the phone to call her youngest daughter. It was just past ten in Tennessee.

"Hello?" Maddy grumbled.

"Good morning," Meredith said brightly. "It sounds like someone slept in."

"Oh. Mom. Hi. I was up late last night. Studying."

"Madison Elizabeth," was all Meredith had to say to make her point.

Maddy sighed. "Okay. So it was a Lambda Chi party."

"I know how fun it all is, and how much you want to experience every moment of college, but your first final is next week. Tuesday morning, right?"

"Right."

"You have to learn to balance schoolwork and fun. So get your lily-white ass out of bed and get to class. It's a life skill—partying all night and still getting up on time."

"The world won't end if I miss one Spanish class."

"Madison."

Maddy laughed. "Okay, okay. I'm getting up. Spanish 101, here I come. *Hasta la vista* . . . ba-by."

Meredith smiled. "I'll call on Thursday and find out how your speech went. And call your sister. She's stressed out about her organic chemistry test."

"Okay, Mom. I love you."

"Love you, too, princess."

Meredith hung up the phone feeling better. For the next three hours, she threw herself into work. She was rereading the latest crop report when her intercom buzzed.

"Meredith? Your dad is on line one."

"Thanks, Daisy." She picked up the call. "Hi, Dad."

"Mom and I were wondering if you could come to the house for lunch today."

"I'm swamped here, Dad—"

"Please?"

Meredith had never been able to deny her father. "Okay. But I have to be back by one."

"Excellent," he said, and she could hear the smile in his voice.

She hung up and went back to work. Lately, with production up and demand down, and costs for both export and transportation skyrocketing, she often spent her days putting out one fire after another, and today was no exception. By noon, a low-grade stress headache had crawled into the space at the base of her skull and begun to growl. Still, she smiled at her employees as she left her office and walked through the cold warehouse.

In less than ten minutes, she pulled up in front of her parents' garage.

The house was like something out of a Russian fairy tale, with its turretlike two-story veranda and elaborate fretwork trim, especially this time of year, when the eaves and railings glittered with Christmas lights. The hammered copper roof was dulled today by the gray winter weather, but on a bright day it shone like liquid gold. Surrounded by tall, elegant poplar trees and situated on a gentle rise that overlooked their valley, this house was so famous that tourists often stopped to photograph it.

Leave it to her mother to build something so absurdly out of place. A Russian dacha, or summerhouse, in Western Washington State. Even the orchard's name was absurd. Belye Nochi.

White Nights indeed. The nights here were as dark as new asphalt.

Not that Mom cared about what was around her. She got her way, that was all. Whatever Anya Whitson wanted, her husband gave to her, and apparently she'd wanted a fairy-tale castle and an orchard with an unpronounceable Russian name.

Meredith knocked and went inside. The kitchen was empty; a big pot of soup simmered on the stove.

In the living room, light spilled through the two-story rounded wall of windows at the north end of the room—the famous Belye Nochi turret. Wood floors gleamed with the golden beeswax that Mom insisted on using, even though it turned the floors into a skating rink if you dared to walk in stockinged feet. A huge stone fireplace dominated the center wall; clustered around it was a grouping of richly upholstered antique sofas and chairs. Above the fireplace hung an oil painting of a Russian troika—a romantic-looking carriage drawn by matching horses—sailing through a field of snow. Pure *Doctor Zhivago.* To her left were dozens of pictures of Russian churches, and below them was her mother's "Holy Corner," where a table held a display of antique icons and a single candle that burned year-round.

She found her father in the back of the room, alongside the heavily decorated Christmas tree, in his favorite spot. He lay stretched out on the burgundy mohair cushions of the ottoman bed, reading. His hair, what he had left of it at eighty-five, stuck out from his pink scalp in white tufts. Too many decades in the sun had blotched and pleated his skin and he had a basset-hound look even when he was smiling, but the sad countenance fooled no one. Everyone loved Evan Whitson. It was impossible not to.

At her entrance, his face lit up. He reached out and squeezed her hand tightly, then let go. "Your mom will be so glad to see you."

Meredith smiled. It was the game they'd played for years. Dad pretended that Mom loved Meredith and Meredith pretended to believe him. "Great. Is she upstairs?"

"I couldn't keep her out of the garden this morning."

Meredith wasn't surprised. "I'll get her."

She left her father in the living room and walked through the kitchen to the formal dining room. Through the French doors, she saw an expanse of snow-covered ground, with acres of dormant apple trees in the distance. Closer, beneath the icicle-draped branches of a fifty-year-old magnolia tree, was a small rectangular garden defined by antique wrought-iron fencing. Its ornate gate was twined with brown vines; come summer, that gate would be a profusion of green leaves and white flowers. Now it glittered with frost.

And there she was: her eighty-something-year-old mother, bundled up in blankets, sitting on the black bench in her so-called winter garden. A light snow began to fall; tiny flakes blurred the scene into an impressionistic painting where nothing looked solid enough to touch. Sculpted bushes and a single birdbath were covered in snow, giving the garden a strange, otherworldly look. Not surprisingly, her mother sat in the middle of it all, motionless, her hands clasped in her lap.

As a child it had scared Meredith—all that solitude in her mother—but as she got older it had begun to embarrass, then irritate her. A woman of her mother's age had no business sitting alone in the cold. Her mother claimed it was because of her ruined vision, but Meredith didn't believe that. It was true that her mother's eyes didn't process color—she saw only white and black and shades of gray—but that had never struck Meredith, even as a girl, as a reason for staring at nothing.

She opened the door and went out into the cold. Her boots sank in the ankle-deep snow; here and there, crusty patches crunched underneath and more than once she almost slipped. "You shouldn't be out here, Mom," she said, coming up beside her. "You'll catch pneumonia."

"It takes more cold than this to give me pneumonia. This is barely below freezing."

Meredith rolled her eyes. It was the sort of ridiculous comment her mother always made. "I've only got an hour for lunch, so you'd better come in now." Her voice sounded sharp in the softness of the falling snow, and she winced, wishing she had rounded her vowels more, tempered her voice. What was it about her mother that brought out the worst in her? "Did you know he invited me for lunch?"

"Of course," her mother said, but Meredith heard the lie in it.

Her mother rose from the bench in a single fluid motion, like some ancient goddess used to being revered and adored. Her face was remarkably smooth and wrinkle-free, her skin flawless and almost translucent. She had the kind of bone structure that made other women envious. But it was her eyes that defined her beauty. Deep-set and fringed by thick lashes, they were a remarkable shade of aqua flecked with bits of gold. Meredith was sure that no one who had seen those eyes ever forgot them. How ironic it was that eyes of such remarkable hue were unable to see color.

Meredith took her mother's elbow and led her away from the bench; only then, when they were walking, did she notice that her mother's hands were bare, and turning blue.

"Good God. Your hands are blue. You should have on gloves in this cold—"

"You do not know cold."

"Whatever, Mom." Meredith bustled her mother up the back steps and into the warmth of the house. "Maybe you should take a bath to warm up."

"I do not want to be warm, thank you. It is December fourteenth."

"Fine," Meredith said, watching her shivering mother go to the stove to stir the soup. The ragged gray wool blanket fell to the floor in a heap around her.

Meredith set the table, and for a few precious moments there was noise in the room, an approximation of a relationship, at least.

"My girls," Dad said, coming into the kitchen. He looked pale and slight, his once-wide shoulders whittled down to nothing by weight loss. Moving forward, he put a hand on each woman's shoulder, bringing Meredith and Mom in close. "I love it when we're together for lunch."

Mom smiled tightly. "As do I," she said in that clipped, accented voice of hers.

"And me," Meredith said.

"Good. Good." Dad nodded and went to the table.

Mom brought a tray of still-warm feta cheese corn bread slices, drizzled with butter, put a piece on each plate, and then brought over bowls of soup.

"I walked the orchard this morning," Dad said.

Meredith nodded and took a seat beside him. "I guess you noticed the back of Field A?"

"Yep. That hillside's been giving us some trouble."

"I've got Ed and Amanda on it. Don't worry about the harvest."

"I wasn't, actually. I was thinking of something else."

She sipped her soup; it was rich and delicious. Homemade lamb meatballs in a savory saffron broth with silken egg noodles. If she didn't exercise extreme caution, she'd eat it all and have to run another mile this afternoon. "Oh, yeah?"

"I want to change that field to grapes."

Meredith slowly lowered her spoon. "Grapes?"

"The Golden Delicious are not our best apple anymore." Before she could interrupt, he held up his hand. “I know. I know. We built this place on Golden Delicious, but things change. Hell, it’s almost 2001, Meredith; wine is the new thing. I think we could make ice wine and late harvest at the very least.”

“In these times, Dad? The Asian markets are tightening and it’s costing us a fortune to transport our fruit. Competition is increasing. Hell, our profits were down twelve percent last year and this year doesn’t look any better. We’re barely hanging on.”

“You should listen to your father,” Mom said.

“Oh, please, Mom. You haven’t even been inside the warehouse since we updated the cooling system. And when was the last time you even looked at one of the year-end statements?”

“Enough,” Dad said with a sigh. “I didn’t want to start an argument.”

Meredith stood up. “I need to get back to work.”

Meredith carried her bowl over to the sink, where she washed it. Then she put the leftover soup in a Tupperware container, stored it in the impossibly full refrigerator, and washed the pot. It hit the strainer with a clang that seemed loud in the quiet room. “That was delicious, Mom. Thanks.” She said a quick good-bye and left the kitchen. In the entryway, she put her coat back on. She was out on the porch, breathing in the sharp, frigid air, when her dad came up behind her.

“You know how she gets in December and January. Winters are hard for her.”

“I know.”

He pulled her into his arms and held her tightly. “You two need to try harder.”

Meredith couldn’t help being hurt by that. She’d heard it from him all her life; just once she wanted to hear him say that Mom should try harder. “I will,” she said, completing their little fairy tale as she always did. And she *would* try. She always did, but she and her mother would never be close. There was just too much water under that bridge. “I love you, Dad,” she said, kissing his cheek.

“I love you, too, Meredoodle.” He grinned. “And think about grapes. Maybe I can still be a vintner before I die.”

She hated jokes like that. "Very funny." Turning away, she went to her car and started the engine. Putting the SUV in reverse, she swung around. Through the lacy snow on the windshield, she saw her parents through the living room window. Dad pulled her mother into his arms and kissed her. They began to dance haltingly, although there was probably no music in the house. Her dad didn't need any; he always said he carried love songs in his heart.

Meredith drove away from the intimate scene, but the memory of what she'd seen stayed with her. All the rest of the workday, while she analyzed different facets of the operation, looking for ways to maximize profit, and as she sat through endless management and scheduling meetings, she found herself remembering how in love her parents had looked.

The truth was, she had never been able to understand how a woman could be capable of passionately adoring her husband while simultaneously despising her children. No, that wasn't right. Mom didn't despise Meredith and Nina. She just didn't care about them.

"Meredith?"

She looked up sharply. For a moment there, she'd been so lost in her own life that she'd forgotten where she was. At her desk. Reading an insect report. "Oh. Daisy. I'm sorry. I guess I didn't hear you knock."

"I'm going home."

"Is it that late already?" Meredith glanced at the clock. It was 6:37. "Shit. I mean, dang it. I'm late."

Daisy laughed. "You're always staying late."

Meredith began organizing her paperwork into neat piles. "Drive safely, Miss Daisy"—it was an old joke but they both smiled—"and remember Josh from the Apple Commission will be here at nine for a meeting. We'll need donuts and coffee."

"You got it. Good night."

Meredith got her desk ready for tomorrow and then headed out.

Snow was falling in earnest now, blurring the view through her windshield. The wipers were moving as fast as they could, but it was still difficult to see. Every pair of oncoming headlights momentarily blinded her. Even though she knew this road like the back of her hand, she slowed down and hugged the shoulder. It reminded her of the one and only time she'd tried to teach Maddy to drive in the snow. The memory made her smile. *It's snow, Mom. Not black ice. I don't have to drive this slow. I could walk home faster.*

That was Maddy. Always in a hurry.

At home, Meredith slammed the door shut behind her and hurried into the kitchen. A quick glance at the clock told her she was late. Again.

She put her purse on the counter. "Jeff?"

"I'm in here."

She followed his voice into the living room. He was at the wet bar they'd installed in the late eighties, making himself a drink. "Sorry I'm late. The snow—"

"Yeah," he said. They both knew she'd left late. "Do you want a drink?"

"Sure. White wine." She looked at him, not knowing what she even felt. He was as handsome as ever, with dark blond hair that was only now beginning to gray at the temples, a strong, square jaw, and steel-gray eyes that always seemed to be smiling. He didn't work out and ate like a horse, but he still had one of those wiry, rawhide bodies that never seemed to age. He was dressed in his usual style—faded Levi's jeans and an old Pearl Jam T-shirt.

He handed her a glass of wine. "How was your day?"

"Dad wants to plant grapes. And Mom was in the winter garden again. She's going to catch pneumonia."

"Your mom is colder than any snowfield."

For a moment, she felt the years that bound them, all the connections that time had created. He'd formed an opinion of her mother more than two decades ago, and nothing had happened to change it. "Amen to that." She leaned back against the wall. All at once the crazy/hectic/hurried pattern of her day—her week, her month—caught up with her and she closed her eyes.

"I got a chapter written today. It's short. Only about seven pages, but I think it's good. I made you a copy. Meredith? Mere?"

She opened her eyes and found him looking at her. A small frown creased the skin between his eyes, made her wonder if he'd said something important. She tried to recall but couldn't. "Sorry. Long day."

"You're having a lot of those lately."

She couldn't tell if there was a hint of accusation in his voice or just a simple honesty. "You know what winter is like."

"And spring. And summer."

There was her answer: accusation. Even last year she would have asked him what was wrong with them. She would have told him how lost she felt in the gray minutiae of her everyday life, and how much she missed the girls. But lately that kind of intimacy felt impossible. She wasn't quite sure how it had happened, or when, but distance seemed to be spreading between them like spilled ink, staining everything. "Yeah, I guess."

"I'm going to the office," he said suddenly, reaching for the jacket he'd draped over the back of the chair.

"Now?"

"Why not?"

She wondered if it was really a question. Did he want her to stop him, to give him a reason to stay, or did he want to leave? She wasn't sure, and really, she didn't care right now. It would be nice to take a hot bath and have a glass of wine and not have to try to think of what to say over dinner. Even better not to have to cook dinner at all. "No reason."

"Yeah," he said, kissing her on the cheek. "That's what I thought."

Two

It had taken two weeks hiking through the jungle to find the kill. Bugs had alerted them; and the smell of death.

Nina stood beside the guide who had led her here. For a terrible instant, she experienced it all: the flies buzzing in the clearing, the maggots that turned the bloody carcass almost white in places, the stillness of the African jungle that meant predators and scavengers were nearby, watching.

Then she began to compartmentalize the scene, to see it as a photographer. She pulled out her light meter and ran a quick check. When that was done, she chose one of the three cameras hanging from around her neck and focused on the ruined, bloodied body of the mountain gorilla.

Click.

She stepped around, kept focusing and snapping shots. Changing cameras, adjusting lenses, checking the light. Her adrenaline kicked in. It was the only time she ever really felt alive, when she was taking pictures.

Her eye was her great gift; that and her ability to separate from what was going on around her. You couldn't have one without the other. To be a great photographer you had to see first and feel later.

She paused long enough to put a little more Vicks under her nose and then squatted down closer to focus on the severed neck. From somewhere, she heard the sound of vomiting; it was probably the young journalist who had accompanied Nina. She could hardly worry about that now.

Click. Click.

The poachers wanted only the head, hands, and feet. The money items. There were places in the world where a gorilla's hand was an ashtray in some rich asshole's library.

Click. Click.

For the next hour, Nina framed and shot, changing cameras and lenses as often as she needed to, putting used film into canisters and labeling them before tucking them into her pocketed vest. When dusk finally fell, they began the long, hot, slippery trek back down through the jungle. The air was electric with sounds—bugs, birds, monkeys—and the sky was the color of fresh blood. A tangerine sun played hide-and-seek through the trees. Though they'd all chatted on the way up, the descent was quiet, solemn. The immediate aftermath was always worst for Nina. It was difficult sometimes to forget what she'd seen. Often, in the middle of the night, the images would return as nightmares and waken her from a dead sleep. More often than she liked to admit, she woke with tears on her cheeks.

At the bottom of the mountain, the group came to the small outpost that served as a town in this remote part of Rwanda. There, they climbed into the jeep and drove several hours to the conservation center, where they asked more questions and she took more photos.

"Mrs. Nina?"

She was standing by the center's door, cleaning a lens, when she heard someone say her name. Putting the camera away, she looked up and saw the center's head guide beside her. She smiled as brightly as she could, given how tired she was. "Hello, Mr. Dimonsu."

"I am sorry to bother you when busy things arc happening, but we forgot to give you most important phone message. It from Mrs. Sylvie. She say to tell you to call her."

"Thank you."

Nina took the bulky satellite phone out of her bag and carried all the gear to a clearing in the center of the camp. A quick compass check identified the satellite's direction. She unfolded the dish part of the sat phone, set it on the ground, and pointed it at sixty degrees northeast. Then she hooked the phone up to the dish and turned it on. An LCD panel blinked to orange life, giving her the signal strength. When it looked good, she made the call.

"Hey, Sylvie," she said when her editor answered. "I got the poacher photos today. Sick bastards. Give me, what, ten days to get them to you?"

"You've got six days. We're thinking of the cover."

The cover. Her two favorite words. Some women liked diamonds; she liked the cover of *Time* magazine. Or *National Geographic.* She wasn't picky. She actually hoped someday to get the cover and about sixteen pages for her photographic essay titled "Women Warriors Around the World." Her pet project. As soon as she was done—whenever the hell *that* might be—she'd submit freelance. "You'll have it. And then I'm meeting Danny in Namibia."

"Lucky girl. Have sex for me. But be ready to be back to work next Friday. The violence in Sierra Leone is escalating again. The peace talks are going to fall apart. I want you there before Christmas."

"You know me," Nina said. "Ready to fly at a moment's notice."

"I won't call unless a new war breaks out. I promise," Sylvie said. "Now go get laid while I try to remember what it's like."

A few days later, Nina was in Namibia, in a rented Land Rover, with Danny at the wheel.

It was only seven in the morning and already the December sun was bright and warm. By one o'clock, the temperature would be somewhere around 115 degrees, and it could well be hotter. The road—if you could call it that—was really a river of thick reddish gray sand that sucked at the car's tires and sent them careening one way and then the other. Nina held on to the door handle and sat up straight, trying to make her body work like a shock absorber, rolling with the motion.

She used her other hand to steady the camera that hung around her neck so that the strap didn't bite into her flesh. A T-shirt was wrapped around the camera and lens—not a very professional way to battle dust, but in all her years in Africa, it had proven to be the best compromise between protection and use. Here, sometimes you had only an instant to grab your camera and take the shot. No time to fumble with straps and cases.

She stared out at the desolate, blistering landscape. As the hours passed, taking them farther and farther from any semblance of civilization and deeper into one of the last true wildernesses of southern Africa, she noticed more herds of starving animals standing by dry riverbeds. In this summer heat, they were dropping to their knees, dying where they stood as they waited for the rains to come. Bleaching bones lay everywhere.

"You sure you want to find the Himba?" Danny asked, flashing her a grin as they slammed sideways and almost found themselves stuck in the sand. The dirt on his face made his white teeth and blue eyes look startlingly bright. Dust powdered his collar-length black hair and shirt. "We haven't had a week to ourselves in months."

The so-called road became passable again, and she brought up her camera, studying him through the viewfinder. Focusing on him, widening the shot just a little, she saw him as clearly as if he'd been a stranger: a handsome thirty-nine-year-old Irishman with pronounced cheekbones and a nose that had been broken more than once. *Pub fights as a lad*, he always said, and just now, when he was looking ahead, concentrating on the road, she could see the tiny frown lines around his mouth. He was worried that he'd followed bad advice on the wrong road, though he'd never say such a thing. He was a war correspondent and used to being "in the shit," as he liked to say, used to following a story to hell and back. Even if it wasn't his story.

She took the shot.

He flashed her a smile and she took another. "Next time you want to photograph women, I suggest waitresses at a poolside bar."

She laughed and put the camera in her lap again, covering the lens with its cap. "I owe you one."

"Indeed you do, love, and I'll be collecting, you c'n be sure."

Nina leaned back into the torn, uncomfortable seat and tried not to close her eyes, but she was exhausted. After two weeks tracking poachers through the jungle and four weeks before that in Angola watching people kill each other, she was tired to the bone.

And still, she loved it. There was nowhere in the world she'd rather be and nothing she'd rather be doing. Finding "the shot" was an adrenaline-fueled fun ride, and one she never tired of, no matter what sacrifices she had to make along the way. She'd known that sixteen years ago, when at twenty-one, with a journalism degree under her belt and a used camera in her backpack, she'd gone in search of her destiny.

For a while she'd taken any job that required a photographer, but in 1985 she'd gotten her big break. At Live Aid, the concert for famine relief, she'd met Sylvie Porter, then a newbie editor at *Time*, and Sylvie introduced Nina to a different world. The next thing Nina knew, she was on her way to Ethiopia. What she saw there changed everything.

Almost immediately her pictures stopped being only images and began to tell stories. In 1989, when Typhoon Gay smashed into Thailand, leaving more than one hundred thousand people homeless, it was Nina's photograph of a single woman, up to her chest in dirty water, carrying her crying baby above her head, that graced the cover of *Time* magazine. Two years ago, she'd won the Pulitzer Prize for her coverage of the famine in Sudan.

Not that it came easily, this career of hers.

Like the Himba tribe of this region, she'd had to become a nomad. Soft mattresses and clean sheets and running water were luxuries she'd learned to live without.

"Look. There," Danny said, pointing.

At first all she saw was an orange and red sky, full of dust. The world felt scorched and smelled of smoke. Gradually, the silhouettes on the ridge materialized into thin people, standing tall, gazing down at the dirty Land Rover and its even dirtier occupants.

"That them?" he asked.

"Must be."

Nodding, he closed the last distance between them and the ridge, and at the bend in a dry riverbed he parked the vehicle and got out.

The Himba tribe stood back, watching.

Danny walked slowly forward, knowing the chief would present himself. Nina followed his lead.

At the elder's hut, they paused. The sacred fire burned in front of it, sending a stream of smoke into the now-purple sky. They both bent down, moved carefully, making sure not to pass in front of the fire. That would be seen as disrespectful.

The chief approached them and, in halting Swahili, Nina sought permission to take pictures, while Danny showed the tribe the fifteen gallons of water he had brought as a gift. For a people that walked miles for a handful of water, it was an overwhelming gift, and suddenly Nina and Danny were welcomed like old friends. Children surged at them, surrounded Nina in a giggling, jumping pack. The Himbas swept her and Danny into the village, where they were fed a traditional meal of maize porridge and sour milk and were entertained by the tribe. Later, when the night was blue with moonlight, they were led to a rounded mud hut, called a rondoval, where they lay together on a mat of woven grass and leaves. The air smelled sweet, of roasted corn and dry earth.

Nina rolled onto her side to face Danny. In the shadowy blue light, his face looked young, although, like her, he had old eyes. It was a hazard of the trade. They'd seen too many terrible things. But it was what had brought them together. What they had in common. The yearning to see everything, no matter how terrible, to know everything.

They'd met in an abandoned hut in the Congo, during the first war, both of them taking cover from the worst of the fighting; she to reload her camera, him to bandage a wound in his shoulder.

That looks bad, she'd said. *Can I wrap it for you?*

He'd looked up at her. *All that prayin' must have worked. God has sent me my own angel.*

From then on, they'd been together all over the world. In the Sudan, Zimbabwe, Afghanistan, Congo, Rwanda, Nepal, Bosnia. They'd both become specialists on Africa, but wherever the big news was happening, they were likely to be there. Both had London apartments that did little more than collect junk mail, messages, and dust. Often their interests took them to separate hot spots—him to civil wars, her to humanitarian tragedies—and they spent months without seeing each other, which was just fine with Nina. It only made the sex better.

"I'm going to be forty next month," he said quietly.

She loved his accent. The simplest sentence sounded edgy and sexy when he said it. *Ah'm goin' t' be farhty next moonth.*

"Don't worry, twenty-five-year-olds still swoon when they see you. It's the I-used-to-be-in-a-rock-band look of you."

"It was a punk rock band, love."

She snuggled closer to him, kissed his neck while her hand slid down his bare chest. His body responded as quickly as she expected, and within moments he had her undressed and they were doing what they'd always done best.

Afterward, Danny pulled her close. "How come we can talk about anything but us?"

"Who was talking about us?"

"I said I was almost forty."

"And I'm supposed to see that as a conversation starter? I'm thirty-seven."

"What if I miss you when you're gone?"

"You know who I am, Danny. I told you at the very beginning."

"That was more than four years ago, for God's sake. Everything in the world changes except you, I guess."

"Exactly." She rolled over, spooning her body against his. She'd always felt safe in his arms, even when gunfire was exploding all around them and the night was full of screaming. Tonight, though, there was only the sound of a fire crackling outside, and of bugs buzzing and chirping in the dark.

She moved the tiniest bit away from him, but his arms closed around her, held her in place.

"I didn't ask for anything," he whispered into her ear.

You did, she thought, closing her eyes. An unfamiliar anxiety settled in the pit of her stomach. *You just don't know it yet.*

On a ridge high above the makeshift village, Nina squatted on the crumbling edge of a riverbed. Her thighs burned from the effort it took to remain motionless. It was six in the morning, and the sky was a gorgeous blend of aqua and orange; already the sun was gaining strength.

Below her, a Himba woman walked through the village with a heavy pot balanced on her head and a baby positioned in a colorful sling at her breast. Nina raised the camera to her eye and zoomed in the telephoto lens until she could see perfectly. Like all the women of this nomadic African tribe, the young woman was bare-breasted and wore a furry goatskin skirt. A large conch-shell necklace—handed down from mother to daughter through the generations, a valued possession—showed the world that she was married, as did the style of her hair. Covered from head to toe in red ochre dust and butterfat to protect her skin from the terrorizing sun, the young mother's skin was the color of old bricks. Her ankles, considered her most private part, were hidden beneath a row of thin metal bands that made a tinkling sound when she walked.

Unaware of Nina, the woman paused at the riverbank and looked out over the scar on the land where water should run. Her expression sharpened, turned desperate as she reached down to touch the child in her arms. It was a look Nina had seen in women all over the world, especially in times of war and destruction. A bone-deep fear for her child's future. There was nowhere to go to find water.

Nina caught it on film and kept shooting until the woman walked on, went back to her rounded mud hut and sat down in a circle of other women. Together, talking, the women began crushing red ochre on flat rocks, collecting the sandy residue in calabash bowls.

Nina covered the lens and stood up, stretching her aching joints. She'd taken hundreds of pictures this morning, but she didn't need to look through them to know that The One was of the woman at the riverbank.

In her mind, she cropped, framed, printed, and hung the image among the great ones she'd collected. Someday her portraits would show the world how strong and powerful women could be, as well as the personal cost of that strength.

She unloaded the film, labeled the canister, tucked it away and reloaded, then walked through the village, smiling at people, handing out the candies and ribbons and bracelets she always carried. She took another great picture of four Himba women emerging from the smoke-and-herb sauna that was their method of keeping clean in a land devoid of water. In the picture, the women were holding hands and laughing. It was an image that captured a universal feminine connection.

She heard Danny come up beside her. "Hey, you."

She leaned against him, feeling good about her shots. "I just love how they are with their kids, even when the odds are impossible. The only time I cry is when I see their faces with their babies. Why is that, with all we've seen?"

"So it's mothers you follow. I thought it was warriors."

Nina frowned. She'd never thought of it that way, and the observation was unsettling. "Not always mothers. Women fighting for something. Triumphing over impossible odds."

He smiled. "So you are a romantic after all."

She laughed. "Right."

"You ready to go?"

"I think I got what I needed, yeah."

"Does this mean we can go lie by a pool for a week?"

"There's nothing I'd rather do." She put her camera equipment away and repacked their gear while Danny spoke to the village elder and thanked him for the pictures. She set up her satellite phone on the desert floor, unfolding the silver wings and positioning it until she found a signal.

As she expected, the magazine offices were closed, so she left a message for her editor and promised to call from the Chobe River Lodge in Zambia. Then she and Danny climbed back into the busted-up old Land Rover, drove through the lunar landscape of Kaokoveld, and hopped on a plane headed south. By nightfall, they were at the Chobe River Lodge, on their own private deck, watching the sun set over a herd of elephants on the opposite shore. They were being served gin and tonics while a hundred yards away lions were hunting in the tall grass.

In a bikini that had seen better days, Nina stretched out on the luxurious two-person lounge chair and closed her eyes. The night smelled of murky water and dry grass and mud baked to stone by the unforgiving sun. For the first time in weeks, her pixie-cut black hair was clean and there was no red dirt under her fingernails. Pure luxury.

She heard Danny coming through their room toward the deck. He took an almost imperceptible pause before each step, a tiny favoring of the right leg, which had taken a bullet in Angola. He pretended it didn't bother him, told people there was no pain, but Nina knew about the pills he swallowed and the way he sometimes couldn't find a comfortable position in which to sleep. When she massaged his body, she put extra effort into that leg, although he didn't ask her to, and she didn't admit that she'd done it.

"Here you go," he said, putting two glasses onto the teak table beside her.

She tilted her face up to thank him and noticed several things at once: he hadn't brought a gin and tonic. Instead, he'd put down a straight shot so big it was practically a tumblerful of tequila. He'd forgotten the salt, and worst of all, he wasn't smiling.

She sat up. "What's wrong?"

"Maybe you should take a drink first."

When an Irishman told you to take a drink first, there was bad news coming.

He sat down beside her on the lounger. She eased sideways to make room for him.

The stars were out now, and in the pale silvery glow she could see his sharp features and hollow cheeks, his blue eyes and curly hair. She realized in that moment, when he looked so sad, how much he laughed and smiled, even when the sun was broiling or the dust was choking or the gunshots were exploding in the air. He could always smile.

Except now he wasn't.

He handed her a smallish yellow envelope. "Telegram."

"Did you read it?"

"Course not. But it can't be good news, now, can it?"

Journalists and producers and photojournalists the world over knew about telegrams. It was how your family delivered bad news, even in this satellite phone and Internet age. Her hands were unsteady as she reached for the envelope. Her first thought was, *Thank God*, when she saw that it had come from Sylvie, but that relief died as she read on.

> NINA.
> YOUR FATHER HAS HAD A HEART ATTACK.
> MEREDITH SAYS IT LOOKS BAD.
> SYLVIE.

She looked up at Danny. "It's my dad. . . . I need to go now—"

"Impossible, love," he said gently. "The first flight out of here is at six. I'll get us tickets to Seattle from Johannesburg. Is it best to drive from there?"

"Us?"

"Aye. I want to be there for you, Nina. Is that so terrible?"

She didn't know how to respond to that, what to say. Relying on people for comfort had never felt natural to her. The last thing she wanted was to give someone the power to hurt her. Self-preservation was the one thing she'd learned from her mother. So she did what she always did at times like these: she reached down for the buttons on his pants. "Take me to bed, Daniel Flynn. Get me through this night."

Interminable was the word that came to mind to describe the wait, but that only made Meredith think *terminal*, which made her think *death*, which brought up all the emotions she was trying to suppress. Her usual coping mechanism—keeping busy—wasn't working for her now, and she'd tried. She'd buried herself in insurance information, researched heart attacks and survival, and come up with a list of the best cardiologists in the country. The second she put her pen down or looked away from the screen, her grief came rushing back. Tears were a constant pressure behind her eyes. So far, though, she'd kept them from falling. Crying would be its own defeat and she refused to give up.

She crossed her arms tightly, staring at the multicolored fish in the waiting room tank. Sometimes, if she was lucky, one of them actually caught her attention and for a nanosecond she forgot that her father might be dying.

She felt Jeff come up behind her. Though she hadn't heard footsteps on the carpet, she knew he was there. "Mere," he said quietly, putting his hands on her shoulders. She knew what he wanted: for her to lean back into him, to let herself be held. There was a part of her that wanted it, too, longed for that comfort, in fact, but the larger part of her—the part that was hanging on to hope one breath at a time—didn't dare soften. In his arms, she might fall apart, and what good would that do?

"Let me hold you," he said into her ear.

She shook her head. How was it he didn't understand?

She worried about her father in a way that consumed her. It felt as if a knife had plunged deep in her chest, tearing past bone and muscle; the sharp point lay poised at her heart. One wrong move and the tender organ would be punctured.

Behind her, she heard him sigh. He let go. "Did you get hold of your sister?"

"I left messages everywhere I could. You know Nina. She'll be here when she's here." She looked at the clock again. "What is taking that damn doctor so long? He should be giving us a report. In ten minutes I'm calling the head of the department."

Jeff started to say something (honestly she was barely listening; her heart was beating so fast she couldn't hear much above it), but before he was finished, the door to the waiting room opened, and Dr. Watanabe appeared. In an instant, Meredith, Jeff, and Mom came together, walked to the doctor.

"How is he?" her mother asked in a voice that carried throughout the room. How could she possibly sound so strong at a time like this? Only the heaviness of her accent showed that she was upset. Otherwise, she looked as calm as ever.

Dr. Watanabe smiled briefly, barely, and said, "Not good. He had a second heart attack when we were taking him to surgery. We were able to resuscitate him, but he's very weak."

"What can you do?" Meredith asked.

"Do?" Dr. Watanable said, frowning. The compassion in his eyes was terrible. "Nothing. The damage to his heart is too extensive. Now we just wait . . . and hope he makes it through the night."

Jeff slipped his arm around Meredith's waist.

"You can see him if you'd like. He's in the cardiac care unit. But one at a time, okay?" Dr. Watanabe said, taking Mom by the elbow.

Details, Meredith thought, watching her mother walk down the hallway. *Focus on the details. Find a way to fix this.*

But she couldn't do it.

Memories gathered at the periphery of her vision, waiting to be invited near. She saw her dad in the stands at her high school gymnastic meets, cheering with embarrassing vigor, and at her wedding, weeping openly as he walked her down the aisle. Only last week he'd taken her aside and said, "Let's go get a couple of beers, Meredoodle, just the two of us, like we used to."

And she'd blown him off, told him they'd do it soon. . . .

Had it really been so important to drop off the dry cleaning?

"I guess we should call the girls," Jeff said. "Fly them home."

On that, Meredith felt something inside her break, and although she knew it was irrational, she hated Jeff for saying it. He'd given up already.

"Mere?" He pulled her into his arms and held her. "I love you," he whispered.

She stayed in his arms as long as she could bear and then eased away.

Saying nothing, not even looking at him, she followed the path her mother had walked, feeling utterly, dangerously alone in the austere, busy CCU. People in blue scrubs moved in and out of her field of vision, but she had eyes only for her father.

He lay in a narrow bed, surrounded by tubes and IV lines and machines. Beside him, her mother stood vigil. Even now, as her husband lay connected to life by the most tenuous strands, she looked strangely, almost defiantly, serene. Her posture was perfect and if there was a shaking in her hands it would take a seismologist to detect it.

Meredith wiped her eyes, unaware until that moment that tears were seeping out. She stood there as long as she could. The doc had said one at a time and Meredith wasn't one to break rules, but finally she couldn't stand it. She went to him, stopped at the foot of his bed. The whir of machinery seemed absurdly loud. "How is he?"

Her mother sighed heavily and walked away. Meredith knew her mom would head straight for a window somewhere and stare out into the snowy night, alone.

Normally, it pissed Meredith off, how alone her mother liked to be, but just now she didn't care, and for once, she didn't judge her mother harshly. Everyone broke—and held themselves together—in their own way.

She reached down and touched her father's hand. "Hey, Daddy," she whispered, trying her best to smile. "It's your Meredoodle. I'm here, and I love you. Talk to me, Daddy."

The only answer was the wind, tapping on the glass while the snow flurried and danced beneath the outside light.

Three

Nina stood in the confusing jumble that was the Johannesburg airport and looked up at Danny. She knew he wanted to go with her, but she couldn't imagine why. She had nothing to give him right now, nothing to give anyone. She just needed to go, to be gone, to be home. "I need to do this alone."

She could see that she'd hurt him.

"Of course you do," he said.

"I'm sorry."

He ran a deeply tanned hand through his long, messy black hair, and stared down at her with an intensity that made her draw in a sharp breath. It got through, that look, hit her hard. He reached out slowly, pulled her into his arms as if they were alone, two lovers with all the time in the world. He claimed her with a kiss that was deep and intimate, almost primal in its power. She felt her heartbeat quicken and her cheeks heat up, although it made no sense, that reaction. She was a grown woman, not a scared virgin, and sex was the last thing on her mind.

"Remember that, love," he said, drawing back but not looking away.

It was a kiss that almost softened her grief for a second, lessened her load. She almost said something, almost changed her mind, but before she found even the start of a word, he was pulling away, turning his back on her, and then he was gone. She stood there a minute, almost frozen; then she grabbed her backpack from the floor beside her feet and started walking.

Thirty-four hours later, she parked her rental car in the dark, snow-coated hospital parking lot and ran inside, praying—as she had for every hour of the transcontinental flight—that she wasn't too late.

In the waiting room on the third floor, she found her sister positioned like a sentinel next to an absurdly cheery aquarium full of tropical fish. Nina skidded to a stop, afraid suddenly to say anything. They'd always handled things differently, she and Meredith. Even as girls. Nina had fallen often and picked herself back up; Meredith had moved cautiously, rarely losing her balance. Nina had broken things; Meredith held them together.

Nina needed that now, needed her sister to hold her together. "Mere?" she said quietly.

Meredith turned to her. Even with the length of the waiting room between them and bad fluorescent lighting above, Nina could see how drawn and tired her sister looked. Meredith's chestnut-brown hair, usually so flawlessly styled, was a mess. She wore no makeup, and without it, her brown eyes looked too big for her pale face, her oversized mouth was colorless. "You're here," she said, moving forward, taking Nina into her arms.

When Nina drew back, she was unsteady, her breathing was a little erratic. "How is he?"

"Not good. He had a second massive heart attack. At first they were going to try to operate . . . but now they're saying he won't survive it. The damage is too extensive. Dr. Watanabe doesn't think he'll make it through the weekend. But they didn't really think he'd make it through the first night, either."

Nina closed her eyes at the pain of that. Thank God she had made it home in time to see him.

But how could she lose him? He was her level ground, her North Star. The one person who was always waiting for her to come home.

Slowly, she opened her eyes and looked at her sister again. "Where's Mom?"

Meredith stepped sideways.

And there she was—a beautiful white-haired woman sitting in a cheap upholstered chair. Even from here, Nina could see how controlled her mother was, how scarily contained. She hadn't risen to welcome her youngest child home, hadn't even looked her way. Rather, she was staring straight ahead; those eerie blue eyes of hers seemed to glow against the pallor of her skin. As usual, she was knitting. They probably had three hundred sweaters and blankets, each neatly folded in stacks in the attic.

"How is she?" Nina asked.

Meredith shrugged, and Nina knew what that movement meant. Who knew about Mom? She was alien to them, indecipherable, and God knew they'd tried. Meredith most of all.

Until the night of the Christmas play, all those years ago, Meredith had followed Mom like an eager puppy, begging to be noticed. After that humiliating night, her sister had drawn back, kept her distance. In the years between then and now, nothing had changed; neither had softened. If anything, the distance between them had grown. Nina had handled it differently. She'd given up on the hope of intimacy earlier and chosen to accept her mother's solitude. In many ways they were alike, she and Mom. They didn't need anyone except Dad.

Nodding at her sister, Nina left her and crossed the room. At her mother's side, she sank to her knees. An unfamiliar longing caught her off guard. She wanted to be told that he would be okay.

"Hey, Mom," she said. "I got here as quickly as I could."

"Good."

She heard a tiny fissure in her mother's voice and that slim weakness connected them. She dared to touch her mother's thin, pale wrist. The veins were blue and thick beneath the white skin, and Nina's tanned fingers looked almost absurdly vibrant against it. Maybe for once it was Mom who needed to be comforted. "He's a strong man with a will to live."

Her mother looked down at her so slowly it was as if she were a robot with a dying battery. Nina was shocked by how old and weary her mother looked, yet how strong. It should have been an impossible combination, but her mother had always been a woman of contradictions. She'd worried acutely about letting her children leave the yard, but hardly looked at them when they were in the house; she'd claimed that there was no God even as she decorated her holy corner and kept its lamp lit; she ate only enough food to keep her body moving, but wanted her children to eat more than they could stand. "You think that is what matters?"

Nina was taken aback by the ferocity in her mother's voice. "I think we have to believe he'll get better."

"He is in room 434. He has been asking for you."

Nina took a deep breath and opened the door to her father's room.

It was quiet except for the mechanical sound of machines. She moved slowly toward him, trying not to cry.

He looked small, a big man who'd been whittled down to fit in a child's bed.

"Nina." His voice was so soft and breathy she hardly recognized it. His skin was frighteningly pale.

She forced herself to smile, hoping it looked real. Her father was a man who valued laughter and joy. She knew it would hurt him to see her in pain.

"Hey, Daddy." The little-girl word slipped out; she hadn't said it in years.

He knew; he knew and he smiled. It was a faded, tired version of his smile and Nina reached down to wipe the spittle from his lip. "I love you, Daddy."

"I want . . ." He was breathing hard now. "Go . . . home."

She had to lean close to hear his quietly spoken words. "You can't go home, Dad. They're taking good care of you here."

He reached for her hand, holding it tightly. "Die home."

This time she couldn't will her tears away. She felt them streak down her face and land in tiny gray petals on the white blanket. "Don't . . ."

He stared up at her, still breathing hard; she saw the light go out of his eyes and the weakening of his will, and that hurt more than words had.

"It won't be easy," she said. "You know Meredith likes everything in its place. She'll want you here."

The smile he gave her was so sad and sloppy it broke her heart. "You . . . hate easy."

"I do," she said quietly, stung by the sudden thought that without him, no one would know her that well.

He closed his eyes and exhaled slowly. For a second, Nina thought she'd lost him, that he'd simply fallen away from her and sunk into the darkness, but this time the machines soothed her. He was still breathing.

She sank into the chair beside him, knowing why he'd asked this favor of her. Mom could do it, of course, could force his move home, but Meredith would hate her mother for it. Dad had spent his life trying to create love where none existed—between his wife and his daughters—and he couldn't give up even now. All he could do was hand his need to her and hope she could accomplish what he wanted. She remembered how often he'd called her his rule-breaker, his spitfire, and how proud he'd been of her courage to go into battle.

Of course she would do as he'd asked. It was perhaps the last thing he'd ask of her.

That night, after the arrangements had been made to have Dad discharged, Nina went out to her rental car. She sat there a long time, alone in the dark parking lot, trying to let go of the fight she and Meredith had had about moving Dad. Nina had won, but it hadn't been easy. Finally, with a tired sigh, she started the engine and drove away from the hospital. Snow patterned her windshield, disappearing and reappearing with each swipe of the wiper blades. Even with limited visibility, her first view of Belye Nochi made her breath catch.

The house looked as beautiful and out of place as ever in its snowy valley, tucked as it was in a vee of land between the river and the hills. Christmas lights made it even more beautiful, almost magical.

It had always reminded her of the fairy tales they'd once been told, full of dangerous magic and handsome princes and dragons. In short, it reminded her of her mother.

On the porch, she stomped the snow off her leather hiking boots and opened the door. The entry was cluttered with coats and boots. The kitchen counters were a graveyard of coffee cups and empty plates. Her mother's precious brass samovar glinted in the light from an overhead fixture.

She found Meredith in the living room, all alone, staring at the fireplace.

Nina could see how fragile her sister was right now. Her photographer's eye noticed every tiny detail: the trembling hands, the tired eyes, the stiff back.

She reached out and pulled her sister into a hug.

"What will we be without him?" Meredith whispered, clinging to her.

"Less," was all Nina could think of to say.

Meredith wiped her eyes, straightening suddenly, pulling away as if she'd just realized that she'd gone weak for a moment. "I'll stay the night. Just in case Mom needs something."

"I'll take care of her."

"You?"

"Yes. We'll be fine. Go make wild, crazy love to that sexy man of yours."

Meredith frowned at that, as if perhaps the idea of pleasure were impossible to contemplate. "You sure you'll be okay?"

"I'm sure."

"Okay. I'll be back over early to get the place ready for Dad. He'll be home at one, remember?"

"I remember," Nina said, walking Meredith to the door. As soon as her sister was gone, she grabbed her backpack and camera bags off the kitchen table and headed up the steep, narrow stairway to the second floor. Passing her parents' room, she went into the bedroom she and Meredith had shared. Although it appeared symmetrical—two twin beds, a pair of matching desks, and two white dressers—a closer look revealed the two very different girls who'd lived here and the separate paths their lives would take. Even as girls, they'd had little in common. The last thing Nina really remembered them doing together was the play.

Mom had changed that day and so had Meredith. True to her word, her sister had never listened to another of Mom's fairy tales, but it had been an easy promise to keep, as Mom never told them a story again. That was what Nina had missed the most. She'd loved those fairy tales. The White Tree, the Snow Maiden, the enchanted waterfall, the peasant girl, and the prince. At bedtime, on the rare nights Mom could be coaxed into telling them a story, Nina remembered being entranced by her mother's voice, and comforted by the familiarity of the words. All the stories were memorized and were the same every time, even without a book from which to read. Mom had told them that it was a Russian tradition, the ability to tell stories.

After the play, Nina had tried to repair the breach caused by Mom's anger and Meredith's hurt feelings, as had her dad. It hadn't worked, of course, and by the time Nina was eleven, she understood. By then, Nina's own feelings had been so hurt so often she'd pulled back, too.

She left the room and shut the door.

At her parents' bedroom, she paused and knocked. "Mom? Are you hungry?"

There was no answer.

She knocked again. "Mom?"

More silence.

She opened the door and went inside. The room was neat as a pin, and spartan in decor. A big king-sized bed, an antique dresser, one of those ancient Russian trunks, and a bookcase overflowing with small hardcover novels from the club her mother belonged to.

The only thing missing was her mother.

Frowning, Nina went downstairs again, calling out for her mother. She was just beginning to panic when she happened to glance outside.

There she was, sitting on her bench in the winter garden, looking down at her own hands. Tiny white Christmas lights entwined the wrought-iron fence, made the garden look like a magical box in the middle of all that night. Snow fell softly around her, making the substantial look illusory. Nina went to the entryway and grabbed some snow boots and a coat. Dressing quickly, she went outside, trying to ignore the tiny burn-like landings of snowflakes on her cheeks and lips. This was exactly why she worked near the equator.

"Mom?" she said, coming up beside her. "You shouldn't be out here. It's cold."

"It is not cold."

Nina heard the exhaustion in her mother's voice and it reminded her of how tired she was, and how terrible this day had been, and the awful day that was coming, and so Nina sat down beside her mother.

For what seemed like an eternity, neither one of them spoke. Finally, Mom said, "Your father thinks I cannot handle his death."

"Can you?" Nina asked simply.

"You would be amazed at what the human heart can endure."

Nina had seen the truth of that all over the world. Ironically, it was what her warrior women photographs were all about. "That doesn't mean the pain isn't unbearable. In Kosovo, during the fighting, I talked to—"

"Do not tell me about your work. These are discussions you have with your father. War does not interest me."

Nina wasn't hurt by that; at least that was what she told herself. She knew better than to reach out to her mother. "Sorry. Just making conversation."

"Do not." Mom reached down to touch the copper column that stood amid a messy coil of dead brown vines. Here and there red holly berries peeked through the snow, framed by glossy green leaves. Not that her mother could see these colors, of course. Her birth defect precluded her seeing the true beauty in her garden. Meredith had never understood why a woman who saw the world in black and white would care so much about flowers, but Nina knew the power of black and white images. Sometimes a thing was its truest self when the colors were stripped away.

"Come on, Mom," Nina said. "I'll make us some dinner."

"You do not cook."

"And whose fault is that?" Nina said automatically. "A mother is supposed to teach her daughter how to cook."

"I know, I know. It is my fault. All of it." Mom stood up, grabbed her knitting needles, and walked away.

Four

The dogs greeted Meredith as if she'd been gone for a decade. She scratched their ears without any real enthusiasm and went into the house, turning on the lights as she made her way from the kitchen to the living room.

"Jeff?" she called out.

Silence answered her.

At that, she did exactly what she didn't want to do: she made herself a rum (heavy on the rum) and Diet Coke and walked out to the porch. There, she sat down on the white love seat and stared out at the moonlit valley. In this light, the orchard looked almost sinister, all those bare, crooked limbs jutting up from the dirty layer of snow.

Reaching down to the left, she grabbed the old wool blanket from its place in a basket and wrapped it around her. She didn't know how to survive this grief, how to accept what was coming.

Without her father, Meredith feared she would be like one of those dormant apple trees: bare, vulnerable, exposed. She wanted to believe she wouldn't be alone with her grief, but who would be there for her? Nina? Jeff? Her children? Mom?

That was the biggest laugh of all. Mom had never been there for Meredith. Now it would be the two of them alone, connected by the thin strand of a dead man's love and precious little more.

Behind her, the door squeaked open. "Mere? What are you doing out here? It's freezing. I've been waiting for you."

"I needed to be alone." She saw that she'd hurt him, and she wanted to take it back, undo it, but the effort was beyond her. "I didn't mean that."

"Yes, you did."

She stood up so quickly the blanket fell away from her shoulders and landed in a heap on the love seat. Forcing a smile, she edged past him and went inside.

In the living room, she sat down in one of the club chairs by the fireplace, grateful that he'd made a fire. She was suddenly freezing. Her fingers tightened around the glass and she took a big gulp of her drink. It wasn't until he came up beside her, and looked down, that she realized she should have sat on the sofa so he could be beside her.

He made himself a drink and sat down on the hearth. He looked tired. And disappointed, too. "I thought you'd want to talk about it," he said quietly.

"God, no."

"How can I help?"

"He's dying, Jeff. There, I said it. We're talking. I feel much better now."

"Damn it, Mere."

She looked at him, knowing she was being a bitch, and unfair, too, but she couldn't stop herself. She just wanted to be alone, to crawl into some dark place where she could pretend this wasn't happening. Her heart was breaking. Why couldn't he see that, and why did he think he could somehow hold it together in his hands? "What do you want from me, Jeff? I don't know how to handle this."

He moved toward her then, pulled her to her feet. The ice rattled in her glass—she was shaking; why hadn't she known that?—and he took the drink from her, put it on the table beside her chair.

"I talked to Evan today."

"I know."

"He's worried."

"Of course he's worried. He's . . ." She couldn't say it again.

"Dying," Jeff said softly. "But that's not what's bothering him. He's worried about you and Nina and your mother and me. He's afraid this family will fall apart without him."

"That's ridiculous," she said, but the softness of her voice betrayed her.

"Is it?"

At the touch of his lips to hers, she remembered how much she'd once loved him, how much she wanted to love him now. She wanted to put her arms around him and cling to him, but she was so cold. Numb.

He held her as he hadn't held her in years, as if he'd fall apart if she let him go, and he kissed her ear, whispering, "Hold me."

She almost cracked right there, almost broke apart. She tried to lift her arms and couldn't do it.

Jeff drew back, letting her go. He stared at her a long time, so long she wondered what it was he saw.

For a moment, he looked like he was going to say something, but in the end, he just walked away.

What was there to say, really?

Her father was dying. Nothing could change that. Words were like pennies, fallen into corners and down the cracks, not worth the effort of collecting.

Nina had spent a lot of time with injured or dying people, standing witness, revealing universal pain through individual suffering. She was good at it, too, able to somehow be both completely in the moment and detached enough to record it. As terrible as it had often been, her place beside makeshift hospital beds, watching people with catastrophic injuries, everything that came before paled in comparison to this moment, when she was suffering herself. On this day when her father came home from the hospital, she couldn't hold back, couldn't put her grief in a box and lock it shut.

She was standing in her parents' bedroom, beside the big window that overlooked the winter garden and the orchard beyond. Outside, the sky was a bold cerulean blue; cloudless. A pale winter sun shone down, its warm breath melting the crusty layer of yellowing snow. Water dripped from the eaves, no doubt studding the snow along the porch rail below.

She brought the camera to her eye and focused on Meredith, who was looking down at Dad, trying to smile; Nina captured the frailty in her sister's face, the sadness in her eyes. Next, she focused on her mother, who stood beside the bed, looking as regal as Lauren Bacall, as cold as Barbara Stanwyck.

From his place in the big bed, with stark white pillows and blankets piled around him, Dad looked thin and old and fading. He blinked slowly, his mottled eyelids falling like flags to half-mast and then lifting again. Through the viewfinder, Nina saw his rheumy brown eyes focus on her. The shock of it, of the directness of his gaze, surprised her.

"No cameras," he said. His voice was frayed and tired, not his voice at all, and somehow that loss, the very *sound* of him, was worse than all the rest. She knew why he'd said that. He knew her, knew why the camera was important to her now.

Nina lowered the camera slowly, feeling naked suddenly, vulnerable. Without that thin layer of a glass lens, she was *here* instead of there, looking at her father, who was dying. She moved in toward the bed, stood beside Meredith. Mom was on the other side. All of them were tucked in close.

"I will be back in a moment," Mom said.

Dad nodded at her. The look that passed between her parents was so intimate that Nina felt almost like an intruder.

As soon as Mom was gone, Dad looked at Meredith. "I know you're afraid," he said quietly.

"We don't need to talk about it," Meredith said.

"Unless you *want* to talk about it," Nina said, reaching down for his hand. "You must be afraid, Dad . . . of dying."

"Oh, for God's sake," Meredith said, stepping back from the bed.

Nina didn't want to explain to her sister, not now, but she'd lived alongside death for years. She knew there were peaceful passings and angry, desperate ones. As hard as it was for her to contemplate his dying, she wanted to help him. She brushed the white hair away from his age-spotted forehead, remembering suddenly how he'd looked as a younger man, when his face had been tanned from working in his orchard. All except for his forehead, which was always pale because of the hats he wore.

"Your mom," he said, speaking with obvious effort. "She'll break without me. . . ."

"I'll take care of her, Dad. I promise," Meredith said unsteadily. "You know that."

"She can't do it again . . . ," Dad said. He closed his eyes and let out a tired sigh. His breathing became labored.

"Can't do what again?" Nina asked.

"Who are you, Barbara Walters?" Meredith snapped. "Back off. Let him sleep."

"But he said—"

"He told us to take care of Mom. Like he even had to ask." Meredith busied herself with his blankets and fluffed his pillows. She was like an über-competent nurse. Nina understood; Meredith was so afraid that she had to keep busy. Next, she knew, her sister would run away.

"Stay," Nina said. "We need to talk—"

"I can't," Meredith said. "The business doesn't stop just because I want it to. I'll be back in an hour."

And then she was gone.

Nina reached instinctively for her camera and started taking pictures; not to show anyone, just for herself. As she looked down at him, focused on his pale face, the tears she'd been fighting turned him into a gray and white smear in the midst of that huge four-poster wooden bed. She wanted to say, *I love you, Dad*, but the words had hooks that wouldn't let go.

Quietly, she left his room and shut the door. In the hallway, she passed her mother, and for a split second, when their pain-filled gazes met, Nina reached out.

Mom lurched away from Nina's hand and went into the bedroom, shutting the door behind her.

There it was. The whole of her childhood repeated in a too-quiet hallway. The worst part was, Nina knew better.

Her mother was not a woman one reached out to.

Meredith and Jeff met the girls at the train station that night. It was a subdued homecoming, full of sad looks and unspoken words, not what it should have been at all.

"How's Grandpa?" Jillian asked when the car doors shut and they were all together in the quiet.

Meredith wanted to lie, but it was too late to protect them. "Not good," she said quietly. "He'll be glad to see you, though."

Maddy's eyes filled with tears. Of course they did; her youngest daughter had always been the emotional one. No one laughed louder or cried harder than Maddy. "Can we see him tonight?"

"Of course, honey. He's waiting for us. And your aunt Nina is here, too."

Maddy smiled at that, but it wasn't her real smile; it was a tattered version of it. "Cool."

And somehow, with all of it, that quiet, subdued *cool* hurt Meredith most of all. In it was the change that was coming, the grief that would reconfigure their family. Maddy and Jillian adored Nina. Usually they treated her like a rock star.

But now it was just that quiet, whispered *cool*.

"Maybe he should see another specialist," Jillian said. Her voice was soft and calm, and in it Meredith heard an echo of the doctor her daughter would someday become. Steady and collected. That was Jillian.

"He's seen several really good doctors," Jeff said. He waited a minute, let those words sink in, and then he started the car.

Usually, they would have talked and laughed and told stories on the drive, and once at home they would have gathered around the kitchen table for a game of hearts or in the living room to watch a movie.

Tonight, though, the drive was quiet. The girls tried to make conversation, told dull stories about classes and sorority rules and even the weather, but their words had trouble rising above the pall that hung in the car.

At Belye Nochi, they went into the house and made their way up the narrow stairway to the second floor. At the top of the stairs, Meredith turned to them and almost warned them that he looked ill. But that was what a mother did with young children. Instead, with a little nod, she opened the door and led the way into the bedroom. "Hey, Dad. Look who is here to see you."

Nina was sitting on the stone hearth, her back to a bright orange fire. At their entrance, she stood. "These can't be my nieces," she said, but her usual booming laugh was gone.

She went to the girls, hugged them tightly. Then she hugged her brother-in-law.

"Your grandfather has been waiting for you two," Mom said, rising from her place in the rocking chair by the window. "As have I."

Meredith wondered if she was the only one who heard the change in her mother's voice when she spoke to the girls.

It had always been like that. Mom was as warm to her granddaughters as she was cold to her daughters. For years it had wounded Meredith, that obvious preference for Jillian and Maddy, but in the end she'd been grateful that her mother made the girls feel cared for.

The girls took turns hugging their grandmother and then turned to face the big four-poster bed.

In it, Dad lay motionless, his face startlingly pale, his smile unsteady.

"My granddaughters," he said quietly. Meredith could see how affected they were by the sight of him. For the whole of their lives he'd been like one of the apple trees on this property. Sturdy and dependable.

Jillian was the first to lean down and kiss him. "Hey, Grandpa."

Maddy's eyes were damp. She reached over for her sister's hand and held it. When she opened her mouth to say something, no words came out.

Dad reached up a mottled, shaking hand and pressed it to her cheek. "No crying, princess."

Maddy wiped her eyes and nodded.

Dad tried to sit up. Meredith went to his bedside to help him. She fluffed and arranged the pillows behind him.

Coughing hard, he said, "We're all here." Then he looked at Mom. "It's time, Anya."

"No," Mom said evenly.

"You promised," he said.

Meredith felt something swirling about the room like smoke. She glanced at Nina, who nodded. So she felt it, too.

"*Now*," Dad said with a sternness that Meredith had never heard before.

Mom folded beneath that command, just sank into the rocking chair.

Meredith barely had time to process the stunning capitulation when her father spoke again.

"Your mother has agreed to tell us one of her fairy tales. After all these years. Like she used to."

He looked at Mom; his smile was so loving it broke Meredith's heart to see. "The peasant girl and the prince, I think. That was always my favorite one."

"No," Meredith said—or maybe she just thought it. She took a step back from the bed.

Nina crossed the room and sat down on the floor at Mom's feet, just as she'd done years ago. As they'd both done.

"Here, Mad," Nina said, patting the floor. "Come sit by me."

Jeff was the next to move. He chose the big armchair by the fireplace and Jillian snuggled in alongside him. Only Meredith had yet to move, and she couldn't seem to make her legs work. For decades she'd told herself that her mother's fairy tales meant nothing; now she had to admit what a lie that had been. She'd loved hearing those stories, and during the telling, she'd accidentally loved her mother. That was the truth about why Meredith had stopped listening. It hurt too much.

"Sit . . . Meredoodle," Dad said gently, and at the nickname, she felt her resistance give way. Woodenly, she crossed the room and sat on the Oriental rug, as far away from her mother as possible.

In the rocking chair, Mom sat very still, her gnarled hands tented in her lap. "Her name is Vera and she is a poor peasant girl. A nobody. Not that she knows this, of course. No one so young can know such a thing. She is fifteen years old and she lives in the Snow Kingdom, an enchanted land that now is rotting from within. Evil has come to the kingdom; he is a dark, angry knight who wants to destroy it all."

Meredith felt a chill move through her. She remembered suddenly how it once had been: Mom would come into their room at night and tell them wondrous tales of stone hearts and frozen trees and cranes who swallowed starlight. Always in the dark. Her voice was magic back then, as it was now. It would bring them all together for a time, but in the morning, those bonds would be gone, the stories never spoken of.

"He moves like a virus, this knight; by the time the villagers begin to see the truth, it is too late. The infection is already there; winter snow turns a terrible purplish black, puddles in the street grow tentacles and pull unwary travelers down into the muck, trees argue among themselves and stop bearing fruit. The fair villagers can do nothing to stop this evil. They love their kingdom and are the kind of people who

keep their heads down to avoid danger. Vera does not understand this. How can she, at her age? She knows only that the Snow Kingdom is a part of her, like the soles of her feet or the palms of her hands. On this night, for some reason she cannot name, she wakes at midnight and gets out of bed quietly, so as not to waken her sister, and she goes to her bedroom window, opening it wide. From here, she can see all the way to the bridge.

In June, when the air smells of flowers, and the night itself is as brief as the brush of a butterfly's wing, she cannot help imagining her own bright future.

It is the time of white nights, when at its darkest the sky is a deep, royal purple smattered with stars. In these months, the streets are never quiet. At all hours, villagers gather on the streets; lovers walk across the bridge. Courtiers leave the cafés very late, drunk on mead and sunlight.

But as she is breathing in the summer night, she hears her parents arguing in the other room. Vera knows she should not listen, but she cannot help herself. She tiptoes to the chamber door, pushing it open just a crack. Her mother stands by the fire, wringing her hands as she looks up at Papa.

"You cannot keep doing these things, Petyr. It is too dangerous. The Black Knight's power is growing. Every night, it seems, we hear of villagers who are turned to smoke."

"You cannot ask me to do this."

"I do ask you. I do. Write what the Black Knight tells you to. They are just words."

"Just words?"

"Petyr," her mother says, crying now, and that frightens Vera; never has she heard her mother weep. "I am afraid for you." And then, even more softly, "I am afraid of you."

He takes her in his arms. "I am careful, always."

Vera closes the door, confused by what she has heard. She does not understand all of it, or perhaps even part of it, but she knows that her strong mother is afraid, and that is something she has never seen before.

But Papa will never let anything bad happen to them. . . .

She means to ask her mother about the argument the next day, but when she wakens, the sun is shining and she forgets all about it. Instead, she rushes outside.

Her beloved kingdom is in bloom and so is she. How can anything be bad when the sun shines?

She is so happy that even taking her younger sister to the park doesn't bother her.

"Vera, look! Watch me!" twelve-year-old Olga calls out to her, launching into a series of cartwheels.

"Nice," Vera says to her sister, but in truth she is barely watching. She leans back into the bench and tilts her chin upward to the sun, closing her eyes. After a long, cold winter, this heat feels wonderful on her face.

"Two roses do I bring to thee."

Vera opens her eyes slowly and finds herself looking up at the most handsome boy she has ever seen.

Prince Aleksandr. Every girl recognizes his face.

His clothes are perfectly made and decorated in golden beads. Behind him stands a gleaming white carriage, drawn by four white horses. And in his hand, two roses.

She responds with the poem's next line, grateful that her father has made her read so much.

"You are young to know poetry," he says, and she can tell that he is impressed. "Who are you?"

She straightens, sitting up, hoping he notices her new breasts. "Veronika. And I am not that young."

"Really? I'll wager your father would not let you go walking with me."

"I don't need anyone's permission to go out, Your Highness," she lies, feeling her cheeks redden.

He laughs, and it is a sound like music.

"Well, then, Veronika, I will see you tonight. At eleven o'clock. Where shall I find you?"

Eleven o'clock. She is supposed to be in bed by then. But she cannot say that. Perhaps she can feign an illness and put blankets in her place in bed and climb out the window. And she will need some kind of magic to find a dress worthy of a prince. Surely he will not want to go walking with a poor peasant girl in a worn linen gown. Perhaps she can sneak over to the Alakee Swamp, where the witches sell love for the price of a finger. At that, her glance shoots to her sister, who has noticed the prince and is walking this way.

"On the Enchanted Bridge," she says.

"I think you will leave me standing there alone."

Olga comes closer, yells her name.

"No. Honestly, I won't." She glances at Olga, wincing at her approach. "I won't. Go, Prince Aleksandr. I'll see you then."

"Call me Sasha," he says.

And just like that, she falls in love with this smiling young man who is all wrong for her. Above her station. And dangerous to her family, as well. She looks down at her pale, slim hands, seeing calluses from washing clothes on rough stones, and she wonders: Which finger would she lose for love . . . and how many will it take to make the prince love her in return?

But these are questions that have no answers and do not matter, not to Vera, anyway, for already love has begun. She and her handsome prince sneak away and fall in love and get married, and they live happily ever after.

Mom stood up. "The end."

"Anya," Dad said sharply. "We agreed—"

"No more." Mom smiled briefly at her granddaughters and then walked out of the room.

Honestly, Meredith was relieved. Against her best intentions, the fairy tale had sucked her in again. "Let's go, girls. Your grandpa needs his rest."

"Don't run away," Dad said to her.

"Run away? It's almost ten, Dad. The girls have been traveling all day. They're exhausted. We'll be back early in the morning." She went to his bedside, leaned down to kiss his stubbly cheek. "Get some sleep, okay?"

He touched her face, let his dry palm linger on her cheek as he stared up at her. "Did you listen?"

"Of course."

"You need to listen to her. She's your mother."

She wanted to say she didn't have time for fairy tales and listening to a woman who rarely spoke wasn't easy, but instead she smiled. "Okay, Dad. I love you."

He pulled his hand back slowly. "Love you, too, Meredoodle."

The fairy tales had always been among Nina's best childhood memories, and though she had not heard one in decades, she remembered them well.

But why would her father bring them back up now? Surely he knew it would end badly. Meredith and Mom hadn't been able to leave the room fast enough.

She went to stand beside him. They were alone now. Behind her, the fire snapped and a log crashed downward, crumbling to orangey black bits.

"I love the sound of her voice," he said.

And Nina suddenly understood. Her father had employed the only device known to actually make Mom talk. "You wanted us all to be together."

Dad sighed. It was a sound as thin as tissue, and afterward, he seemed to grow even more pale. "You know what a man thinks about . . . now?"

She reached for his hand, held it. "What?"

"Mistakes."

"You didn't make many of those."

"She tried to talk to you girls. Until that god-awful play . . . I shouldn't have let her hide. She's just so broken and I love her so much."

Nina leaned forward and kissed his forehead. "It doesn't matter, Dad. Don't worry."

He grabbed her hand and looked up at her through watery brown eyes. "It matters," he said, his mouth trembling, his voice so weak she could barely hear him. "She needs you . . . and you need her. Promise me."

"Promise you what?"

"After I'm gone. Get to know her."

"How?" They both knew that there was no way to get close to her mother. "I've tried. She won't talk to us. You know that."

"Make her tell you the story of the peasant girl and the prince." As he said it, he closed his eyes again, and his breathing turned wheezy. "All of it this time."

"I know what you're thinking, Dad. Her stories used to bring us together. For a while, I even thought . . . but I was wrong. She won't—"

"Just try, okay? You've never heard it all."

"But—"

"Promise me."

She touched the side of his face, feeling the prickly white outcroppings of a beard that hadn't been shaved and the wet trail of his tears. She could tell that he was almost asleep. This afternoon, and maybe this conversation, had cost him too much and he was fading into the pillows again. He'd always wanted his daughters and his wife to love each other. He wanted it so much he was trying to believe a nice story hour would make it happen. "Okay, Dad. . . ."

"Love you," he whispered, his voice slurred. Only the familiarity of the words made them decipherable.

"I love you, too." Leaning down, she kissed his forehead again and pulled the covers up to his chin. Turning off the bedside light, she slipped her camera around her neck and left him.

Drawing in a deep, steadying breath, she went downstairs. In the kitchen, she found her mother standing at the counter, chopping beets and yellow onions. A giant pot of borscht simmered on the stove.

Of course. In times of trouble Meredith did chores, Nina took photographs, and Mom cooked. The one thing the Whitson women never did was talk.

"Hey," Nina said, leaning against the doorway.

Her mother turned slowly toward her. Her white hair was drawn back from her angular face and coiled in a ballerina bun at the nape of her neck. Against the pallor of her skin, those arctic-blue eyes seemed impossibly sharp for a woman of her age. And yet, there was a brittle look to her that Nina didn't remember noticing before, and that new fragility made her bold.

"I always loved your stories," she said.

Mom wiped her hands on her apron. "Fairy tales are for children."

"Dad loves them. He told me once that you told him a story every Christmas Eve. Maybe you could tell me one tomorrow. I'd love to hear the rest of the peasant girl and the prince."

"He is dying," Mom said. "It is a little late for fairy tales, I would say."

Nina knew then: her promise couldn't be kept, no matter how hard she tried. There was simply no way to get to know her mother. There never had been.

Five

Meredith threw back the covers and got out of bed. Reaching for the robe on her bathroom door, she was careful to brush her teeth without looking in the mirror. Reflective surfaces would not be her friend today.

The minute she left her room, she heard noise: the dogs were jumping downstairs, barking, and a television was on somewhere. Meredith smiled. For the first time in months, it felt like home again.

Downstairs, she found Jillian in the kitchen, setting the table. The dogs were positioned beside her, waiting for breakfast scraps.

"Dad told me to let you sleep," Jillian said.

"Thanks," Meredith said. "Where's your sister?"

"Still in bed."

Jeff handed Meredith a cup of coffee. "You okay?" he asked quietly.

"Rough night," she said, looking at him above the rim of her cup. The fairy tale had stirred up a lot of old emotions, and that, combined with her worry about her dad's weakness, had caused a restless night. "Did I keep you awake?"

"No."

She remembered how entwined they used to sleep. Lately, they slept far enough apart that one's restless night didn't affect the other.

"Mom?" Jillian said, putting down napkins. "Can we go see Grandpa and Baba again this morning?"

Meredith reached past Jeff to the stack of buttered toast on the counter. Tearing off a tiny piece, she said, "I'm going to go now. Why don't you all come after breakfast?"

Jeff nodded. "We'll take the dogs for a walk and be right down."

She nodded and took her coffee upstairs, where she exchanged her robe and pajamas for a pair of comfortable jeans and a cable-knit turtleneck sweater. Saying a last quick good-bye, she hurried out of the house.

It was a surprisingly sunny day. Her breath was visible as she walked the quarter mile downhill to her parents' house. All night she'd dreamed about her dad. Maybe she'd been awake, really, and it had been memories that spiraled through her mind. Or maybe a combination of the two. All she really knew for sure was that she needed to sit beside him, let him tell her some stories from his life so she could hold that knowledge close and pass it on someday. They'd forgotten to do that—pass along family stories, put photographs in scrapbooks; that kind of thing. They knew a little about Dad's relatives in Oklahoma and how the Great Depression had ruined them. They knew he'd joined the army and met Mom while on active duty, but that was pretty much it. Most of their family stories dated from the start of Belye Nochi, and Meredith, like many kids, had been more concerned with her own life than his.

Now she needed to rectify that mistake. And she wanted to apologize for running out after the fairy tale. She knew it had hurt his feelings and she hated that. This morning she'd give him a kiss and tell him how much she loved him and how sorry she was. If it mattered to him, she'd listen to every damn stupid story her mother had to tell.

At the front door, she knocked once and went inside.

"Mom?" She called out, closing the door behind her. She could tell immediately that coffee hadn't been made.

"Nice, Nina," she muttered.

She put the coffee on and went upstairs. At her parents' closed bedroom door, she knocked. "Hey, guys. I'm here. Are you in there?" There was no answer, so she opened the door and found her parents cuddled together in bed.

"Morning. I've got coffee going downstairs, and I started the samovar." She went to the windows and threw open the heavy curtains. "The doctor said Dad should try to eat. How do poached eggs and toast sound?"

Sunlight shone through the huge bowed windows, illuminating the honeyed oak floors and landing on the ornate Eastern European bed that dominated the room. As with most of the house, there were few splashes of color in here. Just white bedding and dark wood. Even the chair and ottoman in the corner were upholstered in snowy white damask. Mom had done the decorating, and since she didn't see color, she tended not to use it. The only art on the walls were Nina's more famous photographs, all in black and white, framed in black walnut.

Turning, she looked at her parents again. They lay spooned together, with Dad on his left side, facing the dresser, and Mom tucked up against his back with her arms around him. She was whispering to him; it took Meredith a second to realize that Mom was speaking Russian.

"Mom?" Meredith said, frowning. For all of her mother's Russianness, she never spoke that language in the house.

"I am trying to warm him up. He is so cold." Mom rubbed her hands vigorously along Dad's arms, his sides. "So cold."

Meredith couldn't make herself move. She thought she'd known pain before, but she hadn't; not until this moment.

Her father lay too still in bed, his hair a mess, his mouth slack, his eyes closed. He looked peaceful, as if he were simply sleeping late, but a pale blue cast rimmed his lips; it was just barely there, but she, who had looked at this face so often, saw that the man she loved wasn't there anymore. His skin was a terrible gray color. He'd never reach for her again and pull her into a bear hug and whisper, *I love you, Meredoodle.* At that, her knees buckled. She remained standing only by force of will.

She went to the bed, touched his pale, pale cheek.

He was cold.

Mom made a sobbing sound and rubbed his shoulder and arms harder. "I have some bread saved for you. Wake up."

Meredith had never heard her mother sound so desperate. In truth, she'd never heard *anyone* sound like that, but she understood: it was the sound you made when the floor dropped out from beneath you, and you were falling.

The last thing Meredith wanted to think about was what she should have said to her father, but there it was, a shadowy reminder of last night, standing beside her, whispering poison. Had she told him she loved him?

She felt the sting of tears, but knew she couldn't give in now. If she did, she'd be lost. She wished sharply, desperately, that it could be different, just this once, that she could be the child, taken into her mother's arms, but that wasn't how this would go. She went to the phone and dialed 911.

"My father has died," she said softly into the receiver. When she'd given out all the information, she returned to the bed and touched her mother's shoulder. "He's gone, Mom."

Her mother looked up at her, wild-eyed.

"He's so cold," Mom said, sounding plaintive and afraid, almost childlike. "They always die cold. . . ."

"Mom?"

Her mother drew back, staring uncomprehendingly at her husband. "We'll need the sled."

Meredith helped her mother to her feet. "I'll make you some tea, Mom. We can have it while they . . . take him."

"You found someone to take him away? What will it cost us?"

"Don't worry about that, Mom. Come on. Let's go downstairs." She took her mother by the arm, feeling like the stronger of the two for the first time ever.

"He is my home," her mother said, shaking her head. "How will I live without him?"

"We'll all still be here, Mom," Meredith said, wiping away her own tears. It was a hollow reassurance that did nothing to ease this pain in her chest. Her mother was right. He was home, the very heart of them. How would they stand life without him?

Nina had been out in the orchard since before dawn, trying to lose herself in photography. For a short time, it had worked. She'd been mesmerized by the skeletal fruit trees, turned into crystalline works of art by the icicles that hung from the limbs. Against a tangerine and pink dawn sky, they were stunning. Her dad would love these portraits of his beloved trees.

She would do today what she should have done decades ago—she'd enlarge and frame a series of apple tree shots. Each tree was a representative of her father's life's work, and he'd love the reminders of how much he'd accomplished. Maybe she could even go through the family photos (not that there were many) and find old pictures of the orchard.

Recapping her lens, she turned slightly, and there was Belye Nochi, its peaked roof on copper fire in the new light. It was too early yet to take her dad some coffee, and God knew her mother wouldn't want to sit at the kitchen table with her youngest daughter, so Nina packed up her gear and walked the long way up to her sister's house. She'd started from a spot deep in the back of the orchard; by the time she reached the road, she was actually breathing hard.

Really, she couldn't believe that her sister did this run every day.

When she reached the old farmhouse, she couldn't help smiling. Every inch of the place was decorated for Christmas. Poor Jeff must spend months putting up lights.

It wasn't a surprise. Meredith had always loved the holidays.

Nina knocked on the front door and opened it.

The dogs appeared immediately, greeting her with enthusiasm.

"Aunt Nina!" Maddy ran toward her, throwing her arms around

Nina and giving her a big hug. Last night's meeting had been too reserved for both of them.

"Hey, Mad," Nina said, smiling. "I hardly recognize you, kiddo. You're gorgeous."

"And I was what, a total bow-wow before?" Maddy teased.

"Total." Nina grinned. Maddy took her by the hand and led her into the kitchen, where Jeff was at the table reading *The New York Times* and Jillian was making pancakes.

Nina actually paused. Last night had been so artificial—with the dark room and the fairy tale and all that unspoken grief—that Nina hadn't had time to really *see* her nieces. Now she did. Maddy looked young, still gangly and coltish, with her long, wild brown hair and thick eyebrows and oversized mouth, but Jillian was a woman, serious and composed. It was already easy to picture Jillian as a doctor. There was an invisible line, straight and true, from the pudgy blond girl who'd caught bugs all summer and studied them in jars, to the tall young lady at the stove. And Maddy was still the spitting image of Meredith at that age, but more buoyant than Meredith had ever allowed herself to be.

Strangely enough, Nina felt the passing of her own years when she looked at her nieces' adult faces. It occurred to her for the first time that she was edging toward the middle of her life. She wasn't a kid anymore. Of course, she should have had this thought before, but when you lived alone and did what you wanted, when you wanted, time seemed somehow not to pass.

"Hey, Aunt Neens," Jillian said, removing the last pancake from the griddle.

Nina hugged Jillian, took a cup of coffee from her, and went to stand by Jeff. "Where's Meredith?" she asked, squeezing his shoulder lightly.

He put the paper on the table. "She went down to see your dad. Twenty minutes ago, maybe."

Nina looked at Jeff. "How is she?"

"I'm not the one you should be asking," he said.

"What do you mean?"

Before Jeff could answer, Maddy was beside her. "You want some pancakes, Aunt Nina?"

"No, thanks, hon. I better get down to the folks' house. Your mom is going to tear me a new one for not making coffee."

Maddy's wide mouth stretched into a smile. "She sure will. We'll be down in thirty."

Nina kissed both girls, said good-bye to Jeff, and headed down the road.

Back at the house, she hung her borrowed coat on the entryway hook and called out for her sister. The smell of freshly brewed coffee drew her into the kitchen.

Her sister was standing at the sink with her head bowed, watching the water run.

"Aren't you going to yell at me for not making coffee?"

"No."

Something about the way her sister said it made Nina stop. She glanced back at the stairs. "Is he awake?"

Meredith turned slowly. The look in her eyes was all Nina needed; the world tilted off its axis.

"He's gone," Meredith said.

Nina drew in a sharp breath. Pain that was unlike anything she'd ever known collected in her chest, in her heart maybe. An absurd memory flashed through her mind. She was eight or nine, a black-haired tomboy following her dad through the orchard, wishing she could be anywhere else. Then she'd fallen—caught her toe and gone flying. *Nice trip, Neener Beaner*, he'd said. *See you in the fall.* Laughing, he'd scooped her into his arms and positioned her on his big shoulders and carried her away.

She walked forward, her vision blurred by tears, and stepped into her big sister's arms. When she closed her eyes, he was beside them, in the room with them. *Remember when he taught us to fly kites in Ocean Shores?* but like the other, it was a silly memory, not the best by far, but it was here now, making her cry. Had she said everything to him last night? Had she told him how deeply she loved him, explained enough why she was gone so much?

"I don't remember if I told him I loved him," Meredith said.

Nina drew back, looked into her strong sister's ruined face and tear-filled eyes. "You told him. I heard you. And he knew it anyway. He knew."

Meredith nodded, wiped her eyes. "They'll be . . . coming for him soon."

Nina watched her sister regain composure. "And Mom?"

"She's up with Dad. I couldn't get her to leave him."

They exchanged a look that said everything and Nina said, "I'll go try. And then . . . what?"

"We start making plans. And phone calls."

The thought of it, of watching his life turn into the details of death, was almost more than Nina could bear. Not that she had a choice. She told her sister she'd be back and left the kitchen. Every step took effort and by the time she reached the second floor, she was crying again. Softly, quietly, steadily.

She knocked on the door and waited. At the silence, she turned the knob and went inside.

Surprisingly, the room was empty except for her father, lying in the bed, with the covers drawn so tightly to his chin that they looked like a layer of new-fallen snow on his body.

She touched his face, pushed a snow-white strand of hair away from his closed eyes, and then leaned down and kissed his forehead. The cold of his skin shocked her and the thought slipped in: *He'll never smile at me again.*

She drew in a deep breath and straightened, staring down at him for a long time, memorizing every detail. "Good-bye, Daddy," she said softly. There were more words, of course, hundreds of them, and she knew when she'd say them later: at night, when she felt lonely and disconnected and far away from home.

Backing away from the bed (she had to, had to make herself move, leave, now before she completely broke), she picked up the phone to call Danny but hung up before she'd even heard a tone. What would she say to him? How could words ease a pain like this? Out of the corner of her eye, she saw a blur of movement in the yard; dark blurring across white.

She moved to the window.

Mom was out there, in the snow, trudging toward the greenhouse.

Nina hurried downstairs and slipped back into her borrowed coat and wet boots, then walked across the porch, passing the kitchen window. Inside, she saw Meredith talking on the phone, her face chalky, her lips trembling. Nina didn't even know if her sister saw her pass by.

She went down the side steps and into the thick snow at the corner of the house. After a few feet, she picked up Mom's trail and stepped in her footsteps.

At the greenhouse, she stopped just long enough to gather courage and then opened the door.

Her mother was in her lawn nightgown and snow boots, kneeling in the dirt, pulling up tiny potatoes and throwing them in a pile.

"Mom?"

Nina said it twice more, and got no answer; finally, sharply, she said, "Anya," and moved closer.

Mom stopped and looked back. Her long white hair was unbound and fell in tangles around her pale face. "There are potatoes. Food will help him. . . ."

Nina knelt beside her mother in the dirt. It scared her to see her mother this way, but in a strange way, it soothed her, too. For once, they were feeling the same thing. "Hey, Mom," she said, touching her shoulder.

Mom stared at her, slowly frowning. Confusion clouded those brilliant blue eyes. She shook her head and made a sound, like a hiccup. Fresh tears glazed her eyes and the confusion lifted. "Potatoes won't help."

"No," Nina said quietly.

"He's gone. Evan is gone."

"Come on," Nina said, taking her by the elbow, helping her to her feet. They walked out of the greenhouse and into the snowy yard.

"Let's go inside," Nina said.

Mom ignored her and walked into the calf-deep snow, her hair and nightgown billowing out behind her in the slight breeze. At last she sat on the black bench in her garden.

Of course.

Nina followed her mother. Unbuttoning her own coat, she took it off and draped it over Mom's thin shoulders.

Shivering, Nina drew back and sat down. She thought she knew what her mother loved about this garden: it was contained and orderly. In the sprawling acreage of the orchard, this one square felt safe. The only color in the garden, besides summertime and autumn leaves, belonged to a single copper column, simple in design and accentuated with scripted decorations, that supported a white marble bowl that, come spring, would be filled with white, trailing flowers.

"I do not want him buried," her mother said. "Not in ground that freezes. We'll scatter his ashes."

Nina heard the familiar steel in her mother's voice again, and she almost missed the craziness of a minute ago. At least the woman in the greenhouse *felt* things. This woman, her mother, was back in control. Nina longed to lean against her, to whisper, *I'm going to miss him, Mommy,* as she might have done as a little girl, but some habits were so ingrained by childhood that there was no way to break them, even decades later. "Okay, Mom," she said finally.

A minute later, she stood up. "I'm going to go in. Meredith will need some help. Don't stay out here too long."

"Why not?" her mother said, staring at the copper column.

"You'll catch pneumonia."

"You think I could die from the cold? I am not a lucky woman."

Nina put a hand on her mother's shoulder, felt her flinch at the contact. As ridiculous as it was, that little flinch hurt Nina's feelings. Even now, with Dad's death between them, Mom wanted only to be alone.

Nina went back into the house and found Meredith still in the kitchen making calls. At her entrance, Meredith hung up and turned.

In the look that passed between them was the realization that this was who they were now. The three of them—she and Mom and Meredith. From now on they'd be a triangle, distantly connected, instead of the circle he'd created. The thought of that made her want to run for the airport. "Give me a list of numbers. I'll help with the calls."

More than four hundred people filled the small church to say good-bye to Evan Whitson; several dozen of them had come back to Belye Nochi to show their respects and raise a glass. Judging by the dishes Meredith had washed, a lot of glasses had been raised. As expected, Nina had been a marvelous host, drinking easily and letting people talk about Dad; Mom had moved through the crowd with her head held high, rarely stopping for longer than a moment; and Meredith had done all the heavy lifting. She'd organized and set out all of the food people had brought; she'd made sure there were plenty of napkins, plates, utensils, and glasses on hand, as well as ice; and she'd washed dishes almost continuously. There was no doubt that she was doing what she always did when stressed: hiding out behind endless organizing and chores. But honestly, she wasn't ready to mingle with friends and neighbors yet, to listen to memories about her father. Her grief was too new, too fragile to be handed back and forth in drunken hands.

She was elbow-deep in soapy water when, at about midnight, Jeff came into the kitchen to find her. He took her in his arms and hugged her. It was like coming home after a long journey and the tears she'd held back during the last few days, and the wrenching memorial service today, came pouring out. He held her, stroking her hair as if she were a child and saying the great lie, *It will be okay*, over and over again. When there was nothing left inside, she drew back, feeling shaky, and tried to smile. "I guess I've been holding that in."

"That's what you do."

"You say that like it's a bad thing. Should I fall apart?"

"Maybe."

Meredith shook her head. It only made her feel more separate when he said things like that. He seemed to think she was a vase that could break and be glued back together, but she knew that if the worst happened—if she shattered like glass—some pieces could be lost forever.

"I've been there," he said. "You helped me through my parents' deaths. Let me help you."

"I'm fine. Really. I'll fall apart later."

"Meredith—"

"Don't." She hadn't meant to say it so sharply, and she could tell she'd hurt his feelings, but she was barely hanging on here. She had no energy to worry about anyone else. "I mean, don't worry about it. I'll take care of things here. The girls are tired. Why don't you take them home?"

"Fine," he said, but there was a guarded look in his eyes she didn't recognize.

After everyone had gone, Meredith stood in the clean, orderly kitchen, alone, and wished almost immediately that she'd made a different choice. How hard would it have been to say, *Sure, Jeff, take me home and hold me . . .*

She threw the dishrag on the counter and left the hiding place of her mother's kitchen.

In the living room, she found Nina alone, standing in front of a large easeled picture of Dad. In a pair of crumpled khaki pants and a black sweater, with her short black hair a mess, she looked more like a teenager ready for her first safari than a world-famous photographer.

But Meredith saw the grief in her sister's bottle-green eyes. It was like too much water in a glass, spilling over, and she knew Nina was like her: neither of them knew how to express it or even really feel it as fully as they should, and she hurt for both of them, and for the woman who lay upstairs in her empty bed, feeling the same loss. She wished that they could come together, dissipate some of this pain by pooling it. But that wasn't who they were. She put down her wineglass and went to Nina, the little sister who'd once begged her to remember Mom's fairy tales and tell them in the dark when she couldn't sleep. "We have each other," Meredith said.

"Yeah," Nina agreed, although their eyes betrayed them both. They knew it wasn't enough.

Later that night, when Meredith was at home, tucked into bed beside her husband, it occurred to her that she'd made a terrible mistake, and regret haunted her, kept her awake. She'd been wrong to attend her father's wake as a caterer instead of as a daughter. She'd been so afraid of her feelings that she'd boxed them up and shoved them away, but it had made her miss it. Unlike Nina, Meredith hadn't heard the stories his friends had had to tell.

Sometime around three in the morning, she got out of bed and went to the porch, where she sat wrapped in a blanket, staring at little beyond the vapor of her own breath. But it wasn't cold enough to numb her grief.

For the next three days, Nina tried to be a real part of this family, but her every attempt was a failure. Without Dad, they were like random pieces of a board game, without a common goal or a rule book. Mom stayed in bed, staring straight ahead, knitting. She refused to come down for meals and only Meredith could coax her into showering

Nina had always felt vaguely useless next to her sister's über-competence, but it had never been as apparent as it was now. Meredith was like Ms. Pac-Man, moving steadily forward, ticking chores off her list. Somehow, impossibly, she'd gone back to work the very day after the funeral, so she was running the orchard and warehouses, taking care of her family, and still she managed to come to Belye Nochi at least three times a day to micromanage Nina's chores.

Nothing Nina did was right; Meredith did everything again. Vacuum, dishes, laundry. All of it. Nina would have said something, but honestly, she didn't give a shit, and Meredith moved like a frightened bird, all wing-flapping and chirping. She looked scared, too, like a woman on a cliff about to jump or fall.

But all of that, Nina could handle.

It was the grief that was killing her.

She thought, *He's gone*, at the oddest times, and it hurt so badly she caught her breath or stumbled or dropped a glass. (Meredith had *loved* that.)

She needed to get the hell out of here. That was all there was to it. She wasn't doing anyone any good, least of all herself.

Once she'd had that thought, there was no getting rid of it. All day today, she tried to talk herself out of it, told herself she couldn't run away, certainly not so close to Christmas, but at three o'clock, she went upstairs to her room, closed the door behind her, and called Sylvie in New York.

"Hey, Sylvie," she said when her editor answered.

"Hi, Nina. I've been thinking about you. How's your dad?"

"Gone." She tried not to react to that word, but it took effort. She went to the window of her girlhood room and stared out at the falling snow. It was midafternoon, and already it was darkening.

"Oh, Nina. I'm sorry."

"Yeah, I know." Everyone was sorry. What else was there to say? "I need to get back to work."

There was a pause. "So soon?"

"Yeah."

"Are you sure? You can never get this time back."

"Believe me, Sylvie, the last thing I want is this time back."

"All right. Let me do some checking. I know I need someone in Sierra Leone."

"A war zone sounds perfect," Nina said.

"You have serious issues, you know that, right?"

"Yeah," she said. "I know."

They talked for a few more minutes and Nina hung up. Feeling better—and worse—she went downstairs and found Meredith in the kitchen, doing the dishes. *Of course.*

Nina reached for a towel. "I was going to do that, you know."

"These are lunch and dinner dishes from yesterday, Nina. When exactly were you going to wash them?"

"Whoa, slow down. It's dishes, not—"

"People dying of hunger. I know. I get it. You do things that *matter.* Me, I just run the family business and take care of our parents and clean up after my important sister."

"I didn't mean that."

Meredith turned to her. "Of course not."

Nina felt impaled by that look, as if all her faults had just been laid bare. "I'm here, aren't I?"

"No. Not really." Meredith reached for the cleanser and began scrubbing the white porcelain sink.

Nina moved toward her sister. "I'm sorry," was all she could think to say.

Meredith turned to face her again. She wiped her forehead with the back of her hand, leaving a soapy trail behind. "How long are you staying?"

"Not long. The situation in Sierra Leone—"

"Spare me. You're running away." Meredith finally almost smiled. "Hell, I'd do the same thing if I could."

Nina felt as bad about herself as she ever had. She *was* running—from her ice-cold mother, from this too-empty house, from her brittle, competent sister, and from the memories that lived here. Perhaps those most of all. She cared about what her selfishness would cost her sister, and about the promise to her father she was ignoring, but God help her, she didn't care enough to stay. "What about his ashes?"

"She wants to scatter them on his birthday in May. When the ground isn't frozen."

"I'll come back for that."

"Twice in one year?" Meredith said.

Nina looked at her. "It's some year."

For a moment, it looked like Meredith might crumble, just let go and cry, and Nina felt the start of her own tears.

Then Meredith said, "Be sure and say good-bye to the girls. You know how much they idolize you."

"I will."

Meredith nodded curtly and wiped her eyes. "I have to be back at work in an hour. I'll vacuum before I go."

Nina wanted to say she'd do it—make one last effort—but now that she'd decided to leave, she was like a Thoroughbred at the starting gate. She wanted to run. "I'll go pack."

Late that night, when Nina's few things had been put in her backpack and stowed in the rental car, she finally went in search of her mother.

She found her wrapped in blankets, sitting in front of the fire.

"So you are leaving," her mother said without looking up.

"My editor called. They need me for a story. It's terrible, what's happening in Sierra Leone." She sat down on the hearth; her body shivered at the sudden heat. "Someone needs to show the world what's happening there. People are dying. It's so tragic."

"You think *your* photographs can do that?"

Nina felt the sting of that remark and the insult. "War is a terrible thing, Mom. It's easy to sit here in your nice, safe home and judge my work. But if you'd seen what I've seen, you'd feel differently. What I do *can* make a difference. You can't imagine how some people suffer in the world, and if no one sees it—"

"We'll scatter your father's ashes on his birthday. With or without you."

"Okay," Nina said evenly, thinking, *Dad understood*, and hurting all over again.

"Good-bye, then. Happy Christmas to you."

On that note, Nina left Belye Nochi. At the porch she paused, looking up the valley, watching the snow fall. Her practiced eye took it all in, cataloging and remembering every detail. In thirty-nine hours, it would be dust that rained down on her shoulders and swirled around her boots, and the images of this place would bleach out like bones beneath a punishing sun, until, in no time at all, they'd be too pale to see at all. Her family—and especially her mother—would become shadowy memory beings whom Nina could love . . . from a distance.

Six

In the weeks following her father's death, Meredith held herself together by strength of will alone. That, and a schedule as tight and busy as a boot camp recruit's.

Grief had become her silent sidekick. She felt its shadow beside her all the time. She knew that if she turned toward that darkness just once, embraced it as she longed to, she'd be lost.

So she kept moving. Doing.

Christmas and New Year's had been disastrous, of course, and her insistence on following tradition hadn't helped. The turkey-and-all-the-fixings dinner had only highlighted the empty place at the table.

And Jeff didn't understand. He kept saying that if she'd just cry she'd be okay. As if a few tears could help her.

It was ridiculous. She knew crying wouldn't help, because she cried in her sleep. Night after night she woke with tears on her cheeks, and none of it helped one bit. In fact, the opposite was true. The expression of grief didn't help. Only its suppression would get her through these hard times.

So she went on, smiling brightly at work and moving from one chore to the next with a desperate zeal. It wasn't until the girls went back to school that she realized how exhausted she was by the pretense of ordinary life. It didn't help, of course, that she hadn't slept through the night since the funeral, or that she and Jeff were having trouble finding anything to talk about.

She'd tried to explain it to him, how cold she felt, how numb, but he refused to understand. He thought she should "let it out." Whatever the hell that meant.

Still, she wasn't trying very hard to talk to him, that much was true. Sometimes they went whole days with little more than a nod in passing. She really needed to try harder.

She rinsed out her coffee cup, put it in the strainer, and went to the downstairs office he used for writing. Knocking quietly, she opened the door.

Jeff sat at his desk—the one they'd bought at least a decade ago, dubbed his *writer's space*, and christened by making love on it.

You'll be famous someday. The new Raymond Chandler.

She smiled at the memory, even as it saddened her to think that somewhere along the way their dreams had untangled, gone on separate paths.

"How's the book going?" she asked, leaning against the doorframe.

"Wow. You haven't asked me that in weeks."

"Really?"

"Really."

Meredith frowned at that. She'd always loved her husband's writing. In the early days of their marriage, when he'd been a struggling journalist, she'd read every word he wrote. Even a few years ago, when he'd first dared to try his hand at fiction, she'd been his first, best critic. At least that was what he'd claimed. That book hadn't sold to a publisher, but she'd believed in it, in him, heart and soul. And she was glad that he'd finally started another book. Had she told him that? "I'm sorry, Jeff," she said. "I've been a mess lately. Can I read what you have so far?"

"Of course."

She saw how easy it was to make him smile and felt a pang of guilt. She wanted to lean down and kiss him. It used to be as easy as breathing, kissing him, but now it felt strangely bold, and she couldn't quite make herself move toward him. She mentally added *Read Jeff's Book* to her To-Do list.

He leaned back in his chair. The smile he gave her was a good effort; only their twenty years together allowed her to see the vulnerable underside to it. "Let's go to dinner and a movie tonight. You need a break."

"Maybe tomorrow. Tonight I need to pay Mom's bills."

"You're burning the candle at both ends."

Meredith hated it when he said ridiculous things like that. What exactly was she supposed to stop doing? Her job? Caring for her mother? The chores at home? "It's only been a few weeks. Cut me some slack."

"Only if you cut yourself some."

She had no idea what he meant by that, and right now she didn't care. "I gotta go. See you tonight." She bent down, patted his shoulder, and left the house. She put the dogs in the fenced part of their yard and then drove down to her parents' house.

Her mother's house.

The reminder came with a pinch of grief that she pushed aside.

Inside, she closed the door behind her and called out for her mother.

There was no answer, which was hardly a surprise.

She found her mother in the rarely used formal dining room, muttering to herself in Russian. On the table, spread out in front of her, were all the pieces of jewelry Dad had bought her over the years, as well as the ornately decorated jewelry box that had been a long-ago Christmas gift from her daughters.

Meredith saw the mess grief had made of her mother's beautiful face: it had sucked in her cheeks and made her bones appear more prominent; it had drawn the color from her skin until her flesh nearly matched her hair. Only her eyes—startlingly blue against all that pallor—held any semblance of who she'd been a month ago.

"Hey, Mom," Meredith said, coming up to her. "What are you doing?"

"We have these jewels. And the butterfly is somewhere."

"Are you getting dressed up for something?"

Her mother looked up sharply. Only then, when their gazes really met, did Meredith see the confusion in those electric-blue eyes. "We can sell them."

"We don't need to sell your jewelry, Mom."

"They'll stop handing out money soon. You'll see."

Meredith leaned over and gently scooped up the costume jewelry. There was nothing of real value here: Dad's gifts had always been more heartfelt than expensive. "Don't worry about the bills, Mom. I'll be paying them for you."

"You?"

Meredith nodded and helped her mother to her feet, surprised at the easy acquiescence. Mom let herself be led up the stairs easily.

"Is the butterfly safe?"

Meredith nodded. "Everything is safe, Mom," she said, helping her mother into bed.

"Thank God," Mom said with a sigh. She closed her eyes.

Meredith stood there a long time, staring down at her sleeping mother. She reached out finally and felt her brow (it wasn't hot), and gently brushed the hair from her eyes.

When she was confident that Mom was sleeping deeply, she went downstairs and called the office.

Daisy answered on the first ring. "Meredith Whitson Cooper's office."

"Hey, Daisy," Meredith said, still frowning. "I'm going to work from Belye Nochi today. My mom's acting a little strange."

"Grief will do that to a person."

"Yeah," Meredith said, thinking of the tears that were always on her cheeks when she woke. Yesterday she'd been so exhausted she'd added orange juice to her coffee instead of soy milk. She'd drunk half the cup before she even noticed. "It will."

If Meredith had been burning the candle at both ends then, by the end of January, there was nothing left but the flame. She knew Jeff had grown impatient with her, even angry. Time and again, he told her to hire someone to help take care of her mother, or to let him help her, or—worst of all—to make time for them. But how was she supposed to accomplish that amid all her other chores? She'd tried to get Mom a housekeeper, but that had been a disaster. The poor woman had worked at Belye Nochi a week and quit without giving notice, saying that she couldn't stand the way Mom watched her all the time and told her to quit touching things.

So, with Nina gone off God knew where and Mom growing stranger and colder every day, Meredith had no choice but to pick up the slack. She'd made a promise to her father to care for Mom and she would never let him down. So she kept moving, doing everything that needed to be done. As long as she was moving, she could contain her grief.

Her routine had become her salvation.

Every morning she woke early, ran four miles, made her husband and her mother breakfast, and left for work. By eight o'clock, she was at her desk, working. At noon, she returned to Belye Nochi to check on Mom, pay a few bills, or do a little cleaning. Then it was back to work until six, grocery shopping on her way home, stop at Mom's until seven or eight, and—if Mom wasn't acting too weird—home by eight-thirty for whatever dinner she and Jeff could throw together. Without fail, she fell asleep on the sofa by nine and woke up at three in the morning. The only good part about this crazy routine was that she could call Maddy early because of the time-zone difference. Sometimes, just hearing her daughters' voices could get her through the day.

Now it was barely noon and she was already exhausted as she hit the intercom button and said, "Daisy, I'm going home for lunch. I'll be back in an hour. Can you get the shed reports to Hector and remind Ed to get me that information on grapes?"

The door to her office opened. "I'm worried about you," Daisy said, closing the door behind her.

Meredith was touched. "Thank you, Daisy, but I'm fine."

"You're working too hard. He wouldn't like it."

"I know, Daisy. Thanks."

Meredith watched Daisy leave the office, then gathered up her purse and keys.

Outside, snow was falling again. The parking lot was a slushy, muddy mess, as were the roads.

She drove slowly out to her mom's house, parked, and went inside. At the entryway, she took off her coat and hung it up, calling out, "Mom, I'm here."

There was no answer.

She dug through the refrigerator, found the pierogies she'd defrosted last night and a Tupperware container full of lentil soup. She popped the pierogies in the microwave and warmed them up. She was just about to go upstairs when she caught a glimpse of a dark shape in the winter garden.

This was getting old. . . .

She got her coat and trudged through the falling snow to the garden. "Mom," she said, hearing the exasperation in her voice and unable to temper it. "You've got to quit this. Come on inside. I'll make some pierogies and soup for you."

"From the belt?"

Meredith shook her head. Whatever the hell *that* meant. "Come on." She helped her mother to her feet—bare again, and blue with cold—and led her into the kitchen, where she wrapped her up in a big blanket and sat her down at the table. "Are you okay?"

"I am not the one to be worrying about, Olga," Mom said. "Check on our lion."

"It's me, Meredith."

"Meredith," she said, as if trying to make sense of the name.

Meredith frowned. Her mother seemed more confused than made sense. This wasn't just ordinary grief. Something was wrong. "Come on, Mom. I think we need to see Dr. Burns."

"What have we to trade?"

Meredith sighed again and took the plate of pierogies from the microwave. Placing the golden lamb-filled pastries on a cooler plate, she set them in front of her mother. "They're hot. Be careful. I'm going to get your clothes and call the doctor. Stay here. Okay?"

She went upstairs for some clothes, and while she was there, she called Daisy and asked her to make an emergency appointment with Dr. Burns. Then she came down with the clothes and helped Mom to her feet.

"You ate all of them?" Meredith said, surprised. "Good." She put a sweater on Mom, then helped her into socks and snow boots. "Put on your coat. I'll go warm up the car."

When she came back into the house, Mom was in the entryway, buttoning up her coat incorrectly.

"Here, Mom." Meredith unbuttoned the coat and rebuttoned it. She had almost finished when she realized that the coat was warm.

She reached into the pockets and found the pierogies, still hot from the oven, wrapped in greasy paper towels. *What the hell?*

"They're for Anya," Mom said.

"I know they're yours," Meredith said, frowning. "I'll leave them right here for you, okay?" she said, putting them in the ceramic bowl on the entry table. "Come on, Mom."

She led her mother out of the house and into the SUV.

"Just lean back, Mom. Go to sleep. You must be exhausted." She started up the car and drove to town, parking in one of the angled spots in front of the Cashmere Medical Group's brick office.

Inside, Georgia Edwards was at the desk, looking as perky and beautiful as she had in her cheerleading days at Cashmere High. "Hey, Mere," she said, smiling.

"Hi, Georgia. Did Daisy get an appointment for my mom?"

"You know Jim. He'd do anything for you Whitsons. Take her down to Exam A."

As they approached the exam room, Mom seemed to realize suddenly where they were. "This is ridiculous," she said, yanking her arm away.

"Disagree all you want," Meredith said, "but we're seeing the doctor."

Her mother straightened, lifted her chin, and walked briskly to the first exam room. There, she took the only seat for herself.

Meredith followed her inside and closed the door.

A few moments later, Dr. James Burns walked into the room, smiling. Bald as a cue ball, with compassionate gray eyes, he made Meredith think of her father. They'd been golf partners for years; Jim's father had been one of her father's best friends. He hugged Meredith tightly; in the embrace was their shared grief and a silent *I miss him, too.*

"So," he said when he stepped back. "How are you today, Anya?"

"I am fine, James. Thank you. Meredith is jumpy. You know this."

"Do you mind if I examine you?" he asked.

"Of course it is fine," Mom said. "But unnecessary."

Jim conducted an ordinary flu-type examination. When he finished with that, he made a few notes on her chart and then said, "What day is it, Anya?"

"January thirty-first, 2001," she said, her gaze steady and clear. "Wednesday. We have a new president. George Bush, the younger. And Olympia is the state capital."

Jim paused. "How are you, Anya? Really?"

"My heart beats. I breathe. I go to sleep and I wake up."

"Maybe you should see someone," he said gently.

"Who?"

"A doctor who will help you talk about your loss."

"Death is not something to talk about. You Americans believe words change a thing. They do not."

He nodded.

"My daughter needs help, perhaps."

"Okay," he said, making a few more notes on the chart. "Why don't you go to the waiting room while I speak to her?"

Mom left the room immediately.

"There's something wrong with her," Meredith said as soon as they were alone. "She's confused a lot. She's hardly sleeping. Today she put her lunch in her pockets and talked about herself in the third person. She's constantly worried about a lion, and she called me Olga. I think she's confusing the fairy tales with real life. Last night I heard her reciting one of them to herself . . . as if Dad were listening. You know she's always been depressed in the winter, but this is something else. Something's wrong. Could she have Alzheimer's?"

"Her mind seems to be fine, Meredith."

"But—"

"She's grieving. Give her some time."

"But—"

"There's no normal way to handle a thing like this. They were married for five decades and now she's alone. Just listen to her, if you can; talk to her. And don't let her be alone too much."

"Believe me, Jim, my mom is alone whether I am in the room or not."

"So be alone together."

"Yeah," Meredith said. "Right. Thanks, Jim, for seeing us. Now I need to get her home and get back to work. I have a two-fifteen meeting."

"Maybe you should try slowing down. I can give you a sleeping pill prescription if you'd like."

Meredith wished she had ten bucks for every time someone—especially her husband—had given her that advice. She'd be on a Mexican beach with the money. "Sure, Jim," she said. "I'll stop and smell the roses."

On a blistering hot day, more than one month after she'd left Washington State, Nina stood amid a sea of desperate, starving refugees. As far as she could see, there were people huddled in front of dirty, sagging tents. Their situation was critical; many of them had come in bleeding or shot or raped, but their stoicism was remarkable. Heat and dust beat down on them; they walked miles for a bucket of water, waited hours for a measure of rice from the Red Cross, but still there were children playing in the dirt; every now and then the sound of laughter rose above the crying.

Nina was as filthy and tired and hungry as those around her. She'd lived in this camp for two weeks now. Before that, she'd been in Sierra Leone, ducking and hiding to avoid being shot or raped herself.

She squatted down in the dry, dirty red soil. The humming sound of the camp was overwhelming, a combination of bugs and voices and distant machinery. Off to the left, a tattered medical flag fluttered above an army-issue tent. Hundreds of injured people stood patiently in line for help.

In front of her, sprawled half in and half out of a tent, an old, wizened black man lay in his wife's arms. He'd recently lost a leg, and the bloody stump seeped red beneath the blanket that was wrapped around him. His wife had been with him for hours, propping him up, although her own emaciated body had to be aching. She tipped precious drops of water into his mouth.

Nina capped her lens and stood up. Staring out over the camp, she felt an exhaustion that was new for her. For the first time in her career, the tragedy of it all was nearly unbearable. It wasn't worse here than where she'd been before. That wasn't it. The situation hadn't changed. She had. She carried grief with her everywhere, and the burden of it made compartmentalization impossible.

People usually thought her work was about *being* there, as if anyone could just point and shoot, but the truth was that her photographs were an extension of who she was, what she thought, how she felt. It took perfect concentration to capture the exquisite pain of personal tragedy on film. You had to be there one hundred percent, in the moment—but it had to be *their* moment.

She opened her pack and pulled out her satellite phone. Walking as far east as she dared, she set up the equipment, positioned the satellite, and called Danny.

At the sound of his voice, she felt something in her chest relax. "Danny," she said, yelling to be heard over the static.

"Nina, love. I thought you'd forgotten me. Where are you?"

She winced at that. "Guinea. You?"

"Zambia."

"I'm tired," she said, surprising herself. She couldn't remember ever saying that before, not while she was working.

"I can be at Mnemba Island by Wednesday."

Blue water. White sand. Ice. Sex. "I'm in."

She disconnected the call and packed her phone back up. Slinging the strap over her shoulder, she headed back to the camp. A line of new Red Cross trucks had arrived and the pandemonium of food distribution was going on. She sidestepped a pair of women carrying a box of supplies and went past the tent where she'd been taking pictures.

The man in the bloody bandages had died. The woman still sat behind him, rocking him in her arms, singing to him.

Nina stopped and took a picture, but this time the lens was no protection, and when she eased the camera from her eye, she realized she was crying.

From her comfortable, air-conditioned seat in the back of an SUV, Nina stared through the window at the scenery of Zanzibar. The narrow, twisting streets were teeming with people: women draped in the traditional Muslim veils and robes, schoolchildren in blue and white uniforms, men standing in groups. On the side of the road, vendors tried to sell anything they could, from fruits and vegetables to tennis shoes to barely used T-shirts. In the jungle behind the road, women—most with babies on their backs or in their arms—picked cloves; the spices lay in cinnamon-colored swatches on the sides of the road, drying in the hot sun.

When the cab finally left the main road and turned onto the dirt path that led to the beach, Nina hung on to the door handle for dear life. The road here was pure coral—as was the island—and tires could blow in a second. Their speed slowed; they inched past villages set up in the middle of nothing; cattle penned in makeshift corrals, women in brightly colored veils and dresses gathering sticks, children pumping together at the well for water. The houses were small and dark and made of whatever was handy—sticks, mud, chunks of coral—and everything wore the red cast of the dirt.

At the end of the road, the beach was a hive of activity. Wooden boats bobbed in the shallow water, while men tended to nets spread out on the sand. Raggedly dressed boys haunted the area, hoping for tourists, offering to pose for photographs in exchange for American dollars.

The minute she stepped onto the sleek white motorboat, she realized how tense she'd been. A knot in her neck relaxed. She felt the sea air on her dirty face, whipping through her matted hair as they sped across the flat sea. It occurred to her, as she breathed in the salty air, how lucky she was in this life, even with her grief. She could leave the terrible places behind, change her future with a phone call and an airplane ticket.

The private island—Mnemba—was a small atoll in the Zanzibar archipelago, and when she arrived, the island's manager, Zoltan, was there with a glass of white wine and a cool, wet rag. When he saw Nina, his dark, handsome face broke into a wide grin. "I am glad to see you again."

She jumped out of the boat and into the warm water, making sure to hold her gear bag high above her head. "Thanks, Zoltan. I'm glad to be here." She took the wine from him. "Is Danny here?"

"He's in number seven."

She slung the camera bag and backpack strap over her shoulder and made her way down the beach. The sand was as white as the coral from which it had been formed, and the water was a remarkable shade of aquamarine. Almost exactly the color of her mother's eyes.

There were nine private bandas on the island—thatch-roofed, open-sided cottages—each hidden from view by dense vegetation. The only time guests saw each other, or the staff, was for meals in the dining hut or at sunset, when cocktails were set up on a table at the beach in front of each banda.

Nina saw the discreet #7 sign on the beachside lounge chairs and followed the sand path to the banda. A pair of tiny antelope, no larger than rabbits, with antlers as sharp as ice picks, bounded across the path and disappeared.

She saw Danny before he saw her. He was in one of the woven bamboo chairs, with his bare feet propped on a coffee table, sipping a beer and reading. She leaned against the wooden railing. “That beer isn't quite the best-looking thing in the room, but it's close.”

Danny tossed down his book and stood up. Even in his worn, overwashed khaki shorts, with his long black hair in need of a good cutting, and his shadowy, stubble-coated jaw, he looked beautiful. He pulled her into his arms and kissed her until she pushed him away, laughing. “I'm filthy,” she said.

“It's what I love best about you,” he said, kissing the grimy palm of her hand.

“I need a shower,” she said, unbuttoning her shirt. He took her by the hand and led her through the bedroom and down the wooden walkway to the bathroom and the outside shower. Beneath the spray of hot water, she peeled out of her bra and shorts and panties, kicking the sopping garments aside. Danny washed her in a way that was pure foreplay, and when the soap was still sliding down her slick body, and she reached for him, all it took was a touch. He picked her up and carried her to the bedroom.

Later, when they both could breathe again, they lay entwined on the net-draped bed. “Wow,” she said, her head cradled in the crook of his arm. “I forgot how good we are at that.”

“We're good at a lot of things.”

“I know. But we're *really* good at that.”

There was a pause, and in it she knew he was going to say what she didn't want to hear. “I had to hear from Sylvie that your da died.”

“What was I supposed to do? Call and cry? Tell you he was dying?”

He rolled onto his side, pulling her with him until they lay facing each other. His hand slid down her back and rested on the curve of her hip. “I'm from Dublin, remember? I know about losin' people, Nina. I know how it sits inside you like battery acid, burnin' through. And I know about runnin' from it. You're not the only one in Africa, are you?”

“What do you want from me, Danny? What?”

“Tell me about your da.”

She stared at him, feeling cornered. She wanted to give him what he wanted, but she couldn't. Her feelings, her loss, were so intense that if she let herself feel all of it, she'd never find a way back.

"I don't know how. He was . . . my sun, I guess."

"I love you like that," he said quietly.

Nina wished that made her feel better, but it didn't. She knew about unequal love, how you could be crushed from the inside if one person was more in love than the other. Hadn't she sometimes seen that kind of wreckage in Dad's eyes when he looked at Mom? She was sure she had. And once you'd seen that kind of pain, you didn't forget it. If Danny ever looked at her like that it would break her heart. And he would. Sooner or later he'd figure out that she might have loved her dad, but she was more like her mom.

"Can't we just—"

"For now," he said, but she knew it wouldn't end here.

The thought of losing him made her feel strangely anxious, so she did what she always did when her emotions were too sharp to bear: she let her hands slide down his bare chest, to the line of hair from his navel and still downward, and when she touched him and felt how hard he was for her, she knew he was still hers.

For now.

The sky is slate-gray and swollen with clouds. A lone seagull wheels overhead, battling the wind, cawing. She is little, a girl with long brown pigtails and skinned knees. Running after him. A kite skips on the sand in front of her, twisting; it flips away before she can reach it.

"Daddy," she yells, knowing he is too far ahead. He can't hear her. "I'm back here—"

Meredith awoke in a panic. She sat up in bed and looked around, knowing he wouldn't be here. It was another dream.

Still tired and aching from a night spent turning beneath the covers, she eased out of bed, being careful not to waken Jeff. She went to the window and stared out at the darkness. Dawn hadn't shown its face yet. She crossed her arms tightly, trying to hold herself together. It felt as if pieces of her soul were falling away lately, like some ugly form of spiritual leprosy.

"Come back to bed, Mere."

She didn't look back. "I'm sorry. I didn't mean to wake you."

"Why don't you sleep in today?"

It sounded good, the idea that she could bury herself in his arms and under the blankets and just sleep while life ticked on without her. "I wish I could," she said, already thinking of what she needed to do this morning. As long as she was up, she could get to work on the quarterly taxes. She had a meeting with the accountant next week and she needed to be ready.

Jeff got out of bed and came up behind her. She saw a silvered image of their faces in the blackened window.

"You take care of everything and everyone, Mere. But who takes care of you?"

She turned to him, let him hold her. "You do."

"Me?" he said sharply. "I'm one more thing on your To-Do list."

At another time—last year, maybe—she would have told him that wasn't fair, fought with him about it, but she was too depleted now to bother.

"Not now, Jeff," was all she could think to say. "I can't have this conversation."

"I know how much you're hurting—"

"Of course I'm hurting. My dad died."

"There's more to it than that. You're doing too much," he said quietly. "You're still hell-bent on getting her attention, just like—"

"What am I supposed to do? Ignore her? Or maybe I should quit my job?"

"Hire someone. She doesn't give a shit if you're there. I know it hurts, baby, but she's never cared."

"I can't. She won't let me. And I promised Dad."

"What if she breaks you? Is that what your dad wanted? Does she ever even *look* at you?"

She knew he was right. In times like these she wished they hadn't been together so long, that he hadn't seen so much. But he'd been there on the night of the play—and other nights like it—and he knew her heart and how much pain it sometimes held. "It's not about her, even. You know that. It's about me. Who I am. I just can't let it . . . let her go."

"Your dad was worried about this, remember? He was afraid our family would break apart without him, and he was right. We're falling apart. *You're* falling apart and you won't let anyone help you."

"Doc Burns says Mom will be okay in a little while. Once she's fine, I promise I'll hire someone to clean her house and pay her bills, okay?"

"You promise?"

She kissed him lightly on the lips. It was over. For now. "I'll be back for breakfast, okay? I'll make us omelets and fruit. Just you and me."

Easing away from him, she headed for the bathroom. As she was closing the door, she thought she heard him say something. She caught the word *worried* and closed the door.

In the dark, she dressed in her running clothes and left the bedroom. Downstairs, she turned on the coffeepot and collected the dogs and headed out into the cold early February darkness.

She pushed herself harder than ever before, desperate to clear her mind. Physical pain was so much easier to handle than heartache. Beside her, the dogs yelped and played with each other, occasionally running off into the deep snow on the sides of the road, but always coming back. By the time she had come to the golf course and doubled back, dawn had gilded the valley. It hadn't snowed in almost two weeks and the top layer was crusty and glittery in the pale sunlight.

She veered into Belye Nochi and fed the dogs on Mom's porch. It was one of the many changes in Meredith's new schedule. She always did at least two things at once. She slipped out of her running shoes and went into the kitchen, where she started the samovar, and then climbed the stairs. She was still red-faced and breathing heavily when she opened Mom's door.

And found the bed empty.

"Shit."

Meredith went outside to the winter garden and sat beside her mother, who wore the lacy nightdress that Dad had given her for Christmas last year, with a blue mohair blanket draped around her shoulders. Her lower lip was bleeding from where she'd bitten it. Her feet were covered in stockings that were gray with damp and brown with dirt.

Meredith dared to reach out and cover her mother's cold, cold hand with her own, but she couldn't find any words to go along with the intimate act. "Come on, Mom, you need to eat something."

"I ate yesterday."

"I know. Come on." She held her mother's hand and helped her to rise. After too much time spent on this metal bench, her mother's body straightened slowly, popping and creaking at the new movement.

As soon as she was fully upright, Mom pulled away from Meredith and walked up the flagstone path toward the house.

Meredith let her go on ahead.

Meredith followed her into the kitchen, where she called Jeff and told him she wouldn't be home for breakfast after all. "Mom was in the garden again," she said. "I think I better work here today."

"Big surprise."

"Come on, Jeff. Be fair—"

He hung up.

Stung by the sound of the dial tone, she called Jillian instead. They immediately fell into their easy routine, talking about school and Los Angeles and the weather. Meredith listened to her eldest daughter in amazement. As was happening more and more often lately, she heard this confident young woman talking about chemistry and biology and medical schools, and Meredith wondered how it had happened, this growing up and moving on. Only yesterday, Jillie had been a pudgy girl with gaps in her teeth who could spend an entire afternoon staring at an apple bud, waiting for it to blossom. *It's coming, Mommy. The flower will be here any second. Should I go get Grandpa?*

And teaching Jillian to drive had taken about ten minutes. *I read the manuals, Mom. You don't have to grit your teeth. Trust me.*

"I love you, Jillie," Meredith said, realizing a second too late that she'd interrupted her daughter. She'd been saying something about enzymes. Or maybe ebola. Meredith laughed; she'd been caught not listening. "And I'm really proud of you."

"I'm putting you into a coma, aren't I?"

"Just a deep sleep."

Jillian laughed. "Okay, Mom. I gotta run anyway. Love you."

"Love you, too, Beetle."

When Meredith hung up, she felt better. Whole again. Talking to her girls was always the best prescription for the blues. Except, of course, when those same conversations caused the blues. . . .

For the rest of the day, she worked from her mother's kitchen table; in addition to paying taxes and reading crop reports and overseeing warehouse costs, she cajoled her mother into eating and paid her bills and washed her clothes.

Finally, at eight o'clock, when the dinner dishes were done and the food was put away, she went into the living room.

Mom sat in Dad's favorite chair, knitting. A floor lamp glowed beside her; the light gave her face a softness that was illusory. To her left, the candle on the altar of the Holy Corner sputtered and sent smoke spiraling upward.

Mom's eyes were closed, even while her fingers wielded the knitting needles. Shadowy lashes fanned down her pale cheeks, giving her an eerily sad look.

"It's time for bed, Mom," Meredith said, striving to sound neither impatient nor tired. She flicked on the ceiling light and in an instant the intimacy of the room was gone.

"I can manage my own schedule," Mom said.

And so it began, the endless grind of getting Mom upstairs into bed. They fought about all of it: brushing teeth, changing clothes, taking off socks.

At just past nine, Meredith finally got her mom settled into bed. She pulled the covers up to her chin, just as she'd once done for Jillian and Maddy. "Sleep well," Meredith said. "Dream of Dad."

"It hurts to dream," Mom said quietly.

Meredith didn't know what to say to that. "So dream of your garden. The crocuses will be blooming soon."

"Are they edible?"

That was how it happened lately; one moment her mother was there, behind her blue eyes, and then just as suddenly she'd be absent.

Meredith wanted to believe it was grief that was causing these changes in her mother, all of this confusion. With grief, there would be an end to it.

But each day it went on, each time Mom seemed disconnected to the world and confused by it, Meredith lost a little bit of faith in Dr. Burns's assessment. She worried that it *had* to be Alzheimer's instead of grief. How else to explain her mother's sudden obsession with leather shoes and pounds of butter (which Meredith now found hidden all through the house), and the fairy-tale lion that she sometimes found her mother talking about?

Meredith touched her not-mother again, soothing her as she would a frightened child. "It's okay, Mom. We have plenty of food downstairs."

"I'll sleep for a minute, then I'll go to the roof."

"No going to the roof," Meredith said tiredly.

Mom sighed and closed her eyes. Within moments, she was asleep.

Meredith went around the room picking up the blankets and other items Mom had dropped.

Downstairs, she put a load of clothes in the washer so they'd be ready to go when she got here tomorrow. Then she finished the two care packages for Jillian and Maddy.

It was ten o'clock by the time she was done.

At home, she found Jeff in his office, working on his book.

"Hey," she said, coming into the room.

He didn't turn around. "Hey."

"How's the book going?"

"Great."

"I still haven't read it."

"I know." He turned to her then.

The look he gave her was familiar, full of disappointment, and suddenly she saw the two of them and this moment from a distance, and the new perspective changed everything. "Are we in trouble, Jeff?"

She could see that he was a little relieved by her question, that he'd been waiting for her to ask it. "Yeah."

"Oh." She could see that she'd disappointed him again, that he wanted to talk about these troubles she'd suddenly excavated and tripped over, but she didn't know what to say. Frankly, this was the last thing she needed now. Her mom was crossing the road into crazy and her husband thought they were in trouble.

Knowing it was a mistake and unable to correct it, she left his office—and his sad, disappointed look—and went up to the bedroom they'd shared for so many years. She stripped down to her underwear and put on an old T-shirt, and climbed into bed. A pair of sleeping pills should have helped, but they didn't, and later, when he crawled into bed, she knew he knew she was still awake.

She rolled over and pressed up against his back, whispered, "Good night."

It wasn't enough, wasn't anything, and they both knew it. The conversation they needed to have was out there, like a storm cloud, gathering mass in the distance.

Seven

In mid-February, green was the color of defiance. White crocuses and snowdrops blossomed overnight, their thin, velvety green stalks pushing up through the glittering white blanket of snow.

Every day, Meredith vowed to talk to Jeff about their troubled marriage, but each time she made such a promise to herself something would happen that moved her in a different direction. And the truth was that she didn't want to talk about it. Not really. She had enough on her plate with her mother's increasing confusion and weird behavior. A newlywed might not be able to understand how troubles in a marriage could be ignored, but any woman who'd been married for twenty years knew that almost anything could be overlooked if you didn't mention it.

One day at a time; that was how you made it through. Like an alcoholic who doesn't reach for the first drink, a couple could simply not say the sentence that would begin a conversation.

But it was always there, hanging in the air like secondhand smoke, an unexpected carcinogen. And today, finally, Meredith had decided to begin it.

She left the office early, at five o'clock, and ignored the errands that needed to be done on the way home. The dry cleaning could be picked up later and they could go a day without groceries. She drove straight to her mother's house and parked out front.

As expected, she found Mom in the winter garden, dressed in two nightgowns and wrapped in a blanket.

Meredith buttoned her coat as she went out there. Nearing her mother, she heard the soft, melodic cant of her voice saying something about a hungry lion.

The fairy tale again. Her mother was out here alone, telling stories to the man she loved.

"Hey, Mom," Meredith said, daring to place a hand on her mother's shoulder. She'd learned lately that she could touch her mother at times like this; sometimes Meredith's touch could even help ease the confusion. "It's cold out here. And it will be dark soon."

"Don't make Anya go alone. She's afraid."

Meredith let out a sigh. She was about to say something else when she noticed the new addition to the garden. There was a bright new copper column standing next to the old verdigris-aged one. "When did you order that, Mom?"

"I wish I had some candy to give him. He loves candy."

Meredith helped her mother to her feet. She led her back into the bright, warm kitchen, where she made her a cup of hot tea and reheated a bowl of soup for her.

Her mother huddled over the table, shivering almost uncontrollably. It wasn't until Meredith gave her a slice of bread, slathered with butter and honey, that she finally looked up.

"Your father loves bread and honey."

Meredith felt a surprising sadness at that. Her father had been allergic to honey, and the fact that Mom had forgotten something so concrete was somehow worse than the previous confusions. "I wish I could really talk to you about him," she said, more to herself than to her mother. Meredith needed her father lately, more than ever. He was the one she could have talked to about the trouble in her marriage. He would have taken her hand and walked out in the orchard with her and told her what she needed to hear. "He'd tell me what to do."

"You know what to do," her mother said, tearing off a chunk of bread and putting it in her pocket. "Tell them you love them. That's what matters. And give them the butterfly."

It was perhaps the loneliest moment of Meredith's life. "That's right, Mom. Thanks."

She busied herself around the kitchen while her mother finished eating. Afterward, she helped Mom up the stairs to her bedroom and brushed her teeth for her, just as she used to do for her daughters when they were small, and like them, her mother did as she was bid. When Meredith began to undress her, the usual battle began.

"Come on, Mom, you need to get ready for bed. These nightgowns are dirty. Let me get you something clean."

"No."

For once, it was too much for Meredith—she was too tired to fight—so she gave in and let her mother go to bed in a dirty nightgown.

Outside the bedroom door, she waited until her mother fell asleep, began to softly snore, and then she went downstairs and locked up the house for the night.

It wasn't until she was in the car, driving home, that she really thought about what her mother had said to her.

You know what to do.

Tell them you love them.

The words might have been tossed in a bowl of crazy salad, but it was still good advice.

When had she last said those precious words to Jeff? They used to be commonplace between them; not lately, though.

If reparations had to be started, and a conversation undertaken, those three words had to be the beginning.

At home, she called out for Jeff and got no answer.

He wasn't home yet. She had time to get ready.

Smiling at that, she went upstairs to shower, not realizing until she reached for her razor how long it had been since she'd shaved. How had she let herself go so much?

She dried and curled her hair and put on makeup and then slipped into a pair of silk pajamas that she hadn't worn in years. Barefooted, smelling of gardenia body lotion, she opened a bottle of champagne. She poured herself a glass and went into the living room, where she started a fire in the fireplace and sat down to wait for her husband.

Leaning back into the sofa's soft down cushions, she put her feet up on the coffee table and closed her eyes, trying to think of what else she would say to him, the words he needed to hear.

She was wakened by the dogs barking. They were running down the hallway, falling over each other in their haste to get to the door.

When Jeff walked into the house, he was engulfed by the dogs, their tails thumping on the hardwood floor as they struggled to greet him without jumping up.

"Hey," Meredith said when he came into the room.

Without looking up from Leia, whose ears he was scratching, he said, "Hey, Mere."

"Would you like a drink?" she said. "We can, you know . . . talk."

"I've got a killer headache. I think I'll just take a shower and crash."

She knew she could remind him that they needed to talk and he'd change course. He'd sit down with her and they'd begin this thing that so frightened her.

She probably should force it, but she wasn't sure she wanted to hear what he had to say anyway. And what difference would a day make? He was clearly exhausted, and she knew that feeling in spades. She could show him how much she loved him later. "Sure," she said. "Actually, I'm tired, too."

They went up to bed together, and she snuggled close to him. For the first time in months she fell into a deep and dreamless sleep.

At five forty-five, she was awakened by the phone. Her first thought was *Someone's hurt*, and she sat up sharply, her heart racing.

She grabbed the phone and said, "Hello?"

"Meredith? It's Ed. I'm sorry to bother you so early."

She flicked on the bedside lamp. Mouthing *Work* to Jeff, she leaned back against the headboard. "What is it, Ed?"

"It's your mother. She's in the back of the orchard. Field A. She's . . . uh . . . dragging that old toboggan of yours."

"Shit. Stop her. I'll be right there." Meredith threw back the covers and got out of bed. Running around the room, she looked for something to put on.

"What the hell?" Jeff said, sitting up.

"My eighty-some-year-old mother is out *sledding*. But I'm wrong. She doesn't have Alzheimer's. She's just grieving."

"Yeah, right."

"I've *told* Jim." She found a pair of sweats on the floor of her closet and started dressing. "He's seen her three times in the last month and every time she's as rational as a judge. He says it's just grief. She saves her crazy for me."

"She needs professional help."

She grabbed her purse off the bench at the end of the bed and ran out without saying good-bye.

By spring, Meredith and Jeff had settled into silence. They both knew they were in trouble—the knowledge was in every look, every non-touch, every fake smile, but neither of them brought it up. They worked long hours and kissed each other good night and went their separate ways at dawn. Mom's bouts of confusion had become less frequent lately; so much that Meredith had begun to hope that Dr. Burns was right and that she was finally getting better.

Meredith closed the ledger on her desk and put her mechanical pencil in the drawer. Then she hit the intercom. "I'm going to the house for lunch, Daisy. I should be back in an hour."

"Sure thing, Meredith."

She grabbed her hooded parka and headed down to her car.

It was a lovely late March day that lifted her spirits. Last week a warm front had swept through the valley, pushing Old Man Winter aside. Sunlight had left its indelible mark on the landscape: ice-blue water ran in gullies on either side of the roadways; sparkling droplets fell from the wakening apple trees, creating lacy patterns in the last few patches of slushy snow.

She turned onto Mom's driveway, parked, and walked up to the gate. Off to her right, a man in coveralls was checking the red smudge pots. She waved to him and covered her mouth and nose as she walked through the thick black smoke.

Inside the house, she called out, "Mom. I'm here," as she took off her coat.

In the kitchen, she stopped short.

Her mother was standing on the counter, holding a piece of newspaper and a roll of duct tape.

"Mom! What the hell are you doing? Get down from there." Meredith rushed over and reached out, helping her mother climb down. "Here. Take my hand."

Mom's face was chalky; her hair was a mess. She was dressed in at least four layers of mismatched clothes but her feet were bare. Behind her, on the stove, something was boiling over, popping and hissing. "I need to go to the bank," Mom said. "We need to take our money out while we can. We haven't much to trade."

"Mom . . . your hands are bleeding. What have you done?"

Mom glanced toward the dining room.

Meredith walked slowly forward, past the cold samovar and the empty fruit basket on the counter and into the dining room. The large oil painting of the Neva River at sunset had been taken down and propped against the table. Wallpaper had been torn away in huge strips. In places, dark blotches stained the blank walls. Dried blood? Had her mother worked so feverishly that she'd scraped the skin off her fingertips? Ragged strips of wallpaper had been placed in a bowl on the center of the table, like some weird wilted floral arrangement.

Behind her, the pot on the stove continued to boil over, water sizzling and popping. Meredith rushed to the stove and turned it off, seeing now that the pot was full of boiling water and strips of wallpaper.

"What in the hell . . . ?"

"We will be hungry," Mom said.

Meredith went to her mother, gently took hold of her bloody hands. "Come on, Mom. Let's get you washed up. Okay?"

Mom seemed hardly to hear. She kept mumbling about the money in the bank and how badly she wanted it, but she let Meredith lead her upstairs to the bathroom, where they kept the first-aid kit. Meredith sat Mom on the closed toilet seat and then knelt in front of her to wash and bandage her hands. She could see several precise cuts—slices—to the fingertips. These wounds hadn't been caused by feverish scraping. They were cuts. Slices. "What happened, Mom?"

Her mother kept looking around. "There's smoke. I heard a gunshot."

"It's the smudge pots. You know that. And you probably heard Melvin's truck backfire. He's here to make sure the pots are all working."

"Pots?" Mom frowned at that.

When Meredith had her mother cleaned and bandaged, she put her into bed and pulled up the covers. That was when she noticed the bloodied X-Acto knife on the bedside table. Mom had cut herself on purpose.

Oh, God.

Meredith waited until her mother closed her eyes. Then she went downstairs and just stood there, looking at the damage around her—the boiling wallpaper, the ruined walls, the freaky table arrangement—and fear settled in. She went out to the porch just as Melvin drove away. It took every scrap of willpower she had not to scream out loud.

Instead, she pulled the cell phone out of her pocket and called Jeff at work.

"Hey, Mere. What is it? I'm just about ready to—"

"I need you, Jeff," she said quietly, feeling as if she were coming apart. She'd tried so hard to do everything right, to fulfill her promise to her father, and somehow she had failed. She didn't know how to handle this alone.

"What is it?"

"Mom has gone way around the bend this time. Can you come over?"

"I'll be there in ten minutes."

"Thanks."

She made a call to Dr. Burns next and told him she needed him to come over immediately. She didn't hesitate to use the word *emergency.* This definitely qualified as one in her book.

As soon as the doctor said he'd be right over, Meredith disconnected that call and dialed Nina's number. She had no idea what time it was in Botswana or Zimbabwe—wherever her sister was now—and she didn't care. She only knew that when Nina answered, Meredith was going to say, *I can't do this alone anymore.*

But Nina didn't answer. Instead, her perky recorded voice said, "Hey, thanks for calling. God knows where I am right now, but leave a message and I'll get back to you when I can."

Beep.

Meredith hung up the phone without leaving a message.

What was the point?

She stood there, the phone in her hand, staring through the slowly dissipating smoke. It stung her eyes, but it hardly mattered. She was crying anyway. She didn't even remember when it had started, her crying, and for once, she didn't care.

True to his word, Jeff showed up in less than ten minutes. He got out of the car and came toward her. At the top of the porch steps, he opened his arms and she walked into them, letting his embrace hold her together.

"What did she do?" he finally said.

Before she could answer, there was a loud crash in the kitchen.

Meredith spun on her heels and ran back inside.

She found her mother sprawled on the dining room floor, clutching a strip of wallpaper in one hand and her ankle in the other. A chair lay on its side beside her. She must have fallen off of it.

Meredith went to her, bent down. She tested the already-swelling ankle. "Help me get her into the living room, Jeff. We'll put her on the ottoman bed."

Jeff bent down to her mother. "Hey, Anya," he said in a voice so gentle it made Meredith remember what a wonderful father he was, how easily he'd dried his daughters' tears and made them laugh. He was such a good man; after all Mom had put him through over the years, all the silence she'd heaped on him, still he managed to care about her. "I'm going to carry you into the living room, okay?"

"Who are you?" Mom said, searching his gray eyes.

"I'm your prince, remember?"

Mom calmed down instantly. "What have you brought for me?"

Jeff smiled down at her. "Two roses," he said, scooping her into his arms. He carried her into the living room and put her down on the ottoman bed.

"Here, Mom," Meredith said. "I've got an ice pack. I'm going to put it on your ankle, okay? Keep your feet on this pillow."

"Thank you, Olga."

Meredith nodded and let Jeff lead her into the kitchen.

"She fell off the chair?" he asked, glancing into the ruined dining room.

"That would be my guess."

"Wow."

"Yeah." She stared at him, not quite knowing what to say.

She heard Dr. Burns drive up and relief propelled her forward.

He came into the house, looking more than a little harried, holding a half-eaten sandwich. "Hello, you two," he said as he came inside. "What happened?"

"Mom was tearing down wallpaper and fell off a chair. Her ankle is swelling up like a balloon," Meredith said.

Dr. Burns nodded and set his sandwich down on the entryway table. "Show me."

But when they went into the living room, her mother was sitting up, knitting, as if this were just an ordinary afternoon instead of the day she'd tried to cook wallpaper and cut her own flesh.

"Anya," Jim said, going to her. "What happened here?"

Mom gave him one of her dazzling smiles. Her blue eyes were completely clear. "I was redecorating the dining room and I fell. Silly of me."

"Redecorating? Why now?"

She shrugged. "We women. Who knows?"

"May I take a look at your ankle?"

"Certainly."

He gently examined Mom's ankle and wrapped it in an Ace bandage.

"This pain is nothing," she said.

"And what about your hands?" he asked, examining her fingertips. "It looks like you cut yourself on purpose."

"Nonsense. I was redecorating. I told you this."

Dr. Burns studied her face for a few more minutes and then smiled gently. "Come on. Let Jeff and me help you to your room."

"Of course."

"Meredith, you stay here."

"Gladly," she said, watching nervously as they made their way up the stairs and disappeared.

Meredith paced impatiently, chewing on her thumbnail until it started to bleed.

When Jeff and Dr. Burns came back down the stairs, she looked at the doctor. "Well?"

"She's sprained her ankle. It will heal if she stays off it."

"That's not what I mean, and you know it," Meredith said. "You saw her fingers. And I found an X-Acto knife by her bed. I think she did it on purpose. She *must* have Alzheimer's. Or some kind of dementia anyway. What do we do?"

Jim nodded slowly, obviously gathering his thoughts. "There's a place in Wenatchee that could take her for a month or six weeks. We could call it rehabilitation for her ankle. Insurance would cover that, and at her age, healing is slow. It's not a long-term solution, but it would give her—and you—some time to deal with what's happened. It's possible that time away from Belye Nochi and the memories here might help."

"You mean a nursing home?" Meredith said.

"No one likes a nursing home," the doctor said. "But sometimes it's the best answer. And remember, it's only a short-term solution."

"Will you tell her she's going there because she needs rehab?" Jeff asked, and Meredith could have kissed him. He knew how hard this decision was for her.

"Of course."

Meredith drew in a deep breath. She knew she would replay this moment over and over, probably hating herself more every day. She knew her father would never make this choice and wouldn't have wanted her to make it. But she couldn't deny how much this would help her.

She sleeps outside . . . tears down wallpaper . . . falls off chairs . . . what will be next?

"God help me," she said softly, feeling alone even with Jeff right beside her. She'd never known before how profoundly a single decision could separate you from other people. "Okay."

That night, Meredith couldn't sleep. She heard the clicking of digital minutes into one another as she lay in bed.

Everything about her decision felt wrong. Selfish. And that was what it was in the end: her decision.

She stayed in bed as long as she could, trying to relax; at two o'clock, she dropped the pretense and got up.

Downstairs, she roamed through the shadowy, quiet house, looking for something to help her sleep or to occupy her mind while she was awake: TV, a book, a cup of tea . . .

Then she saw the telephone and knew exactly what she needed: Nina's complicity. If Nina agreed about the nursing home, Meredith would shoulder only half the guilt.

She dialed her sister's international cell phone number and sat down on the sofa.

"Hello?" said a heavily accented voice. Irish, Meredith thought. Or Scottish.

"Hello? I'm calling Nina Whitson. Did I get the wrong number?"

"No. This is her phone. Who am I speakin' to?"

"Meredith Cooper. I'm Nina's sister."

"Ah, brilliant. I'm Daniel Flynn. I suppose you've heard of me."

"No."

"That's disappointing, isn't it? I'm a . . . good friend of your sister's."

"How good a friend are you, Daniel Flynn?"

His laugh was low and rumbling. Sexy as hell. "Daniel's me old man, and a mean son of a bitch he was. Call me Danny."

"I notice you didn't answer my question, Danny."

"Four and a half years. Give or take."

"And she never mentioned you or brought you home?"

"More's the pity, eh? Well, it was grand talkin' to you, Meredith, but your sis is givin' me the evil eye, so I'd best hand her the phone."

As Meredith said good-bye, she heard a rustling sound, as if Danny and Nina were fighting over the phone.

Nina answered, sounding a little breathless; laughing. "Hey, Mere. What's up? How's Mom?"

"Honestly, Neens, that's why I'm calling. She's not good. She's confused lately. Calls me Olga half the time and recites that damn fairy tale as if it means something."

"What does Doc Burns say?"

"He thinks it's ordinary grief, but—"

"Thank God. I wouldn't want her to end up like Aunt Dora, stuck in that pathetic nursing home, eating old Jell-O and watching game shows."

Meredith flinched at that. "She fell and sprained her ankle. Luckily I was there to help, but I can't always be there."

"You're a saint, Mere. Really."

"No, I'm not."

"That's what Mother Teresa said to me, too."

"I'm no Mother Teresa, Nina."

"Yes, you are. The way you're taking care of Mom and running the orchard. Dad would be proud."

"Don't say that," she whispered, unable to put any power in her voice. She wished now that she hadn't called.

"Look, Mere. I really can't talk now. We're just on our way out. Do you have something important?"

This was her moment: she could blurt out the truth and be judged (Saint Mere, cramming Mom in a home) or she could say nothing. And what if Nina disagreed? Meredith hadn't thought about that possibility before, but now she saw it clearly. Nina would not support her, and that would only make matters worse. To be called selfish by Nina was more than she could bear. "No, nothing important. I can handle it."

"Good. I'll be home for Dad's birthday, don't forget."

"Okay," Meredith said, feeling sick. "See you then."

Nina said, "Good-bye," and their conversation broke.

Meredith hung up the phone. With a sigh, she turned off the lights and went back upstairs, where she crawled into bed with her husband.

. . . stuck in that pathetic nursing home . . .

Saint Mere

She lay there a long time, in the dark, trying not to remember those wretched, long-ago visits to Aunt Dora.

She was certain she had never fallen asleep, but at seven A.M., the alarm clock jolted her awake.

Jeff stood by the bed with a cup of coffee. "You okay?"

She wanted to say no, to scream it, maybe even to burst into tears, but what good would that do? The worst part of all was that Jeff knew it; he was giving her his sad look again, his I'm-waiting-for-you-to-need-me look. If she told him the truth, he'd hold her hand and kiss her and tell her she was doing the right thing. And then she'd really lose it. "I'm fine."

"I thought you'd say that," he said, stepping back. "We need to go in about an hour. I've got an appointment at nine."

She nodded and shoved the hair out of her face. "Okay."

For the next hour, she got ready as if this were any ordinary day, but when she climbed into the driver's seat of her big SUV, she suddenly lost the ability to pretend. The truth of her choice swept through her, chilling her.

In front of her, Jeff started up his truck, and together they drove in their separate cars to Belye Nochi.

Inside, she found Mom in the living room, standing at her Holy Corner. Dressed in a black woolen sheath, with a white silk scarf around her throat, she managed to look both elegant and strong. Her back was straight, her shoulders firm. Her snow-white hair had been drawn back from her face, and when she turned to look at Meredith, there wasn't a drop of confusion in those arctic-blue eyes.

Meredith's resolve slipped; doubt surged up in its place.

"I want the Holy Corner brought to my new room," Mom said. "The candle must be kept burning." She reached over for the crutches Dr. Burns had brought her. Settling them in place under her arms, she limped slowly toward Meredith and Jeff.

"You need help," Meredith said as she approached. "I can't be here all the time."

If Mom heard, or cared, there was no sign of it. She limped past Meredith and went to the front door. "My bag is in the kitchen."

Meredith should have known better than to seek absolution from her mother. How well she knew that whatever she needed from Mom, she wouldn't get it. Maybe this most of all. She walked past her mother and went into the kitchen.

It was the wrong bag. Meredith had packed the big red suitcase only last night. She bent down and opened this one.

Her mother had packed it full of butter and leather belts.

Eight

Nina woke to the sound of gunfire.

Rounds exploded just outside her window; the dingy, peeling walls of her hotel room shuddered. A shower of plaster and wattle rained down on the floor. Somewhere a window shattered and a woman screamed. Nina got out of bed and crawled over to the window.

Tanks were rolling down the rubble-strewn street. Men in uniforms—boys, really—walked alongside, shooting their machine guns, laughing as people tried to find shelter.

She turned around and leaned against the rough wall, then slid down to a sit on the powdery floor. A rat scurried along the floorboards and crept into the shadows along her so-called closet.

God, she was tired of this.

It was the end of April. Only a month ago she'd been in Sudan with Danny, but it felt like a lifetime.

Her cell phone rang.

She crawled across the dirty floor and sat against the side of the bed. Reaching up to the nightstand, she found the checkbook-sized phone and flipped it open. "Hello?"

"Nina? Is that you? I can barely hear you."

"Gunfire. Hey, Sylvie, what's up?"

"We're not using your photos," Sylvie said. "There's no way to sugar-coat it. They're not good enough."

She couldn't believe what she'd just heard. "Shit. You've got to be kidding me. I'm better on my worst day than most of the assholes you use."

"These are worse than your worst day, kiddo. What's going on?"

Nina pushed the hair out of her eyes. She hadn't had a haircut in weeks, and her hair was so dirty that when she pushed it aside, it stayed. The water in her hotel—in the whole block—had been out for days. Ever since the fighting had escalated. "I don't know, Sylvie," she finally said.

"You shouldn't have gone back to work so quickly. I know how much you loved your father. Is there anything I can do to help?"

"Getting the cover always makes me feel better."

Sylvie's silence said it all. "A war zone is no place to grieve, Nina. Maybe you've lost your edge because there's somewhere else you need to be."

"Yeah. Well . . ."

"Good luck, Nina. I mean that."

"Thanks," she said, and hung up.

She looked around the dark, dingy room, feeling the echo of machine-gun fire along her spine, and she was tired of all of it. Exhausted. It was hardly surprising that her latest photos were crap. She was too tired to concentrate, and when she did finally fall asleep, dreams of her father invariably wakened her.

His last words nagged at her lately, the promise he'd elicited. Maybe that was her problem. Maybe that was why she couldn't concentrate.

She'd failed to keep that promise.

No wonder she'd lost her mojo.

It was back in Belye Nochi, in the hands of a woman she'd promised to get to know.

In the first week of May—only a few days earlier than she'd planned—at just past seven in the morning, Nina drove into the Wenatchee Valley. The jagged Cascade Mountain Range was still covered in snow but everything else was dressed for spring.

At Belye Nochi, the orchard was in full bloom. Acres of apple trees boasted bright flowers. As she drove toward the house, she imagined her father there, walking proudly between the rows with a small, black-haired girl beside him, asking questions. *Are they ready yet, Daddy? I'm hungry.*

They're ready when they're ready, Neener Beaner. Sometimes you have to be patient.

She'd matured alongside those trees, learning along the way that she wasn't patient, and that farming didn't interest her; that her father's life's work would never be hers.

In the driveway, she pulled up in front of the garage and parked.

The orchard was alive with workers who moved through the trees, checking for bugs or rot or whatever it was they looked for.

Nina slung her camera bag over her shoulder and headed for the house. The yard was a vibrant green so bright it was almost hard to look at. All along the fence line and on either side of the walkway, white flowers grew in clumps.

At the house, she didn't bother knocking. "Mom?" she called out, flipping on the entryway light and taking off her boots.

There was no answer.

She went into the kitchen.

The house smelled musty, vacant. Upstairs it was as quiet and empty as below.

Nina refused to feel disappointed. She knew when she'd decided to surprise Mom and Meredith that it might be a little dicey.

She went back out to the rental car and drove up the road toward her sister's house. At the vee in the road, a truck came toward her.

She pulled over, waiting.

The truck slowed down and stopped beside her, and Jeff rolled down his window. “Hey, Neens. This is a surprise.”

“You know me, Jeff. I move like the wind. Where’s Mom?”

Jeff glanced in his rearview mirror as if someone were coming up on his tail.

“Jeff? What’s wrong?”

“Meredith didn’t tell you?”

“Tell me what?”

He finally looked at her. “She had no choice.”

“Jeff,” Nina said sharply. “I don’t know what the hell you’re talking about. Where is my mom?”

“Parkview.”

“The nursing home? Are you kidding me?”

“Don’t rush to conclusions, Nina. Meredith thought—”

Nina gunned the engine and spun the car around in the dirt and drove off. In less than twenty minutes she pulled into the nursing home’s gravel driveway and parked. She grabbed her heavy canvas camera bag off the passenger seat and marched across the parking lot and into the building.

Inside, the lobby was defiantly cheery and obscenely bright. Fluorescent bulbs stretched like glowworms along the beige ceiling. To the left was a waiting room—with primary-colored chairs and an old RCA television. Directly in front of her was a big wooden desk. Behind it, a woman with tightly permed hair talked animatedly on the phone, clacking her polka-dot fingernails on the fake wood surface of the desk.

“I mean it, Margene, she has really packed on the pounds—”

“Excuse me,” Nina said tightly. “I’m looking for Anya Whitson’s room. I’m her daughter.”

The receptionist paused long enough to say, “Room 146. To your left,” and then went back to her conversation.

Nina walked down the wide hallway. On either side of her were closed doors; the few that were open revealed small hospital-like rooms inhabited by elderly people in twin beds. She remembered when Aunt Dora had been here. They'd visited her every weekend, and Dad had hated every second. *Death on the layaway plan*, he used to say.

How could Meredith have done this? And how dare she not tell Nina about it?

By the time she reached room 146, Nina was in a rage. It felt good; it was the first real fire she'd felt since Dad's death. She knocked sharply.

A voice said, "Come in," and she opened the door.

Her mother sat in an unattractive plaid recliner, knitting. Her white hair was unkempt and her clothes didn't match, but her blue eyes were bright. At Nina's entrance, she looked up.

"Why the hell are you here?" Nina said.

"Language, Nina," her mother said.

"You should be at home."

"You think so? Without your father?"

The reminder was delivered softly, like a drop of acid. Nina moved forward woodenly, feeling her mother's gaze on her. She saw the re-created Holy Corner set up on an old oak dresser.

Behind her, the door opened again and her sister walked into the small room, carrying a tote bag bulging over with Tupperware containers.

"Nina," she said, coming up short. Meredith looked flawless, as usual, her chestnut hair styled in a classic bob. She was wearing crisp black pants and a pink shirt that was tucked in at the waist. Her pale face was expertly made up, but even so, she looked tired. And she'd lost too much weight.

Nina turned on her. "How could you do this? Was it *easier* to just dump her here?"

"Her ankle—"

"Who gives a shit about her ankle? You know Dad would hate this," Nina said sharply.

"How dare you?" Meredith said, her cheeks flushing with anger. "*I'm* the one who—"

"Stop it," Mom hissed. "What is wrong with you two?"

"She's an idiot," Meredith responded. Ignoring Nina completely, she moved toward the table, where she set down a big grocery bag. "I brought you some cabbage pierogies and okroshka, Mom. And Tabitha sent you some new yarn. It's in the bottom of the bag, along with a pattern she thought you'd like. I'll be back again after work. As usual."

Mom nodded, but said nothing.

Meredith left without another word, shutting the door firmly behind her.

Nina hesitated a moment and then followed. Out in the hallway, she saw Meredith hurrying away; her heels clattered on the linoleum floor. "Meredith!"

Her sister flipped her off and kept going.

Nina went back into the pathetic little room with its twin bed and its ugly recliner and its battered wood dresser. Only the Russian icons and candle gave a hint about the woman who lived here. The woman whom Dad had thought was so broken . . . and whom he'd loved.

"Come on, Mom. You're getting the hell out of here. I'm taking you home."

"You?"

"Yeah," Nina said firmly. "Me."

"That *bitch*. How could she say those things to me? And especially in front of Mom?" Meredith was in the small, cramped office from which her husband oversaw the newspaper's city beat. Not that there was much city, or much beat, either. A stack of paper by his computer reminded her that he'd been working hard on his novel. The one she hadn't yet found time to read.

She continued pacing, chewing her thumbnail until it hurt.

"You should have told her the truth. I told you that."

"This is not the time for I-told-you-so's."

"But you talked to her, what? Two or three times since you put your mom in Parkview? Of course Nina's pissed. You would be, too." He leaned back in his chair. "Let Nina spend time with her. By tomorrow night, she'll understand why you made the choice you did. Your mom will dish up a big pile of crazy and Nina will fall all over herself to apologize."

Meredith stopped pacing. "You think?"

"I know. You didn't stick your mom there because it was hard on you to care for her, although it was. You put her there to keep her safe. Remember?"

"Yeah," she said, wishing she felt stronger about it. "But she's been better in the nursing home. Even Jim said that. No walking in the snow barefooted or peeling off wallpaper or cutting her fingers. She saved the good stuff for me."

"Maybe she's ready to come home, then," he said, but she could tell that he wasn't really engaged in the conversation anymore. Either he had something on his mind, or he'd heard it too many times. Probably the latter; she'd spent a lot of time in the last month worrying about her mother, and Jeff had heard it all. Actually, it was the only thing she could remember talking to him about lately.

"I've got to run," he said. "Interview in twenty minutes."

"Oh. Okay."

She let him walk her out of the newspaper's grungy, crowded office and to her car. She climbed into the driver's seat and started the engine.

It wasn't until she was at her desk, looking over the orchardists' pruning report, that she realized Jeff hadn't kissed her good-bye.

As she drove toward Belye Nochi, Nina glanced sideways at her mother, who sat in the passenger seat of the rental car, knitting.

They were in foreign terrain now, she and her mother. Their togetherness implied a kind of partnership, but such a connection had never before existed and Nina didn't really believe that mere proximity could give rise to a new kind of relationship. "I should have stayed," she said. "Made sure you were okay."

"I hardly expected that from you," her mother said.

Nina didn't know if it was a put-down, with the emphasis on *you*, or a simple statement of fact. "Still . . ." She didn't know what to say next. Once again, she was a kid, hovering in her mother's orbit, waiting for something—a look, a nod, some gratitude or grief. Anything but the *click click click* of those needles.

At the house, she watched her mother gather up her knitting, grab the bag of icons from her Holy Corner, and open the car door. With the bearing of a queen, she walked across the grassy lawn, up the stone path, and into her home, closing the door behind her.

"Thanks for springing me, Nina," Nina muttered, shaking her head.

By the time she made it into the house with the luggage, the Holy Corner was set up again, the candle was burning, and her mother was nowhere to be found.

Nina went upstairs, dragging the suitcase behind her. Pausing at her mother's open bedroom door, she listened, hearing the clatter of knitting needles and a soft, singsongy voice: Mom was either talking to herself or she was on the phone.

Either way, apparently it was better than talking to her daughter. She dropped her mom's suitcase on the floor and then put her own backpack and camera gear in her old bedroom and went downstairs again. On her dad's favorite ottoman bed, she spread out, fluffed up the pile of pillows behind her to make a headrest, and turned on the TV.

In seconds, she was asleep. It was the best, most dreamless sleep she'd had in months, and when she awoke, she felt refreshed and ready to take on the world.

She went upstairs and knocked on the bedroom door. "Mom?"

"Come in."

Nina opened the door and found her mother in the wooden rocking chair by the window, knitting. "Hey, Mom. Are you hungry?"

"I was last night and again this morning, but I made sandwiches. Meredith has asked me not to use the stove."

"I slept for a whole day? Shit. Promise me you won't tell Meredith."

Mom looked at her sharply. "I do not make promises to children." At that, she went back to her knitting.

Nina left the bedroom and took a long, hot, only-in-America shower.

Afterward, even though she was dressed in her crumpled, ancient khakis, she felt human.

Downstairs, she meandered around the kitchen, trying to figure out what to make for lunch.

In the freezer, she found dozens of containers of food, each one marked and dated in black ink. Her mother had always cooked for a platoon instead of a family, and nothing from the Whitson table was ever thrown away. Everything was packed up, dated, and frozen for later use. If Armageddon ever came, no one at Belye Nochi would go hungry.

Her eye went straight to the stroganoff and homemade noodles.

Comfort food. Exactly what they needed. She put some water on to boil for the noodles and popped the sauce in the microwave to thaw it. She was about to set the table when a blast of sunlight caught her attention. At the window, she looked down and saw the orchard in full bloom.

She ran for her camera bag, chose one, and went outside, where she immediately lost herself in the choices presented. She took pictures of everything, the trees, the blossoms, the smudge pots, and with every click of the shutter, she thought of her dad and how much he loved this time of year. When she finished, she covered her lens and walked idly back toward the house, passing her mother's so-called winter garden.

On this surprisingly sunny day, the garden was a riot of white blossoms upheld by lush green stems and leaves. Something sweet-smelling was in bloom and its perfume mixed with the fecund smell of fertile soil. She sat down on the ironwork bench. She'd always thought of this garden as solely her mother's domain, but just now, with the apple trees blooming all around her, she felt her father's presence as keenly as if he were sitting beside her.

She picked up her camera again and began taking pictures: a pair of ants on a green leaf, a flawless, pearlescent magnolia blossom, the copper column that had always been center stage in this garden, with its blue-green patina—

Nina lowered the camera.

There were two columns now. The new one was bright, shiny copper, with an elegant scroll stamped into it.

She brought the camera to her eye again and focused on the new column. In the upper half there was an ornate etching. Scrollwork. Leaves, ivy, flowers.

And the letter *E*.

She turned slightly and faced the other column. Pushing the vines and flowers aside, she studied the scrollwork.

She'd seen it dozens of times in her life, but now, for the first time, she studied it closely. There were Russian letters entwined in the scrollwork. An *A* and what appeared to be the *P* symbol, a circle—which might be an *O*—and something that looked like a spider. There were also a few she didn't recognize.

She was just about to reach for it when she remembered the water she'd put on to boil.

"Shit." Nina grabbed her camera and ran for the house.

Nine

Meredith came up with a plan and stuck to it. She'd decided that two afternoons and an evening with Mom would be enough time for Nina to understand the nursing home decision. Yes, Mom had gotten better in the past few weeks, but Meredith didn't believe for a second that she was well enough to care for herself yet.

And it was important—crucial, even—that Nina understood the situation. Meredith didn't want to carry the burden of this decision alone any longer. Mom had been in the home for almost six weeks and her ankle was fully healed. Soon a permanent choice would have to be made, and Meredith refused to do it alone.

At four-thirty, she left the office and drove to the nursing home. Once there, she waved at Sue Ellen, the receptionist, and sailed past, her head held high, her keys in one hand, her handbag in the other. At Mom's room, she paused just long enough to tell herself she didn't really have a headache, and then she opened the door.

Inside, a pair of blue-coverall-clad men were cleaning: one was mopping the floor, the other was wiping down the window. All of Mom's personal items were gone. On the bed, instead of the brand-new bedding Meredith had bought, there was a plain blue mattress.

"Where's Mrs. Whitson?"

"She moved out," one of the men said without looking up. "Didn't give us much warning."

Meredith blinked. "Excuse me?"

"Moved out."

Meredith spun on her heel and walked back to the front desk. "Sue Ellen," she said, pressing two fingertips to her left temple. "Where is my mother?"

"She left with Nina. Moved out, just like that. No notice or nothing."

"Well. This is a mistake. My mother will be back—"

"There's no room now, Meredith. Mrs. McGutcheon is taking her place. We never know for sure, of course, but we don't expect to have a room available again until after July."

Meredith was too mad to be polite. Saying nothing, she marched out of the building and got in her car. For the first time in her life, she didn't give a shit about the posted speed limit, and in twelve minutes she was at Belye Nochi and out of her car.

Inside, the whole house reeked of smoke. In the kitchen, she found dirty plates piled in the sink and an open pizza box on the counter. More than half of the pizza was left in the box.

But that wasn't the worst of it.

A misshapen pot sat slumped over the front burner. Meredith didn't need to reach for it to know that it had melted to the burner.

She was about to charge up the stairs when she glanced out at the side yard. Through the wood-paned French doors, she saw them: Mom and Nina were sitting together on the iron bench.

Meredith opened one of the French doors so hard it clattered against the wall.

As she crossed the yard, she heard her mother's familiar story voice, and knew immediately that the bouts of confusion weren't over.

"... she mourns the loss of her father, who is imprisoned in the red tower by the Black Knight, but life goes on. This is a terrible, terrible lesson that every girl must learn. There are still swans to be fed in the ponds of the castle garden, and white summer nights when the lords and ladies meet at two in the morning to stroll the riverbanks. She doesn't know how hard one winter can be, how roses can freeze in an instant and fall to the ground, how girls can learn to hold fire in their pale white hands—"

"That's enough of the story, Mom," Meredith said, trying not to sound as pissed off as she was. "Let's go inside."

"Don't stop her—" Nina said.

"You're an idiot," Meredith said to Nina, helping Mom to her feet, leading her into the house and up the stairs, where she got her settled in the rocker with her knitting.

Back downstairs, she found Nina in the kitchen. "What in the *hell* were you thinking?"

"Did you hear the story?"

"What?"

"The story. Was that the peasant girl and the prince? Do you remem—"

Meredith took her sister by the wrist and pulled her into the dining room, switching on the lights.

It looked exactly as it had on the day Mom fell off the chair. Strips of wallpaper were gone; the blank valleys looked like old wounds next to the vibrant color of what remained. Here and there, reddish black smears stained both the wallpaper and the vacant strips.

Outside, somewhere in the fields, a truck backfired.

Meredith turned to Nina, but before she could say anything, she heard footsteps thundering down the stairs.

Mom ran into the kitchen, carrying a huge coat. "Did you hear the guns? Downstairs! Now!"

Meredith took her mother by the arm, hoping her touch would help. "That was just a truck backfiring, Mom. Everything is fine."

"My lion is crying," Mom said, her eyes glassy and unfocused. "He's hungry."

"There's no hungry lion here, Mom," Meredith said in an even, soothing voice. "Do you want some soup?" she asked quietly.

Mom looked at her. "We have soup?"

"Lots of it. And bread and butter and kasha. No one is hungry here."

Meredith gently took the coat from her mother. Tucked inside the pocket, she found four bottles of glue.

The confusion left as quickly as it had come. Mom straightened, looked at her daughters, and then walked out of the kitchen.

Nina turned to Meredith. "What the fuck?"

"You see?" Meredith said. "She goes . . . crazy sometimes. That's why she needs to be someplace safe."

"You're wrong," Nina said, still staring at the doorway through which Mom had just passed.

"You're so much smarter than I am, Nina. So tell me, what am I wrong about?"

"That wasn't nuts."

"Oh, really? And just what was it?"

Nina finally faced her. "Fear."

Nina was hardly surprised when Meredith started cleaning the kitchen, and with a martyr's zeal. She knew her sister was pissed. She should have cared about that, but she couldn't.

Instead, she thought about the promise she'd made to her father.

Make her tell you the story of the peasant girl and the prince.

At the time it had seemed pointless, really; impossible. A dying man's last desperate hope to make three women sit down together.

But Mom *was* falling apart without him. He'd been right about that. And he'd thought the fairy tale could help her.

Meredith banged a pot down on one of the remaining burners and then swore. "We can't use the damn stove until we can get rid of this pot you melted."

"Use the micro," Nina said distractedly.

Meredith spun around. "That's your answer? Use the micro. That's all you have to say?"

"Dad made me promise—"

Meredith dried her hands on a towel and threw it on the counter. "Oh, for God's sake. We aren't going to help her by making her tell us fables. We'll help her by keeping her safe."

"You want to lock her away again. Why? So you can have lunch with the girls?"

"How dare you say that to me? *You*." Meredith moved closer, her voice lowering. "He used to pore through magazines, looking for his 'little girl's' pictures. Did you know that? And he checked the mail and messages every day for calls that hardly ever came. So don't you *dare* call me selfish."

"Enough."

Mom was standing in the doorway, dressed in her nightgown, with her hair uncharacteristically unbound. Her collarbone stuck out prominently beneath her veiny skin; a small three-tiered Russian-style cross hung from a thin gold strand coiled around her neck. With all that pallor—white hair, pale skin, white gown—she looked almost translucent. Except for those amazing blue eyes. Now they were alight with anger. "Is this how you honor him, by fighting?"

"We're not fighting," Meredith said, sighing. "We're just worried about you."

"You think I have gone crazy," Mom said.

"*I* don't," Nina said, looking up. "I noticed the new column in the winter garden, Mom. I saw the letters."

"What letters?" Meredith demanded.

"It is nothing," Mom said.

"It's *something*," Nina said.

Her mother made no sign of having heard. No sigh. No flinch. No looking away. She simply walked over to the kitchen table and sat down.

"We don't know anything about you," Nina said.

"The past does not matter."

"It's what you've always said, and we let you. Or maybe we didn't care. But now I do," Nina answered.

Mom looked up slowly, and this time there was no mistaking the clarity in her eyes, nor the sadness. "You will keep asking me, won't you? Of course you will. Meredith will try to stop you because she is afraid, but there is no stopping you."

"Dad made me promise. He wanted us to hear one of your fairy tales all the way to the end. I can't let him down."

"I know better than to make promises to the dying. Now you have learned this lesson, too." She stood up, her shoulders only a little stooped. "It would break your father's heart to hear you two fighting. You are lucky to have each other. Act like it." Then she walked out of the room.

They heard her door slam shut upstairs.

"Look, Nina," Meredith said after a long silence. "I don't give a shit about her fairy tales. I'll take care of her because I promised Dad and because it's the right thing to do. But what you're talking about—trying to get to know her—it's a kamikaze mission and I've crashed once too often. Count me out."

"You think I don't know that?" Nina said. "I'm your sister. I know how hard you tried with her."

Meredith turned abruptly back to the stove, attacking the melted pot as if treasure lay beneath it.

Nina got up and went to her sister. "I understand why you put her in that terrible place."

Meredith turned. "You do?"

"Sure. You thought she was going looney tunes."

"She *is* looney tunes."

Nina didn't know what to say, how even to frame her opinion so that it made sense. All she knew was that she'd lost some essential piece of herself lately, and maybe fulfilling the promise to her father would help her get it back. "I'm going to get her to tell me that fairy tale—all of it—or die trying."

"Do what you want," Meredith said finally, sighing. "You always do."

At work, Meredith tried to lose herself in the everyday minutiae of running the orchard and the warehouses, but nothing she did was right. It felt as if there were a valve in her chest tightening with every breath she took. The pressure building up behind it was going to blow any minute. After the third time she yelled at an employee, she gave up and left before she could do more damage. She tossed a packet of papers on Daisy's desk, said tensely, "File this, please," and walked away before Daisy could ask a question.

She got in her car and just drove. At first she had no idea where she was going; somewhere along the way, she found herself following an old forgotten road. In some ways, it led back to her youth.

She parked in front of the Belye Nochi gift shop. It was a lovely little building set back from the highway and ringed by ancient, flowering apple trees.

Long ago, it had been a roadside fruit stand; here, Meredith had spent some of the best summers of her life, selling their ripe, perfect apples to tourists.

She stared through the windshield at the white clapboard building, its eaves strung with white lights. Come summer, there would be flowers everywhere—in planters by the door, in baskets on the porch, twined up the fence line.

It had been her idea to convert this fruit stand into a gift shop. She still remembered the day she'd approached Dad with the plan. She'd been a young mother with a baby on each hip.

It'll be great, Dad. Tourists will love it.

That's a killer idea, Meredoodle. You're going to be my shining star. . . .

She'd poured her heart and soul into this place, choosing every item they sold with exquisite care. And it had been a rousing success, so much so that they'd added on twice and still they didn't have enough room to sell all the beautiful souvenirs and crafts made in this valley.

When she'd quit the gift shop and moved into the warehouse, it had been to make her father happy.

Looking back on it now, that was when it had begun, this life of hers that seemed to be about everyone else. . . .

She put the car in reverse and drove away, wishing vaguely that she hadn't stopped by. For the next hour, she just drove, seeing the changes spring had made on the landscape. By the time she pulled into her own driveway, it was dusk, and the view was slowly darkening.

Inside the house, she fed the dogs and started dinner and then took a bath, lying in the water so long it grew cold.

She was still so confused and upset by today's events that she didn't know what to do or what to want. All she really knew for sure was that Nina was screwing everything up, making Meredith's life harder. And there was no doubt in her mind that it would all collapse into a big fat mess that Meredith would have to clean up.

She was sick to death of being where the buck stopped.

She dried off and slipped into a pair of comfortable sweats and left the bathroom. As she was toweling off her hair, she glanced at the big king-sized bed along the far wall.

She remembered, with a sharp longing, the day she and Jeff had bought that bed. It had been too expensive, but they'd laughed about the expense and paid for it with a credit card. When the bed had been delivered, they'd come home from work early and fallen onto it, laughing and kissing, and christening it with their passion.

That was what she needed now: passion.

She needed to rip off her clothes and fall into bed and forget all about Nina and Mom and nursing homes and fairy tales.

The second she had the thought, it calcified into a plan. Feeling excited for the first time in months, she changed into a sexy nightgown and went downstairs, where she made a fire and poured herself a glass of wine and waited for Jeff to get home from work.

At eleven o'clock that night, she was still waiting. And that sense of excitement had slowly melted into anger.

Where in the hell was he?

By the time he finally walked into the living room, she'd had three glasses of wine and dinner was ruined.

"Where the hell have you been?" she said, rising.

He frowned. "What?"

"I made a romantic dinner. It's ruined now."

"You're pissed that I'm home late? You've got to be kidding me."

"Where were you?"

"Researching my book."

"In the middle of the night?"

"It's hardly the middle of the night. But, yeah. I've been doing it since January, Mere. You just haven't noticed. Or cared." He walked away from her and went into his office, slamming the door behind him.

She followed him, throwing the door open. "I *wanted* you tonight," she said.

"Well, pardon me all to hell for not giving a shit. You've ignored me for months. It's been like living with a goddamn ghost, but now all of a sudden, because you're horny, I'm supposed to change gears and be here for you? It doesn't work that way."

"Fine. I hope you're comfortable here tonight."

"It'll be a hell of a lot warmer than *your* bed."

She walked out of the office and slammed the door behind her, but with that crack of sound, the anger left her, and without it, she felt lost. Lonely.

She should say she was sorry, tell him about her shitty day. . . .

She was about to do that when she saw the pale bluish light slide along beneath the door. He'd turned his computer on and started writing.

She turned from the door and went upstairs, crawling into their bed. In twenty years of marriage, it was the first time he'd slept on the sofa after a fight, and without him, she couldn't sleep.

At five o'clock, she finally gave up trying and went downstairs to apologize.

He was already gone.

That morning, Meredith went for a run (six miles this time; she was feeling particularly stressed out), called both of her daughters, and still got to work before nine. As soon as she was at her desk, she called Parkview and spoke to the director, who was none too happy about Mom's sudden exit. She learned—again—that they didn't expect an opening in the near future. Things could change, of course (which meant someone could die; someone else's family could be shattered), but there was no way to guarantee a spot.

Nina would never stay long enough to actually help. In the past fifteen years, Meredith couldn't remember her sister staying at Belye Nochi longer than a week, ten days at most. Nina might be world-famous and renowned in her field, but she was not reliable. She'd even bailed as Meredith's maid of honor—at the last minute, with no time to get a replacement—because of some assassination in Central America. Or Mexico. Meredith still didn't know; all she knew was that one minute Nina was there for her, trying on bridesmaid dresses, and the next minute she was gone.

There was a knock at the door. Meredith looked up just in time to see Daisy waltz in carrying a manila folder. "I've got the field and orchardist reports here."

"Great," Meredith said. "Just leave them on my desk."

Daisy hesitated and Meredith thought, *Oh, no. Here it comes.* She'd known Daisy since childhood, and hesitant she was not. "I heard," Daisy said, closing the door behind her. "About Nina kidnapping your mom."

Meredith smiled tiredly. "That's a bit overly dramatic. I'll handle it."

"Of course you will, but honey, should you?" Daisy put the folder down on the desk. "I can run this place, you know," she said quietly. "Your dad trained me. All you have to do is ask for help."

Meredith nodded. It was true, although she'd never really thought about it before. Daisy *did* know the orchard and its operation better than anyone except Meredith herself. She'd worked here for twenty-nine years. "Thanks."

"But you don't really know how to do that, do you, Meredith?"

Meredith fought the urge to roll her eyes. It was what Jeff said to her all the time. Was that really such a flaw? To do what needed to be done? "Can you get Dr. Burns on the phone for me, Daisy?"

"Of course." Daisy headed for the door.

A moment later, Daisy put through the call and Jim answered.

"Hey, Jim," she said. "It's Meredith."

"I expected you to call. I heard from Parkview today." He paused. "Nina?"

"Naturally. She's seen *The Great Escape* one too many times. They don't know when they'll have another opening, and there's no way we can afford live-in help. Can you recommend another nursing home?"

It was a moment before Jim said, "I've spoken to her doctor at Parkview, and with the physical therapist who worked with her. I also visited Anya once a week."

Meredith felt herself tensing up. "And?"

"None of us witnessed any significant confusion or dementia. The only time she got a little rattled was when that storm hit last month. Apparently the thunder scared her and she told everyone she needed to get to the roof. But a lot of the residents were upset by the noise." He drew in a deep breath. "Your dad used to say that Anya battled depression every winter. Something about the cold and the snow bothering her. That, plus the grief . . . anyway, bottom line: I don't believe she is suffering from Alzheimer's or even severe dementia. I can't diagnose what isn't visible to me, Meredith."

Meredith felt as if a huge weight had suddenly been placed on her shoulders. "Now what? How can I take care of her and keep her safe? I can't run Belye Nochi and my own home and be there for Mom all the time. She was cutting herself, for God's sake."

"I know," he said gently. "I've made some calls. There's a senior complex in Wenatchee that's really nice. It's called Riverton. She would have an apartment with a backyard that's big enough for some gardening. She has the choice of cooking her meals or going to the complex's dining room. There's an opening in mid-June for a one-bedroom. I asked the manager to reserve it for you, but they'll need a deposit quickly. Ask for Junie."

Meredith wrote it all down. "Thank you, Jim. I really appreciate your help."

"No problem." He paused. "How are *you*, Meredith? You didn't look so good the last time I saw you."

"Thanks, Doc." She tried to laugh. "I'm tired, but that's to be expected."

"You do too much."

"The story of my life. Thanks again." She hung up before he could say more. Reaching down to the floor, she picked up her purse and headed out of her office.

At Belye Nochi, she found Nina in the kitchen, reheating a pot full of goulash.

Nina smiled at her. "I'm watching it, see? No fire yet."

"I need to talk to you and Mom. Where is she?"

Nina cocked her head toward the dining room. "Guess."

"The winter garden?"

"Of course."

"Damn it, Neens." Meredith walked through the damaged dining room and went out to Mom, who was sitting on the iron bench. At least she was dressed for the cool weather this time.

"Mom?" Meredith said. "I need to talk to you. Can we go inside?"

Mom straightened; only then did Meredith realize how soft and rounded she'd looked before.

Together, neither touching nor speaking, they walked back into the house. In the living room, Meredith got Mom settled in a chair and then built a fire. By the time she was finished, Nina was with them, sprawled out on the sofa, with her stockinged feet propped on the coffee table.

"What's up, Mere?" she asked, flipping through an old *National Geographic*. "Hey, here's my shot. The one that won the Pulitzer," she said, smiling, showing off the two-page spread.

"I spoke with Dr. Burns today."

Nina set the magazine aside.

"He . . . agrees with me that the nursing home isn't the right place for Mom."

"Uh. Duh," Nina said.

Meredith refused to rise to the bait. She kept her gaze on Mom. "But we both think this house is too much for you to handle alone. Jim found a nice place in Wenatchee. A senior condominium-like complex. He says you could have a lovely little one-bedroom unit that would have its own kitchen. But if you didn't feel like cooking, there's a dining room, too. It's right downtown. You could walk to the stores and the knitting shop."

"What about my winter garden?" Mom asked.

"There's a backyard with the unit. You could build a winter garden there. The bench, the fencing, the columns; everything."

"She doesn't need to move," Nina said. "This is her home and I'm here to help out."

Meredith finally snapped. "Really, Nina? How long can we count on you? Or will this be like my wedding?"

"There was an assassination that week," Nina said, looking uncomfortable suddenly.

"Or like Dad's seventieth birthday? What happened that time? A flood, wasn't it? Or was that the earthquake?"

"I'm not going to apologize for my work."

"I'm not asking you to. I'm just saying that you might have the best intentions in the world, but if something terrible happened in India tomorrow, all we'd see of you is your ass as you walked out of the door. I can't be with Mom every second and she can't be alone all the time."

"And this would make it easier on you," Mom said.

Meredith searched her mother's face for sarcasm or judgment, or even confusion, but all she saw was resignation. It had been a question, not an indictment. "Yes," she said, wondering why the affirmation made her feel as if she'd failed her father.

"Then I will go. I do not care where I live anymore," Mom said.

"I'll pack up everything you need," Meredith said. "So you're ready to go next month. You won't have to do a thing."

Mom stood up. She looked at Meredith, her blue eyes soft with emotion. It was a look that lasted a heartbeat—and then was gone. Turning on her heel, she went upstairs. The bedroom door slammed shut behind her.

"She doesn't belong in some glorified nursing home," Nina said.

Meredith honestly hated her sister for that. "What are you going to do about it?"

"What do you mean?"

"Are you going to pay for a live-in companion, someone who can do all the shopping and cleaning and bill-paying? Or maybe you're going to promise to stick around for years? Oh, wait. Your promises don't mean shit."

Nina slowly stood, faced Meredith. "I'm not the only one who breaks promises in this family. You promised him you'd take care of Mom."

"And that's what I'm doing."

"Oh, really? What if he were here right now, listening to you talk about moving the winter garden and packing up her things and moving her into town? Would he be *proud* of you, Meredith? Would he say, *Well done. Thanks for keeping your word?* I don't think so."

"He'd understand," Meredith said, wishing her voice were stronger.

"No. He wouldn't, and you know it."

"Fuck you," Meredith said. "You have no idea how hard I tried . . . how much I wanted to . . ." Her voice broke and tears gathered in her throat. "Fuck you," she said again, whispering it this time. She spun around and practically ran for the front door, noticing that the goulash was burning as she yanked the door open and went outside.

In her car, she slammed the door shut and clutched the steering wheel. "It's easy to be self-righteous when you're *gone*," she muttered, starting up the car.

The drive home took less than two minutes.

The dogs greeted her exuberantly and she knelt down to pet them both, letting their enthusiasm at her return be a balm on her rattled nerves.

"Jeff?" she called out. Getting no answer, she took off her coat and poured herself a glass of wine. In the living room, she turned on the gas fireplace and sat on the marble hearth, letting the real heat from a fake fire warm her back.

For years she'd tried to love her mother in the same unconditional way she had loved her father. That desire to love—and be loved—was the cornerstone of her youth, and its first true failure.

Nothing she'd done had ever been right in her mother's eyes, and for a girl who desperately wanted to please, this failure had left scars. The worst of them—besides the night of the Christmas play—had come on a sunny spring day.

Meredith didn't recall how old she was exactly, but Nina had just started her swimming lessons, so maybe ten, and Dad had taken her sister to the pool, so Meredith was alone with Mom in that big, rambling house. She'd snuck out after lunch, with tools in her hand and a packet of seeds in her pocket. Alone in the winter garden, humming with excitement, she'd pulled out all the ivy that grew over everything and dragged away the old verdigris copper column that gave the garden a jumbled, messy look. Attacking the muddy black earth with her trowel, she'd carefully planted flower seeds in neat and tidy rows. She could picture how they would grow and bloom, how they'd give a bright and pretty order to the messy green and white so-called garden.

She'd been pleased with herself for coming up with the idea and executing it so well. As she worked the dirt and divided up the seeds and carefully placed them in the ground, she imagined her mother coming out here, seeing this gift, and—finally—hugging her.

So intent was she on the dream that she didn't hear the house door slam shut or footsteps on the stepping-stones. The first notice she'd had that she wasn't alone was when Mom yanked her to her feet so hard and fast that Meredith stumbled and fell sideways.

What have you done to my garden?

I wanted to make it pretty for you. I—

Meredith would never forget the look on her mother's face as she dragged her across the yard and up the porch steps. All the way into the house, Meredith was crying, saying she was sorry, asking what she'd done that was so bad, but her mother said nothing, just pushed her into the house and slammed the door shut.

Meredith stood at the dining room window after that, crying, watching her mother attack the dirt, throwing the seeds away as if they held some kind of poison. Mom worked like a mad person, in a frenzy; she brought all the ivy back, cradling it in her hands with a gentleness she'd never shown her children, and when that was all returned to its place, she went for the column, dragging it back, muscling it into its place. When the winter garden looked as it had, she dropped to her knees in front of the column and stayed there all afternoon, with her head bowed as if in prayer. She was still there when night fell and rain started.

When she finally came back into the house, her hands black with dirt, her fingers bleeding, her face streaked by mud and rain, she didn't even look at Meredith, just walked up the stairs and closed her bedroom door.

They never spoke of that day again. And when Dad came home, Meredith threw herself into his arms and cried until he said, *What is it, Meredoodle?*

Maybe if she'd said something, told him the truth, it would have changed things, changed her, but she couldn't do it. *I just love you, Daddy,* she'd said, and his booming laugh had grounded her once again.

And I love you, he'd said. She wanted that to be enough, prayed for it to be enough, but it wasn't, and she felt her own sense of failure blossom, take over, until all she could do was try to stop loving her mother.

She closed her eyes, rocking just a little. Nina was wrong. Dad *would* understand....

A thump sounded nearby, and she looked up, expecting to see Luke or Leia in the room, tail thumping a quiet greeting, begging for a little attention.

Jeff stood in the doorway, still dressed in the worn Levi's and blue crew-neck sweater he'd put on yesterday morning.

"Oh. You're home."

"I'm going," he said quietly.

She didn't know whether to be relieved or disappointed that they wouldn't be together tonight. "Do you want me to hold dinner?"

He took a deep breath and said, "I'm leaving."

"I heard you. I don't—" It sunk in suddenly and she looked up. "Leaving? Me? Because of last night? I'm sorry about that. Really. I shouldn't have—"

"We need some time apart, Mere."

"Don't do this," she whispered, shaking her head. "Not now."

"There's never a good time. I waited because of your father, and then because of your mother. I told myself you still loved me, that you were just busy and overwhelmed, but . . . I just don't believe it anymore. There's a wall around you, Mere, and I'm tired of trying to climb it."

"It'll be better now. In June—"

"No more waiting," he said. "We only have a few weeks before the girls come home. Let's use the time to figure out what the hell we want."

She felt herself falling apart but the thought of giving in to that scared her to death. For months now she'd been burying her emotions and God knew what would happen if she ever stopped. If she let herself cry she might wail like a banshee and turn to stone like one of her mother's fairy-tale characters. So she held it together and nodded, said in as even a voice as she could muster, "Okay."

She saw the way he looked at her then, the disappointment, the resignation. His gaze said, *Of course that's what you'd say.* It hurt her almost more than she could stand, letting him go, but she didn't know how to stop him, what to say, so she stood up and walked past him, past the suitcase at the front door (the thump she'd heard) and went into the kitchen.

Her heart was actually missing beats as she stood at the sink, staring at nothing. It was hard to catch her breath. Never in all their years of marriage had it occurred to her that Jeff would leave her. Not even last night when he'd let her sleep alone. She'd known he wasn't happy—and neither was she, really—but that seemed separate somehow, an ordinary bad patch.

But this . . .

He came up behind her. "Do you still love me, Mere?" he asked quietly, turning her by the shoulders until they were facing each other.

She wished he'd asked her that an hour ago, or yesterday, or last week. Anytime except now, when even the ground beneath her felt unreliable. She'd thought his love was a bulkhead that could hold back any storm, but like everything else in her life, his love was conditional. All at once she was that ten-year-old girl again, being dragged out of the garden, wondering how she'd gone so wrong.

He let go of her and started for the door.

Meredith almost called out for him, almost said, *Of course I love you. Do you love me*? but she couldn't make her mouth open. She knew she should grab the suitcase from him or throw her arms around him. Something. But she just stood there, dry-eyed and uncomprehending, staring at his back.

At the last minute, he turned to look at her. "You're like her, you know that, don't you?"

"Don't say that."

He stared at her a moment longer, and she knew it was an opening, a chance he was giving her, but she couldn't take it, couldn't make herself move or reach out or even cry.

"Good-bye, Mere," he finally said.

She stood there a long time, was still there, at her sink, staring out at the dark nothingness of her yard, long after he'd driven away.

You're like her, he'd said.

It hurt so much she couldn't stand it, as he must have known it would.

"He'll be back," she said to no one except herself. "Couples take breaks sometimes. It will all be okay." She had to figure out how to fix it, what needed to be done. She went to the closet and grabbed the vacuum and dragged it into the living room and turned it on. The sound drowned out the voices in her head and the erratic beating of her heart.

Ten

When Nina finished showering and unpacking, she went downstairs. In the kitchen, she found her mother already seated at the table, where a cut-crystal decanter waited. "I thought we'd have a drink. Vodka," her mother said.

Nina stared at her. It was one of those moments when you glimpsed something unexpected, like a face in the shadows. In all her thirty-seven years, Nina had never been offered a drink by her mother. She hesitated.

"If you'd rather not . . ."

"No. I mean yes," Nina said, watching as her mother poured two shot glasses full of vodka.

She tried to see *something* in her mother's beautiful face, a frown, a smile; something. But the blue eyes revealed nothing.

"The kitchen smells of smoke," Mom said.

"I burned the first dinner. Too bad you never taught me to cook," Nina said.

"It is reheating, not cooking."

"Did your mother teach you to cook?"

"The water is boiling. Put in the noodles."

Nina went to the stove and poured some of her mother's homemade noodles into the boiling water. Beside them, a saucepan bubbled with stroganoff sauce. "Hey, I'm cooking," she said, reaching for a wooden spoon. "Danny would laugh his ass off right now. He'd say, *Watch it, love. People're goin' t' eat that.*" She waited for her mom to ask who Danny was, but all that rebounded was silence, and then a slow tapping.

She looked back, saw her mother tapping a fork on the table.

Nina returned to the table, took a place opposite her mother. "Cheers," she said, lifting her glass.

Mom lifted the small heavy glass, clinked it against Nina's, and downed the vodka in a swallow.

Nina did the same. Minutes passed in silence. "So what do we do now?"

"Noodles," was Mom's reply.

Nina rushed back to the stove. "They're floating," she said.

"They're done."

"Another cooking lesson. This is awesome," Nina said, pouring the noodles and water into a strainer in the sink. Then she dished up two plates, grabbed the salad, and returned to the table, carrying a bottle of wine with her.

"Thank you," Mom said. She closed her eyes in prayer for a moment and then reached for her fork.

"Have you always done that?" Nina said. "Prayed before dinner?"

"Quit studying me, Nina."

"Because that's the kind of thing a parent generally passes on to their children. I don't remember praying before dinner except at the big holidays."

Mom began to eat.

Nina wanted to keep questioning her mother, but the savory scent of the stroganoff—rich beef chunks, perfectly browned and then simmered for hours in a sauce of sherry wine, fresh thyme, heavy cream, and mushrooms—wafted up to her, and her stomach growled in anticipation. She practically dived into this meal that so represented her childhood. "Thank God you have enough food in the freezer to feed a starving nation," she said, pouring them both some wine. When silence answered her, she said, "Thank you, Nina, for saying so."

Nina tried to concentrate on the food, but the silence got to her. She had never been a patient woman. It was strange; she could sit still for hours waiting for the perfect shot, but without a camera in her hand, she needed something to do. Finally, she couldn't take it anymore. "Enough," she said so sharply that Mom looked up. "I'm not Meredith."

"I am aware of that."

"You were too tough for us when we were girls, and Mere, well, she stuck around and she never changed much. I left. And you know what? You don't scare me or hurt me so much anymore. I'm here now to take care of you. If Mere has her way, I'll be here until you move into Senior World, and I'll be damned if I'll eat every meal under a cone of silence."

"A what?"

"We must have talked at dinner when I was a kid. I remember talking. Even laughing."

"That was the three of you."

"How come you never really look at me or Meredith?"

"You are imagining things now." Mom took a drink of wine. "Eat."

"Okay, I'll eat. But we are going to talk, and that's that. Since you are a lemon in the conversation game, I'll start. My favorite movie is *Out of Africa*. I love watching giraffes move across the sunset in the Serengeti, and I'm surprised to admit that sometimes I miss the snow."

Mom took another drink of her wine.

"I could ask about the fairy tales instead," Nina said. "I could ask about how it is that you know the stories word for word or why you only told them to us with the lights out, or why Dad—"

"My favorite author is Pushkin. Although Anna Akhmatova reads my mind. I miss . . . the true *belye nochi*, and my favorite movie is *Doctor Zhivago*." Her accent softened on the Russian words, turned them into a kind of music.

"So we have something in common after all," Nina said, reaching for her wine, watching her mother.

"What is that?"

"We like big love stories with unhappy endings."

Her mother pushed back from the table suddenly and stood up. "Thank you for dinner. I am tired now. Good night."

"I'll ask again, you know," Nina said as she passed her. "For the fairy tale."

Mom paused, took a slowed step, and then kept going, around the corner and up the stairs. When her bedroom door thudded closed, Nina stared up at the ceiling. "You're afraid, aren't you?" she mused aloud. "Of what?"

Bundled up in her old terry-cloth robe, Meredith sat out on her porch, rocking in a wicker chair. The dogs lay beside her feet, tangled together. They appeared to be sleeping, but every now and then one of them whined and looked up. They knew something was wrong. Jeff was gone.

She couldn't believe he'd done this to her *now*, in the wake of her father's death and in the midst of her mother's meltdown. She wanted to latch on to that anger, but it was ephemeral and hard to hold. She kept imagining one scene, over and over and over.

They would be at the dining room table, she and Jeff and the girls. . . .

Jillian would have her nose buried in a book; Maddy would be tapping her foot, asking when they could go. All of that teenage impatience would disappear when Jeff said, "We're breaking up."

Maybe that wasn't exactly how he would say it, or maybe he'd chicken out and let Meredith say the poisonous words. That had certainly been their parenting pattern. Jeff was the "fun" one; Meredith laid down the law.

Maddy would burst into uncontrollable sobbing.

Jillian's tears would be the silent, heartbreaking type.

Meredith drew in a deep, shuddering breath. She knew now why unhappily married women stayed in their marriages. It was because of the scene she'd just imagined and the pain of it.

In the distance, she could see the first copper glimmer of dawn. She'd been out here all night. Tightening her robe around her, she went inside, milled throughout the house, picking up objects and putting them down. The crystal award Jeff had won last year for investigative journalism . . . the reading glasses he'd recently begun to use . . . the picture of them at Lake Chelan last summer. Before, when she'd looked at that photo, all she'd seen was that she was getting older; now she saw the way he was holding her, the brightness of his smile.

She put the picture down and went upstairs. Though bed beckoned her, she didn't even go close to it, not to that king-sized mattress where his shape lingered, and his scent. Instead, she put on her running clothes and ran until she couldn't breathe without pain and her lungs felt like jelly.

At home, she went straight to the shower, where she stayed until the water turned cold.

When she was dressed, she knew that no one would be able to look at her and know that her husband had left her in the night.

She was holding her car keys, standing in her kitchen, when she realized it was Saturday.

The warehouse would be dark and freezing. Closed. Oh, she could go to work anyway, try to lose herself in the minutiae of insect and pruning reports, of crop projections and sales quotas. But she would be alone, in the quiet, with only her own thoughts to distract her.

"No way."

She went out to the car and started it up, but instead of driving to town, she drove to Belye Nochi and parked.

The living room light was on. A plume of smoke rose from the chimney. Of course Nina was up. She was still running on Africa time.

Meredith felt a wave of self-pity. With all her heart, she wished she could talk to her sister about this, that she could hand her pain off to someone else who might find the words to soften or reshape it.

But Nina was not that person. Neither would Meredith tell her friends. It was humiliating and painful enough without the addition of becoming a bit of town gossip. And besides, she wasn't the kind of woman who talked about her problems; wasn't that part of the reason she was alone now?

She yanked open the car door and got out.

Inside the house, she noticed the lingering smell of smoke. Then she saw the dirty dishes piled in the sink and the open decanter of vodka on the counter.

It pissed her off. Suddenly. Sharply. Disproportionately. But it felt good, this anger. She could hold on to it, let it consume her. She attacked the dishes so loudly that pans clanged together as she threw them in the soapy water.

"Whoa," Nina said, coming into the room. She was wearing a pair of men's boxer shorts and an old Nirvana T-shirt. Her hair stuck out like a black Chia Pet and her face crinkled in a smile. She looked like Demi Moore in *Ghost*; almost impossibly pretty. "I didn't think pot-tossing was your sport."

"Do you think I have nothing better to do than clean up your messes?"

"It's a little early for high drama."

"That's right. Make a joke. What's it to you?"

"Meredith, what's wrong?" Nina said. "Are you okay?"

Meredith almost gave in. The softness of her sister's voice, the unexpected question . . . she almost said, *Jeff left me*.

And then what?

She drew in a deep breath and folded the hand towel in precise thirds before draping it over the oven's handle. "I'm fine."

"You don't act fine."

"Honestly, Nina, you don't know me well enough to say that. How was Mom last night? Did she eat?"

"We drank vodka together. And wine. Can you believe it?"

Meredith felt a sharp pang at that; it took her a moment to realize she was jealous. "Vodka?"

"I know. Shocked the shit out of me, too. And I found out her favorite movie is *Doctor Zhivago*."

"I don't think alcohol is her best bet these days, do you? I mean, she doesn't know where the hell she is half the time."

"But does she know *who* she is. That's what I want to know. If I could just get her to tell us the fairy tales—"

"Screw the fairy tales," Meredith said, more sharply than she should have. At Nina's surprised look, she realized she might even have yelled it. "I'm going to start packing her things for the move next month. I think she'll be more comfortable there if she has her stuff around her."

"She won't be comfortable," Nina said, and now she looked angry. "It doesn't matter how neat and tidy and organized you are. You're still putting her away."

"You going to stay, Nina? Forever? Because if you are, I'll cancel the reservation."

"You know I can't do that."

"Yeah. Right. You can criticize but you can't solve."

"I'm here now."

Meredith glanced at the sinkful of soapy water and the now-clean dishes in the strainer. "And what a help you've been to me. Now, if you'll excuse me, I'm going to get some boxes from the garage. I'll start in the kitchen. You're more than welcome to help."

"I'm not going to pack her life into boxes, Mere. I want to open her up, not close her away. Don't you get it? Don't you care?"

"No," Meredith said, pushing past her. She left the house and walked over to the garage. While she waited for the automatic door to open, she had trouble breathing. It swelled up in her, whatever the feeling was, until her chest ached and her arm tingled and she thought, *I'm having a heart attack.*

She doubled over and sucked in air. In and out, in and out, until she was okay. She started into the darkness of the garage, glad that she'd controlled herself and that she hadn't lost it in front of Nina, but when she turned on the light, there was Dad's Cadillac. The 1956 convertible that had been his pride and joy.

Frankie's his name, after Sinatra. I stole my first kiss in Frankie's front seat. . . .

They'd gone on a dozen family road trips in old Frankie. They'd gone north to British Columbia, east to Idaho, and south to Oregon, always in search of adventure. On those long, dusty drives, with Dad and Nina singing along to John Denver, Meredith had felt all but invisible. She didn't like exploring roads or making wrong turns or running out of gas. It had always seemed to end up that way, too, with Dad and Nina laughing like pirates at every escapade.

Who needs directions? Dad would say.

Not us, Nina would reply, bouncing in her seat and laughing.

Meredith could have joined in, could have pretended, but she hadn't. She'd sat in the back, reading her books and trying not to care when a hubcap flipped off or the engine overheated. And whenever they stopped for the night and camp was set up, Dad would always come for her; while he smoked his pipe, he'd say, *I thought my best girl would like to take a walk. . . .*

Those ten-minute walks were worth a thousand miles of bad road.

She touched the shiny cherry-red hood, felt its smoothness. No one had driven this car in years. "Your best girl would like to take a walk," she whispered.

He was the one person she would have told about what happened last night. . . .

With a sigh, she went to his workbench and looked around until she found three big cardboard boxes. She carried them back into the kitchen, set them down on the hardwood floor, and opened the cupboard closest to her. She knew it was too early to start packing, but anything was better than being alone in her empty house.

"I heard you and Nina fighting."

Meredith slowly closed the cupboard and turned around.

Her mother stood in the doorway, dressed in her white nightgown with a black woolen blanket draped like a cape around her shoulders. Light from the entryway shone through the cotton fabric, outlining her thin legs.

"I'm sorry," Meredith said.

"You and your sister are not close."

It was a statement rather than a question, as it certainly should be, but Meredith heard something sharp in her mother's voice, a judgment, perhaps. Her mother wasn't looking past Meredith for once, or beside her; she was staring right at her, as if seeing her for the first time.

"No, Mom. We're not close. We hardly ever see each other."

"You will regret this."

Thank you, Yoda. "It's fine, Mom. Can I make you some tea?"

"When I am gone, you will only have each other."

Meredith walked over to the samovar. That was the last thing she wanted to think about today—her mother's death. "It will be hot in a moment," she said without turning around.

After a while, she heard her mother walk away, and Meredith was alone again.

Nina planned to wear her mother down. If Meredith the martyr's performance in the kitchen had proven anything, it was that time was of the essence. With every rip of newspaper or clang of a pot, Nina knew that another piece of her mother's life was being wrapped up and put away. If Meredith had her way, there would soon be nothing left.

Dad had wanted something else, though, and now Nina wanted it, too. She wanted to hear the peasant girl and the prince in its entirety; in truth, she couldn't remember ever wanting anything more.

At breakfast, she'd gone into the kitchen, stepping carefully around her ice-cold sister. Ignoring Meredith, she made Mom a cup of sweetened tea and a piece of toast and carried them upstairs. Inside her mother's bedroom, she found Mom in bed, her gnarled hands folded primly on the blanket over her stomach, her white hair a bird's nest that hinted at a restless night. With the door open, they could both hear Meredith packing up the kitchen.

"You could help your sister."

"I could. If I thought you should move. I don't." She handed her mother the tea and toast. "You know what I realized when I made your breakfast?"

Mom sipped tea from the delicate silver-encased glass cup. "I suppose you will tell me."

"I don't know if you like honey or jam or cinnamon."

"All are fine."

"The point is, I don't know."

"Ah. That is the point," Mom said, sighing.

"You're not looking at me again."

Mom said nothing, just took another sip of tea.

"I want to hear the fairy tale. The peasant girl and the prince. All of it. Please."

Mom set the tea down on the bedside table and got out of bed. Moving past Nina as if she were invisible, she walked out the room, across the hall, and went into the bathroom, closing the door behind her.

At lunch, Nina tried again. This time, Mom picked up her sandwich and carried it outside.

Nina followed her out to the winter garden and sat beside her. "I mean it, Mom."

"Yes, Nina. I know. Please leave me."

Nina sat there another ten minutes, just to make her point, then she got up and went inside.

In the kitchen, she found Meredith still packing pots and pans into a box. "She'll never tell you," she said at Nina's entrance.

"Thanks for that," Nina said, reaching for her camera. "Keep boxing up her life. I know how much you want everything to be neat and labeled. You're a barrel of laughs. Honest to God, Mere, how can your kids and Jeff stand it?"

Nina came back into the house at just past six. In the last bit of copper-colored evening light, the apple blossoms glowed with a beautiful opalescence that gave the valley an otherworldly look.

The kitchen was empty except for the carefully stacked and labeled cardboard boxes that were tucked neatly into the space between the pantry and fridge.

She glanced out the window and saw that her sister's car was still here. Meredith must be in another room, knee-deep in boxes and newsprint.

Nina opened the freezer and burrowed through the endless rows of containers. Meatball soup, chicken stew with dumplings, pierogies, lamb and vegetable moussaka, pork chops braised in apple wine, potato pancakes, red pepper paprikash, chicken Kiev, stroganoff, strudels, ham-and-cheese rolls, homemade noodles, and dozens of savory breads. Out in the garage, there was another freezer, equally full, and the basement pantry was chock-full of home-canned fruit and vegetables.

Nina chose one of her favorites: a delicious slow-cooked beef pot roast stuffed with bacon and horseradish. She defrosted the roast in the microwave, with all the root vegetables and rich beef broth, then ladled it to a baking dish and put it in the oven. She set the oven for 350 degrees, figuring it couldn't be too far wrong, and then filled a pot of water for homemade noodles. There were few things on the planet better than her mom's noodles.

While dinner was in the oven, she set the table for two and then poured herself a glass of wine. With this meal, the aroma would bring Mom to her.

Sure enough, at six forty-five, Mom came down the stairs.

"You made dinner?"

"I reheated it," Nina said, leading the way into the dining room.

Mom looked around at the ravaged wallpaper, still smeared with streaks of blood that had dried black. "Let us eat at the kitchen table," she said.

Nina hadn't even thought about that. "Oh. Sure." She scooped up the two place settings and put them down on the small oak table tucked into the nook in the kitchen. "There you go, Mom."

Meredith walked in then; she noticed the two place settings and her face scrunched in irritation. Or maybe relief. With Meredith it was hard to tell.

"Do you want to eat with us?" Nina asked. "I thought you'd need to get home, but there's plenty. You know Mom. She always cooked for an army."

Meredith glanced through the window, up in the direction of her house. "Sure," she finally said. "Jeff won't be home tonight . . . until late."

"Good," Nina said, watching her sister closely. It was odd that she'd stay for dinner. Usually she all but ran for home when she had the chance. "Great. Here. Sit." The minute her sister was seated, Nina quickly set another place at the table and then got the crystal decanter. "We start with a shot of vodka."

"What?" Meredith said, looking up.

Mom took the decanter and poured three shots. "It does no good to argue with her."

Nina sat down and picked up her glass, holding it up. Mom clinked hers to it. Reluctantly, Meredith did the same. Then they drank.

"We're Russian," Nina said suddenly, looking at Meredith. "How come I never thought about that before?"

Meredith shrugged, clearly disinterested. "I'll serve," she said, getting to her feet. She was back a few moments later with the plates.

Mom closed her eyes in prayer.

"Do you remember that?" Nina asked Meredith. "Mom praying?"

Meredith rolled her eyes this time and reached for her fork.

"Okay," Nina said, ignoring the awkward silence at the table. "Meredith, since you're here, you have to join in a new tradition Mom and I have come up with. It's revolutionary, really. It's called dinner conversation."

"So we're going to talk, are we?" Meredith said. "About what?"

"I'll go first so you can see how it goes: My favorite song is 'Born to be Wild,' my best childhood memory is the trip to Yellowstone where Dad taught me how to fish." She looked at her sister. "And I'm sorry if I make my sister's life harder."

Mom put down her fork. "My favorite song is 'Somewhere Over the Rainbow,' my favorite memory is a day I watched children making snow angels in a park, and I'm sorry that you two are not friends."

"We're friends," Nina said.

"This is stupid," Meredith said.

"No," Nina said. "Staring at each other in silence is stupid. Go."

Meredith gave a typically long-suffering sigh. "Fine. My favorite song is 'Candle in the Wind'—the Princess Di version, not the original; my favorite childhood memory is when Dad took me ice-skating on Miller's Pond . . . and I'm sorry I said we weren't close, Nina. But we aren't. So maybe I'm sorry for that, too." She nodded, as if in saying it, she checked something off her To-Do list. "Now, let's eat. I'm starving."

Eleven

Nina wasn't even finished eating when Meredith got to her feet and began clearing the table. The second her sister was up, Mom followed suit.

"I guess dinner is over," Nina said, reaching for the butter and jam before Meredith snatched it away.

Mom said, "Thank you for dinner," and left the kitchen. Her footsteps on the stairs were quick for a woman of her age. She must have been practically running.

Nina couldn't really blame Meredith. As soon as their little conversational jumper cables had been used—the so-called new tradition—they had fallen into their familiar silence. Only Nina had even tried to make small talk, and her amusing stories about Africa had been met with a lukewarm response from Meredith and nothing at all from Mom.

Nina left the table just long enough to get the decanter of vodka. Thumping it down on the table, she said, "Let's get drunk."

Meredith, elbow-deep in soapy water, said, "Okay."

Nina must have misheard. "Did you say—"

"Don't make a lunar mission out of it." Meredith walked over to the table, plucked up Nina's plate and silverware, and went back to the sink.

"Wow," Nina said. "We haven't gotten drunk together since . . . Have we *ever* gotten drunk together?"

Meredith dried her hands on the pink towel that hung from the oven door. "You've gotten drunk while I was in the room, does that count?"

Nina grinned. "Hell, no, that doesn't count. Pull up a chair."

"I'm not drinking vodka, though."

"Tequila it is." Nina got up before Meredith could change her mind; she ran into the living room, grabbed a bottle of tequila from the wet bar, and then snagged salt, limes, and a knife on her way back through the kitchen.

"Aren't you going to mix it with something?"

"No offense, Mere, but I've seen you drink. If I mix it with anything, you'll just sip it all night and I'll end up drunk and you'll be your usual cool, competent self." She poured two shots, sliced a lime, and pushed the glass toward her sister.

Meredith wrinkled her nose.

"It's not heroin, Mere. Just a shot of tequila. Take a walk on the wild side."

Meredith seemed to decide all at once. She reached out, grabbed the shot, and downed it.

When her eyes bulged, Nina handed her the lime. "Here. Bite down on this."

Meredith made a whooshing sound and shook her head. "One more."

Nina drank her own shot and poured them each another, which they drank together.

Afterward, Meredith sat back in her chair, pushing a hand through her perfectly smooth hair. "I don't feel anything."

"You will. Hey, how do you manage to keep looking so . . . neat all the time? You've been packing boxes all day, but you still look ready for lunch at the club. How does that happen?"

"Only you can make looking nice sound like an insult."

"It wasn't an insult. Honestly. I just wonder how you stay so . . . I don't know. Forget it."

"There's a wall around me," Meredith said, reaching for the tequila, pouring herself another shot.

"Yeah. Like a force field. Nothing reaches your hair." Nina laughed at that. She was still laughing when Meredith drank her third shot, but when her sister gulped it down and glanced sideways, Nina saw something that made her stop laughing. She didn't know what it was, a look in Meredith's eyes, maybe, or the way her mouth kind of flitted downward.

"Is something wrong?" Nina asked.

Meredith blinked slowly. "You mean besides the fact that my father died at Christmas, my mom is going crazy, my sister is pretending to help me, and my husband . . . is gone tonight?"

Nina knew it wasn't funny, but she couldn't help laughing. "Yeah, besides that. And anyway, you know your life rocks. You're one of those wonder women who do everything right. That's why Dad always counted on you."

"Yeah. I guess," Meredith said.

"It's true," Nina said with a sigh, thinking suddenly about her dad again, and how she'd let him down. She wondered how long it would last, this sudden bobbing up of her grief. Would it ever just submerge?

"You can do everything right," Meredith said quietly, "and still end up in the wrong. And alone."

"I should have called Dad more from Africa," Nina said. "I knew how much my phone calls meant to him. I always thought there was time. . . ."

"Sometimes the door just slams shut, you know? And you're all by yourself."

"There is something we can do now to help him," she said.

Meredith looked startled. "Help who?"

"Dad," Nina said impatiently. "Isn't that who we're talking about?"

"Oh. Is it?"

"He wanted us to get to know Mom. He said she—"

"Not the fairy tales again," Meredith said. "Now I know why you're so successful. You're obsessive."

"And you aren't?" Nina laughed at that. "Come on. We can *make* her tell us the story. You heard her tonight: she said there was no point arguing with me. That means she's going to give up fighting."

Meredith stood up. She was a little unsteady on her feet, so she clutched the back of the chair for support. "I *knew* better than to try to talk to you."

Nina frowned. "You were talking to me?"

"How many times can I say it: I am not listening to her stories. I don't care about the Black Knight or people who turn into smoke or the handsome prince. That was *your* promise to Dad. Mine was to take care of her, which I'm going to do right now. If you need me, I'll be in the bathroom, packing up her things."

Nina watched Meredith leave the kitchen. She couldn't say she was surprised—her sister was nothing if not consistent—but she was disappointed. She was certain that this task was something Dad had wanted them to do together. That was the point, wasn't it? Being together. What else but the fairy tales had ever accomplished that?

"I tried, Dad," she said. "Even getting her drunk didn't help."

She got to her feet, not unsteady at all. Tucking the decanter of vodka under one arm, and grabbing Mom's shot glass, she went upstairs. At the bathroom's half-open door, she paused, listening to the clink and rattle that meant Meredith was back at work.

"I'll leave Mom's door open," she said, "in case you want to listen in."

No answer came from the bathroom, not even a pause in crinkling of newspaper.

Nina walked across the hallway to her mother's room. She knocked on the door but didn't wait for an invitation. She just walked in.

Mom sat up in bed, propped up on a mound of white pillows, with the white comforter drawn up to her waist. All that white—her hair, her nightgown, her bedding, her skin—contrasted sharply with the black walnut headboard and bed. Against it, she looked ethereal, otherworldly; an aged Galadriel with intense blue eyes.

"I did not invite you in," she said.

"Nope. But here I am. It's magic."

"And you thought I would want vodka?"

"I know you will."

"Why is that?"

Nina moved to the side of the bed. "I made a promise to my dying father." She saw the effect of her words. Her mother flinched as if she'd been struck. "You loved him. I know you did. And he wanted me to hear your fairy tale about the peasant girl and the prince. All of it. On his deathbed, he asked me. He must have asked you, too."

Her mother broke eye contact. She stared down at her blue-veined hands, coiled together atop the blankets. "You will give me no peace."

"None."

"It is a child's story. Why do you care so much?"

"Why did he?"

Mom didn't answer.

Nina stood there, waiting.

Finally Mom said, "Pour me a drink."

Very calmly, Nina poured her mother a shot and handed it to her.

Mom drank the vodka. "I will do it my way," she said, setting the empty glass aside. "If you interrupt me, I will stop. I will tell it in pieces and only at night. We will not speak of it during the day. Do you understand?"

"Yes."

"In the dark."

"Why always—"

The look Mom gave her was so sharp Nina stopped abruptly. "Sorry." She went to the light switch and turned it off.

It was a moonless night, so no silver-blue glow came through the glass. The only light was from the crack of the open door.

Nina sat on the floor, waiting.

A rustling sound filled the room: her mother getting comfortable in the bed. "Where should I begin?"

"In December, you ended when Vera was going to sneak out to meet the prince."

A sigh.

And then came her mother's story voice, sweet and mellifluous: "After she comes home from the park, Vera spends the rest of that day in the kitchen with her mother, but her mind is not on the task at hand. She knows her mama knows this, that she is watching her carefully, but how can a girl concentrate

on straining goose fat into jars when her heart is full of love?

"Veronika, pay attention," her mama says.

Vera sees that she has spilled a big blob of fat on the table. She wipes it up with her hand and throws it into the sink. She hates goose fat anyway. She prefers rich, homemade butter any day.

"And you throw it away? What is wrong with you?"

Her sister giggles. "Maybe she is thinking of boys. Of a boy."

"Of course she is thinking of boys," Mama says, wiping the moisture from her brow as she stands at the stove, stirring the simmering lingonberries. "She is fifteen."

"Almost sixteen."

Her mama pauses in her stirring and turns around.

They are in the kitchen, in the last days of summer, preserving food for winter. The tables are full of berries to be turned into jam; onions, mushrooms, potatoes, and garlic to be put in the cellar; cucumbers to be pickled; and beans to be canned in brine. Later, Mama has promised to teach them how to make blini with a sweet cherry filling.

"You are almost sixteen," Mama says, as if it had not occurred to her before. "Two years younger than I was when I met Petyr."

Vera puts down the slippery pot of goose fat. "What did you feel when you first saw him?"

Mama smiles. "I have told this story many times."

"You always say he swept you away. But how?"

Mama wipes her brow again and reaches out for the wooden chair in front of her. Pulling it back a little, she sits down.

Vera almost makes a sound; that's how shocked she is by this. Her mother is not a woman who stops working to talk. Vera and Olga have grown up on stories of responsibility and duty. As peasants beholden to the imprisoned king, they have been taught their place. They must keep their heads down and their hands working, for the shadow of the Black Knight falls with the swiftness of a steel blade. It is best never to draw attention to oneself.

Still, her mother is sitting down now. "He was a tutor then, and so good-looking he took my breath away. When I told your baba this, she tsked and said, 'Zoya, be careful. You will need your breath.' "

"Was it love at first sight?" Vera asks.

"I knew when he looked at me that I would take his hand, that I would follow him. I say it was the mead we drank, but it wasn't. It was just . . . Petyr. My Petya. His passion for knowledge and life swept me away and before I knew it, we were married. My parents were horrified, for the kingdom was in turmoil. The king was in exile then, and we were afraid. Your father's ambition scared them. He was a poor country tutor, but he dreamed of being a poet."

Vera sighs at the romance of it. Now she knows she must sneak out tonight to meet the prince. She even knows that her mother will understand if she finds out.

"All right," her mother says, sounding tired again. "Let's get back to work, and Veronika, be careful with that goose fat. It is precious."

As the hours pass, Vera finds her mind more and more distracted. While she prepares the beans and cucumbers, she imagines an entire love story for her and Sasha. They will walk along the edge of the magic river, where images of the future can sometimes be seen in the blue waves, and they will pause under one of the streetlamps, as she has often seen lovers do. It will not matter that he is a prince and she a poor tutor's daughter.

"Vera."

She hears her name being called out and the sound of it is impatient. She can tell that it is not the first time she had been spoken to. Her father is standing in the room, frowning at her.

"Papa," she says. He looks tired, and a little nervous. His black hair, usually so neatly combed, stands out in all directions, as if he has been rubbing his head repeatedly, and his leather jerkin is buttoned crookedly. His fingers, stained blue with ink, move anxiously.

"Where is Zoya?" he asks, looking around.

"She and Olga went for more vinegar."

"By themselves?" Her father nods distractedly and chews on his lower lip.

"Papa? Is something wrong?"

"No. No. Nothing." Taking her in his arms, he pulls her into an embrace so tight that she has to wiggle out of it or gasp for breath.

In the years to come, Vera will replay that embrace a thousand times in her mind. She will see the jewel-tone jars in the candlelight, smell the dusty, sun-baked leather of her father's jerkin, and feel the scratch of his stubbly jaw against her cheek. She'll imagine herself saying, I love you, Papa.

But the truth is that she has romance and sneaking out on her mind, so she says nothing to her father and goes back to work.

That night, Vera cannot lie still.

Every nerve ending in her body seems to be dancing. Sounds float in through her open window: people talking, the distant patter of hooves on cobblestoned streets, music from the park. Someone is playing a violin on this warm, light night, probably to woo a lover, and upstairs, someone is moving around—maybe dancing. The floorboards creak with every step.

"Are you scared?" Olga asks for at least the fifth time.

Vera rolls over onto her side. Olga does the same. In their narrow bed, they are face-to-face. "When you are older, you'll see, Olga. There is a feeling in your heart when you meet the boy you'll love. It's like . . . drowning and then coming up for air."

Vera hugs her sister and plants a kiss on her plump cheek. Then she throws back the covers and springs out of bed. With a small hand mirror, she tries to check her appearance, but she can see herself only in pieces—long black hair held away from her face with leather strings, ivory skin, pink lips. She is wearing a plain blue gown with a lace collar—a girl's costume, but it is the best she has. If only she had a beret or a pin or, best of all, some perfume.

"Oh, well," she says, and turns to her sister. "How do I look?"

"Perfect."

Vera smiles broadly. She knows it is true. She is a pretty girl, some even say beautiful.

She goes to her bedroom door and listens. No sound reaches her ear. "They are in bed," she says. Moving cautiously, she tiptoes over to her window, which is always left open in the summer. She blows her sister a kiss and climbs out onto the tiny ironwork grate. With every careful step, she is sure that someone from the street below will look her way and point and shout out that a girl is sneaking out to meet a boy.

But the people on the street are drunk on light and mead and they barely notice her climbing down from the building's second floor. When she jumps the last few feet and lands on the small patch of grass, she cannot contain her excitement. It spills over in a giggle, which she stifles with her hand as she runs across the cobblestoned street.

There he is. Standing by the streetlamp at this end of the Fontanka Bridge. From here, everything about him is golden: his hair, his jerkin, his skin.

"I didn't think you'd come," he says.

She cannot seem to talk. The words, like her breath, are trapped in her chest. She looks at his handsome lips and it is a mistake. In a flash, she is closing her eyes, leaning toward him, and still it is a surprise when he kisses her. She gasps a little, feels herself start to cry, and though her tears turn into tiny stars and embarrass her, there is nothing she can do to stop them from falling.

Now he will know that she is a silly peasant girl who has fallen in love over nothing and cried at her first kiss.

She starts to make an excuse—she is not even sure what it will be, but before she can speak, Sasha pulls her down into a crouch and says, "Be quiet," in a voice so sharp she feels stung by it. "Look."

A shiny black carriage, drawn by six black dragons, is moving slowly down the street. Silence falls all at once. People freeze in their tracks, retreat into shadows. It is the Black Knight. . . .

The carriage moves like a hunting animal, the dragons breathing fire. When it stops, Vera feels a chill move through her. "That is where I live," she says.

Three hulking green trolls in black capes get out of the carriage and come together on the sidewalk, talking for a moment before they go to the front door. "What are they doing?" she whispers as they go inside the building. "What do they want?"

The minutes tick by slowly until the door opens again.

Vera sees it all in some kind of slow motion. The trolls have her father. He is not fighting, not arguing, not even talking.

Her mama stumbles down the steps behind them, sobbing, pleading. Windows in the building above her are slamming shut.

"Papa!" Vera cries out.

Across the street, her father looks up and sees her. It is as if he alone heard her cry out.

He shakes his head and holds out his hand as if to say, Stay there, *and then he is shoved into the carriage and he is gone.*

She elbows Sasha one last time and he lets her go. Without a backward glance, she runs across the street. "Mama, where have they taken him?"

Her mother looks up slowly. For a second, she seems not to recognize her own daughter. "You should be in bed, Vera."

"The trolls. Where are they taking Papa?"

When her mother doesn't answer, she hears Sasha's voice behind her. "It's the Black Knight, Vera. They do what they want."

"I do not understand," Vera cries. "You are a prince—"

"My family has no power anymore. The Black Knight has imprisoned my father and my uncles. You must know that. It is dangerous to be a royal in the Snow Kingdom these days. No one can help you," he says. "I am sorry."

She starts to cry, and this time her tears are not starlight; they are tiny black stones that hurt when they form.

"Veronika," her mother says. "We need to get inside. Now." She grabs Vera's hand and pulls her away from Sasha, who just stands there watching her. "She is fifteen years old," Mama says to him, putting an arm around Vera, holding her close as they climb the steps to the door.

When Vera looks back out to the street, her prince is gone.

From then on, Vera's family is changed. No one smiles anymore, no one laughs. She and her mother and her sister try to pretend that it will get better, but none believes it.

The kingdom is still beautiful, still a white, walled city filled with bridges and spires and magical rivers, but Vera sees it differently now. She sees shadows where there had been light, fear where there had been love. Before, the sound of students laughing on a warm white night could make her cry with longing. Now she knows what is worth crying over.

Days melt into weeks and Vera begins to lose all hope that her father will return. She turns sixteen without a celebration.

"I hear they are looking for workers at the castle," her mother

says one day while they are eating supper. "In the library and in the bakery."

"Yes," Vera says.

"I know you wanted to go to university," her mother says.

Already that dream is losing substance. It is something her father had dreamed for her, that one day she, too, would be a poet. Finally, she is the grown-up she'd longed to be, and she has no choices now. Not a peasant girl like her. She understands this at last.

Her future has been changed by this arrest; fixed. There will be no schooling for her, no handsome boys carrying her schoolbooks or kissing her under streetlamps. No Sasha. "I do not want to smell like bread all day."

She feels her mother's nod. They are connected like that now, the three of them. When one moves, they all feel it. Ripples in a pond.

"I will go to the royal library tomorrow," Vera says.

She is sixteen. How can she possibly understand the mistake she has just made? Who could have known that people she loved would die because of it?

Twelve

"What do you mean, people will die? What's her mistake?" Nina said when her mother fell silent. "We've never heard that part of the story before."

"Yes, you have. It scared Meredith, so I sometimes skipped it."

Nina got up and went to the bed, turning on the lamp. In the soft light, her mother looked like a ghost, unmoving, her eyes closed.

"I am tired. You will leave me now."

Nina wanted to argue. She could sit in the dark and listen to her mother's voice for hours. About that, her father had been right. The fairy tale connected them somehow. And her mother might be feeling it, too; Nina was certain Mom was elaborating, going deeper into the story than ever before. Did she, like Nina, want to keep it going? Had Dad asked that of her?

"Can I bring you anything before I go?" Nina asked.

"My knitting."

Nina looked around, saw the bulging bag stuffed alongside the rocking chair. Retrieving it, she went back to the bed. In no time, Mom's hands were moving over the coil of blue-green mohair yarn. Nina left the room, hearing the *click click click* of the needles as she closed the door.

She stopped by the bathroom and pushed the door open. The room was empty.

Alone, she went downstairs and put a log on the dwindling fire. She poured herself a glass of wine and sat down on the hearth.

"Wow," she said. "Wow."

It was a hell of a story, worth listening to, if for no other reason than to hear her mother speak with such passion and power. The woman who told that story was someone else entirely, not the cold, distant Anya Whitson of Nina's youth.

Was that the secret her father wanted her to glimpse? That somewhere, buried beneath the silent exterior, lay a different woman? Was that her father's gift? A glimpse—finally—at the woman with whom he had fallen in love?

Or was there more to it? The story was so much richer and more detailed than she remembered. Or maybe she hadn't really listened before. The story had always been something she'd taken for granted; like a picture you saw so often you never wondered who it was that had taken it, or who that was standing in the background. But once you'd noticed the oddity, it threw everything else into question.

Meredith hadn't intended to listen to her mother's fairy tale, but as she sat in the ridiculously overstocked bathroom, going through drawers full of over-the-counter and prescription medications dating back to 1980, she heard The Voice.

That was how she'd always thought of it, even as a girl.

Without making a conscious decision, she finished packing the box, marked it BATHROOM, and dragged it into the hallway. There she heard the words from her childhood float through the open door.

Maybe she is thinking of boys. Of a boy. . . .

Meredith felt a shiver. She recognized her own longing; it was familiar to her, that feeling of wanting something from her mother. She had known it all of her life.

She knew she should leave the bathroom and walk down the hallway and out of the house, but she couldn't do it. The lure of Mom's voice, as sweet and honeyed as any fairy-tale witch's, snared her as it always had, and before she really thought about it, she found herself crossing the hallway, standing at the partially open door, listening.

It wasn't until she heard Nina's sharp voice say, "What do you mean, people will die?" that the spell broke. Meredith backed away from the door quickly—she definitely did not want to be caught eavesdropping; Nina would take it as interest and pounce.

Hurrying down the stairs, she was home in no time.

The dogs greeted her with dizzying enthusiasm. She was so relieved to have been missed that when she let them inside, she dropped to her knees on the mudroom floor and hugged them both, letting their nuzzling and face-licking substitute for the sound of her husband's voice.

"Good puppies," she murmured, scratching the soft hair behind their ears. Getting tiredly to her feet, she went to the closet beside the washer and dryer and got the giant bag of dog food—

Jeff's job

—and poured some into their silver bowls. After a quick check that they had plenty of fresh water, she went into the kitchen.

The room was empty, quiet, with no lingering scents. She stood there in the darkness, paralyzed by the thought of the night to come. No wonder she'd stayed for the story. Anything was better than facing her empty bed.

She called each of her daughters, left I-love-you messages, and then made herself a cup of tea. Grabbing a heavy blanket, she went outside to sit on the porch.

At least the quiet out here felt natural.

She could lose herself in the endless starlit sky, in the smell of rich black earth, in the sweet scent of new growth. In this month that was a pause between spring and summer, the first tiny apples were out on the trees. In no time, the orchards would be full of fruit and workmen and pickers. . . .

It was her dad's favorite time of year, this moment when everything was possible and he could still hope for the best crop ever. She had tried to love Belye Nochi as her father had. She loved him, so she tried to love what he had loved, and what she'd ended up with was a facsimile of his life, lacking the passion he had brought to it.

She closed her eyes and leaned back. The wicker swing back bit into her neck, but she didn't care. The rusty old chains on either side squeaked as she pushed off with her feet.

You're like her.

That was what Jeff had said.

Wrapping the blanket more tightly around her, she finished her tea and went upstairs, letting the dogs come up the stairs behind her. In her room, she took a sleeping pill and crawled into bed, pulling the covers up past her chin. Curling into a fetal position, she tried to focus on the chuffing sound of the dogs' breathing.

Finally, somewhere past midnight, she fell into a troubled, fitful sleep, until her alarm went off at 5:47.

Batting the off button, she tried to go back to sleep, but it was a wasted effort, so she got up, dressed in her running clothes, and ran for six miles. When she got home she was exhausted enough to climb back into bed, but she didn't dare take that route.

Work was the key. Keeping busy.

She thought about going in to work, although on the beautiful sunny Sunday, someone was liable to see her car, and if Daisy found out that Meredith had come in on a Sunday, the inquisition would begin.

She decided to go to Belye Nochi and make sure Nina was taking good care of Mom. There was still plenty of packing to be done.

An hour later, dressed in an old pair of jeans and a navy-blue sweatshirt, she showed up at Mom's house, calling out, "Hello," as she came into the kitchen.

Nina was at the kitchen table, wearing the same clothes she'd been in yesterday, with her short black hair spiked out in all directions. There were several books open on the table and pieces of paper lay scattered about, with Nina's bold scrawl covering most of the sheets.

"You look like the Unabomber," Meredith said.

"Good morning to you, too."

"Have you slept at all?"

"Some."

"What's wrong?"

"I know you don't care, but it's the fairy tale. I can't get it out of my head." Nina looked up. "She mentioned the Fontanka Bridge last night. It was always the Enchanted Bridge before, wasn't it? Does that seem odd to you?"

"The fairy tale," Meredith said. "I should have known."

"Listen to this: 'The Fontanka is a branch of the River Neva, which flows through the city of Leningrad.' "

Meredith poured herself a cup of coffee. "She's Russian. The story takes place in Russia. Stop the presses."

"You should have been there, Mere. It was amazing. Last night was all new."

No, it wasn't. "Maybe you were just too young to remember. I am not getting sucked into this."

"How can you not be interested? We've never heard the end of it."

Meredith turned around slowly, looking at her sister. "I'm tired, Neens. I don't know if you know how that feels, really. You're always so in love with everything you do. But I've spent most of my life on this piece of property, and I've tried to get to know Mom. She won't let it happen. That's the answer, the end. She'll lure you in, make you think there's something more—you'll see sadness in her eyes sometimes or a softening in her mouth, and you'll seize on it and believe in it because you want to so much. But it's all a lie. She just doesn't . . . love us. And frankly, I've got problems of my own right now, so I'll have to say a polite no, thank you, on your fairy-tale quest."

"What problems?"

Meredith looked down at her coffee. She'd forgotten for a split second that it was Nina to whom she was speaking. Nina, with her journalist's knack for getting to the heart of a thing instantly and her fearlessness in asking questions. "Nothing. It was just an expression."

"You're lying."

Meredith gave a tired smile and went to the table, sitting down across from her sister. "I don't want to fight with you, Neens."

"So talk to me."

"You'd be the last person who would understand, and I'm not being a bitch. It's just the truth."

"Why do you say that?"

"Danny Flynn. You've been with him for more than four years, but none of us ever even heard of him. I know about the places you've been and the photographs you've taken, even the beaches you like, but I don't know anything about the man you love."

"Who said I loved him?"

"Exactly. I don't know if you've ever been in love. It's stories that matter to you. Like this thing with Mom. Of course you're hooked." She made a sweeping gesture with her hand, indicating the books spread out on the table. "Just don't expect all of this to mean anything, because it doesn't. She won't let it, and please, *please* quit trying to make me care. I can't. Not like that, about her. Not again. Okay?"

Nina stared at her; the pity in her eyes was almost unbearable. "Okay."

Meredith nodded and got to her feet. "Good. Now I'm going to run to the grocery store and then I'll come back and do some more packing."

"You need to keep busy," Nina said.

Meredith ignored the knowing tone in her sister's voice. "It doesn't look like I'm the only one. I'll see you in a few hours. Make sure Mom eats a good meal." Smiling tightly, she headed for her car.

Nina spent the rest of the day alternately taking pictures of the orchard and surfing the Internet. Unfortunately, the dial-up connection at Belye Nochi was impossibly slow, so it took forever to look things up. Not that there was much to find. What she'd learned was that Russia had a rich fairy-tale tradition that was different in many ways from the Grimms' type of stories that were more familiar to Americans. There were literally dozens of peasant girl and prince stories, and often they ended unhappily to teach a lesson.

None of it illuminated the story Nina was being told.

Finally, as night fell outside, Meredith opened the study door and said, "Dinner's ready."

Nina winced. She'd meant to quit earlier and help with dinner. But as usual, once she started researching something, time fell away from her. "Thanks," she said, and closed down the computer. Then she went into the kitchen, where she found Mom seated at the table. There were three place settings.

Nina looked at her sister. "You're staying for dinner again? Should we call Jeff down and invite him?"

"He's working late," Meredith said, taking a casserole out of the oven.

"Again?"

"You know news. The stories happen at all hours."

Nina got the decanter of vodka and three shot glasses and brought them to the table. She sat down next to Mom, poured.

Her hands in puffy, insulated gloves, Meredith carried the hot casserole dish to the table and set it down on a pair of trivets.

"Chanakhi," Nina said, leaning close, breathing in the savory aroma of the lamb and vegetable casserole. It had come out of Mom's freezer, so it would taste exquisite, even reheated. The vegetables would be perfectly tender, their flavors merged into a silken tangle of tomatoes, sweet peppers, string beans, and Walla Walla sweet onions; all of it swimming in a rich garlic-and-lemon-tinged lamb broth with big chunks of succulent meat. It was one of Nina's favorites. "Great choice, Meredith."

Meredith pulled up a chair and sat down between them.

Nina handed her a straight shot of vodka.

"Again?" Meredith said, frowning. "Wasn't last night enough?"

"It's a new tradition."

"It smells like pine needles," Meredith said, wrinkling her nose as she smelled it.

"The taste is quite different," Mom said.

Nina laughed at that and raised her shot glass. They dutifully clinked the glasses together and drank. Then Nina reached for the serving spoon. "I'll dish up. Meredith, why don't you start?"

"The three things again?"

"You can do as many as you want. We'll follow your lead."

Mom said nothing, just shook her head.

"Fine," Meredith said as Nina ladled the casserole into her sister's white china bowl. "My favorite time of day is dawn. I love sitting on my porch in the summer, and Jeff . . . thinks I run too much."

While Nina was figuring out her response to that, Mom surprised her by saying, "My favorite time of day is night. *Belye nochi.* I love cooking. And your father thinks I should learn to play the piano."

Nina heard the word *thinks* and it made her look up. For a moment they all looked at each other.

Mom was the first to glance away. "He *thought* this. Do not rush me to the doctor's, Meredith," she said. "I know he is not here."

Meredith nodded but said nothing.

Nina filled in the awkward silence. "My favorite time of day is sunset. Preferably in Botswana. In the dry season. I love answers. And I think there's a reason Mom hardly ever looks at us."

"It is meaning you want?" Mom said. "You will be disappointed. Now eat. I hate this dish when it is cold."

Nina recognized her mother's tone. It meant that the frivolity of their little tradition had come to an end. The rest of the meal proceeded in silence; the only sounds were spoons scraping on fine china and wineglasses being set down on the wooden table, and when dinner was over, Meredith rose to her feet and went to the sink. Mom walked gracefully away.

"I'm going to hear more of the story tonight," Nina said to Meredith, who was drying the silverware.

Her sister didn't turn around, neither did she answer.

"You could—"

"I need to go through Dad's study," Meredith said. "I need some of his files at the office."

"Are you sure?"

"I'm sure. I've been putting it off."

There were places in every home that belonged to a single individual. No matter how many family members might use a space, or come and go through it, there was one in the group to whom it truly belonged. In Meredith's home, the porch was hers. Jeff and the girls used it on occasion, but rarely: summertime parties and such. Meredith loved that porch and sat in the wicker rocker throughout the year.

In Belye Nochi, almost every room belonged to her mom. Her damaged eyesight was reflected in all the decorations and furniture, from the kitchen with its pale walls and white tile counters to its antique wooden table and chairs. Where there was color in this house, it came in splashes—the nesting dolls in the windowsill, the gilded icons in the Holy Corner, the painting of the troika.

Of all the rooms in Belye Nochi, only one could truly be called her father's, and it was this room, his study.

Meredith stood in the doorway. She didn't have to close her eyes to imagine him at this desk, laughing, talking to the two little girls at play on the floor at his feet.

The echo of his voice was strong in here. She could almost smell the sweet tang of his pipe smoke.

Don't tell your mom, now, you know she hates it when I smoke.

She went to the center of the room and knelt on the thick forest-green carpet. A pair of blackwatch-plaid club chairs stood cocked toward each other, facing the giant mahogany desk that dominated the room. The walls were a rich cobalt blue with black trim, and everywhere she looked was a family photograph, framed in forest-green leather.

She sat back on her heels, overcome for a moment at the idea of what she was to do in here. Only his clothes would be more difficult to go through.

But it had to be done and she was the one to do it. She and Mom would both need documents from this room in the coming months and years. Insurance information, bill records, tax records, and banking information, just to name a few.

So Meredith took a deep breath and opened his file drawer. For the next hour, as night fell outside, she carefully picked through the paper trail of her parents' lives, sorting everything into three piles: *Keep*, *Maybe*, and *Burn*.

She was grateful for the concentration it took to do the sorting. Only rarely did she find her mind wandering into the swamp of her own broken marriage.

Like now, as she stared down at a picture that had somehow fallen into the property tax file. In the photograph, Dad, Nina, Jeff, Jillian, and Maddy were playing catch in the front yard. The girls were small—barely taller than the mailbox—and dressed in matching pink snowsuits. Christmas lights and evergreen boughs decorated the fences, and everyone was laughing.

But where was she? She'd probably been in the dining room, setting the table with Martha Stewart–level obsessiveness, or wrapping gifts or rearranging the decorations.

She hadn't been where it mattered, making memories with her husband and children. Maybe she'd thought time was more elastic, or love more forgiving. She set the picture on the file and opened another drawer. As she reached inside she heard footsteps, the thump of the front door, and the sound of Nina's voice in the living room.

Of course. Night had fallen and driven Nina back into the house, where her sister would undoubtedly exchange one obsession—her camera—for another. The fairy tale.

Meredith grabbed a file and pulled it out, seeing that the label had been partially ripped. The part she could make out read: ВераПеТроВНа. She was pretty sure that the letters were Russian.

Inside, she found a single letter, postmarked twenty years ago from Anchorage, Alaska, and addressed to Mrs. Evan Whitson.

Dear Mrs. Whitson,

Thank you for your recent reply to my query. While I am certain that you could provide invaluable insight into my Leningrad study, I certainly understand your decision. If, however, you ever change your mind, I would welcome your participation.

Sincerely,
Vasily Adamovich
Professor of Russian Studies
University of Alaska

Behind her, and through the open door, she heard Nina say something to Mom; then there was a long, drawn-out silence. Finally her mother said something, and Nina answered, and her mother began to speak again.

The fairy tale. There was no mistaking the sound of it.

Meredith hesitated, telling herself to stay where she was, that none of this mattered to her, that it couldn't matter, that Mom wouldn't let it, but when she heard *Vera*, she folded the strange letter, put it back in its envelope, and dropped it onto the *Keep* pile.

Then she got to her feet.

Thirteen

Nina put her camera on the coffee table and walked over to her mother, who sat in Dad's favorite chair, knitting. Even on this warm May evening, a chill hung in the living room, so Nina built a fire.

"Are you ready?" she asked her mother.

Mom looked up. Her face was pale, her cheeks a little drawn, but her eyes were as bright and clear as ever. "Where did we leave off?"

"Come on, Mom. You remember."

Mom stared at her for a long time, and then said, "The lights."

Nina turned off all the lights in the living room and entryway. The fire gave the darkness a blazing heart, and she sat on the floor in front of the sofa. For a moment the house was almost preternaturally silent, as if it, too, were waiting. Then the fire crackled and somewhere a floorboard creaked; the house settled in for the story.

Her mother began slowly. "In the year following her father's imprisonment in the Red Tower, Vera becomes somebody, and in the Snow Kingdom, in these dark times, that is a dangerous thing to be. She is no longer just an ordinary

peasant girl, the daughter of a poor country tutor. She is the eldest daughter of a banned poet, a relative of an enemy of the realm. She must be careful. Always.

The first weeks without Papa are strange. Their neighbors will no longer make eye contact with Vera. When she comes up the stairs at night, doors clap shut in a sound like falling cards.

The black carriages are everywhere these days, as are the whispered stories of arrest, of people being turned to smoke and lost forever. By the time she is seventeen, Vera can recognize other families of criminals. They move like victims, with their shoulders hunched and their eyes cast downward, trying to make themselves smaller, unremarkable. Unnoticeable.

This is how Vera moves now. No more does she spend time in front of a mirror, trying to be pretty for boys.

She just tries to get by. She wakens early every morning and dresses in a black, shapeless dress. Clothes do not matter to her anymore; neither does it matter that her shoes are ugly and her socks do not match. Like this, she makes kasha in the morning for her sister, who has become a pale shadow of Vera, and for her mother, who rarely speaks anymore. The sound of her crying can be heard most nights. For months, Vera tried to comfort her mother, but it was a wasted effort. Her mother cannot be comforted. None of them can.

So they go on, doing what they must to survive. Vera works long days at the castle library. In rooms scented by dust, leather, and stone, she turns in the last of her father's dreams for her—that she will become a writer—she hands it in like an overdue book and takes joy in the words of others. Whenever she has time, she disappears into a corner and pores through stories and poems, but she cannot do this often or for long. Vera can never forget that she is being watched, always. Lately, even children are being arrested. In this way are parents made to confess. Vera is terrified that one day the black carriages with the three trolls will arrive at her building again and that they will have come for her. Or worse—for Olga or Mama. It is only when she is truly alone—in her bed at night with Olga snoring gently beside her—that she allows herself to even remember the girl she'd once imagined herself to be.

It is then, in the quiet darkness, with cold winter air sweeping through the thin glass of her closed window, that she thinks of Sasha and how his kiss made her cry.

She tries to forget about him, but even as months pass with no word from him, she cannot forget.

"Vera?" her sister whispers in the dark.

"I'm awake," she answers.

Olga immediately snuggles closer to her. "I'm cold."

Vera puts her arms around her younger sister and holds her close. She knows she should say something comforting. As the older sister it is her job to lift Olga's spirits and it is an obligation she takes seriously, but she is so tired. She hasn't enough of herself left to share.

Finally Vera gets out of bed and dresses quickly. Hiding her long hair beneath a kerchief, she goes into the cold kitchen, where a pot of water-thinned kasha sits on the stove.

Mama is gone already. Earlier than usual, even. She leaves every morning well before dawn for her job at the royal food warehouse; when she finally comes home at night, she is too tired to do more than kiss her girls and go to bed.

Vera reheats the kasha for her sister, sweetening it with a big dollop of honey, and takes it to her. Sitting together on the bed, they eat breakfast in silence.

"Today, again?" Olga finally says, scraping the bowl for the last speck of food.

"Today," Vera confirms. It is the same thing she has said to her sister every Friday since their papa was taken away. She has no words to add to it; Olga knows this. Hope is a fragile thing, easily broken if handled too much. So, saying no more, they dress for work and leave the building together.

Outside, winter is gnashing its teeth.

Vera lifts her collar upward and walks briskly forward, her body angled into the wind. Snowflakes scald her cheeks. On the frozen river, she sees scores of fishermen hunched around holes in the ice. At the corner, she and Olga go their separate ways.

Moments later, Vera hears the distant roar of a dragon and sees a black carriage turning onto this street, its color vivid amid the falling snow and the white stone of their walled kingdom. She dives into the shadowy snowbank beneath a crystal tree.

Someone is being arrested; someone's family is being ruined, and all Vera can think is, Thank God it is not my family this time. She waits until the carriage is gone and gets back to her feet. In the slicing snow, she takes the trolley across town to a place that has become as familiar to her as her own arm.

At the entrance to the Great Hall of Justice, she pauses just long enough to square her shoulders. She opens the huge stone door and goes inside. The first thing she sees is a queue of woolen-clad women wearing felt boots and clapping their mittened hands together to keep warm. They move forward, always forward; people in line, waiting for their turn.

The next two hours pass in a gray blur, until at last Vera is at the front of the line. She gathers her courage and straightens as she walks up to the gleaming marble desk where a goblin sits in a tall chair, his face as pale and shapeless as melting wax, his golden eyes opening and closing like those of a serpent.

"Name," he says.

She answers in as even a voice as she can.

"Your husband?" he says, his voice a hiss in the quiet.

"Father."

"Give me your papers."

She slides her papers across the cold desk, watching his slim, hairy hand close over them. It takes courage to stand there while he studies her paperwork. What if he has her *name on a list? Or if they've been waiting for her? It is dangerous to keep coming here, or so her mother tells her. But Vera cannot stop. Coming here is the only hope she has now.*

He hands her papers back to her. "The case is being studied," he says, and then yells, "Next."

She stumbles away from the window quickly, hearing an old woman come up beside her and ask about her husband.

It is good news. Her father is alive. He has not been sentenced and sent to the Barrens . . . or worse. Soon, the Black Knight will realize his error. He will learn that her father is no traitor.

She flips her collar up and goes back out into the cold. If she hurries, she can be to work by noon.

Friday after Friday, Vera goes to see the goblin. Each time the answer is the same. "The case is being studied. Next."

And then her mother tells her they must move.

"There is nothing to be done about it, Vera," her mother says, sitting slumped in a chair at the kitchen table. The past year has taken a toll on her, left its mark in wrinkles. She smokes a cheap cigarette and seems hardly to care that ashes flutter to the wood floor. "My wages at the storehouse have been cut. We cannot pay the bills here anymore."

Vera would like to argue with her mother as she used to, but there is not enough money for firewood at night and they are cold.

"Where will we go?" Vera asks. Beside her she hears Olga whine.

"My mother offered."

Vera is actually surprised by this. Even Olga looks up.

"We don't even know her," Vera says.

Her mother takes another long drag on the cigarette and exhales the thin blue smoke. "My parents did not approve of your father. Now that he is gone . . ."

"He's not *gone," Vera says, deciding right then that she will never like this grandmother, let alone love her.*

Though her mother says nothing, the look in her dark eyes is easy to read: he is gone.

Olga touches Vera, whether for support or in comfort, Vera is unsure. "When do we move?"

"Tonight. Before the landlord comes to collect the rent."

Once, Vera would have talked back or argued. Now she sighs quietly and goes into her room. There is little enough to pack up. A few clothes, some blankets, a hairbrush, and her old felt boots, which she has almost outgrown.

In no time, they are outside, dressed in layers that represent almost all of their clothing; they trudge through the snow toward their new home.

At last they arrive. The building is small and it looks unkempt. A stone façade on the stoop is crumbling away. Cheap fabric curtains hang at odd angles in several of the windows.

Up the stairs they go, to the last apartment on the second floor.

The woman who answers is heavy and sad-looking, wearing a floral housecoat that has seen better days. Her gray hair is covered by a pale green kerchief. She is smoking a cigarette, and her fingers are discolored where it rests between them.

"Zoya," the woman says. "And these are my grandchildren. Veronika and Olga. Which is which?"

"I am Vera," she says, standing tall beneath her new grandmother's scrutiny.

The woman nods. "There will be no problem with you, yes? We do not need the trouble you have had."

"There will be no trouble," Mama says quietly, and they are shown inside.

Vera stops dead. Olga bumps into her and giggles. But her laughter stops abruptly.

The apartment is a single room with a small wood-burning stove and a sink, a wooden table with four mismatched chairs, and a narrow bed pushed against the wall. A curtainless window stares out at the brick wall across the alley. In the corner, a half-open door reveals an empty closet. There is no bathroom; it must be a communal one for the building.

How can they all live here, crammed together like rats in a shoe box?

"Come," her grandmother says, grinding out the butt of her cigarette in a saucer overflowing with ashes. "I will show you where to put your things."

Hours later, on this first night in their new home, in the room that smells of boiled cabbage and too many people, Vera makes a bed of blankets on the floor and snuggles close to her sister.

"A man from work will bring our furniture over tomorrow," Mama says tiredly. Olga begins to cry. They all know that furniture will not matter much.

Vera takes hold of her sister's hand. Outside, a cart crashes into something, a man yells out a curse, and Vera can't help thinking that they are the sounds of a dying dream.

After that, Vera is angry all of the time, and although she tries to hide her displeasure with life, she knows she fails to do so. She is sharp-tempered and quick to criticize. She and her mother and Olga sleep together in their narrow bed, crammed so close that they must turn in unison or not at all.

She works from dawn until dark, and when she gets back to the apartment it is more of the same. She cooks dinner with her mother and grandmother, then carries firewood to the stove for the night and washes the dishes. Working, working, working. Only on Fridays is it different.

"You should quit going there," her mother says as they leave the apartment. It is five in the morning and dark as jet in the streets.

As they pass a café, a group of drunken young noblemen stumble out, laughing and hugging one another, and Vera feels an ache in her chest at the sight of them. They are so young, so free, and yet they are older than she, who trudges along beside her mother and sister going to work at dawn instead of drinking coffee and arguing politics and writing important words.

Her mother reaches out and takes Vera's hand. "I'm sorry," she says quietly.

Rarely do they touch on the truth of their lives or the loss. Vera squeezes her mother's hand. She wants to say, I know, or It's okay, but she is afraid she'll cry, so she just nods.

"Well. Good-bye, then," her mother finally says, turning toward her trolley stop.

"See you tonight."

The three of them go their separate ways to work.

Alone, Vera walks the last few blocks to the Great Hall of Justice. She enters the long queue and waits her turn.

"Name," says the goblin at the desk when it is her turn.

At her answer, he takes her papers and reads them. Abruptly, he gets up from his chair and leaves. Down the hall, in a great glassed chamber, she can see him talking to other goblins and then to a man in long black robes.

Finally, the goblin returns, takes his seat, and pushes the papers back to her. "There is no one of that name in our kingdom. You are mistaken. Next.*"*

"But you do *have him, my lord. I have been coming here for more than a year. Please check again."*

"No one of that name is known here."

"But—"

"He's not here," the goblin says, sneering. "Gone. Get it? Now move on." He cranes his head to look around her. "Next."

Vera wants to sink to her knees and cry out, but it is not good to draw attention to oneself, so she wipes the tears from her eyes and straightens her shoulders and heads for work.

Her father is gone.

There one moment and disappeared the next. The truth is that he is dead, that they have killed him; whoever they are. The trolls in their shiny black carriages and the Black Knight, for whom they work. Questions cannot be asked, though, not even the ordinary questions of a grieving family. They cannot beg to bury him or visit his grave site or dress his body for burial. All of that would draw attention to them and to this execution that the Black Knight wants to deny. In the library, she goes about her work and says nothing about her father.

On her walk home—no trolleys for her today; she wants this journey to last—it seems as if winter is rising from the ground itself. Brittle black leaves fall from the trees and hang suspended in the chilly air. From a distance, there are so many of them it looks like a flock of crows flying too low. Beneath a leaden sky, buildings look drab and hunkered down. Even the mint-green castle looks forlorn in this weather.

By the time she gets home, the snow is accumulating on the cobblestoned street and on the bare tree limbs.

At her door, she pauses just long enough to catch her breath. In that instant, she imagines the conversation she will have and exhaustion presses down on her. Still, she straightens her spine and walks inside.

The room is crowded with furniture from their old life. Her grandmother's bed is pushed up to the wall and stacked with quilts. Their own narrower bed abuts the closet. When they want to open the closet door, they must move the bed. A bureau that her mother has hand-painted and a pair of lamps line the wall beneath the window that won't open. The only beautiful piece of furniture in the apartment—a gorgeous mahogany writing desk that was her father's—is covered with jars of pickles and onions.

She finds her mother at the stove. Olga is at the table, peeling potatoes.

Her mother takes one look at her and moves the pot off the stove, then wipes her hands on the apron tied about her waist. Although her dress is baggy and old, and her hair is unkempt after a day at the food storehouse, her eyes are keen and the look in them is knowing. "It is Friday," she says at last.

Olga rises from her chair. In a dress that is too tight, she looks like a flower sprouting from a seed shell. Vera can't help thinking that her sister is a child at fifteen, and yet she remembers it as the age when she met Sasha. She had thought she was full-grown then. A woman standing on a bridge with the man she intended to love.

"Did you learn something?" Olga asks.

Vera can feel the color draining from her face.

"Come, Olga," Mama says briskly. "Put on your coat and your valenki. *We are going for a walk."*

"But my boots are too small for me," Olga whines. "And it is snowing."

"No argument," her mother says, walking over to the big rounded wood and leather chest by their bed. "Your grandmother will be home soon from work."

Vera stands back, saying nothing while her mother and sister dress for the cold. When everyone is ready, they go outside, into the blurry white world. The hush of the falling flakes mutes everything around them. Even the whine and clatter of the trolley sounds distant. In this whispered world, they seem isolated, separate. They are even more alone as they enter the Grand Park. By the time they arrive, streetlamps are lit throughout the square. There are no people out here on this cold early evening, only the gilded row of noble houses in the distance.

They come to the centerpiece of the park: the giant bronze statue of a winged horse. It rises up from the snow in defiance, dwarfing everyone who looks upon it.

"These are dangerous times," Mama says when they are in front of the statue. "There are things . . . people that cannot be spoken of in the closeness of an apartment or the confines even of a friendship. We will speak of it . . ." She pauses, draws in a breath, and softens her voice. "Him . . . now and not again. Yes?"

Olga stamps her foot in the snow. "What is going on?"

Mama looks to Vera for the answer.

"I went to the Great Hall today, to ask about Papa," she says, feeling tears sting her eyes. "He is gone."

"What does that mean?" Olga says. "Gone? Do you think he escaped?"

It is Mama who has the strength to shake her head. "No, he has not escaped." She glances around again and moves closer, so that the three of them are touching each other, huddled together in the shadow of the statue. "They have killed him."

Olga makes a terrible sound like she is choking, and Vera and Mama hug her tightly. When they draw back, all are crying.

"You knew," Vera says, not bothering to wipe her eyes, although her tears are freezing instantly, sticking her eyelashes together until she can hardly see.

Mother nods.

"When they took him away?"

She nods again.

"You let me go every Friday," Vera says. "If I had known—"

"You had to learn in your way," her mother says. "And I hoped . . . of course . . ."

"I do not know what to do now," Vera says. She feels disconnected from herself, from her own life.

"I have been waiting for you to ask me this," Mama says. "You both have been waiting. Hoping. Now you know: this is our life. Our Petya will not come back. This is who we are now."

"What does that mean?" asks Olga.

"Live," Mama says quietly.

And Vera understands. It is time for her to quit marking time and start doing something with it.

"I do not know what to dream about," Vera says. "It all seems so impossible."

"Dreams are for men like your father. They are the reason we mourn him now, in private and secretly, as if we are criminals. He planted in your head all kinds of fantasies. Let that go. Quit being his children and become women of this kingdom. There are things to do out there; I promise you this."

Their mother pulls them into a fierce hug and kisses both their cheeks. When they are close, she whispers, "He loved you two more than his words, more than his own breath. That will never die."

"I miss him," Olga says, starting to cry again.

"Yes," Mama says in a throaty voice. "Forever. That's how long we'll have an empty place at the table." She draws back at last. "But we will not speak of him again. Not ever. Not even to each other."

"But . . . you cannot just stop your feelings," Vera says.

"Perhaps," her mother says, "but you can refuse to express them, and that is what we will do." She puts her hand into the big pocket of her wool coat and pulls out a cloissoné butterfly.

Vera has never seen anything so beautiful. This is not the kind of piece their family can own—it is something from the kings or the wizards at least.

"Petyr's father made this," her mother says, revealing a family history they knew nothing about. "It was to be for the little princess, but the king thought it shoddy work, so your grandfather was fired and learned to make bricks of clay instead of pieces of art. He gave it to your father on our wedding day. And now it is what we have to remember someone in our family who is lost to us. Sometimes, if I close my eyes when I hold it, I can hear our Petya's laugh."

"It's just a butterfly," Vera says, thinking it is not so lovely as she'd thought; certainly it is not a substitute for her papa's laughter.

"It is all we have," her mother says gently.

Vera wraps herself in grief as only a teenage girl can, but as the winter wanes and spring blooms across the kingdom, she begins to feel burdened by her melancholy.

"It is not fair that I cannot go to university," she whines to her mother one warm summer day, many months after their makeshift funeral at the park. They are kneeling in the black earth weeding their small garden. Both have already worked a full day in the city; this is their summertime routine. A day's labor in the kingdom and then a two-hour cart ride beyond the walled city to the countryside, where they rent a small patch of ground.

"You are too old to be whining about fairness, and obviously you know better," her mother says.

"I want to study the great writers and artists."

Her mother sits back on her heels and looks at Vera. In the syrupy golden light that falls at ten o'clock at night, she looks almost pretty again. Only her brown eyes remain stubbornly old. "You live in the Snow Kingdom," she says.

"I think I know this."

"Do you? You work in the greatest library in the world—there are three million books at your fingertips each day. The royal museum is on your way home. And your sister works there. Anytime you wish you can see the masters' paintings. Galina Ulanova is dancing this season, and do not forget the opera." She makes a tsking sound. "Do not tell me that a young woman of this kingdom needs to go to university to learn. If you believe such a thing, you are not"—her voice lowers—"his daughter." It is the first time her mother has mentioned Father and it has the intended effect.

Vera slides sideways off her own heels and sits in the warm dirt, looking down at the fragile green rosette of a baby cabbage beside her.

I am Petyr Andreyevich’s daughter, *she thinks, and in that reclamation, she remembers the books her father had read to her at night, and the dreams he’d encouraged her to dream,*

For the remainder of that week, Vera contemplates the discussion in the garden. At work she wanders around the library, walking amid the stacks with the ghost of her father beside her. She knows that all she needs is someone to help her understand the words she reads. It is as if she is a seedling, with a tender green strand pushing up through earth that resists her movement. The sun is up there, though, if only one keeps growing upward.

And then one day she is at the counter organizing parchment rolls when a familiar face appears. It is an aged man, walking with a cane across the marble floor, his tattered brown cleric’s robes trailing along behind him. At a table near the wall, he sits down and opens a book.

Vera approaches him slowly, knowing that her mother would not approve of her plan, but a plan it suddenly is.

“Excuse me,” she says softly to the man, who looks up at her through rheumy eyes.

“Veronika?” he says after a long moment.

“Yes,” she says. This man used to come by the house, in older, better days. She does not think to mention her father, but he is here between them, as surely as the dust. “I am sorry to bother you, but I seek a tutor. I haven’t much money.”

The cleric removes his glasses. It takes him a while to speak, and when he does, his voice is barely more than a whisper. “I cannot help you myself. It is the times in which we live. I should stop writing.” He sighs. “As if I could . . . but I know some students perhaps who are not so afraid as an old man. I will ask.”

"Thank you."

"Be careful, young Veronika," he says, putting on his glasses. "And tell no one of this conversation."

"This secret is safe with me."

The cleric doesn't smile. "No secret is safe."

Fourteen

It was almost midnight when Meredith finally got home. Exhausted by the length of the day and yet captivated by tonight's story, she fed the dogs, played with them for a while, then changed into a comfortable pair of sweats. She was in the kitchen making herself a cup of tea when a car drove up.

Jeff. Who else would it be at twelve-thirty?

She stood there, her hands gripping the sink's porcelain rim, her heartbeat going crazy as the front door opened.

Nina walked into the kitchen, looking vaguely pissed off.

Meredith felt a rush of disappointment. "It's past midnight. What are you doing here?"

Nina walked over to the counter, grabbed a bottle of wine, found two coffee mugs in the sink, rinsed them out, and poured two glasses full. "Well, I'd *like* to talk about the story, which is becoming pretty damn detailed for a fairy tale, but since you're afraid of it, I'll say what I came for. We need to talk."

"Tomorrow is—"

"Now. Tomorrow you'll be armored up again and I'll be intimidated by your competence. Come on." Then she took Meredith by the arm and led her into the living room, where she got a fire going by pressing a button.

Whoosh went the gas flames, and on came the heat and light.

"Here," she said, handing Meredith a cup of wine.

"Don't you think it's a little late for wine?"

"I'm not even going to answer that. You're lucky it's not tequila, the way I'm feeling."

Nina. Always the drama.

Meredith sat on one end of the sofa, her back tilted against the armrest. Nina sat on the opposite end. In the middle, their toes brushed against each other.

"What do you want, Nina?" Meredith asked.

"My sister."

"I don't know what you mean."

"You were the one who took me trick-or-treating when Dad was working, remember? You always made my costume. And remember, when I tried out for cheerleader, you helped me with my routine for weeks, and when I made it you were happy for me, even though you hadn't made the squad when you tried out? And when Sean Bowers asked me to the prom, you were the one who told me not to trust him. We might not have had much in common, but we were *sisters.*"

Meredith had forgotten all of that, or at least, she hadn't thought of it in years. "That was a long time ago."

"I went away and left you. I get it. And Mom is not an easy person to be left with. And we don't know each other very well, but I'm here now, Mere."

"I see you."

"Do you? Because frankly, you've been a bitch the last few days. Or maybe not a bitch, just kind of mopey, and one woman who won't talk to me at dinner is pretty much my quota." Nina leaned forward. "I'm here and I miss you, Mere. It's like you don't want to look at me or talk to me at all, I think—"

"Jeff left me."

Nina sat back abruptly. "What?"

Meredith couldn't say it again. She shook her head, felt the sting of tears. "He's living at the motel by his office."

"That *prick*," Nina said.

Meredith actually laughed. "Thanks for not assuming it was my fault."

The look Nina gave Meredith was caring and compassionate, and Meredith knew suddenly why so many strangers opened up to her sister. It was that look, the one that promised to comfort and care, but not to judge.

"What happened?" Nina asked quietly.

"He asked me if I still love him."

"And?"

"I didn't answer," Meredith said. "I didn't answer. And I haven't called him yet, haven't gone after him or written him a passionate letter or even begged him to come back. No wonder he left me. He even said . . ."

"What?"

"That I was like Mom."

"So now I think he's a prick and an asshole."

"He loves me," Meredith said. "And I've hurt him. I could tell. That's why he said it."

"Who gives a shit about his feelings? That's your problem, Mere, you care too much about everyone else. What do *you* want?"

She hadn't asked herself that question in years. She'd gone to the college they could afford, not the one she'd wanted; she'd married younger than planned because she'd gotten pregnant; she'd come home to Belye Nochi because Dad needed her. When had she ever done what she wanted?

Strangely, she thought about the early days at the orchard, when she'd started the gift shop and stocked it with things she loved.

"You'll figure it out, Mere. I promise." Nina came over and hugged her.

"Thanks. I mean it. You helped."

Nina sat back. "Remember that the next time I burn the hell out of the stove or leave a mess in the kitchen."

"I'll try," Meredith said, leaning forward to clink her glass against Nina's. "To new beginnings."

"I'll drink to that," Nina said.

"You'll drink to anything."

"Indeed I will. It's one of my best traits."

For the next two days, Mom shut down, turned from quiet into stone-like, even refusing to come down for dinner. Nina would have been upset by it, and maybe even done something about it, but the reason was obvious. All of them were feeling the same way. As the days turned to night and moved forward, Nina found herself unable even to think about the fairy tale.

Dad's birthday was approaching.

The day of it dawned bright and sunny, with a cloudless blue sky.

Nina pushed the covers back and got out of bed. Today was the day she'd come home for. None of them had mentioned it, of course, they being the kind of women who didn't talk about their pain, but it had been between them always, in the air.

She went to her bedroom window and looked out. The apple trees seemed to be dancing; millions of green leaves and white blossoms shimmied in the light.

She grabbed her clothes from a heap on the floor, dressed quickly, and left the bedroom. She wasn't entirely sure what she'd say to her mother on this tenderest of days; she just knew that she didn't want to be alone with her thoughts. Her memories.

Across the hall, she knocked on Mom's door. "Are you up?"

"Sunset," Mom said. "I'll see you and Meredith then."

Disappointed, Nina went down to the kitchen. After a quick breakfast, she set off up the driveway to Meredith's house, but all she found there were the huskies, sleeping in sunny patches on the porch. Of course, Meredith had gone to work.

"Shit."

Since the last thing she wanted to do was roam through this quiet house on Dad's birthday, she returned to Belye Nochi, plucked her car keys from the bowl on the entry table, and set off for town, looking for anything to occupy her time until sunset. Along the way she stopped now and then to take photographs, and at noon she ate greasy American food at the diner on Main Street.

Before the day ended, though, she was back at Belye Nochi. She slung her camera bag over her shoulder and went inside, where she found Meredith in the kitchen, putting something into the oven.

"Hey," Nina said.

Meredith turned to her. "I made dinner. And set the table. I thought . . . afterward . . ."

"Sure," Nina said, walking over to the French doors, looking out. "How do we do this?"

Meredith came up beside her, putting an arm around her shoulders. "I guess we just open the urn and let the ashes fall. Maybe you could say something."

"You're the one who should say something, Mere. I let him down."

"He loved you so much," Meredith said. "And he was proud of you."

Nina felt tears start. Outside, the sky seemed to fold across the orchard in ribbons of salmon pink and the palest lavender. "Thanks," she said, leaning against her sister. She had no idea how long they stood there, together, saying nothing.

"It is time," Mom finally said behind them.

Nina eased away from Meredith, steeling herself for whatever was to come. As one, she and her sister turned.

Mom stood in the doorway, holding a rosewood box inlaid with ivory. She was practically unrecognizable in a purple chiffon evening blouse and canary-yellow linen pants. A red and blue scarf was coiled around her neck.

"He liked color," Mom said. "I should have worn more of it. . . ." She smoothed the hair from her face and glanced out the window at the setting sun. Then she drew in a deep breath and walked toward them. "Here," she said, holding out the box to Nina.

It was just a box full of ashes, not really her dad, not even all she had left of him, and yet, when she took it from her mother, the grief she'd been suppressing rolled over her.

She heard Mom and Meredith leave the kitchen and walk out through the dining room. She followed slowly behind them.

A cool breeze came through the open French doors, brushing her cheek, bringing with it the scent of apples.

"Come on, Nina," Meredith called from outside.

Nina repositioned the camera strap around her neck and headed for the garden.

Meredith and her mother were already there, standing stiffly by the iron bench beneath the magnolia tree. The last bit of sunlight illuminated the new copper column and turned it into a vibrant flame.

Nina hurried across the grass, noticing a second too late that it was slippery out here. It all happened in an instant: her toe caught on a rock and she started to fall and she reached out to stop it and suddenly the box was flying through the air. It crashed into one of the copper columns and shattered.

Nina hit the ground hard enough to taste blood. She lay there, dazed, hearing Meredith's *Oh, no,* repeat over and over.

And then her mother was pulling her to her feet, saying something in Russian. It was the gentlest voice she'd ever heard from her mother.

"I dropped it," Nina said, wiping her face, smearing the grit across her cheek, and at the thought of that she started to cry.

"Do not cry," Mom said. "Just think if he were here. He would say, *What the hell did you expect, Anya, waiting until dark?*"

Her mother actually smiled.

"We'll call it an ash-tossing," Meredith said, her mouth quirking up.

"Some families scatter. We fling," Nina said.

Mom was the first to laugh. The sound was so totally foreign that Nina gasped, and then she started to laugh, too.

They stood there, the three of them, laughing together in the middle of the winter garden, with the apple trees all around them, and it was the best tribute to him they could have made. And later, when Mom and Meredith had gone inside, Nina stood there alone, in the quiet, staring down at a velvety white magnolia blossom dressed in gray ash. "Did you hear us laughing? We've never done that before, not the three of us, not together. We laughed for you, Dad. . . ."

She would have sworn she felt him beside her then, heard his breathing in the wind. She knew what he would have said to her tonight. *Nice trip, Neener Beaner. See you in the fall.* "I love you, Dad," she whispered as a single apple blossom floated on the breeze and landed at her feet.

Meredith took the chicken Kiev out of the oven and set the pan on the cold stove to cool.

Drying her hands on a plaid towel, she took a deep breath and went into the living room to be with her mom. "Hey," she said, sitting down beside her on the sofa.

The look her mother gave her was staggering in its sadness.

It connected them for a moment, enough that Meredith reached out and touched her mother's hand.

For once, her mother didn't pull away.

Meredith wanted to say something—just the right thing to ease their pain, but of course there were no such words.

"We should eat now," Mom said at last. "Go get your sister."

Meredith nodded and went out to the winter garden, where Nina was photographing the ash-dusted magnolia blossom.

Meredith sat down on the bench beside her. The bronze sky had darkened so that all they could really see were white flowers, which looked silver in the fading light.

"How are you doing?" Nina asked.

"Shitty. You?"

Nina recapped her lens. "I've been better. How's Mom?"

Meredith shrugged. "Who knows?"

"She's better lately, though. I think it's the fairy tale."

"You would think that." Meredith sighed. "How the hell would we know? I wish we could really talk to her."

"I don't think she's *ever* really talked to us. We don't even know how old she is."

"How come we didn't think that was weird when we were kids?"

"I guess you get used to what you're raised with. Like those feral kids who actually think they're dogs."

"Only you could find a way to work feral children into a conversation like this. Come on," Meredith said.

They went back into the house and found Mom at the table, with dinner served. Chicken Kiev with au gratin potatoes and a green salad. There was a decanter of vodka and three shot glasses in the center of the table.

"That's my kind of centerpiece," Nina said, taking a seat while Mom poured three shots of vodka.

Meredith sat down beside her sister.

"A toast," her mother said quietly, raising her shot glass.

There was a moment of awkward silence as they looked at one another. Meredith knew that each of them was thinking about what to say, how to honor him without either making it hurt more or sound sad. He wouldn't have wanted that.

"To our Evan," Mom said at last, clinking her glass against the others. She downed the alcohol in one swallow. "Your father loved it when I drank."

"It's a good night for alcohol," Meredith said. She drank her vodka and held her empty glass out for more. The second shot burned down her throat. "I miss hearing his voice when I come into the house," she said.

Mom immediately poured herself another shot. "I miss the way he kissed me every morning."

"I got used to missing him," Nina said quietly. "Pour me another."

By the time she finished her third shot of vodka, Meredith felt a buzzing in her blood.

"He would not want us speaking about him in this way," Mom said. "He would want . . ."

In the silence that followed, they all looked at each other. Meredith knew they were thinking the same thing: how did you just go on?

You just do, she thought, and so she said, "My favorite holiday is Thanksgiving. I love everything about it—how my kids look forward to it, the decorations, hearing the first Christmas album, the food. And I'll say it now: I hated those damn family road trips we used to take. Eastern Oregon was the worst. Remember the time we stayed in teepees? It was one hundred degrees and Nina sang 'I think I Love You' for four hundred miles."

Nina laughed. "I *loved* those camping trips because we never knew where we were going. Christmas is my favorite holiday because I can remember the date. And the thing I miss most about Dad is that he was always waiting for me."

Meredith had never known that sometimes Nina felt alone, that for all her gallivanting about the globe, she liked to know that someone was waiting for her.

"I loved your father's adventurous spirit," Mom said. "Although those camping trips were hell. Nina, you should never sing in front of people if they cannot leave."

"Ha!" Meredith said. "I knew I wasn't crazy. Your singing was like listening to a dental drill."

"Yeah? Well, David Cassidy wrote me a letter."

"His signature was stamped." Meredith smiled at the coup de grâce.

Across the table, Mom sighed as if she were hardly listening to them. "He always promised to take me to Alaska. Did you know that? To see again the Belye Nochi and the northern lights. That is the thing I remember most about Evan. He saved me."

She looked up suddenly, as if realizing all at once that she'd shown something of herself. She pushed back from the table and stood up.

"I always wanted to go to Alaska, too," Meredith said. She didn't want her mother to leave the table, not now.

"I am going to my room," Mom said.

Meredith rushed forward to take her arm. "Here, Mom—"

Mom pulled away. "I am not an invalid."

Meredith stood there, watching Mom walk out of the kitchen and disappear. "She confuses the hell out of me."

"You said a mouthful there, sister."

That night, Meredith and Nina stayed up late, talking about Dad and trading childhood memories. Both were trying in their way to hold on to the day, to really celebrate his birthday, and afterward, when Meredith lay in her lonely bed, she began what she knew would be a new life habit: talking to her dad in the quiet times. She couldn't get advice from him, perhaps, but somehow just saying the words aloud helped. She told him about Jeff and her confusion and her inability to say what her husband wanted to hear. And she knew what her dad would have asked her. It was the same question Nina had posed.

What do you want?

It was something she hadn't thought seriously about in years. She'd spent the last decade considering what she would make for dinner, where the girls should go to school, how to package apples for the foreign markets. She'd thought fruit production and college entrance essays, house repairs and how to save for tuition and taxes.

The minutiae had consumed the whole.

But all the next day, as she tried to concentrate on work, the question came back to her, until finally she had an answer of sorts.

She didn't know exactly what she wanted, but she knew suddenly what she *didn't* want. She was tired of running too fast and hiding behind a busy schedule, tired of pretending problems didn't exist.

After work, she drove across town to the *Wenatchee World* building.

"Hey," she said from the doorway of Jeff's office.

He looked up from the paperwork on his desk. She could tell that he hadn't been sleeping well, and his shirt was in need of washing. His unshaven jaw made him look different, younger, hipper; someone she didn't know.

He ran a hand through his sandy blond hair. "Meredith."

"I should have come sooner."

"I expected you to."

She glanced out the window, at the cars rolling past. "You were right to leave. We need to figure out where to go from here."

"Is that what you came to tell me?"

Was it? Even now she wasn't sure.

He got up from the desk and came toward her. She felt his gaze on her face, searching her eyes for something. "Because that's not what I'm waiting to hear."

"I know." She hated to disappoint him, but she couldn't give him what he wanted, even though it would be easier to say the words and get her life back and think about it later. "I'm sorry, Jeff. But you changed things, and you got me thinking. For once, I don't want to do what's expected. I don't want to put everyone's happiness above my own. And right now I don't know what to say to you."

"Can you say you *don't* love me?"

"No."

He thought about that, not quite frowning. "Okay." He sat down on the edge of his desk, and she felt the distance between them suddenly in a way she hadn't before. "Maddy said you sent her a care package last week."

"Jillian got hers the week before."

He nodded, looked at her. "And your dad's birthday?"

"I got through it. I'll tell you about it someday. There's a funny Nina story in it."

Someday.

She was about to ask him about his book when there was a knock at his door. A beautiful young woman with messy blond hair poked her head in his office. "You still up for pizza and beer, Jeff?" she asked, curling her fingers around the doorframe.

Jeff looked at Meredith, who shrugged.

For the first time, she wondered about what he was doing while they were apart. It had never occurred to her that he might forge a new life, make new friends. She smiled a little too brightly and said good-bye in a steady voice. Nodding briefly to Miss Journalism USA in the tight jeans and V-neck sweater, she left the office and drove home. There, she fed the dogs and paid some bills and put in a load of wash. Dinner was a bowl of Raisin Bran, which she ate while standing in front of the sink. Afterward, she called each of the girls and heard about the classes they were taking and the boys they thought were hot.

It was Jillian who asked about Jeff.

"What do you mean, how's Dad?" Meredith said, stammering, realizing a second too late that it had been an innocent question.

"You know, his allergies. He was coughing like crazy last night."

"Oh, that. He's fine."

"You sound weird."

Meredith laughed nervously. "Just busy, baby. You know how the apple biz gets this time of year."

"What does that have to do with Dad?"

"Nothing."

"Oh. Well. Tell him I love him, okay?"

Thc irony of that was not lost on Meredith. "Sure."

She hung up the phone and stared out her kitchen window at the darkness. On the wall beside her, the kitchen clock ticked through the minutes. For the first time, she felt the truth of this situation: she and Jeff were separated. Separate. Apart. She should have realized that before, of course, but somehow she hadn't really owned it until now. There'd been so much going on at Belye Nochi that the problems in her own marriage had taken a backseat.

And suddenly she didn't want to be here alone, didn't want to watch some sitcom and try to be entertained.

"Come on, puppies," she said, reaching for her coat, "we're going for a walk."

Ten minutes later she was at Belye Nochi. She settled the dogs on the porch and went inside, calling out for Nina.

She found Mom in the living room, knitting.

"Hey, Mom."

Her mother nodded but didn't look up. "Hello."

Meredith tried not to feel disappointed. "I'm going to start packing again. Do you need anything? Have you eaten?"

"I am fine. Nina made dinner. Thank you."

"Where is she?"

"Out."

Meredith waited for more, got nothing, and said, "I'll be upstairs if you need me."

Dragging boxes upstairs, she went into her parents' closet. The left side was Dad's: a row of brightly colored cardigans and golf shirts. She touched them gently, let her fingers trail across the soft sleeves. Soon his clothes would have to be packed up and given away, but the thought of that was more than Meredith could bear right now.

So she faced Mom's side. *This* was where she would start.

She went to the stack of sweaters on the shelf above the dresses. Scooping them up, she dropped the heap onto the carpeted floor. Kneeling, she began the arduous task of choosing, culling, and folding. She was so intent on her job that she barely noticed the passing of time, and was surprised when she heard Nina's voice.

"Are you comfortable, Mom?" Nina said.

Meredith moved to the closet door, opening it just a crack.

Mom was in bed, with the bedside lamp on beside her. Her white hair was unbound, tucked behind her ears. "I am tired."

"I've given you time," Nina said, sitting on the floor in front of the cold black hearth.

Meredith didn't move; instead, she flicked off the closet light and stayed where she was.

Mom sighed. "Fine," she said, turning off the bedside light.

"*Belye nochi*," Mom said, turning the words into liquid magic, full suddenly of passion and mystery. "It is a season of light in the Snow Kingdom, where fairies glow on bright green leaves and rainbows swirl through the midnight sky. The streetlamps come on, but they *are decorations only, golden oases positioned along streets burnished beneath them, and on the rare days when rain falls, everything is mirrored in the light.*

On such a day is Vera cleaning the glass cases in the elves' great lost-manuscript chamber. She has asked for this work. The rumor is that sometimes the elves appear to those who believe in them, and Vera wants to believe again.

Alone in the manuscript room (in these dangerous new times, few scholars dare to ask about the past anymore), she hums a song that her father taught her.

"The library is to be quiet."

Vera is so startled by the voice that she drops her rag. The woman facing her is storklike: tall and rail-thin, with a beak of a nose. "I am sorry, ma'am. No one ever comes in here. I thought—"

"Do not. You never know who is listening."

Vera cannot tell if the words are a warning or a rebuke. It is difficult to recognize such nuances these days. "Again, I apologize, ma'am."

"Good. Madam Dufours tells me that a student from the college requests your assistance. Cleric Nevin has sent him. Help him but do not neglect your duties."

"Yes, ma'am," Vera says. On the outside she is calm, but inside she is like a puppy leaping to be let outside. The cleric has found a student who will teach her! She waits for the librarian to leave and then puts away her cleaning supplies.

Moving too quickly (she tries to slow down but cannot; it has been so long since she felt this excited), she barely touches the wooden railing as she hurries down the wide marble steps. Downstairs, the main hall of the library is full of tables and people moving about. A queue snakes back from the head librarian's desk.

"Veronika." She hears her name and turns slowly.

He looks exactly as she remembers: with his shock of golden hair that is too long and curly. His wide jaw has been freshly shaven; a tiny red nick on his neck attests to a hurried job. But it is his green eyes that capture her once again.

"Your Highness," she says, trying to sound casual. "It is good to see you. How long has it been?"

"Don't."

"Don't what?"

"You know what happened on the Fontanka Bridge."

Her smile slips; she tries to find it again. She will not show herself to be naïve and silly. Not again. "That was just a night. Years ago."

"It was no ordinary night, Vera."

"Please. Don't tease me, Your Highness." To her horror, her voice breaks just a little. "And you never came back."

"You were fifteen," he says. "I was eighteen."

"Yes," she says, frowning. Still she does not understand what he is trying to say.

"I have been waiting for you."

For the first time in her life, Vera pretends to be ill. She goes to the librarian and complains about gnawing pains in her stomach and begs to be allowed to go home early.

It is a terrible thing to do, and dangerous. If Mama knew of it, Vera would be in trouble, both for the lie and for the choices that will inevitably follow the lie. What if Vera is seen outside when supposedly she is ill?

But a girl her age cannot act out of fear when love is at hand.

Still, she is smart enough to go directly home when she is let go from work. On the trolley, she stands at the brass pole, holding tightly as the car lurches and sways. At the apartment, she opens the door slowly and peers inside.

Her grandmother stands in front of the stove, stirring something in a big black cauldron. "You are home early," she says, us-

ing the back of her plump hand to push the damp gray hair away from her eyes.

The sweet smell of simmering strawberries fills the apartment. On the table, at least a dozen glass jars stand clustered in readiness, their metal tops spread out alongside.

"The library was not busy," Vera says, feeling her face redden at the lie.

"Then you can—"

"I'm going out to the country," Vera says. At her grandmother's sharp look, she adds, "I will pick some cucumbers and cabbage."

"Oh. Very well, then."

Vera stands there a moment longer, looking at her grandmother's stern profile. Her baggy dress is ragged at the hem and her stockings are pocked with tears and snags. A tattered blue kerchief covers her frizzy gray hair.

"Tell Mama I will be out late. I will not be home in time for supper, I am sure."

"Be careful," her grandmother says. "You are young . . . and his daughter. It does not do well to be noticed."

Vera nods to conceal the flushing of her cheeks—again. She goes to the corner of the apartment, where their rusted old bicycle stands propped against the wall. She carries the bike to the door and leaves the apartment.

Never has she flown so on her rickety bicycle down the streets of her beloved Snow Kingdom. Tears blur her eyes and disappear into her waving hair. When people move in front of her, she pings the bell on her handlebars and darts around them. All the way through the city, along the river, and over the bridge, she can feel the rapid beating of her heart and his name repeats in her head.

Sasha. Sasha. Sasha.

He has been waiting for her, just as she has been waiting for him. The luck of this seems impossible, a bit of gold found in the dirty road of her life. At the intricate black scrollwork entrance of the Summer Garden, she eases to a stop and slips off her bike.

The beauty of the castle grounds amaze her. Bordered on three sides by water, the park is a magnificent green haven in the walled city. The air smells of limes and hot stone. Exquisite marble statues line the well-groomed paths.

She does as they have planned: she walks her bike down the path, trying to look calm, as if this is an ordinary early evening stroll through a place where peasants rarely go. But her pulse is racing and her nerve endings feel electrified.

And then he is there, standing beside a lime tree, smiling at her.

She misses a step and stumbles, hitting her bike. He is beside her in an instant, holding her arm.

"This way," he says, leading her to a spot deep in the trees, where she sees he has laid out a blanket and a basket.

At first they sit cross-legged on the warm plaid wool, their shoulders touching. Through the green bower, she can see sunlight dappling the water and gilding a marble statue. Soon, she knows, the paths will be full of lords and ladies and lovers eager to walk outside in the warm light of a June night.

"What have you been doing since . . . I last saw you?" she asks, not daring to look at him. He has been in her heart for so long it is as if she knows him already, but she doesn't. She does not know what to say or how to say it, and suddenly she is afraid that there is a wrong way to move forward, a mistake that once made cannot be undone.

"I am at the cleric's college, studying to be a poet."

"But you are a prince. And poetry is forbidden."

"Do not be afraid, Vera. I am not like your father. I am careful."

"He said the same thing to my mother."

"Look at me," Sasha says quietly, and Vera turns to him.

It is a kiss that, once begun, never really ends. Interrupted, yes. Paused, certainly. But from that very moment onward, Vera sees the whole of her life as only a breath away from kissing him again. On that night in the park, they begin the delicate task of binding their souls together, creating a whole comprising their separate halves.

Vera tells him everything there is to know about her and listens rapturously to his own life story—how it was to be born in the northern wilds and left in an orphanage and found later by his royal parents. His tale of deprivation and loneliness makes her hold him more tightly and kiss him more desperately and promise to love him forever.

At this, he turns a little, until he is lying alongside her, their faces close. "I will love you that long, Vera," he says.

After that there is nothing more to be said.

They walk hand in hand through the pale purple glow of early morning. The alabaster statues look pink in the light. Out in the city, they are among people again, strangers who feel like friends on this white night when the wind blowing up from the river rustles through the leaves. Northern lights dance across the sky in impossible hues.

At the end of the bridge, beneath the streetlamp, they pause and look at each other.

"Come tomorrow night. For dinner," she says. "I want you to meet my family."

"What if they do not like me?"

There is no cracking in his voice, no physical betrayal of his emotions, but Vera sees his heart as clearly as if it were beating in the pale white cup of her hands. She hears in him the pain of a boy who'd been abandoned and claimed so late that damage was done. "They will love you, Sasha," she says, feeling for once as if she is the older of the two. "Trust me."

"Give me one more day," he says. "Do not tell anyone about us. Please."

"But I love you."

"One more day," he says again.

She supposes it is little enough to agree to, although he is being foolish. And yet, she smiles at the thought of another magical night like this, where there is nothing but the two of them. She can certainly feign illness one more time.

"I'll meet you tomorrow at one o'clock. But do not come inside the library. I need my job."

"I'll be waiting on the bridge over the castle moat. I want to show you something special."

Vera lets go of him at last and walks across the street, with her bike clattering along beside her. Heaving it up the stairs, she tries to be quiet as she goes up to the second floor and opens the door. The old hinges squeak; the bike rattles.

The first thing she notices is the smell of smoke. Then she sees her mother, sitting at the table, smoking a cigarette. An overflowing ashtray is near her elbow.

"Mama!" Vera cries. The bicycle clangs into the wall.

"Hush," her mother says sharply, glancing over at the bed where Grandmother lies snoring.

Vera puts the bicycle away and moves toward the table. There are no lights on, but a pale glow illuminates the window anyway, giving every hard surface in the room a softer edge; this is especially true of her mother's face, which is clamped tight with anger. "And where are your vegetables from the garden?"

"Oh. I hit a bench with my bike and fell into the street. Everything was lost." As the lie spills out, she grabs on to it. "And I was hurt. Oh, my side is killing me. That is why I am so late. I had to walk all the way home."

Her mother looks at her without smiling. "Seventeen is very young, Vera. You are not so ready for life . . . and love . . . as you believe. And these are dangerous times."

"You were seventeen when you fell in love with Papa."

"Yes," her mother says, sighing. It is a sound of defeat, as if she already knows everything that has happened.

"You would do it again, wouldn't you? Love Papa, I mean."

*Her mother flinches at that word—*love.

"No," her mother says softly. "I would not love him again, not a poet who cared more for his precious words than his family's safety. Not if I had known how it would feel to live with a broken heart." She puts out her cigarette. "No. That is my answer."

"But—"

"I know you don't understand," her mother says, turning away. "I hope you never do. Now come to bed, Vera. Allow me to pretend you are still my innocent girl."

"I am," Vera protests.

Her mother looks at her one last time and says, "Not for long, though, I think. For you want to be in love."

"You make it sound as if falling in love is like catching some disease."

Her mother says nothing, just climbs into the narrow bed with Olga, who makes a snoring sound and flings an arm across her.

Vera wants to ask more questions, explain how she feels, but she sees that her mother isn't interested. Is this the reason Sasha asked for one more day? Did he know that Mama would resist?

She brushes her teeth and dresses for bed, plaiting her long hair. Climbing in next to her mother, she eases close, finds warmth in her mother's arms.

"Be careful," her mother whispers into Vera's ear. "And do not lie to me again."

Fifteen

The next morning, Vera wakes early enough to wash her hair in the kitchen sink and painstakingly brushes it dry.

"Where are you going?" Olga says sleepily from the bed.

Vera presses a finger to her lips and makes a shushing sound.

Her mother angles up on one elbow in the bed. "There is no need to shush your sister, Veronika. I can smell the rosewater you used in your hair."

Vera considers lying to her mother, perhaps saying that someone important is expected in the library today, but in the end she simply says nothing.

Her mother throws back the flimsy covers and gets out of the narrow bed. She and Olga peel sideways like synchronized swimmers and stand together in their ragged white nightgowns.

"Bring your young man here on Sunday," Mama says. "Your grandmother will be out."

Vera throws her arms around her and hugs her tightly. Then as they have done each day for more than a year, the three of them eat breakfast and then leave together.

When Mama turns toward the warehouse and walks away, Olga sidles up to Vera. "Tell me."

Vera links arms with her sister. "It is Prince Aleksandr. Sasha. He has been waiting for me to grow up and now that I have, he is in love with me."

"The prince," Olga says in awe.

"I am seeing him again tonight. So tell Mama I am fine and I will be home when I can. I don't want her to worry."

"She'll be mad."

"I know," Vera says. "But what can I do? I love him, Olga."

At the corner, Olga stops. "You will be home, though?"

"I promise."

"Okay, then." Olga gives her a kiss on each cheek and heads down the street toward her own job at the museum.

Vera catches a trolley on the next street and rides it for several blocks. She is busy thinking of ways to sneak out of work early when she enters the library.

The librarian is standing in the magnificent foyer, with her arms crossed and her right foot tapping on the marble floor impatiently.

Vera skids to a stop. "Madam Plotkin. I am sorry to be late."

The librarian looks at the clock on the wall. "Seven minutes, to be precise."

"Yes, ma'am." Vera tries to appear contrite.

"You were seen yesterday in the park."

"Oh, no. Madam Plotkin, please—"

"Do you value this employment?"

"Yes, ma'am. Very much. And I need it. For my family."

"If I were the child of a criminal of the kingdom, I would be careful."

"Yes, ma'am. Of course."

The librarian brushes her hands together, as if they'd gathered dirt somehow during this conversation and now she wants to be clean. "Good. Now go to the storeroom and unpack the boxes there."

"Yes, ma'am."

"I trust you will not be sick again."

Trapped all day in the dark, dusty storage room, Vera feels like a bird banging against a glass window. She imagines Sasha on the bridge, waiting first with a smile and then with a frown.

She is desperate to run out of this oppressive quiet, but her fear is greater than her love, it seems, and that shames her even more. She is the daughter of a criminal of the kingdom, and she cannot draw attention to herself. Her family is barely making it as things are. The loss of this employment would ruin them. And so she stays, moving so erratically sometimes that her fellow workers snap at her to be careful and pay attention.

Hour after hour she stares at the clock, willing the black hand to move . . . to move . . . to click forward, and when her shift is finally over, she drops what she is doing and races for the door, emerging into the bright light of the stairwell. She hurries down the wide marble steps. In the lobby, she forces herself to slow down and moves as casually as she can across the marble floor.

Outside, she runs: down the steps, across the street to the trolley stop. When the car jangles to a halt in front of her, she squeezes into the crowd; there are so many people on board, she doesn't need to hold on to the brass pole.

At her stop, she jumps off and runs for the corner.

The street is empty.

Then she sees the black carriages. Two of them, parked in front of the moat bridge.

Vera does not move. It is as if her knees have forgotten how to bend, and it takes all her courage just to breathe. They know she is a peasant girl, sneaking out to meet a royal, and they have come for her. Or maybe they came for him. Even a prince is not safe from the Black Knight's reach.

"You shouldn't be here."

She hears the words as if from far away, and then someone is grabbing her, forcing her to turn.

A man is beside her. "They've taken him away. You shouldn't be here."

"But—"

"No buts. Whoever he was to you, you should forget him and go home."

"But I love him."

The man's fleshy face softens in sympathy. "Forget about your young man," he says. "And go."

He pushes her with a firmness that makes her stumble sideways. In the old days perhaps such a shove would be rude, but now it is a kindness, a reminder that this is no place to stand and cry. "Thank you, sir," she says quietly as she moves away from him.

Tears sting her eyes and she wipes them away reluctantly. Her eyes are burning when she looks up and sees a wavery image of a young man standing beneath a darkened streetlamp.

From here, it looks like Sasha, with his unruly hair and broad smile and strong jawline. Even as she picks up her pace, she tells herself she is being a fool, that he is gone and from now on all handsome blond-haired young men will remind her of Sasha; still, within a meter or so she is running. A split second before he begins to move toward her, she knows this is no mistake. It is her Sasha, now running toward her.

"Vera," he says, pulling her into his arms, kissing her so deeply she has to push him away to breathe.

"You waited all day?"

"A day? You think that is all I would wait?" He pulls her close.

Together they cross the street. The Royal Theater rises up from the concrete like a green and white spun-sugar confection, its roof adorned with a lyre and crown. A queue is beginning to form along the sidewalk. Vera notices how beautifully the people are dressed—in furs and jewels and white gloves.

Sasha takes her around to a door in the back of the theater. She follows him into a dark hallway and up a flight of stairs.

They skirt the main hall and slip into a private box.

Vera stares across the darkened hall in awe, seeing the gilt decor and crystal chandeliers. In this box—obviously being repaired—even the tools and disarray can't hide the exquisite detail. Plush mohair seats line the box's front; in the back, tucked in the shadows, is an ottoman bed draped in dusty velvet. As she is standing alongside it, she hears the doors open below her, and well-dressed patrons stream into the theater. The buzz of conversation rises to the rafters.

She turns to Sasha. "We have to leave. I do not belong here."

He pulls her into the shadows. Blue velvet curtains cushion their bodies as they lean against the wall. "This box won't be used tonight. If someone comes in, we'll say we are cleaners. There are our brooms."

The lights flicker and a hush falls over the audience. On stage, gold and blue velvet curtains part.

Music begins with a high, pure note and then sweeps into a symphony of radiant sound. Vera has never heard anything as beautiful as this music, and then Galina Ulanova—the great ballerina—leaps across the stage like a ray of light.

Vera leans forward, as close to the velvet curtains of the box as she dares.

For more than two hours, she doesn't move as the romantic story of a princess kidnapped by an evil wizard plays out across the intricately staged set. And when the wizard is brought to his knees by love, Vera finds herself crying for him, for her, for all of it. . . .

"My papa would have loved this," she says to Sasha.

He kisses her tears away and leads her to the ottoman bed.

She knows what is going to happen now; she can feel passion coming to life between them, uncoiling.

She wants him, there's no doubt about that; she wants him the way a woman wants a man, but she doesn't know much more than that. He lies down on the soft cushion, pulling her down on top of him, and when he slides his hand under her dress, she starts to shake a little. It is as if her body is taking charge of itself.

"Are you sure of this, Verushka?" he whispers, and the endearment makes her smile, reminds her that this is Sasha beneath her. She will be safe.

"I am sure."

By Sunday Vera is an entirely different girl. Or perhaps she is a woman. She and Sasha have met secretly after work every day since the ballet, and Vera has fallen so deeply in love with him that she knows there will never be a way out of it. He is the other half of her.

"Are you sure about this, Verushka?" he asks her now, as they climb the steps to her front door.

She takes his hand. She is sure enough for the both of them. "Yes." But when she reaches for the door, he grabs her hand. "Marry me," he says, and she laughs up at him. "Of course I will."

Then she kisses him and tells him to come inside.

The hallway is dark and cluttered with boxes. They climb the narrow wooden stairs to the second floor. At the door to the apartment she pauses just long enough to kiss him and then she opens the door with a flourish.

The small apartment is shabby but spotlessly clean. Her mother has been cooking all day and the sweet, savory scent of boar stew fills the room.

"This is my prince, Mama."

Her mother and Olga stand on the other side of the table,

pressed together, their hands on the chairs in front of them. Both are dressed in pretty floral blouses with plain cotton skirts. Mama has put on a pair of worn, sagging stockings and heels for this meeting; Olga is in her stockinged feet.

Vera sees them through Sasha's eyes: her tired, once-beautiful mother, and Olga, who is ready to burst into womanhood. Her sister is smiling so brightly her big, crooked teeth seem ordinary-sized.

Her mother comes around the table. "We have heard much about you, Your Highness. Welcome to our home."

Olga giggles. "I've really *heard a lot about you. She can't shut up."*

Sasha smiles. "She talks to me of you also."

"That is our Veronika," Mama says. "She is a talker." She shakes Sasha's hand firmly, gazing up at him. When she seems satisfied, she lets go and moves toward the samovar. "Would you like some tea?"

"Yes. Thank you," he says.

"You attend the cleric's college, I hear," Mama says to him. "This must be exciting."

"Yes. I'm a good student, too. I will make a good husband."

Her mother flinches a little but pours the tea. "And what are you studying?"

"I hope to be a poet someday like your husband."

*Vera sees it all as if in slow motion: her mother hears the terrible words together—*poet *and* husband*—and she stumbles. The fragile glass cup in her hand falls slowly, crashes to the ground. Hot tea sprays Vera's bare ankles and she cries out in pain.*

"A poet?" her mother says quietly, as if none of it has happened, as if a treasured family heirloom does not lie broken at her feet. "I thought a prince was dangerous enough, but this . . ."

Vera cannot believe that she forgot to warn Sasha of this. "Don't worry, Mama. You needn't—"

"You say you love her," Mama says, ignoring Vera, "and I can

see in your eyes that you do, but you will do this to her anyway, this dangerous thing that has been done to our family already."

"I wouldn't endanger Vera for anything," he says solemnly.

*"Her father promised me the same thing," Mama says bitterly. Simply the use of the word—*father*—underscores how angry her mother is.*

"You can't stop us from marrying," Vera says.

This time her mother looks at her, and in those eyes she loves is a nearly unbearable disappointment.

Vera feels her confidence ebbing. Ten minutes ago it would have been inconceivable that she should have to choose between Sasha and her family . . . yet wasn't that exactly what her mother had done? Mama had chosen her poet and run away with him, only to come back home in shame. And now, though her mother accepts her, there is little love left between them.

Vera places a hand on her stomach, rubbing it absently. In the months to come, she will remember this moment and understand that already his child is growing inside of her, but all she knows then is that she is afraid of

"Stop." Meredith pushed the closet door open and stepped out of her hiding place. The bedroom was blue with moonlight and in it, Mom looked exhausted. Her shoulders had begun to round, and her long, pale fingers had started to tremble. Worse than all of that, though, was the sudden pallor of her skin. Meredith walked over to the bed. "Are you okay?"

"You were listening," Mom said.

"I was listening," she admitted.

"Why?" Mom asked.

Meredith shrugged. Honestly, she had no answer for that.

"Well. You are right," Mom said, leaning back into the pillows. "I *am* tired."

It was the first time Mom had *ever* said she was right about something. "Nina and I will take care of you. Don't worry." She almost reached out to stroke her mother's hair, as she would have done to a child who looked as worn out as Mom did. Almost.

Nina came up to the bedside and stood beside Meredith.

"But who will take care of you two?" Mom asked.

Meredith started to answer and stopped. It dawned on her both that this was the most caring thing Mom had ever said to them, and that she was right to ask it.

Mom would be gone someday, and only they would be left. Would they take care of each other?

"So," Nina said when they went out into the hallway, "how much of the story have you secretly been listening to?"

Meredith kept moving. "All of it."

Nina followed her down the stairs. "Then why in the *hell* did you stop her?"

In the kitchen, Meredith put water on to boil. "I don't get you," she said to her sister. "When you look through a piece of glass the size of my thumbnail, you see everything."

"Yeah. So?"

"Tonight you sat in the room with Mom for all that time and didn't notice that she was fading right in front of you."

"Says you."

Meredith almost laughed at the immaturity of that. "Look: It's been a hell of a day and I can tell you're itching for a fight, which I definitely don't want to have. So I'm going to go home to my empty bed and try to sleep through the night. Tomorrow we can talk about the fairy tale, okay?"

"Okay. But we *will* talk about it."

"Fine."

Long after Meredith had gone, Nina remained alone in the kitchen, thinking about what her sister had said.

You didn't notice that she was fading right in front of you.

It was true.

If Mom had been fading, Nina hadn't noticed. She could blame it on her interest in the words, or the darkness of the room, but neither answer was quite the truth.

Long ago, Nina had mastered a simple survival skill: she'd learned how to look at her mother without really seeing her. She still remembered the day it had begun.

She'd been eleven years old, and still trying to love her mother unconditionally. Her softball team had won a spot in the statewide tournament, to be held in Spokane.

She'd been so excited, unable to talk about anything else for weeks. She'd thought—foolishly—*Now she'll be proud of me.*

Nina was surprised by how much it hurt to remember that day. Dad had been at work, so Mom was in charge of getting her to the train. They had ridden with Mary Kay and her mom, both of whom talked excitedly all the way to the station. There, Nina remembered slinging her backpack over her shoulder and running forward in a herd of girls, giggling all the way, yelling, "Bye, Mom. I'll wave from the train!"

Once on board, all the girls clustered at the windows to wave good-bye to their parents, who stood on the platform.

Nina's gaze searched the crowd, but her mother wasn't there, wasn't standing with all the other parents.

She hadn't even cared enough about Nina to wave good-bye.

From then on, Nina became like Meredith, a daddy's girl who hardly spoke to her mother and expected nothing of her.

It was the only way she'd found to protect herself from pain.

Now that habit would have to be reconsidered. For years, she'd seen her mother without really looking at her, just as she and Meredith had heard the fairy tale without really listening. They had taken for granted that it was a lovely bit of fiction; they'd listened only to hear their mother's voice.

But everything was different now.

To fulfill the promise she'd made to her father, Nina would have to do better: she'd have to really see and really listen to her mother. Every word.

Sixteen

Nina spent a restless night dreaming of imprisoned kings and black carriages drawn by dragons and girls who cut off their fingers for love.

Finally, she gave up trying to sleep and turned on the bedside lamp. Rubbing her eyes, she pulled out a pad of paper and a pen.

The fairy tale was changing.

Or maybe *changing* wasn't the right word; they'd gotten to a place in the story that was new to Nina. She'd never heard this part of the peasant girl and the prince before. She was sure of it.

And it was so detailed. Not like a fairy tale at all. But what did it all mean?

She wrote: *FONTANKA BRIDGE (real).*

She tapped her pen against the pad and went through the story point by point.

CIGARETTES (since when did fairy-tale mothers smoke? And why hadn't the mom smoked in the earlier segments?)

GALINA SOMETHING. For the life of her, she couldn't remember the ballerina's last name, but it had been Russian.

On that, Nina went down to her dad's office and booted up the computer. The dial-up connection took forever to engage, but when the Internet came up, she ran searches on every word she could think of. She was so caught up in gathering information that when Meredith touched her shoulder, she actually jumped.

"You look like you haven't slept," Meredith said.

Nina pushed back from her chair and looked up. "It's the fairy tale. Last night was all new, right? We've never heard that part before?"

"It was new," Meredith said.

"Did you notice the changes? Vera's mother is smoking cigarettes and wearing sagging stockings, and Vera is pregnant before she gets married. When did you ever hear shit like that in a fairy tale before? And listen to this: Galina Ulanova was a great Russian ballerina who danced at the Mariinsky Theatre in Leningrad until 1944, and after that, she was at the Bolshoi in Moscow. And check out this picture: the theater has a lyre and crown on its cupola."

Meredith leaned closer. "That's exactly how Mom described it."

Nina hit a few keys and a picture of the Summer Garden came up. "Real. In St. Petersburg, which used to be Leningrad. And Petrograd before that. These Russians change the names of everything with every leader. Notice the marble statues and the lime trees? And here's the Bronze Horseman; it's a famous statue in the park. Not a winged horse, but a man on horseback."

Meredith frowned. "I found a letter in Dad's files. From a professor in Alaska. He was asking Mom about Leningrad."

"Really?" Nina scooted closer to the computer, her fingers flying on the keyboard as she pulled up the biography on Galina Ulanova again. "She was most famous in Leningrad in the thirties. If we knew how old mom was, it would help. . . ." She typed in *LENINGRAD 1930.*

On screen, a list of links finally came up. One of them—*GREAT TERROR*—caught Nina's attention and she clicked on it. "Listen to this," she said when the Web site appeared. "The thirties were characterized by the Great Purge of the Communist Party, in which Stalin's secret police arrested peasants, perceived political radicals, ethnic minorities, and artists. It was a time of widespread police surveillance, middle-of-the-night arrests, secretive 'trials,' years of imprisonment, and executions."

"Black vans," Meredith said, leaning over Nina's shoulder to read the rest. "The secret police came to get people in black vans."

"The Black Knight is Stalin," Nina said. "It's a story within a story."

She pushed back from the computer. She and Meredith looked at each other, and in that look, Nina felt the first true connection of their lives. "Some of it is real," Nina said quietly, feeling a shiver move through her.

"And have you noticed that she hasn't been crazy or confused lately?" Meredith said.

"Not since she started the fairy tale. Do you think Dad knew it would help her?"

"I don't know," Meredith said. "I don't know what any of it means."

"I don't know, either, but we're going to find out."

At work, Meredith had trouble concentrating on the details of her job. She didn't think anyone noticed, but while she was in meetings or listening to someone talk on the phone or reading some report, she found her attention wandering back to Mom and the fairy tale.

By the end of the day she was as obsessed as her sister. After work, she drove straight home to feed the dogs and then went to Belye Nochi and into her father's office.

Kneeling on the thick carpet in front of the boxes, she found the one marked FILES, MISC 1970–1980, and opened the flaps.

This was going to be her starting place. Nina might be a whiz at investigative research, but Meredith knew where to look in the house.

If there was one letter about Mom's past, there might be others. Or maybe there were other documents, hidden in mislabeled files, or photographs thrown in with other memorabilia.

She found the file marked BepaΠeTpoBHa and pulled it out. Rereading the letter from Professor Adamovich, she walked over to the computer and sat down. The only link that came up directed her to the University of Alaska Web site.

She picked up the phone and called. It took several attempts, but finally she was routed to the Russian Studies Department and a woman with a heavy accent answered. "May I help you?"

"I hope so," Meredith said. "I'm trying to find Professor Vasily Adamovich."

"Oh, my," the woman said, "there is a name I have not heard in a long time. Dr. Adamovich retired about twelve years ago. He has had several most worthy successors, however, and I would be most happy to connect you to someone else."

"I really need Dr. Adamovich. I have some questions about one of his research studies."

"Oh, well, I guess I cannot help you, then."

"How can I get in touch with the professor directly?"

"I'm afraid I do not have an answer for you on that."

"Thank you," Meredith said, disappointed. She hung up the phone and went to the study window. From here, she could see the corner of the winter garden. On this warm evening, the bench was empty, but as Meredith stood there, Mom crossed the yard, draped in a big blanket, its plaid tail dragging in the grass behind her. In the garden, she touched each of the copper columns, then sat down and pulled her knitting out of her bag.

From this angle, Meredith could see the way Mom's chin was tucked into her body, the way her shoulders were rounded. Whatever strength it took for her mother to stand so straight and tall around her children, she had none of it out there. It looked like she was talking to herself or to the flowers or . . . to Dad. Had she always sat out there alone, talking, or was that new; yet another by-product of a lost love?

"She out there again?" Nina asked, coming into the office. Her hair was damp and she was wearing a big terry-cloth robe and a pair of sheepskin slippers.

"Of course." Meredith reached down for the letter and handed it to Nina. "I called the university. The professor is retired, and the woman I spoke to didn't know much else."

Nina read the letter. "So, we know for sure that Mom has a connection to Leningrad, and the fairy tale takes place there and at least some of it is probably real. So, I'm going to ask the obvious question: Is she Vera?"

There was the sixty-four-thousand-dollar question. "If Mom is Vera, she got pregnant at seventeen. So she had a miscarriage or . . ."

"We have a sibling somewhere."

Meredith stared out the window at the woman who was always so alone. Could she really have other children, and probably grandchildren, out there somewhere? Could she have walked away from them and never gone back?

No. Not even Anya Whitson was that heartless.

Meredith had had two late-term miscarriages in the years after her girls were born. She'd had a terrible time dealing with the losses. She'd seen a counselor for a short time and talked to Jeff until it was obvious that it wounded him too much to keep listening. In the end, she'd had no one—no friend or family member—in whom she could confide. The few times she had mentioned it, people immediately wanted her to "see someone," not understanding that all she'd really wanted to do was remember her boys.

The one person in whom she'd never confided was her mother.

Certainly no woman who'd been through the loss of a child, either in the womb or in the world, could see another woman's similar suffering and say nothing. "I don't believe that," she said finally. "And Vera obviously sees color." As a kid, Meredith had looked up Mom's birth defect in the encyclopedia. Achromatopsia, it was called, and one thing was certain: her mother had never seen a lavender sky. "Maybe Mom is Olga."

"Or maybe Vera is Mom's mom. It's unlikely, but since we don't know how old she is, anything is possible. That would be just like Mom, to tell us her story in a way we don't ever get to know *her.* How will we know?"

"Keep her talking. I'm going to go through this house from stem to stern. If there's anything to find, I'll find it."

"Thanks, Mere," Nina said. "It feels good to be together on this."

During dinner that night, Nina concentrated on acting normal. She drank her vodka and ate her meal and made her pretense at conversation, but all the while she was watching Mom closely, thinking, *Who are you?* It took an act of will not to voice the question out loud. As a journalist, she knew that timing was everything, and you never asked a question until you had a pretty damn good idea of the answer. She could tell that Meredith was fighting the same battle.

So when Mom stood up after the meal and said, "I am too tired for storytelling tonight," Nina was almost relieved.

She helped her sister with the dishes (okay, Meredith did most of the work), then she kissed her good-bye and went into Dad's study, where she got on the Internet. She ran searches on everything she could find about Leningrad in the twenties and thirties. She found a lot of information but no real answers.

Finally, at almost two in the morning, she pushed back from the computer in disgust. She had pages and pages of anecdotal information but no *facts*—other than what she'd known already. The story was taking place in Leningrad under Stalin.

She tapped her pen on the table and talked out loud, going through what she knew. Again. As she went through it all, she glanced at her notes.

The envelope from the professor stuck out from underneath her pad. She picked up the letter and read it again, studying it word by word. *Leningrad. Participation. Study. Understand.*

Her mother knew something, had seen or experienced something important enough to have been the subject of a professorial research project.

But what?

The Great Terror? Stalin's repression? Or maybe she'd been a prima ballerina. . . .

"Stop it," Nina said aloud, turning her attention to the dusty green file folder marked ВераПеТроВНа. Then she stared at the letter. "What did you want to know from her, Vasily Adamovich?"

That was when she saw it, when she said his name out loud.

Nina sat upright.

It was in his signature.

When he signed his name, Vasily, the first letter looked like a *B*.

Nina's heart was pounding as she reached for the file. Was there a space after the *a*? Could it be a first and last name? She broke the word at the second capital letter and was left with *Bepa*.

Vepa.

She ran an Internet search for the Russian alphabet and compared the letters.

Bepa was Vera.

Vera.

Then she translated the rest of the letters. ПеТроВНа.

Petrovna.

A little more research, and she understood Russian names. First was the given name, then the patronymic—a male or female identification of the father—and then the surname. So this file contained two of three names—-*ovna* was the suffix for a daughter. Vera Petrovna meant *Vera, Petyr's daughter.*

Nina sat back in her chair, feeling the adrenaline rush that always came with nailing a key part of a story. Vera was a real person. Real enough to put her name on a file, and important enough to keep that file for twenty years.

It wasn't a complete answer; it didn't answer the big question about Mom's identity, and unfortunately, without a surname, she couldn't locate anything more online. The research study could be about Vera, and Mom could have known her or something about her. Or, of course, she could be Vera. Or Olga. Those answers Nina would have to find somewhere else.

This Vasily Adamovich—Vasily, Adam's son—knew the connection between Mom and Vera, and that connection was important enough to include in a research study.

And with that, Nina came up with a plan.

Seventeen

At 5:47 Meredith went for her run. The dogs raced along with her, eagerly vying for attention.

By seven o'clock, she was out in the orchard and walking the rows with her foreman, checking on the new fruit's early progress, noting frost damage, and assessing the workers' careful hand-wrapping of the apples, and by ten she was at her desk, reading crop projections.

But all she could really think about was the fairy tale.

I'm just going to ask it: Is she Vera?

The idea of that was like a budding apple; it flowered, grew, and gained mass. It seemed impossible that something you'd heard all your life and deemed irrelevant could actually be of value; it was like finding out that the painting above your fireplace was an early Van Gogh.

But it was true; she'd heard the words for years and simply accepted them at face value, never questioning, never looking deeper. Maybe all kids did that with family stories. The more you heard something, the less you questioned the veracity of it.

She put aside the crop reports and turned to her computer. For the next hour she ran random searches. Leningrad, Stalin, Vera, Olga (if she had been looking for Russian mail-order brides, the names would have been pay dirt), Fontanka Bridge, Great Terror. Bronze Horseman statue. Nothing of real value came up, just more and more evidence that the backdrop of the fairy tale was largely real.

She found a long list of Vasily Adamovich's published works. He'd written about almost every facet of Russian and Soviet life, from the earliest days of the Bolshevik revolution, through the murder of the Romanovs and the rise of Stalin and the terrors of his regime, to Hitler's attack during World War II, to the tragedy at Chernobyl. Whatever had happened to Russians in the twentieth century, he'd studied it.

"That's a lot of help," Meredith murmured, tapping her pen. When she added *RETIREMENT* to the search, she came up with an unexpected link to a newspaper article.

> Dr. Vasily Adamovich, a former professor of Russian studies at the University of Alaska in Anchorage, suffered a stroke yesterday at his home in Juneau. Dr. Adamovich is well known in academic circles for his prolific publishing schedule, but friends say he is a master gardener and can tell a mean ghost story. He retired from teaching in 1989 and volunteered frequently at his neighborhood library. He is recovering at a local hospital.

Meredith picked up the phone and dialed information. The operator had no listing for a Vasily Adamovich in Juneau. Disappointed, Meredith asked for the library's number instead.

"There are several listings, ma'am."

"Give me all of them," Meredith answered, making note of each branch's phone number.

On the fourth call, she got lucky. "Hello," she said. "I'm trying to find a Dr. Vasily Adamovich."

"Oh, Vasya," the woman answered. "No one has called for him in a while, I'm sad to say."

"This is the library where he volunteered?"

"Two days a week for years. The high school kids loved him."

"I'm trying to reach him. . . ."

"Last I heard he was in a nursing home."

"Do you know which one?"

"No. I'm sorry. I don't, but . . . are you a friend of Vasya's?"

"My mother is. She hasn't spoken to him in a long time, though."

"You do know about the stroke?"

"Yes."

"I heard he was in pretty bad shape. He has difficulty speaking."

"Okay, well. Thank you for your help." Meredith hung up the phone.

Almost simultaneously, Daisy walked into her office.

"There's a problem down in the warehouse. Nothing urgent, but Hector wants you to stop by sometime today if you can. If you're too busy, I'm sure I can solve it for you."

"Yeah," Meredith said, staring down at her notes. "Why don't you do that?"

"And then I'll go to Tahiti."

"Um. Okay."

"On the company credit card."

"Uh-huh. Thanks, Daisy."

Daisy crossed the room in a burst of energy and sat down in the chair opposite Meredith's desk. "That's it," she said, crossing her arms. "Start talking."

Meredith looked up. Honestly, she was surprised. What had Daisy been saying? "What?"

"I just told you I was going to Tahiti on the company dime."

Meredith laughed. "So you're saying I wasn't listening."

"What's going on?"

Meredith considered that Daisy had been around the Whitsons for as long as anyone could remember. "When did you meet my mom?"

Daisy's overplucked eyebrows lifted in surprise. "Well, let's see. I guess I was about ten. Maybe a little younger. It was all the buzz. I remember that. 'Cause your daddy was datin' Sally Herman when he went off to war and when he came home, he was married."

"So he barely knew her."

"I don't know about that. He was in love with her, though. My mom said she'd never seen a man so in love. She took care of Anya."

"Who did?"

"My mom. For most of that first year."

Meredith frowned. "What do you mean?"

"She was sick. You knew that, right? I think she was in bed for a year or so and then one day she just got better. My mom thought they'd be friends, but you know Anya."

It was stunning news, really. Stunning. She didn't remember her mother ever having so much as a cough. "Sick how? What was wrong with her?" What caused a woman to spend a year in bed? And what made her suddenly get better?

"I don't know. Mom never said much about it, really."

"Thanks, Daisy." She watched Daisy leave the office and close the door behind her.

For the next few hours, Meredith managed to get a little bit of work done, but mostly she was thinking about her mother.

At five o'clock, she gave up the pretense and left the office, saying, "Daisy, will you run the warehouse check for me? If there's a real problem, I'll be on my cell. Otherwise I'm gone for the day."

"You bet, Meredith."

Ten minutes later, when she walked into her mother's house, the smell of baking bread greeted her. She found her mother in the kitchen, draped in her big, baggy white apron, her hands sticky white with flour. As she had always done, she was making enough bread for an army. The freezer in the garage was full of it.

"Hey, Mom."

"You are here early."

"Business was slow, so I thought I'd come here and do some more packing for you. When I get it all organized, you and I should probably go through the giveaway piles."

"If you wish."

"Do you care what I keep and what I get rid of?"

"No."

Meredith didn't even know what to say to that. How could *nothing* be of importance to her mom? "Where's Nina?"

"She said something about errands and left an hour ago. She took her camera, so . . ."

"Who knows when she'll be back."

"Right." Mom turned back to her dough.

Meredith stood there a minute longer, then took off her jacket and hung it on the hook by the door. She started to go down the hall toward Dad's office, but as she approached the open door, she paused. The last time she'd packed up Mom's things, she hadn't looked for anything, hadn't gone through pockets or felt back in the drawers.

Glancing back at the kitchen, seeing Mom still kneading dough, she eased toward the stairs and went up to the master bedroom.

In the long, wide closet, her mother's black and gray clothing lined the right wall. Almost everything was either soft merino wool or brushed cotton. Turtlenecks and cardigans and long skirts and flowy pants. There was nothing trendy or showy or expensive here.

Clothes to hide in.

The thought came out of nowhere, surprising her. It was the sort of thing she would have noticed before, if she'd ever really looked.

This telling of the fairy tale was changing their perceptions of everything, of each other most of all. With that thought came another: what was it about the play—and about the fairy tale—that had upset Mom so much all those years ago? Before, Meredith had always assumed that her mother's Christmas play anger had been directed at Meredith, that in choosing to do the fairy tale as a Christmas play, Meredith had done something wrong.

But what if it hadn't been about Meredith and Nina at all; what if it had been a reaction to seeing the words acted out?

She went deeper into the closet and stood in front of her mother's chest of drawers. There was something in here that would reveal her mother. There had to be. What woman didn't have some memento hidden far from prying eyes?

She closed the door until there was only the slimmest view of the room, and then she returned to the chest, opening the top drawer. Underwear lay neatly folded in three piles: white, gray, black. Socks were organized in similarly colored balls. Several bras filled out the corner. She let her fingers trail beneath it all, feeling the smooth wood of the drawer's bottom. Guilt made her grimace but she continued through the second and third drawers, with their neatly folded sweaters and T-shirts. Kneeling, she opened the bottom drawer. Inside, she found pajamas, nightgowns, and an out-of-date bathing suit.

Nothing hidden. Nothing more personal than undergarments.

Disappointed and vaguely embarrassed, she closed the drawer. With a sigh, she got back to her feet and stood there looking at the clothes. It was all perfectly organized. Everything with a place and in it; the only thing that didn't fit was a sapphire-blue wool coat hanging at the very back of the closet.

Meredith remembered the coat. She'd seen her mother wear it once—to a performance of *The Nutcracker* when she and Nina were little girls. Dad had insisted, had twirled Mom around and kissed her and said, "Come on, Anya, just this once . . ."

She reached back for it, pulled it out. The coat was a bright blue cashmere in a classic forties style, with broad shoulders, a fitted waist, and wide, cuffed sleeves. Intricately carved Lucite buttons ran from throat to waist. Meredith put it on; the silk lining was deliciously soft. Surprisingly, it fit pretty well; wearing it made her imagine her mother as young instead of old, as a smiling girl who would love the feel of cashmere.

But she hadn't loved it, had rarely worn it. Neither, though, had she thrown it away, and for a woman who kept so few mementos, it was an odd thing to have saved. Unless she hadn't wanted to hurt Dad's feelings. It must have been expensive.

She put her hands in the pockets and twirled to look at herself in the full-length mirror behind the door.

That was when she felt it, something hidden, sewn into the lining behind the pocket.

She felt for the fraying edge of the secret compartment and worked it for a few seconds, finally extracting a tattered, creased black and white photograph of two children.

Meredith stared down at it. The image was slightly blurry and the paper was so creased and veined it was hard to see clearly, but it was two children, about three or four years of age, holding hands. At first she thought it was her and Nina, but then she noticed the old-fashioned, heavy coats and boots the kids were wearing. She turned the picture over and found a word written on the back. In Russian.

"Meredith!"

She flushed guiltily before she realized it was Nina, thundering up the stairs like an elephant.

Meredith opened the closet door. "I'm in here, Nina."

Dressed in khaki pants and a matching T-shirt, with hiking boots, Nina looked ready to go on a safari. "There you are. I've been look—"

Meredith grabbed her arm and pulled her into the closet. "Is Mom still in the kitchen?"

"Baking enough bread for a third world country? Yes. Why?"

"Look what I found," Meredith said, holding out the picture.

"You went snooping? Good girl. I wouldn't have thought you had it in you."

"Just look."

Nina took the photograph and stared down at it for a long time and then turned it over. After a quick glimpse at the word, she turned it over again. "Vera and Olga?"

Meredith's heart actually skipped a beat. "You think?"

"I can't tell if they're boys or girls. But this one kinda looks like Mom, don't you think?"

"Honestly? I don't know. What should we do with it?"

Nina thought about that. "Leave it here for now. We'll bring it with us. Sooner or later, we'll ask Mom."

"She'll know I went through her stuff."

"No. She'll know *I* did. I'm a journalist, remember? Snooping is my job description."

"And I found out from Daisy that Mom was sick when she married Dad. They thought she'd die."

"Mom? Sick? She never even gets a cold."

"I know. Weird, huh?"

"Now I'm certain about my plan," Nina said.

"What plan?"

"I'll tell you at dinner. Mom needs to hear this, too. Come on, let's go."

Nina waited with obvious impatience while Meredith returned the photograph to its hiding place and hung the coat back up. Together, they went downstairs.

Their mother was seated at the kitchen table. On the counter, there were dozens of loaves of bread and several bags from the local Chinese restaurant.

Nina carried the Chinese food to the table, positioning the white cartons around the vodka bottle and shot glasses.

"Can I have wine instead?" Meredith said.

"Sure," Nina said absently, pouring two shots instead of three.

"You seem . . . buoyant," Mom said.

"Like a Pekingese when the mailman comes," Meredith added when her sister sat down across from her.

"I have a surprise," Nina said, lifting her shot glass. "Cheers."

"What is it?" Meredith asked.

"First we talk," Nina said, reaching for the beef with broccoli, serving up a portion on her plate. "Let's see. My favorite thing to do is travel. I love passion in all of its guises. And my boyfriend wants me to settle down."

Meredith was shocked by that last bit. It was so intimate. To her surprise, she decided to match it. "I love to shop for beautiful things. I used to dream of opening a string of Belye Nochi gift stores, and . . . my husband left me."

Mom looked up sharply but said nothing.

"I don't know what's going to happen," Meredith said at last. "I think maybe love can just . . . dissolve."

"No, it does not," her mother said.

"So how do—"

"You hang on," her mother said. "Until your hands are bleeding, and still you do not let go."

"Is that how you and Dad stayed happy for so long?" Nina asked.

Mom reached for the chow mein's serving spoon. "Of course that is what I am speaking of."

"Your turn," Nina said to Mom.

Meredith could have kicked her sister. For once they were actually *talking* and Nina turned it right back to the game.

Mom stared down at her food. "My favorite thing to do is cook. I love the feel of a fire on a cold night. And . . ." She paused.

Meredith found herself leaning forward.

"And . . . I am afraid of many things." She picked up her fork and began to eat.

Meredith sat back in amazement. It was impossible to imagine her mother afraid of anything, and yet she'd revealed it, so it must be true. She wanted to ask, *What frightens you?* but she didn't have the courage.

"It's time for my surprise," Nina said, smiling. "We're going to Alaska."

Meredith frowned. "We who?"

"You, me, and Mom." She reached down and produced three tickets. "On a cruise ship."

Meredith was too stunned to say anything. She knew she should argue, say she had to work, that the dogs couldn't be left alone—

anything—but the truth was that she *wanted* to go. She wanted to get away from the orchard and the office and the talk she had to have with Jeff. Daisy could run the warehouse.

Mom looked up slowly. Her face was pale; her blue eyes seemed to burn through the pallor. "You are taking me to Alaska? Why?"

"You said it was your dream," Nina said simply. Meredith could have kissed her. There was such a gentleness in her sister's voice. "And you said it, too, Mere."

"But . . . ," Mom said, shaking her head.

"We need this," Nina said. "The three of us. We need to be together and I want Mom to see Alaska."

"In exchange for the rest of the story," Mom said.

An awkward pause fell over the table.

"Yes. We want to hear the whole . . . fairy tale, Mom, but this is separate. I saw your face when you said you'd always dreamed of going to Alaska. You *have* dreamed of this trip. Let Meredith and me take you."

Mom got up and went to the French doors in the dining room. There, she stared out at the winter garden, which was now in full vibrant bloom. "When do we leave?"

The next morning, Nina stood at the fence line, with her camera in her hands, watching workers stream onto the property. Women headed toward the shed, where they would pack apples from cold storage for shipment around the world; in a few months, Nina knew, they'd be busy sorting the harvest by quality. All up and down the rows, workers in faded jeans, most with jet-black hair, climbed up and down ladders beneath the branches, carefully hand-wrapping the fledgling apples to protect them from bugs and the elements.

She was just about to go back into the house when a dirty blue car pulled in front of the garage and parked. The driver's door opened. All Nina saw was a shock of gray-threaded black hair and she started to run for him.

"Danny!" she cried, throwing herself into his arms so hard he stumbled backward and hit the car, but still he held on to her.

"You're not an easy woman to track down, Nina Whitson."

Smiling, she took him by the hand. "You did okay. Here. Let me show you around the place."

With an unexpected pride, she showed him around the orchard her father had loved. Now and then she shared memories from her past; mostly she told him about the story her mother was telling.

Finally, she said, "Why are you here?"

He smiled down at her. "First things first, love. Where's your bedroom?"

"On the second floor."

"Damn," he said. "You're goin' t' make me work for it."

"I'll make it worth your time. Promise," she said, kissing his ear.

He carried her up the stairs and into her girlhood room.

"A cheerleader, eh?" he said, glancing at the dusty red and white pom-pom lying in the corner. "How come I never knew that?"

She started unbuttoning his shirt. Her hands were frantic as she undressed him. Anticipation of his touch was an exquisite torture, and when they were both naked and in bed, he began caressing her with an ardor that matched her own. She was on fire for him; there was no other way to put it. And when she came, it was so intense it felt as if she were breaking apart.

Afterward, he rolled over onto one elbow and looked down at her. His face was deeply tanned and lined, the creases at his eyes like tiny white knife marks. His hair had taken flight during their lovemaking, turned into dozens of curly black wings. He was smiling, but there was something pinched in it, and the look in his eyes was almost sad. "You asked why I was here."

"Give a girl a chance to breathe, won't you?"

"You're breathing," he said quietly. With those two words, and the look in his eyes, she knew it all.

"Okay," she said, and this time she had to force herself to look at him. "Why are you here?"

"I was in Atlanta. From there, this was nothin'."

"Atlanta?" she said, but she knew what was in Atlanta. Every journalist did.

"CNN. They've offered me my own show. In-depth world stories." He smiled. "I'm tired, Neens. I've been gallivantin' for decades now, and my bum leg hurts all the time and I'm tired of tryin' to keep up with the twenty-year-olds. Mostly, though . . . I'm tired of being alone so much. I wouldn't mind the globe-trottin' if I had a place to come home to."

"Congratulations," she said woodenly.

"Marry me," he said, and the earnestness in his blue eyes made her want to cry. She thought, absurdly, *I should have taken more pictures of him.*

"If I said yes," she said, touching his face, feeling the unfamiliar smoothness of his cheek, "would you forget CNN and stay in Africa with me? Or maybe go to the Middle East, or Malaysia? Could I say on Friday, *I need good Thai food*, and we'd hop on a plane?"

"We've done all that, love."

"And what would I do in Atlanta? Learn to make the perfect peach pie and welcome you home with a glass of scotch?"

"Come on, Neens. I know who you are."

"Do you?" Nina felt as if she were falling suddenly. Her stomach ached, her eyes stung. How could she say yes . . . how could she say no? She loved this man. Of that she was sure. But the rest of it? Settling down? A house in the city or a place in the suburbs? A permanent address? How could she handle that? The only life she'd ever wanted was the one she now had. She simply couldn't plant roots—that was for men like her father and women like her sister, who liked the ground to be level where they stood. And if Danny really loved Nina, he'd know that.

"Just come back to Atlanta with me for the weekend. We'll talk to people, see what's available for you. You're a world-famous photojournalist, for fuck's sake. They'd be crawlin' all over themselves to give you a job. Come on, love, give us a chance."

"I'm going to Alaska with Mom and Meredith."

"I'll have you back in time. I swear it."

"But . . . the fairy tale . . . I have more research to do. I can't just leave the story. Maybe in two weeks, when we're done. . . ."

Danny pulled away from her. "There will always be another story to follow, won't there, Neens?"

"That's not fair. This is my family history, the promise I made to my dad. You can't ask me to give that up."

"Is that what I asked?"

"You know what I mean."

" 'Cause I thought I proposed marriage and didn't get an answer."

"Give me more time."

He leaned down and kissed her; this time it was slow and soft and sad. And when he took her in his arms and made love to her again, she learned something new, something she hadn't known before: sex could mean many things; one of them was good-bye.

Meredith hadn't been on a vacation without Jeff and the girls in years. As she packed and repacked her suitcase, she found her enthusiasm for the trip growing by leaps and bounds. She had always wanted to go to Alaska.

So why had she never gone?

The question, when it occurred to her, made her pause in her packing. She stared down at the open suitcase on her bed, but instead of seeing the neatly folded white sweater, she saw the blank landscape of her own life.

By and large, she'd been the one who planned family vacations, and she'd always let someone else choose the destination. Jillian had wanted to see the Grand Canyon, so they'd gone camping in the summer; Maddy had always been the Tiki-Girl, and two family vacations in Hawaii had cemented that nickname; and Jeff loved to ski, so they went to Sun Valley every year.

But never had they headed north to Alaska.

Why was that? Why had Meredith been so ready to bypass her own happiness? She'd thought there would be time to unwind those choices, that if she put her children first for nineteen years, she could then shift course and be the one who mattered. As easy as changing lanes while driving. But it hadn't been like that, not for her anyway. She'd lost too much of herself in parenthood to simply go back to who she'd been before.

As she looked around her room, there were mementos everywhere, bits and pieces of the life she'd lived—photographs of the family, art projects the girls had made over the years, souvenirs she and Jeff had bought together. There, right by the bed, was a photograph she'd looked at every day of her life and yet not really seen in years. In it, she and Jeff were young—kids, really—a pair of newlyweds with a bald, bright-eyed little girl cradled between them. Jeff's hair was long and wheat-blond, blown by the wind across his sunburned cheeks. And the smile on his face was breathtaking in its honesty.

She's us, he'd said to Meredith on that day, all those years ago, when they'd held their daughter, Jillian, between them. *The best of us.*

And suddenly the thought of losing him was more than she could bear. She grabbed her car keys and drove to his office, but once there, when she looked up at him, she realized she was equally afraid of losing herself.

"I wanted to remind you that we're leaving tomorrow," she said after what had to be the longest silence in the world.

"I know that."

"You're staying at the house, right? The girls are going to be calling you every day, I think. They're sure you can't live without me."

"You think they're wrong?"

He was close, so close she could have touched him with only the slightest effort. She longed suddenly to do it, but she held back. "Are they?"

"When you come home, we'll talk."

"What if—" slipped out of her mouth before she realized even that she was going to speak.

"What if what?"

"What if I still don't know what to say?" she finally said.

"After twenty years?"

"It went by fast."

"It's one question, Mere. Are you in love with me?"

One question.

How could the whole of an adult life funnel down to that?

As the silence expanded, he reached for a framed picture on his desk.

"This is for you," he said.

She looked down at it, feeling the start of tears. It was their wedding picture. He'd kept it on his desk all these years. "You don't want it on your desk anymore?"

"That's not why I'm giving it to you."

He touched her cheek with a gentleness that somehow communicated more than twenty years of being together, of knowing each other, of passion and love and the disappointments that came with both, and she knew he'd given her the picture so that she'd remember them.

She looked up at him. "I never told you I wanted to go to Alaska. I think there were a lot of things I didn't say." She could tell by the way he was looking at her that he understood, and all at once she was reminded of how well he knew her. He'd been at her side through graduation and childbirth and her father's death. He'd been the primary witness to most of her life. When had she stopped talking to him about her dreams? And why?

"I wish you had told me."

"Yeah. Me, too."

"Words matter, I guess," he said finally. "Maybe your dad knew that all along."

Meredith nodded. How was it that her whole life could be distilled down to that simple truth? Words mattered. Her life had been defined by things said and unsaid, and now her marriage was being undermined by silence. "She's not who we thought she was, Jeff. My mom, I mean. Sometimes, when she's telling us the story, it's like . . . I don't know. She melts into this other woman. I'm almost afraid of finding out the truth, but I can't stop. I need to know who she is. Maybe then I'll know who I am."

He nodded and came closer. Leaning down, he kissed her cheek. "Safe travels, Mere. I hope you find what you're looking for."

Eighteen

It was one of those rare crystal-blue days in downtown Seattle when Mount Rainier dominated the city skyline. The waterfront was empty this early in the season; soon, though, the souvenir shops and seafood restaurants along this street would be wall-to-wall tourists. But now the city belonged to locals.

Meredith stared up at the giant cruise ship docked at Pier 66. Dozens of passengers milled around the terminal and lined up for departure.

"You guys ready?" Nina asked, flinging her backpack over one shoulder.

"I don't know how you can travel so light," Meredith said, lugging her suitcase behind her as they made their way to the bellmen waiting by the exit doors. They handed off their luggage and headed for the gangplank. As they reached it, Mom stopped suddenly.

Meredith almost ran into her. "Mom? Are you okay?"

Mom tightened the black, high-collared wool coat around her and stared up at the ship.

"Mom?" Meredith said again.

Nina touched Mom's shoulder. "You crossed the Atlantic by boat, didn't you?" she said gently.

"With your father," Mom said. "I don't remember much of it except this. Boarding. Leaving."

"You were sick," Meredith said.

Mom looked surprised. "Yes."

"Why?" Nina asked. "What was wrong with you?"

"Not now, Nina." Mom repositioned her purse strap over her shoulder. "Well. Let us go find our rooms."

At the top of the gangplank, a uniformed man looked at their documents and led them to their side-by-side cabins. "You have places at the early seating for dinner. Here's your table number. Your luggage will be brought to the cabin. We're serving cocktails on the bow as we pull out of port."

"Cocktails?" Nina said. "We're in. Let's go, ladies."

"I will meet you there," Mom said. "I need a moment to get organized."

"Okay," Nina said, "but don't wait too long. We need to celebrate."

Meredith followed Nina through the glittering burgundy and blue interior to the jutting rounded bow of the ship. There were hundreds of people on deck, gathered around the swimming pool and along the railing. Black-and-white-uniformed waiters carried bright, umbrella-clad drinks on sparkling silver trays. Over in an area by a food stand, a mariachi band was playing.

Meredith leaned against the railing and sipped her drink. "Are you ever going to tell me about him?"

"Who?"

"Danny."

"Oh."

"He was totally hot, by the way, and he flew all the way out to see you. Why didn't he stick around?"

Behind them, the ship's horn honked. People all around them clapped and cheered as the giant ship pulled away from the dock. Mom was nowhere to be seen. Big surprise.

"He wants me to move to Atlanta and settle down."

"You don't sound very happy about that."

"Settle down. Me? I don't just love my career, I live for it. And really, marriage isn't my thing. Why can't we just say we'll keep loving each other and travel until we need wheelchairs?"

Even a month ago, Meredith would have given Nina platitudes, told her that love was the only thing that mattered in life and that Nina was getting to an age where she should start a family, but she had learned a thing or two in the months since Dad's death. Every choice changed the road you were on and it was too easy to end up going in the wrong direction. Sometimes, settling down was just plain settling. "I admire that about you, Neens. You have a passion and you follow it. You don't bend for other people."

"Is love enough? What if I love him but I can't settle down? What if I never want the white picket fence and a bunch of children running around?"

"It's all about choices, Neens. No one can tell you what's right for you."

"If you had it to do over again, would you still choose Jeff, even with all that's happened?"

Meredith had never considered that question, but the answer came effortlessly. Somehow it was easier to admit out here, with nothing but strangers and water around them. "I'd marry him again."

Nina put an arm around her. "Yeah," she said, "but you still think you don't know what you want."

"I hate you," Meredith said.

Nina squeezed her shoulder. "No, you don't. You love me."

Meredith smiled. "I guess I do."

The hostess led them to a table by a massive window. Through the glass was miles of empty ocean, the waves tipped in light from a fading sun. As they took their seats, Mom smiled at the hostess and thanked her.

Meredith was so surprised by the warmth in Mom's smile that she actually paused. For years she'd taken care of her mother, fitting that chore into all the others on her busy schedule. Because of that, she'd rarely really looked at Mom; she'd moved past and around her on the way to Dad. Even in the past months, when so often it had been just the two of them, there were few moments of honest connection. She'd known her mother as distant and icy, and that was how she'd seen her.

But the woman who'd just smiled was someone else entirely. Secrets within secrets. Was that what they'd discover on this trip? That their mother was like one of her precious Russian nesting dolls, and if that were true, would they ever really see the one hidden deep inside?

Handing them menus, the hostess said, "Enjoy your meal," and left.

When their waiter showed up a few minutes later, none of them had spoken.

"We all need drinks," Nina said. "Vodka. Russian. Your very best."

"No way," Meredith said. "I am not drinking vodka straight shots on my vacation." She smiled at the waiter. "I'll have a strawberry daiquiri, please."

Nina smiled. "Okay. I'll have a straight shot of vodka and a margarita on the rocks. Lots of salt."

"The vodka and a glass of wine," Mom said.

"And the A.A. meeting has come to order," Meredith said.

Amazingly, Mom smiled.

"To us," Nina said when the drinks arrived. "To Meredith, Nina, and Anya Whitson. Together for maybe the first time."

Mom flinched, and Meredith noticed that she didn't look at them, not even when they touched their glasses together.

Meredith found herself watching Mom closely; she noticed a tiny frown gather at the edges of her mouth when she looked out at the vast blue sea. Only when night fell did she seem to lose that tension in her face. She followed the conversation, added her three new answers to the pot. She drank a second glass of wine but seemed to grow more agitated than relaxed from the alcohol, and when she finished dessert, she stood up almost immediately.

"I am going back to my room," she said. "Will you join me?"

Nina was on her feet in an instant, but Meredith was slower to respond. "Are you sure, Mom? Maybe you should rest tonight. Tomorrow is okay for the story."

"Thank you," her mother said. "But no. Come." She turned crisply on her heel and walked away.

Meredith and Nina had to rush along behind her through the busy passageways.

They went into their own room and changed into sweats. Meredith had just finished brushing her teeth when Nina came up alongside her, touching her shoulder. "I'm going to show her the picture and ask who the children are."

"I don't think it's a good idea."

"That's because you're a nice girl who follows the rules and tries to be polite." She grinned. "I'm the other sister. You can say you knew nothing about it. Will you trust me on this?"

"Sure," Meredith finally said.

They left their stateroom and went next door.

Mom opened the door and led them into her spacious suite. As expected, the cabin was as neat as a pin; no clothes lay about, no personal items were anywhere. The only unexpected find was a pot of of tea and three cups on the coffee table.

Mom poured herself a cup of tea and then went to a club chair positioned in the corner of the room. She sat down and put a blanket over her lap.

Meredith sat in the love seat opposite her.

"Before you turn out the lights," Nina said, "I have something to show you, Mom."

Mom looked up. "Yes?"

Nina moved closer. In what felt to Meredith like slow motion, Nina pulled the photograph out of her pocket and handed it to Mom.

Mom drew in a sharp breath. What little color her face held drained away. "You went through my things?"

"We know the fairy tale takes place in Leningrad and that some of it is real. Who is Vera, Mom?" Nina asked. "And who are these children?"

Mom shook her head. "Do not ask me."

"We're your daughters," Meredith said gently, trying to soften the questions her sister had asked. "We just want to know you."

"It was what Dad wanted, too," Nina said.

Mom stared down at the photograph, which vibrated in her shaking hand. The room went so still they could hear the waves hitting the boat far below. "You are right. This is no fairy tale. But if you want to hear the rest of it, you will allow me to tell the story in the only way I can."

"But who—"

"No questions, Nina. Just listen." Mom might have looked pale and tired, but her voice was pure steel.

Nina sat down by Meredith, holding her hand. "Okay."

"Okay, then." Mom leaned back in the seat. Her finger moved over the photo, feeling its slick surface. For once, the lights were on as she started to speak. "Vera fell in love with Sasha on that day in the Summer Garden, and for her, this is a decision that will never change. Even though her mother disagrees, is afraid of Sasha's love of poetry, Vera is young and passionately in love with her husband, and when their first child is born, it seems like a miracle. Anastasia, they name her, and she is the light of Vera's life. When Leo is born the next year, Vera cannot imagine that it is possible to be happier, even though it is a bad time in the Soviet Union. The world knows this, they know of Stalin's evil. People are disappearing and dying. No one knows this better than Vera and Olga, who still cannot safely say their father's name. But in June of 1941, it is impossible to worry, or so it seems to Vera as she kneels in the

rich black earth and tends her garden. Here, on the outskirts of the city, she and Sasha have a small plat of land where they grow vegetables to carry them through the long white Leningrad winter. Vera still works in the library, while Sasha studies at university, learning only what Stalin allows. They become good Soviets, or at least quiet ones, for the black vans are everywhere these days. Sasha is only a year away from finishing his degree and he hopes to find a teaching position at one of the universities.

"Mama, look!" Leo calls out to her, holding up a tiny orange carrot, more root still than vegetable. Vera knows she should chastise him, but his smile is so infectious that she is lost. At four he has his father's golden curls and easy laugh. "Put the carrot back, Leo, it still needs time to grow."

*"*I told *him not to pull it up," says five-year-old Anya, who is as serious as her brother is joyous.*

"And you were right," Vera says, struggling not to smile. Though she is only twenty-two years old, the children have turned her into an adult; it is only when she and Sasha are alone that they are really still young.

When Vera finishes with her garden, she gathers up her children, takes one in each hand, and begins the long walk back to their apartment.

It is late afternoon by the time they return to Leningrad, and the streets are crowded with people running and shouting. At first Vera thinks it is just the belye nochi *that has energized everyone, but as she reaches the Fontanka Bridge, she begins to hear snippets of conversation, the start of a dozen arguments, a buzz of anxiety.*

*She hears a squawking sound coming through a speaker and the word—*Attention*—thrown like a knife into wood. Clutching her children's hands, she wades into the crowd just as the announcement begins. "Citizens of the Soviet Union . . . at four A.M. without declaration of war . . . German troops have attacked our country. . . ."*

The announcement goes on and on, telling them to be good Soviets, to enlist in the Red Army, to resist the enemy, but Vera cannot listen to anymore. All she can think is that she must get home.

The children are crying long before Vera gets back to the apartment near the Moika embankment. She hardly hears them. Though she is a mother, holding her own babies' hands, she is a daughter, too, and a wife, and it is her mother and husband whom she wants to see now. She takes her children up the dirty staircase, down hallways that are frighteningly quiet. In their own apartment, no lights are on, so it takes her eyes a moment to adjust.

Mama and Olga, still dressed in their work clothes, are at one of the windows, taping newsprint over the glass. At Vera's return, her mother stumbles back from the window she's been covering, saying, "Thank God," and takes Vera in her arms.

"We have things to do quickly," Mama says, and Olga finishes the window and comes over. Vera can see that Olga has been crying, her freckled cheeks are tracked in tears and her strawberry-blond hair is a mess. Olga has a nervous habit of pulling at her own hair when she is afraid.

"Vera," Mama says briskly. "You take Olga and go to the store. Buy whatever you can that will last. Buckwheat, honey, sugar, lard. Anything. I will run to the bank and get out all our money." Then she kneels in front of Leo and Anya. "You will stay here alone and wait for us to return."

Anya immediately whines. "I want to go with you, Baba."

Mama touches Anya's cheek. "Things are different now, even for children." She gets to her feet and grabs her purse from the other room, checking to make sure that her blue passbook is there.

The three of them leave the apartment, closing the door behind them, hearing the lock click into place. From the other side, there is crying almost immediately.

Vera looks at her mother. "I cannot just leave them here, locked in—"

"From now on, you will do many unimaginable things," her mother says tiredly. "Now let us go before it is too late."

Outside, the sky is a beautiful cloudless blue and the lilacs that grow beneath the first-floor windows scent the air. It seems impossible that war hangs over Leningrad on a day like this . . . until they turn the corner and come to the bank, where people are jammed together in a crowd at the closed door, waving their passbooks in the air and screaming; women are crying.

"We are too late already," Mama says.

"What is happening?" Olga asks, pulling nervously at her hair again, looking around. Beside her, an elderly woman makes a moaning sound and thumps to the ground in a heap. In seconds she is lost amid the crowd.

"The banks are closed for now. Too many people tried to take out their money." Mama chews on her lower lip until blood appears and then leads them down to the grocer's. Here, people are leaving with whatever they can carry. The shelves are practically empty. Already prices are doubling and tripling.

Vera has trouble making sense of this. War has just been announced and yet the supplies are gone already and the people around her look dazed and desperate.

"We have been here before," Mama says simply.

In the store, they have only enough money for buckwheat, flour, dried lentils, and lard. Carrying their meager supplies back through the crowded streets, they make it to the apartment at just past six.

Vera can hear her children crying and it breaks her heart. She opens the door and scoops them up. Leo throws his arms around her neck and hangs on, saying, "I missed you, Mama."

Vera thinks then that she will never again follow her mother's advice about this one thing: she will never leave her children alone.

"Where is your papa?" she asks Anya, who shrugs her small shoulders.

He should have been home by now.

"I'm sure he's fine," her mother says. "It will be difficult to get through the streets."

Worry gnaws at Vera, though, sharpening its bite with every passing minute. Finally, at eight o'clock, he comes into the apartment. The side of his face is dirty and his hair is damp with sweat.

"Verushka," he says, pulling her into his arms, holding her so tightly she cannot breathe. "The trolleys were full. I ran all the way here. Are you okay?"

"Now we are," she says.

And she believes it.

That night, while her grandmother snores in the hot darkness, Vera sits up in her bed. The big crisscross of tape and newsprint on the windows lets only the merest light through. Beyond it, the city is strangely, eerily silent. It is as if Leningrad itself has drawn in a sharp breath and is afraid to exhale.

In this shadowy darkness, their apartment seems even smaller and more jumbled. With three narrow beds in the living area and the children's cots in the kitchen, there is barely room to walk in here anymore. Even at mealtimes they cannot all be together. There isn't enough room at the table or chairs to go around it.

Not far away, Mama and Olga are awake, too, sitting up in their bed. Beside Vera, Sasha is as silent as she's ever seen him.

"I don't know what we're supposed to do," Olga says. At nineteen, she should be thinking of love and romance and her future, not war. "Maybe the Germans will save us. Comrade Stalin—"

"Shhh," Mama says sharply, glancing over at her sleeping mother. Some things can never be said aloud. Olga should know this by now.

"Tomorrow we will go to work," Mama says. "And the next day we do the same, and the next day after that. Now we must go to sleep. Here, Olga, roll over. I will hold you."

Vera hears the squeaking of the tired bed as they settle down to sleep. She stretches out beside her husband, tries to feel safe in his arms. There is too little light to see his face clearly; he is just gray and black patches, but his breathing is steady and sure and the sound of it, in rhythm to the beating of her heart, calms her down. She touches his cheek, feels the soft stubble of new growth, as familiar to her now as the wedding band she wears. She leans forward to kiss him, and for a moment, when his lips are on hers, there is nothing else, but then he draws back and says, "You will have to be strong, Verushka."

"We will be strong," she says, holding him in her arms.

Two nights later they are awakened by gunfire.

Vera launches out of bed, her heart pounding. She falls over her mother's bed as she tries to get to her children. Gunfire rattles the thin windows, and she can hear footsteps in the hallway and people screaming.

"Hurry," Sasha says, sounding surprisingly calm. He herds them all together while Mama takes as much food as she can carry. It is not until they are outside in the street, huddled with the crowd of their neighbors beneath a pale blue sky, that they understand: these are Russian antiaircraft guns, practicing for what is to come.

There are no shelters on their street. It is Mama who organizes the people in her building: tomorrow they will go to the storage area in the basement and make a shelter.

Finally, amid the sound of gunfire and the preternatural silence between bursts, Sasha looks down at Vera. Leo is asleep in his arms (the boy can sleep through anything) and Anya is beside him, worriedly sucking her thumb and caressing the end of her blanket. It is a baby habit that was long gone before the start of the war and is now back.

"You know I have to go," Sasha says to Vera.

She shakes her head, thinking suddenly that this gunfire means nothing; the look on her husband's face is infinitely more frightening.

"I am a university student and poet," he says. "And you are the daughter of a criminal of the state."

"You haven't published any of your poetry—"

"I am suspect, Vera, and you know this. So are you."

"You cannot go. I won't let you."

"It is done, Vera," is what he says. "I joined the People's Volunteer Army."

Mama is beside her then, clutching her arm. "Of course you are going, Sasha," she says evenly, and Vera hears the warning in her mother's tone. Always it is about appearances. Even now, as the gunfire explodes all around them, a black van prowls in the street.

"It is the right thing to do," Sasha says. "We are the Soviet Army. The best in the world. We will kick the Germans' asses in no time and I will be home."

Vera feels little Anya beside her, holding her hand, listening to every word, and so, too, their neighbors, and even strangers. She knows what she is supposed to feel and to say, but doesn't know if she has the strength for it. Her father had once said to her much the same thing: Do not worry, Veronika Petrovna, I will always be here for you.

"Promise you'll come back to me," she says.

"I promise," he says easily.

But Vera knows: there are some promises that are pointless to ask for and useless to receive. When she turns to her mother, this truth passes between them, and Vera understands her own childhood. She will have to be strong for her children.

She looks up at her husband. "It is a promise I will hold you to, Aleksandr Ivanovich."

In the morning, she wakens early; in the quiet darkness, she finds her one photograph of them, taken on the day of their wedding.

She looks down at their bright and smiling faces. Tears blur the image as she takes it out of the frame and folds it in half and then in half again. She tucks it in the pocket of his coat.

She hears footsteps behind her, feels his hands on her shoulders.

"I love you, Veruskhka," he says softly, kissing the side of her face.

She is glad he is behind her. She is not sure she has the strength to look him in the eyes when she says, "I love you, too, Sasha."

Come back to me.

In no time at all, he is gone.

Nineteen

Vera and Olga are lucky in their jobs. Olga works in the Hermitage Museum and Vera in the Leningrad Public Library. Now both of them spend their days in dark, quiet rooms, crating up masterpieces of art and literature so that the history of the Soviet state will never be lost. When work is over for the day, Vera walks home by herself. Sometimes she goes out of her way to see the Summer Garden and remember the day she met Sasha, but it is getting harder and harder to recall. Already the face of Leningrad is changing. The Bronze Horseman is covered in sandbags and wooden planks. Camouflage nets hang over the Smolny; gray paint has been splashed over the golden spires of the Admiralty. Everywhere she looks, people are busy—building air-raid shelters, standing in line for food, digging trenches. The skies overhead are still blue and cloudless, and no bombs have dropped on them yet, but it is coming and they know it. Every day the speakers blare out reports of the advancements of the German troops. No one believes that the Germans will reach Leningrad—not their magical city built on mud and bones—but bombs will fall here. They have no doubt about that.

On her way home, Vera stops by the bank and withdraws the two hundred rubles she is allowed for the month, and when she has her money, she stands in line for three loaves of bread and a tin of cheese. Today she is lucky; there is food at the end of her long wait. Sometimes she gets to the front of the line only to see it close.

When she finally gets home at eight o'clock, she finds Anya and Leo playing war in the living room, jumping from bed to bed, making shooting sounds at each other.

"Mama!" Leo cries when he sees her. His face breaks into a gummy grin and he runs toward her, throwing himself in her arms. Anya is close on his heels, but she doesn't hug Vera so tightly. Anya is aggrieved by this business of war and she wants everyone to know it. She does not like spending her days in nursery school and not coming home until six o'clock, and then with "smelly Mrs. Newsky from next door."

"How are my babies?" Vera asks, pulling Anya into her arms anyway. "What did you two do in school today?"

"I am too old for baby school," Anya informs her, scrunching her face in concentration.

Vera pats her daughter's head and goes into the kitchen. She is at the stove putting water on to boil when Olga comes into the apartment.

"Have you heard?" she says breathlessly.

Vera turns around. "What is it?"

Olga glances nervously at Anya and Leo, who are playing with sticks. "The children of Leningrad," she says, lowering her voice. "They're being evacuated."

On the morning of the evacuation, Vera wakens feeling sick. She cannot do it, cannot put her babies on a train bound for somewhere far away and then just go on with her life. She lies in bed, alone, as private a time as exists in this crowded apartment, staring up at the rust-stained, water-marked ceiling. She can hear her mother turning restlessly and Olga snoring quietly in the bed only two feet away.

"Vera?" Mama says.

Vera turns onto her side.

Mama is looking at her. They are close, in their side-by-side beds, almost close enough to touch. A threadbare blanket falls from Mama's shoulder when Olga rolls over. "You cannot think it," she says, and Vera wonders if one day she will know what her children are thinking before they do.

"How can I not?" Vera says. All her life she has understood what it is to be a good Soviet, how to follow the rules and keep one's head down and make no move that draws attention. But this . . . how can she blindly do this thing?

"Comrade Stalin has eyes everywhere. He is surely watching the Germans, and he knows where our children can go so that they will be safe. And all workers' children must go. That is all there is."

"What if I don't see them again?"

Mama peels back the cover and gets out of bed, crossing the tiny space between them. She gets into bed, takes Sasha's side, and pulls Vera into her arms, stroking her black hair as she used to when Vera was young. "We women make choices for others, not for ourselves, and when we are mothers, we . . . bear what we must for our children. You will protect them. It will hurt you; it will hurt them. Your job is to hide that your heart is breaking and do what they need you to do."

"Sasha told me I would have to be strong."

Mama nods. "I don't think men understand, though. Even your Sasha. They march off with their guns and their ideas and they think they know courage."

"You're talking about Papa now."

"Maybe I am."

They lay for a while longer without talking.

For the first time in a long time, she is thinking about her father. As much as it hurts, it is better than dwelling on what is to come. She closes her eyes and in the darkness she is on the street in front of their old apartment, watching her papa leave.

Her fingers are freezing beneath her woolen gloves and her toes tingle with the cold.

"I want to come to the café with you," she pleads, tilting her face up to him. A light snow is falling around them; flakes land on her bare cheeks.

He smiles down at her, his big black mustache beetling above his lip. "This is no place for a girl, you know this, Veruskha."

"But you'll be reading your poetry. And Anna Akhmatova will be there. She is a woman."

"Yes," he says, trying to look stern. "A woman. You are still a girl."

"One day," he says, pressing a gloved hand to her shoulder, "you will write your beautiful words. By then they will be teaching literature again in our schools instead of this terrible Soviet realism that is Stalin's idea of progress. Be patient. Wave to me when I'm across the street, and then go inside."

She stands there in the snow, watching him go. Tiny kisses of white fire land on her cheeks, almost immediately turning to spots of water that slide downward, slipping like cold fingers beneath her collar.

Soon he is only a blur, a smear of gray wool moving in all that white. She thinks perhaps he has stopped to wave to her, but she cannot be sure. Instead, she sees how night falls on the snow, how it changes the color and textures, and she tries to place this in her memory so that she can describe it in her journal.

"Do you remember when I used to dream of being a writer?" Vera says quietly now.

It is a long time before her mother says, even more softly, "I remember all of it."

"Maybe someday—"

"Shhh," her mother says, stroking her hair. "It will only hurt more. This I know."

Vera hears the disappointment in Mama's voice, and the acceptance. Vera wonders if one day she will sound like that, too, if it will seem easier to give up. Before she can think of what to say, she hears Leo in the kitchen. No doubt he is talking to the stuffed rabbit that is his best friend.

Vera thinks, It has begun. *She feels her mother's kiss, hears words whispered at her ear, but she cannot understand them. The roar in her head is too loud. She eases out from the bed and sits up. Although this morning is warm, as was the night before, she is dressed in a skirt and a sweater. A battered pair of shoes waits at the end of the bed. They are all sleeping in their clothes now. An air raid can come at any time.*

The sound of movements overtake the small apartment: Olga whines that she is still sleepy and her arms ache from loading art into boxes; her grandmother blows her nose; Anya informs everyone that she is hungry.

It is all so ordinary.

Vera swallows the lump that has formed in her throat, but it will not go away. In the kitchen, she sees Leo—the spitting image of his father, with angelic golden curls and expressive green eyes. Leo. Her lion. He is laughing now, telling his poor one-eyed, tattered rabbit that maybe they will get to feed the swans in the Summer Garden today.

"It is war," Anya says, looking impossibly superior for a five-year-old. Her lisp turns the sentence into something softer, but all of Anya's fire is in her eyes. She is pure steel, this girl; exactly how Vera once imagined herself to be.

"Actually," Vera says. "We are going on a walk." She feels physically ill when she says it, but her mother comes up behind her;

with a touch, Vera can go on. She crosses the room and picks up their coats. Last night, Vera stayed up late, sewing money and letters into the lining of her babies' coats.

Leo is on his feet in an instant, gleefully clapping his hands, saying, "Walk!" over and over. Even Anya is smiling. It has only been five days since the announcement of war, but in those days their old life has disappeared.

Breakfast passes like a funeral procession, in quiet glances and lowered gazes. No one except Mama can look at Vera. At the end of the meal, her grandmother rises. When she looks at Vera, her eyes fill with tears and she turns away.

"Come, Zoya," her grandmother says in a harsh voice. "It does not look good to be late."

Vera can see that her mother's lip is bleeding from where she has bitten it. She goes to her grandchildren and kneels down, taking them in her arms and holding them.

"Don't cry, Baba," Leo says. "You can walk with us tomorrow."

Across the room, Olga bursts into tears and tries immediately to control herself. "I am going now, Mama."

Mama lets go slowly and gets back to her feet. "Be good," is the last thing she says to her grandchildren. She hands Vera one hundred rubles. "It is all we have left. I'm sorry. . . ."

Vera nods and hugs her mother one last time. Then she straightens. "Let's go, children."

It is a beautiful sunny day. The six of them walk together for as long as they can; Mama and Baba leave first, turning toward the Badayev food warehouses where they both work; Olga leaves next. She hugs her niece and nephew fiercely and tries to hide her tears and she runs toward her trolley stop.

Now it is just Vera and her children, walking down the busy street. All around her, trenches are being dug, shelters are being built. They stop in the Summer Garden, but the swans are gone from the pond and the statues are sandbagged. There are no children playing here today, no bicycle rings bleating out.

Smiling too brightly, Vera takes her children by the hands and leads them to a part of the city where they have never been.

Inside the building that they enter there is pandemonium. Queues snake through the hall in every direction, flowing away from desks overrun with paperwork, manned by Party members in drab clothing with dour, disappointed faces.

Vera knows they should go directly into the first processing queue and wait their turn, but suddenly she is not as strong as she needs to be. Taking a deep breath, she takes her children to a corner. It is not quiet here—the sounds of people are everywhere—footsteps, crying, sneezing, begging. The whole place smells of body odor and onions and cured meat.

Vera kneels down.

Anya is frowning. "It smells in here, Mama."

"Comrade Floppy doesn't like this place," Leo says, hugging his bunny.

"Do you remember, when Papa went off to join the Peoples' Volunteer Army, he told us we would all have to be strong?"

"I'm strong," Leo says, showing off a pudgy pink fist.

"Yes," Anya says. She is suspicious now. Vera sees that her daughter is looking at the coats in Vera's arms and the suitcase she has brought from home.

Vera takes the heavy red woolen coat and puts it on Anya, buttoning it up to her throat. "It is too hot for this, Mama," Anya whines, wiggling.

"You're going on a trip," Vera says evenly. "Not for long. Just a week or two. And you might need your coat. And here . . . here in this suitcase I have packed a few more clothes and some food. Just in case."

"You are not wearing a coat," Anya says, frowning.

"I . . . uh . . . I have to work and stay at home, but you will be home before you know it and I'll be waiting for you. When you get back—"

"No," Anya says firmly. "I don't want to go without you."

"I don't want to," Leo wails.

"We have no choice. You understand what this means? War is coming, and our great Comrade Stalin wants you children to be safe. You're going to take a short train ride south until our Red Army triumphs. Then you will come home to Papa and me."

Leo is crying now.

"You want us to go?" Anya asks, her blue eyes filling with tears.

No, *Vera thinks, even as she nods. "I need you to take care of your brother," she says. "You are so strong and smart. You will stay with him always, and never wander off. Okay? Can you be strong for me?"*

"Yes, Mama," Anya says.

For the next five hours, they stand in one queue after another. The children are processed and sorted and sent to other lines. By the end of the afternoon, the evacuation center is literally overrun with children and their mothers but the place is strangely quiet. The children sit as they are told, their faces shiny with sweat in the coats they shouldn't need, their legs swinging in front of them. None of the mothers look at each other; it hurts too much to see your own pain reflected in another woman's eyes.

And finally the train arrives. Metal wheels scream; smoke billows into the air. At first the crowd just sits there—no one wants to move—but when the whistle pierces the silence, they run like a herd, mothers bustling past each other, elbowing hard, trying to get their babies seats on the train that will save them.

Vera pushes her way to the front of the queue. The train seems alive beside her, breathing smoke, clanging. Party members patrol the area like sharks, forcing mothers to part with their children. Leo is sobbing, clutching Vera. Anya is crying, too, but in a silent way that is somehow worse.

"Take care of each other and stay together. Do not give your food to anyone else. There is money sewn into your pockets if you

need it, and my name and address, too." She pins little name tags on their lapels.

"Where are we going?" Anya asks. She is trying to be grown-up; it is heartbreaking in one so young. At five, she should be playing with dolls, not standing in lines to leave her home.

"To the country, a summer park near the Luga River. You will be safe there, Anya. And in no time, I will come for you." Vera plays with the tag pinned to Anya's lapel, as if touching the little piece of identification will help.

"Get on board," a comrade yells out. "Now. The train is leaving."

Vera hugs her daughter, and then her son, and then she straightens slowly, feeling as if her bones are breaking as she does it.

Other people are handling her babies now, grabbing them, handing them to other people.

They are crying and waving. Anya is holding Leo's hand; she shows her mama how tightly she is holding on, how strong she is being.

And then they are gone.

At first Vera cannot make herself move. People push her out of the way, muttering desperate, feral curses. Do they not see that she is paralyzed, that she cannot move? Finally someone pushes hard enough that she falls to her knees. She can feel children being handed off over her head, passed from one to another of the adults.

Vera climbs slowly to her feet, noticing dully that her stockings have ripped at the knees. She moves aside, searching the train's windows, starting to run from car to car until she realizes that her children are too little to be seen.

So little.

Has she told them everything?

Keep your coat; winter comes on fast, even though they say you'll be back in a week.

Never be apart from each other.

Brush your teeth.

Eat your food. All of it. And get to the front of the line at every meal.

Watch out for each other.

I love you.

At that, Vera stumbles, almost falls. She didn't tell them she loved them. She'd been afraid it would make them all cry harder, so she'd withheld the precious words, the only ones that really mattered.

She makes a sound. The pain of it comes from someplace deep, deep inside and it just erupts. Screaming, she shoves her way back into the crowd of people, elbows her way past women who stare at her with blank, desperate eyes. She fights her way to the train.

"I am a nonessential worker," she says to the woman at the head of the line, who looks too tired to care.

"Paperwork?"

"I have dropped it in that mess," she says, indicating the crowd. The lie tastes bitter on her tongue and makes her sick to her stomach. It is the kind of thing that draws attention, and nothing—not even war—is as frightening as the attention of the secret police. She draws herself upright. "The workers are not controlling the evacuation. It's not efficient. Perhaps I should report this to someone."

The criticism works. The tired woman straightens, nods briskly. "Yes, comrade. You are right. I will be more careful."

"Good." Vera's heart is pounding in her chest as she walks past her into the train. At every step she is certain that someone will come for her, yell, Fraud! *and haul her away.*

But no one comes and finally she slows down, seeing the sea of children's faces around her. They are packed like sardines in the gray seats, bundled in coats and hats on this sunny summer's day—proof that no one believes they'll be home in two weeks, although no one would dare say it. Their faces are round and sheened with tears or sweat. They are quiet. So quiet. No talking or laughing or playing. They just sit there, looking broken and numb. There are a few women around. Evacuation workers, nursery school teachers, and probably some like Vera, who could neither let their children go nor defy an order of the state.

She does not want to think about what she has done or what it will mean to her family. They desperately need the money she earns at the library. . . .

The train seems to waken beneath her. The whistle blows and she can feel it start to move. Barely touching the seats, unable to make eye contact with the children around her, she keeps going, from one car to another.

"Mama!"

She hears Anya's voice spike above the rattling wheeze of the train. Vera claws her way forward to the small seat where her children sit huddled together, their heads too low to allow them to peer out the window.

She slides into the seat, pulling them both onto her lap and smothering them with kisses.

Leo's round face, wet with sweat and tears, is already dirty, although she cannot imagine how he made that happen. His eyes are damp with tears, but he doesn't cry this time, and Vera wonders if her good-bye did something to him, if now he is less innocent or not quite so young. "You said we had to go."

Vera's throat feels so tight it is all she can do to nod.

"I held his hand, Mama," Anya says solemnly. "Every minute."

Like all good Soviets, Vera does not allow herself to question the government. If Comrade Stalin wants to protect the children by taking them south, she puts them on the train. Her great act of defiance, going with them, seems like a small thing, and the farther she gets from Leningrad, the smaller it seems. She will see

that they are safe at their destination and when she knows that all is well, she will return to her job at the library. If she is lucky it won't take more than a day or two. She will explain to her boss, Comrade Plotkin, that it was her patriotic duty to accompany the children on this state-mandated evacuation.

Words matter here in the Soviet Union. Words like patriotic, efficient, essential. *No one wants to question the wrong thing. If Vera can act certain and fearless, perhaps she will be okay.*

If only Mama will not worry too much. Or Olga.

"Mama, I'm hungry," Leo says grumpily. He is curled into her lap like a tiny fiddlehead fern; his stuffed gray bunny clutched in his arms. He is sucking his thumb and stroking the soft pink satin inside the rabbit's floppy ear.

They have been on the train only a few hours and no one has said a thing about meals or stopping or when they will arrive at their destination.

"Soon, my little lion," Vera says, patting his padded shoulder. She can see the way the children on the train are coming out of their numbness, growing restless. A few whine; someone starts to cry. Vera is about to reach down for the small bag of raisins she has brought with her when the train's whistle shrieks. It doesn't stop this time, doesn't blast once as if at a crossing and then go still. Instead, the sound goes on and on, like a woman's scream. The brakes lock, make a grinding noise, and the train shudders in response, starts to slow.

Gunfire erupts all around them. There is the whine of an airplane engine and the explosions start.

Vera looks outside, sees fire everywhere. Panic breaks out in the train. Everyone is screaming and running to the windows.

A woman in a Party shirt and wrinkled blue wool pants makes her way through the car, saying, "Everyone off of the train. Go. To the barn behind us. Now!"

Vera grabs her children and runs. It occurs to her later, when she is at the front of the line, that she is an adult, that she should have helped the unaccompanied children, but she is not thinking straight. The airplanes keep flying overhead; the bombs drop and fires start.

Outside, all is smoke and screaming. She can hardly see anything but destruction—burning buildings, black and smoldering holes in the ground, ruined houses.

The Germans are here, pushing forward with their tanks and their guns and their bombs.

Vera sees a man coming toward her; he is wearing an army uniform. "Where are we?"

"About forty kilometers south of the Luga River," he yells as he runs past her.

She pulls her children in closer. They are crying now, their faces streaked with black. They run with the crowd to a giant barn and cram together inside.

It is hot in here, and it smells of fear and fire and sweat. They can hear the airplanes overhead and feel the bombs that shake the ground.

"They took us right to the Germans," some woman says bitterly.

"Shhh," comes at once from dozens of others, but it cannot be unsaid. The truth of it sticks in Vera's mind like a shred of metal and cannot be dislodged.

All of these people—children, mostly—waiting for a night that won't fall, for protection that may not come at all. How can you trust a leader who sends his country's children directly into the enemy?

Thank God she is with them. What if they had been alone?

She knows she will think this later, and for a long time; she will probably weep with relief. But later. Now she must act.

"We need to leave this barn," she says, quietly at first, but when another bomb hits close enough to rattle the rafters and send dust raining down on them, she says it again, louder: "We need to leave this barn. If a bomb hits us—"

"Citizen," someone says, "the Party wants us here."

"Yes, but . . . our children." She does not say what is on her mind; she cannot. But many know anyway. She can see it in their eyes. "I am taking my children out of here. I will take anyone who wants to go."

There is grumbling around her. She is hardly surprised. Her country is a place of great fear these days, and no one knows which is more likely to kill you—the Germans or the secret police.

She tightens her hold on her children's hands and begins to move slowly through the crowd. Even the children ease sideways to let her pass. The eyes that meet hers are distrustful and afraid.

"I will come with you," one woman says. She is old and wrinkled, her gray hair hidden beneath a dirty kerchief. Four children stand clustered around her, dressed for winter, their pale faces streaked with ash.

They are the only ones.

Vera and the woman and their six children make their way out of the barn, past all the silent children. Outside, the countryside is gray with smoke.

"We might as well start walking," the woman says.

"How far are we from Leningrad?" Vera asks, wondering if she has done the right thing. She feels exposed now, vulnerable to the airplanes flying overhead. To her left, a bomb falls and a building explodes.

"About ninety kilometers," the woman says. "It will do us no good to talk."

Vera hefts Leo into her arms and holds on to Anya. She knows that she will not be able to carry her son for long, but she wants to start out that way. Just in case. She can feel his strong, steady heartbeat against her own.

In the years to come, she will forget the hardships of that journey, how her children's feet blistered until they bled, how their food ran out, how they slept in hay barns like criminals, listening all night for air raids and falling bombs, how they woke in a panic, thinking they'd been shot, feeling blindly for wounds that were not there. Instead, she will remember the lorry drivers who picked them up, and the people who stopped to give them bread and ask them what they'd seen down south. She will remember how she told them what she hadn't known before: that war is about fire and fear and bodies lying in ditches by the side of the road.

By the time she gets home and stumbles into her mother's welcoming arms, she is battered and tired and bloody; her shoes have worn through in places and the pain in her feet will not ease, even in a pail of hot water. But none of this matters. Not now.

What matters is Leningrad, her wonderful white city. The Germans are moving toward her home. Hitler has vowed to wipe this city off the map.

Vera knows what she must do.

Tomorrow, very early in the morning, she will get out of her narrow bed and dress in layers. She will pack all the sausage and dried fruit she can carry, and like thousands of other women her age, she will go south again to protect all that she loves. It is every citizen's job.

"We have to stop them at Luga," she says to her mother, whose face crumples in understanding. "They need workers there."

Mama does not ask why or how or why you? All of those answers are clear. It is only the first full week of war, and already Leningrad is becoming a city of women. Every man between fourteen and sixty has gone to fight. Now the girls are going off to war, too. "I will take care of the children," is all her mother says, but Vera can hear You come back to us *as clearly as if it had been spoken aloud.*

"I won't be gone long," Vera promises. "The library will call me patriotic. All will be fine."

Mama only nods. They both know it is a fiction, this promise of Vera's, but they say nothing. Both of them want to believe.

Twenty

I think that is enough for tonight," Mom said.

Meredith was the first to stand. Moving almost cautiously, she crossed the small, carpeted space and stood beside Mom. "You don't look as tired tonight."

"Acceptance," Mom said, staring down at her own hands.

The unexpected answer brought Nina to her feet. She moved in beside her sister. "What do you mean by that?"

"You were right, Nina. Your father made me promise to tell you this story. I did not want to. And fighting a thing tires you out."

"Is that why you went so . . . crazy after Dad died?" Meredith asked. "Because you were ignoring his wishes?"

"That is perhaps one of the reasons," her mother said, giving a little shrug, as if to say that reasons didn't matter much.

Nina and Meredith stood there a moment longer, but whatever slim strand of intimacy had been created tonight was gone now. Again, Mom would barely make eye contact with them.

"Okay," Meredith finally said. "We'll come get you in the morning for breakfast."

"I do not want—"

"We do," Nina said in a voice that silenced her mother's protest. "Tomorrow the three of us are going to be together. You can discuss it or argue or yell at me, but you know that I won't change my mind and in the end I'll get my way."

"She's right," Meredith said, smiling. "She's a bitch when she doesn't get her way."

"How would we know?" Mom said.

"Was that a joke?" Nina said, grinning.

It was like seeing the sun for the first time or riding your first two-wheeler. The whole world suddenly brightened.

"Go away," Mom said, but Nina could tell that she was trying not to smile with them, and just that little change gave Nina wings.

"Come on, big sis," she said, slinging an arm around Meredith.

They left Mom's stateroom for their own room.

Their long, narrow room was surprisingly spacious. There was a small sitting area—a love seat that could be made into a bed—a coffee table, a television, and two twin beds. A pair of sliding doors led to their private veranda. Nina turned on the television, which showed the ship's progress on a nautical map. There was no cell phone or Internet service out here in the waters off British Columbia, and no television programming. If they wanted to watch a movie, they needed to borrow one from the ship's library.

"Dibs on the bathroom," Meredith said as soon as they closed the door behind them, and Nina couldn't help laughing. It was a sentence straight from their youth.

Meredith is on my side, Dad, tell her to scoot over.

Nina broke my rock 'em sock 'em robot on purpose.

Don't make me stop this car, you two.

Nina couldn't help smiling at that last one. When Meredith came out of the bathroom, looking squeaky clean and ready for bed in her pink flannel pajamas, Nina took her turn and got ready for bed. For the first time in years, she and her sister ended up in side-by-side twin beds.

"You're smiling," Meredith said.

"I was just thinking about our camping trips."

" 'Don't make me stop this car.' " Meredith said, and they both laughed. For a magical moment, the years fell away and they were kids again, fighting over an inch of space in the backseat of a bright red Cadillac convertible, with John Denver singing about being high in the mountains.

"Mom never joined in," Meredith said, her smile fading.

"How did she stay so quiet?"

"I always thought it was because she didn't give a shit, but now I wonder. Dad was right: the fairy tale is changing everything."

Nina nodded and leaned back. "The picture," she said after a moment. "It's Anya and Leo, right?"

"Probably."

Nina turned to look at her sister. The question that had been beside them all night, gathering weight and mass, was close now, impossible to ignore. "If Mom really is Vera," she said slowly, "what happened to her children?"

Nina had been all over the world, but rarely had she seen scenery to rival the magnificence of the Inside Passage. The water was a deep, mysterious blue, and there were islands everywhere—rough, forested hillocks of land that looked exactly as they had two hundred years ago. Behind it all were rugged, snow-draped mountains.

She had come out early this morning and been rewarded with breathtaking shots of dawn breaking across the water. She caught an orca breaching off the bow of the ship, its giant black and white body a stark contrast to the bronzed early morning sky.

She finally stopped shooting at about seven-thirty. By then her hands were frozen and her teeth were chattering so hard it was difficult to keep the camera steady.

"Would you like some hot chocolate, ma'am?"

Nina turned away from the railing and the exquisite view, and found a fresh-faced young deck steward holding a tray of cups and a thermos of hot chocolate. It sounded so good she didn't even mind that the girl had called her ma'am. "That would be great. Thanks."

The steward smiled. "There are blankets on the deck chairs, too."

"Does it ever get warm up here?" Nina asked, wrapping her cold fingers around the warm cup.

"Maybe in August." The girl smiled. "It's beautiful in Alaska, but the climate isn't too friendly."

Nina thanked the steward and went over to one of the wooden deck chairs. She scooped up a heavy, plaid woolen blanket, swung it around her shoulders, and went back to the railing. There, she stared out at the sparkling blue water. A trio of dolphins swam alongside the ship, jumping and diving in perfect synchronicity.

"That's a sign of good luck," Meredith said, coming up beside her.

Nina opened one arm, let Meredith snuggle under the blanket beside her. "It's cold as hell out here."

"But beautiful."

Up ahead, a lone lighthouse stood at the rugged green end of an island.

"You were restless last night," Meredith said, reaching for Nina's hot chocolate.

"How do you know?"

"I'm an insomniac lately. It's one of the many prizes you find in the Cracker Jack box of a crumbling marriage. I'm always exhausted and I never sleep. So why were you tossing and turning?"

"We're three days away from Juneau."

"And?"

"I found him."

Meredith turned to her. The blanket slipped out of Nina's fingers and slid downward. "What do you mean, you found him?"

"The professor of Russian studies. Dr. Adamovich. He's in a nursing home on Franklin Street in Juneau. I had my editor track him down."

"So that's why we're on this cruise. I should have guessed. Did you speak to him?"

"No."

Meredith bit down on her lip and looked out at the water. "What are we supposed to do? Can we just show up at his door?"

"I didn't really think it through. I know. I know. Big surprise. I just got so amped when I found him. I know he'll have answers for us."

"He wrote to *her*. Not us. I don't think we can tell her. She's . . . fragile, Neens. Dad was right about that."

"I know. That's why I wasn't sleeping. We can't tell her we've been researching her life, and we can't just show up at the professor's nursing home, and we can't sneak away for a day after all the fuss I made about us being together. And if we did sneak away, he might not talk to us anyway. It's her he wanted to see."

"I can see how all that would keep you up. Especially with the rest of it."

"The rest of it?"

"Your nature, Neens. You can't not see him."

"I know. So what do we do?"

"We will go see the professor."

Nina gasped at the sound of her mother's voice and turned around. In her surprise, she caught the side of her cup on the railing and hot chocolate splashed everywhere.

"Mom," Meredith stammered.

"You heard it all?" Nina said, licking chocolate from her fingers. She knew she looked calm—it was one of the many things photojournalism had taught her: how to look calm even if your insides were shaking—but her voice was uneven. Things were going so well with Mom lately; she hated to think she'd ruined that.

"I heard enough," Mom said. "It is the professor from Alaska, yes? The one who wrote to me years ago?"

Nina nodded. She pulled the blanket off of her and Meredith and carried it over to Mom, wrapping it around her thin shoulders. "It was me, Mom. Not Meredith."

Mom held the blanket closed at her breast, her fingers pale against the red plaid. She glanced at the deck chair beside her and sat down, covering herself carefully with the blanket.

Nina and Meredith took chairs on either side of her, flipping the blankets out, too. A steward came by and offered them each a hot chocolate.

"I'm sorry, Mom," Nina said. "I should have told you at the beginning."

"You thought I would not agree to the trip."

"Yes," Nina said. "It's just that I want to get to know you. And not only because I promised Dad."

"You want answers."

"How can I—how can *we*," she said, including Meredith in this, "not want answers? You are part of who we are, and we don't know you. Maybe it's why we don't know ourselves. Meredith can't figure out if she loves her husband or what her own dream is. And I've got a man waiting for me in Atlanta and all I can think about is Vera."

Mom leaned back onto the teak chair. "It is time, I suppose," she said quietly. "Your father spoke to Professor Adamovich, I believe, although I never did. He thought we should talk—*I* should talk. It's probably why he kept the letter all these years."

"What does the professor want to talk about?" It was Meredith who asked this, and although her voice was quiet, the look in her eyes was intent.

"Leningrad," Mom said. "For years the government hid what happened. We Soviets are good at hiding things, and I was afraid to talk about it. But there is no reason for fear now. I am eighty-one years old tomorrow. Why be afraid?"

"Tomorrow is your birthday?" they said at once.

Mom almost smiled. "It was easier to hide everything. Yes, tomorrow is my birthday." She sipped her hot chocolate. "I will go see this professor with you, but you two should know now: you will be sorry you began all of this."

"Why do you say that?" Meredith asked. "How could we be sorry to learn who you are?"

It was a long moment before Mom answered. Slowly, she turned to Meredith and said, "You will."

Ketchikan was a town built on salmon: catching it, salting it, processing it. The rain gauge—called a liquid-sunshine-o-meter—attested to the dampness of the climate.

"Look at that," Meredith said, pointing to a grassy area across the street where a man with long black hair was carving a totem pole. A crowd was gathered around him, watching.

Nina dared to reach for her mother's arm. "Let's go check it out." She was surprised when Mom nodded and let Nina guide her across the street to the small park.

Rain started to fall as they stood there. Most of the crowd dispersed, running for cover, but Mom just stood there, watching the man work. In his capable hands, the metal instrument cut and gouged and changed the wood from rough to smooth. They saw a paw begin to appear.

"It is a bear," Mom said, and the man looked up.

"You have a good eye," he said.

Nina could see now how old he was. His dark skin was lined and leathery, and the hair at his temples was gray.

"This is for my son," the man said, pointing to the beaked bird at the base of the totem pole. "This is our clan. The raven. And this thunderbird brought the storm that washed the road away. And this bear is my son. . . ."

"So it's a family history," Meredith said.

"A burial totem. To remember him."

"It's beautiful," Mom said, and just then, in the falling rain, Nina heard the voice of the fairy tale, and for the first time it made sense. She understood why her mother only told the story in the dark and why her voice was so different: it was about loss. The voice was how her mother sounded when she let her guard down.

They stood there long enough to see the bear's claw take shape. Then they finally walked toward Creek Street. Here, the old red-light district had been transformed into a boardwalk of shops and restaurants positioned above a river. They found a cozy little diner with a view and sat down at a knotty pine table by the window.

The street outside was full of tourists with shopping bags, moving like wildebeests in the migration season from one store to the next, even in the rain. The bells above the store doors were chiming a random tune.

"Welcome to Captain Hook's," said a cute young waitress dressed in bright yellow overalls and a red checked blouse. A yellow fisherman's hat sat firmly on her brown curls. A name tag identified her as Brandi. She handed them each a large laminated menu in the shape of a fishhook.

In no time at all the waitress returned to take their orders, which were three fish-and-chips baskets and iced teas. When she left, Meredith said, "I wonder what our family totem would look like."

There was a moment's pause after that. In it, they all looked up, made eye contact.

"Dad would be the bottom," Nina said. "He was the start of us."

"A bear," Meredith said. "Nina would be an eagle."

An eagle. A loner. Ready to fly away. She frowned a little, wishing she could disagree. Her life had left markers all over the world, but very few at home. No one's totem would include her except this family's, and while that was what she'd always wanted—to be totally free and independent—it felt lonely just now. "Meredith would be a lioness who cares for everyone and keeps the pride together."

"What would you be, Mom?" Meredith asked.

Mom shrugged. "I would not be there, I think."

"You think you left no mark on us?" Nina asked.

"Not one that begs to be remembered."

"Dad loved you for more than fifty years," Meredith said. "That's not nothing."

Mom took a sip of her iced tea and stared out the window at the rain.

The waitress returned with their food. Nina got up quickly and whispered a request, and then sat down again. As they ate the delicious halibut and fries, they talked about the day in Ketchikan—the gold nugget jewelry in the windows of the shops, the ornate First Nations tribal art, the Cowichan sweaters the locals wore, and the bald eagle they'd seen perched on a totem pole in town. It was a conversation that could have been had by any family on vacation in town, but to Nina it felt almost magical. As her mother spoke about things that interested her, she seemed to soften. It was as if every ordinary word loosened something in her until by the end of the meal she was smiling.

The waitress returned and cleared their plates. Instead of placing the bill on the wooden table, she set a piece of birthday cake in front of Mom. Its lit candle danced above the buttercream frosting.

"Happy birthday, Mom," Meredith and Nina said together.

Mom stared down at the candle.

"We always wanted to have a birthday party for you," Meredith said. She reached out and put her hand on Mom's.

"I have made so many mistakes," Mom said softly.

"Everyone makes mistakes," Meredith said.

"No. I . . . I didn't mean to be that way . . . I wanted to tell you . . . but I couldn't even look at you, I was so ashamed."

"You're looking at us now," Nina said, although it wasn't strictly true. Mom was actually staring at the candle. "You want to tell us your story. You always wanted to. That's why you started the fairy tale."

Mom shook her head.

"You're Vera," Nina said quietly.

"No," Mom said, "that girl is not who I am."

"But she's who you were," Nina said, hating herself for saying it, but unable to stop.

"You are a dog with a bone, Nina." She sighed. "Yes. Long ago I was Veronika Petronova Marchenko."

"Why—"

"Enough," Mom said sharply. "This is my first birthday party with my daughters. There will be time later for the rest of it."

Twenty-one

At dinner, they talked about ordinary things. They drank wine and toasted again to Mom's eighty-first birthday. After a delicious meal, they wandered through the Vegas-like glitter of the giant ship and found their way to a theater, where a man in an orange sequined jumpsuit was performing magic. He made his barely clad assistant disappear, gave her paper roses that turned into white doves and flew away, and cut her in several pieces and then put her back together.

Mom clapped enthusiastically at each new trick, smiled like a little kid.

Meredith could hardly take her eyes off her mother. She looked bright and almost happy; for the first time, Meredith understood how cold her mother's beauty had always been before. Her beauty was different tonight: softer, warmer.

When the show was over, they walked back to their staterooms. In the crowded hallways, amid all the chatter of their fellow passengers and the ringing of the casino bells, they were strangely silent. Something had changed today, with that little burning candle on a piece of chocolate cake, but Meredith didn't know quite *what* had changed or how they would be reshaped by it. All she knew was that she had lost the ability to stay separate now. For more than twenty-five years, she'd kept up her side of the wall, too. She had refused to really see or need her mother, and in that distance, she'd found strength. At least a facsimile of strength. Now she had almost none of that left. Truthfully, she was glad it was too late to hear more of the story tonight.

At their door, Nina stopped. "I had a great day, Mom. Happy birthday." She moved forward awkwardly, pulled Mom into an embrace that was over before Mom could lift her own arms.

Meredith wanted to follow suit, but when she looked in her mother's blue eyes, she felt too vulnerable to make a move. "I . . . uh . . . I know you must be tired," Meredith said, smiling nervously. "We should go to bed and get up early. Tomorrow we'll be cruising Glacier Bay. It's supposed to be spectacular."

Mom said, "Thank you for my birthday," so softly they almost couldn't hear, and then she opened the door and went into her room.

Meredith unlocked their door and went inside.

"Dibs on the bathtub," Nina said, grinning.

Meredith barely noticed. She grabbed a blanket from her bed and went out onto the small veranda. From here, even in the darkness, she could make out the coastline. Here and there lights shone, marking peoples' lives.

She leaned back against the sliding door and wondered at the vistas she wasn't seeing. It was all out there—the mystery, the beauty; beyond her ability to see now, but there just the same. It was simply a matter of timing and perspective, what one saw. Like with Mom. Perhaps everything had been there to be seen all along and Meredith had had the wrong perspective, or not enough light.

"I suppose that is you, Meredith."

She was startled by the sound of her mother's voice, coming from the darkness of the veranda to her right. It was another jolt of reality:

there were hundreds of tiny verandas stuck out from the side of this ship, and yet in the dark, each one seemed entirely separate. "Hey, Mom," she said. She could only make out the merest shape of her mother, see only the white sheen of her hair.

They were alike in that way, she and her mom. When they were troubled, both wanted to be outside and alone.

"You are thinking about your marriage," Mom said.

Meredith sighed. "I don't suppose you have any advice for me."

"To lose love is a terrible thing," Mom said softly. "But to turn away from it is unbearable. Will you spend the rest of your life replaying it in your head? Wondering if you walked away too soon or too easily? Or if you'll ever love anyone that deeply again?"

Meredith heard the softening in her mother's voice. It was like listening to melted pain, that voice. "You know about loss," she said quietly.

"We all do."

"When I first fell in love with Jeff, it was like seeing sunlight for the first time. I couldn't stand to be away from him. And then . . . I could. We got married so young. . . ."

"Young has nothing to do with love. A woman can be a girl and still know her own heart."

"I stopped being happy. I don't even know why or when."

"I remember when you were always smiling. Back when you opened the gift shop. Maybe you never should have taken over the business."

Meredith was too surprised to do more than nod. She hadn't thought her mother ever noticed her one way or the other. "It meant so much to Dad."

"It did."

"I made the mistake of living for other people. For Dad and the orchard, and my kids. Mostly for them, and now they are so busy with their own lives they hardly ever call. I have to memorize their schedules and track them down like Hercule Poirot. I'm a bounty hunter with a phone."

"Jillian and Maddy flew away because you gave them wings and taught them to fly."

"I wish I had wings," Meredith said quietly.

"This is my fault," Mom said, standing up. The veranda creaked at the movement.

"Why?" Meredith said, moving closer to the rail that separated the two verandas. She felt her mother come toward her until suddenly they were standing face-to-face, a foot or less apart. Finally, she could see Mom's eyes.

"I am telling my story to explain."

"When it's over, will I know what I did that was so wrong?"

In the uncertain mix of light and shadow, her mother's face seemed to crumple like old wax paper. "You will know, when it is all done, that you are not the one who did anything wrong. Now come inside. I will tell you about the Luga line tonight."

"Are you sure? It's late."

"I am sure." She opened her sliding door and disappeared inside her cabin.

Meredith went back into the brightly lit stateroom and found Nina on her bed, drying her short black hair with a towel.

"You can't see anything out there, can you?"

"Mom wants to tell more of the story."

"Tonight?" Nina jumped up, letting the wet towel slump to the floor, and hurried to the other side of the room.

Meredith picked up the damp towel and carried it to the bathroom, where she hung it back up.

"You ready?" Nina said from the doorway.

Meredith turned to look at her sister. "You have wings."

"Huh?"

"Maybe I'm like some ostrich or dodo bird. I stayed on the ground so long, I lost the ability to fly."

Laughing, Nina put an arm around Meredith and led her out of the stateroom. "You're *not* some damned ostrich, which, by the way, are mean-assed birds who always stand alone."

"So what am I?" Meredith asked as Nina knocked on Mom's door.

"Maybe you're a swan. They mate for life, you know. I don't know if one can fly without the other."

"That's strange, coming from you. You're no romantic."

"Yeah," Nina said, looking at her. "But you are."

Meredith was surprised by that. She would never have called herself a romantic. That was for people like her father who loved everyone unconditionally and never failed at the grand gesture. Or like Jeff, who never forgot to kiss her good night, no matter how late it was or how hard his day had been.

Or maybe it was for girls who found their soul mates when they were young and didn't quite understand how rare that was.

The door opened. Mom stood there waiting, her white hair unbound and her body wrapped in an oversized blue cruise ship robe. The color was so incongruous on Mom that Meredith did a double-take.

And then it struck her. "Vera sees color," she said.

Beside her, Nina gasped. "That's right. So *you* see in color."

"No," Mom said.

"How come—"

"No questions," Mom said firmly. "These were the rules." She walked over to her bed and climbed in, leaning back into a pile of pillows.

Meredith followed Nina into the room and took a seat beside her sister on the love seat. In the silence, she heard waves slapping the side of the boat, and the quiet intake of their combined breathing.

"Vera cannot believe that she must leave her children again," Mom said softly, using her voice to its fullest power. She no longer looked delicate and old. In fact, she was almost smiling and her eyes had drifted shut.

"Especially when she worked so hard to bring them home, but Leningrad is a city of women now, and they must defend against the Germans, and so, on a bright and sunny day, Vera kisses

her babies good-bye for the second time in a week. They are four and five, too young to be left without their mother, but war changes everything, and just as her mother had predicted, Vera is doing what would have been unimaginable even a few months ago. In their small apartment, with all eyes on her, Vera kneels down in front of them. "Aunt Olga and Mama have to go help keep Leningrad safe. You need to be very strong and grown-up while we are gone, yes? Baba will need your help."

Leo's eyes immediately fill with tears. "I don't want you to go."

Vera cannot look in her son's sad eyes, so she turns slightly toward her daughter, whom already she had begun to think of as the strong one.

"What if you don't come back?" Anya says quietly, trying her best not to cry.

Vera reaches into her pocket for the treasure she had thought to take with her. She pulls it out slowly. In her palm sits the beautiful jeweled butterfly. "Here," she says to Anya. "I want you to hold this for Mama. It is my most special thing. When you look at it, you'll think of me and know that I will come back to you and that wherever I am, I am thinking of you and Leo, and loving you both. Don't play with it, or break it. This is who we are, Anya. It proves that I will come back to you. Okay?"

Very solemnly, Anya takes the butterfly, holds it carefully in her small palm.

Vera kisses them both one last time and stands.

Across the room, she meets her mother's gaze. It is all there, in their eyes—the good-bye, the promise to take care and come back, and the worry that this is *good-bye. Vera knows she should hug her mother, but if she does that she'll cry, and she cannot cry in front of her children, so she instead grabs a heavy winter coat off the hook by the door and slings it over her shoulder. In no time at all, she and Olga are crammed together in the back of a transport truck, surrounded by dozens of other young women; many of them are dressed in flowery summer skirts with sandals on their feet. In other times, they would look like girls going off to camp, maybe to the Urals or the Black Sea, but no one would make that mistake of them now. There is not a one of them smiling.*

When they reach the Luga line, there are people—girls and women, mostly—as far as the eye can see; they are building the massive trenches and fortifications that will stop the enemy from reaching Leningrad. Bent above the ground, stabbing at the dirt with pickaxes and shovels, these women are exhausted; their faces are streaked with sweat and dirt and their dresses are ruined. But they are Russians—Soviets—and no one dares to pause or complain. No one even imagines doing such a thing. Vera stands in the sunlight, with the forest only a few miles away, while a comrade tells her what to do.

Olga moves in close to her, takes her hand. They listen like soldiers and look like children, though they do not know this. It is their last moment of peace for many nights. After that, they take up pickaxes and trudge to the line, where the ground has been chewed up already. Dropping into the trench, they become two more in an endless line of girls and women and old men who hack at the earth until their hands blister and bleed, until they cough up blood and cry black tears. Day after day, they dig.

At night, they huddle in a barn with the other girls, who look as dazed and tired and dirty as Vera feels. The whole place smells of dust and mud and sweat and smoke.

On their seventh night, Vera finds a quiet corner in the barn where they stay at night and builds a small fire of twigs. It will not last long, these flames that feed on so little, so she works fast, boiling a cup of water for her sister, handing it to her. The watery cabbage soup they had for dinner has long ago given way to hunger, but there is nothing to be done about that.

Beside them, a heavyset older woman leans against the bales of hay, looking at her dirty fingernails as if she's never seen her own hands before. Her fleshy, dirty face is unfamiliar, but there is something comforting in her eyes.

"Look at my hands," Olga says, putting down her cup of water. "I'm bleeding."

She says it with a kind of confused wonder, as if the pain is not hers, nor really even the blood.

Vera takes her sister's hand, sees the matted blood and broken blisters on her palm. "You have to keep your hands wrapped. I told you this."

"They were watching me today," Olga says quietly. "Comrades Slotkov and Pritkin. I know they know about Papa. I could not stop to adjust the wraps."

Vera frowns. She has heard this from her sister before in the past week, but now she recognizes that something is wrong. Olga does not make eye contact with her. Already they have seen girls die around them. Only yesterday, Olga spent half the day deafened by a bomb that landed too close.

Outside, the alarm blares. The sound of aircraft is a faraway drone at first, not unlike the murmur of a distant bee at a summer picnic. But the sound builds, and fear in the barn becomes palpable. Girls move and shift and lie flat, but really there is nowhere to go.

Bombs drop. Fires flash red and yellow and black through the slats in the barn siding. Somewhere, someone is screaming. The air turns gray and gritty. Vera's eyes sting.

Olga flinches but doesn't move. Instead, she stares at her wounded palm, and begins methodically ripping off the dead, blistered skin. Blood bubbles up from her wounds.

"Don't do that," Vera says, pulling her sister's hand away.

"Honey."

Vera hears the word spoken aloud. At first it makes no sense; all she can really comprehend is the bombing. Near her, someone is crying.

Then she hears it again. "Honey."

The old woman is nearer now. Deep wrinkles bracket her

smoker's mouth and purplish bags buttress her tired eyes. She pulls a small vial from her apron pocket. "Put honey on your sister's wounds."

Vera is stunned by the generosity of the act. Honey is more valuable than gold on this Luga line. Food and medicine in one.

"Why are you doing this?" Vera says after she smears a small drop on Olga's wounds.

The woman looks at her. "We are all we have left," she says, scooting back into her place amid the hay bales.

"What is your name?" Vera says.

"It doesn't matter," the woman says. "Watch your sister closely. I have seen eyes like hers before. She is not doing well."

Vera nods bravely, though the words are like a cold wind. She has been telling herself that this change in Olga is ordinary sleep deprivation and hunger, but now she sees what the old woman sees: the speck of craziness in her sister's wide eyes. Olga cannot stand these days and nights—the screaming, the endless work, the horror of watching a girl your own age blown apart. The suddenness of the danger; that's the worst of it. Olga is unraveling. She talks to herself and hardly ever sleeps. She pulls out her hair in clumps.

"Come here, Olgushka," Vera says, pulling her sister into her arms. They crawl back into their bed of hay, which is neither soft nor sweet-smelling.

"I see Papa," Olga says, her voice dreamy-sounding. It is as if she has forgotten who they are and where they are and of whom they do not speak.

"Shush."

"Tell me a story, Vera. About princesses and boys who bring you roses."

Vera is weary to the bone, but she strokes her sister's dirty, matted hair and uses the only thing she has—her voice—to soothe their spirits. "The Snow Kingdom is a magical, walled city, where night never falls and white doves nest on telephone lines. . . ."

Long after Olga has fallen asleep, Vera is still stringing her pretty words together, changing the world around them in the only way she can. When her own eyes grow too heavy to keep open any longer, she kisses her sister's bloody palm, tasting the metallic blood mixed with the sweetness of the honey. She should have put some of the honey on her own blistered palm, but she didn't think of it. "Sleep now."

"Will we see Mama tomorrow?" Olga asks sleepily.

"Not tomorrow, no," Vera says, tightening her hold. "But soon."

The day is sunny and bright. If not for the Germans bombing everything in sight, and their tanks rolling forward, forward, the birds would be singing here, the pine trees would be green instead of black. As it is, the beauty of the place is long gone. The trench is a huge, gaping slash in the earth, a mortal muddy wound. Girls crawl all around it; soldiers run back and forth between here and the front line, not far away. If this line breaks, if the Germans get past it, Leningrad will fall. This they all believe, so they keep digging, no matter that their hands are bleeding and bombs are as ever-present as sunlight.

Vera is trying not to think about anything except the spoon in her hand. The pickax broke last week. For a while she was lucky enough to find a spade, but she didn't hide it well and one morning when she woke up it was gone, so now she digs with a serving spoon.

All day long. Stab, push, twist, pull. Until her shoulder aches and her neck hurts and her blistered palms burn. No amount of salt water can help (the honey and the old woman are long gone). And now she is having her monthly bleeding as well. Her body is turning against her, it seems, and yet all she can worry about is Olga. Her sister digs without complaint, but she can't sleep or eat, and when the bombs start falling, Olga just stands there with a hand tented across her face, staring up at the planes.

In the past few weeks, Vera has learned that anything can become ordinary—sleeping in the dirt, running for cover, digging holes, watching people die, stepping over bodies, smelling flesh burn. But she cannot accept the new Olga, who moves like the blind and laughs giddily when bombs explode around her.

The air-raid alarm rings out. Girls and women scurry out of the trench and into it. They are screaming to one another, pushing each other aside.

Olga is standing beside the trench, her dress torn and dirty. Her long strawberry-blond hair is filthy, frizzy, and held back from her blackened face by a once-blue kerchief. Overhead, German planes begin to fill the sky, their engines droning.

Vera yells for her sister as she scrambles over the broken earth, leading the way, pushing debris aside. "Come on—"

"It sounds like Mama's sewing machine."

Vera turns at that, looks back. Olga is still standing there, too far away, her hand tented over her eyes.

"Run!" Vera yells at the same time the bomb hits.

Olga is there and gone, flung like a rag doll to the side. She falls in a broken heap on the other side of the trench while debris rains down. . . .

Vera is screaming, crying; she crawls out of the trench and over the broken earth to where her sister lies beneath a pile of dirt and rubble. A brick is on Olga's chest—where did it come from?

Blood gushes from the side of Olga's mouth and slides through the soot and mud on her cheek. Her breathing is a phlegmy, bubbling cough. "Vera," she says, shuddering. "I forgot to get down. . . ."

"You're supposed to listen to me," Vera says. She holds her sister to her chest, trying to keep her alive by loving her. "I am your big sister."

"Always . . . bossing . . ."

Vera kisses her sister's cheek, tries to wipe the blood away, but her hands are so dirty she is just making a mess. "I love you, Olga. Don't leave me. Please . . ."

Olga smiles and coughs. Blood gushes from her nose and mixes with dirt. "Remember when we went—"

And she is gone.

Vera sits there a long time, kneeling in the dirt. Until the soldiers come and take Olga away.

Then she goes back to digging. It isn't that she doesn't care or doesn't hurt.

But what else can she do?

Twenty-two

In August, Vera is released from work on the line. She is one of thousands of dazed, solitary women walking in silent groups for home. The trains are still running, although most of them are full all the time, and only the luckiest find space enough to sit or stand. They are evacuating the children of Leningrad again—this time with their mothers—but Vera does not trust her government anymore and will not follow the evacuation order again. Only last week she heard of a train of children that was bombed near Mga. Maybe it is true, maybe it is not. She does not care. It could be true, and that is enough for her.

She is tougher now, after two months spent digging in the black earth and running for shelter. Tough enough to make her way home through countryside she's never seen. When she is lucky, a transport or a lorry picks her up and takes her as far as they are going, but luck is a thing she has never counted on, and most of the miles to Leningrad, she walks. When she meets soldiers on the road, she asks about Sasha, but she does not get answers. It is no surprise to her.

When she finally makes it to Leningrad, she finds a city as changed as she. Windows are blacked out and crisscrossed in tape. Trenches cut through parks, tearing through grass and flowers. Everywhere she looks are mounds of broken cement—dragon's teeth, they are called—meant to bar the tanks. Huge iron beams crisscross the city boundaries like the ugly, misplaced bars of a prison. And soldiers move in marching columns through the streets. Already many of them look as broken as she feels; they've lost on one front and are moving to another, closer to the city. In their tired eyes, she sees the same fear that is now lodged inside of her: Leningrad is not the impervious city they'd imagined her to be. The Germans are getting closer. . . .

Finally, Vera stands on her own street and looks up at her apartment. Except for the blacked-out windows, it looks as it always did. The trees out front are in full summer bloom and the sky is as blue as a robin's egg.

As she stands there, afraid to go forward, a feeling moves through her, as powerful as hunger or desire: she shivers with it.

It is wanting to turn and run, to hold on to this terrible truth a little longer, but she knows that running will not help, so she takes a deep breath and walks forward, one step at a time, until she is at her own front door.

It opens at her touch and suddenly she is in her home again, as small and cluttered as it is. Never has the broken-down furniture and peeling paint looked so beautiful.

And there is her mama, standing at the stove in a faded dress, with her gray hair all but hidden beneath a threadbare kerchief, stirring something. At Vera's entrance, she turns slowly. Her bright smile is heartbreaking; worse is the way it fades away and is replaced by sorrow. Only one has come home.

"Mama!" Leo screams, coming at her like a windstorm, toys

dropping from his hands. Anya is beside him in an instant and they throw themselves into Vera's arms.

They smell so good, so pure. . . . Leo's cheeks are as soft and sweet as ripe plums and Vera could eat him up. She holds them too long, too tightly, unaware that she has begun to shake and to cry.

"Don't cry, Mama," Anya says, wiping her cheek. "I still have the butterfly. I didn't break it."

Vera slowly releases them and stands up. She is shaking like a leaf and trying not to cry as she stares across the kitchen at her mother. In that look, Vera feels her childhood leave her at last.

"Where's Aunt Olga?" Leo asks, looking past her.

Vera cannot answer. She just stands there.

"Olga is gone," Mama says with only a slight tremble in her voice. "She is a hero of the state, our Olga, and that is how we must think of her."

"But . . ."

Mama takes Vera in her arms, holding her so hard that neither can breathe. There is only silence between them; in that silence, memories pass back and forth like dye in water, moving and fluid, and when they pull back and look at each other, Vera understands.

They will not speak of Olga again, not for a long time, not until the sharp pain rounds into something that can be handled.

"You need a bath," Mama says after a time. "And those bandages on your hands need changing, so come along."

Those first days back in Leningrad seem like a dream to Vera. During the day, she works alongside other library employees, packing up the most valuable books for transport. She, who is so low on the roster, finds herself actually holding a first edition of Anna Karenina. *The pages have an unexpected weight, and she*

closes her eyes for just a moment. In the darkness she sees Anna, dressed in jewels and furs, running across the snow to Count Vronsky.

Someone says her name so sharply she almost drops the treasured volume. Starting, she flushes and lowers her gaze to the floor, mumbling, "Sorry," and goes back to work. By the end of the week, they have packed up more than 350,000 masterpieces and sent them out of harm's way. They've filled the attic with sandbags and moved other important works to the basement. Room after room is cleared out and boarded up and shut down, until only the smallest of the rooms is left open for readers.

By the end of her shift, Vera's shoulders ache from all the lifting and dragging of boxes, but she is far from finished for the day. Instead of going home, she trudges through the busy, camouflaged streets and gets into the first queue she finds.

She doesn't know what they are selling at this market and she doesn't care. Since the start of bread rationing and the limitations placed on the withdrawal of banking accounts, you take what you can get. Like most of her friends and neighbors, Vera has very little money. Her rations allow her four hundred grams of bread a day and six hundred grams of butter a month. On this, they can live. But she thinks often of a decision she made years ago: if she worked now in the bread factory, her family would be better fed. She would be an essential worker, with higher rations.

She stands in line for hours. At just past ten o'clock in the evening, she comes to the front. The only thing left for sale are jars of pickles, and she buys three—the amount she can afford and carry.

In the apartment, she finds her mother and grandmother sitting at the kitchen table, passing a cigarette back and forth between them.

Saying nothing—they all say little these days—she goes past them to the children's beds. Leaning down, she kisses both tender cheeks. Exhausted and hungry, she goes back into the kitchen. Mama has put out a plate of cold kasha for her.

"The last transport left today," Baba says when Vera sits down.

Vera looks at her grandmother. "I thought they were still evacuating the city."

Mama shakes her head. "We could not decide and now it is decided for us."

"The Germans have taken Mga."

Vera knows what this means, and if she did not, the look of despair in her mother's eyes would have been enough to inform her. "So . . ."

"Leningrad is an island now," Mama says, taking a drag off the cigarette and handing it back to Baba. "Cut off from the mainland on all sides."

Cut off from supplies.

"What do we do?" Vera asks.

"Do?" Baba says.

"Winter is coming," Mama says in the silence. "We need food and a burzhuika. *I will take the children and go to the marketplace tomorrow."*

"What will you trade?"

"My wedding ring," Mama says.

"So it has begun," Baba says, stubbing out the cigarette.

Vera sees the way they look at each other, the knowing sadness that passes between mother and daughter, and although it scares her, it comforts her, too. They have been through this before, her mama and her babushka. War is nothing new to Peter's city. They will survive as they have survived before, by being careful and smart.

The city becomes one long line. Everything is disappearing, especially politeness. Rations are consistently being cut, and often there is no food to be had, even with a ration card. Vera, like

everyone else, is tired and hungry and afraid. She wakes at four in the morning to stand in line for bread, and after work, she walks miles to the outskirts of town, bartering with peasants for food—a liter of vodka for a bag of withered potatoes; an outgrown pair of valenki *for a pound of lard—and digging up whatever forgotten vegetables she can find.*

It is not safe and she knows it, but there is nothing to be done. This search for food is all there is. No one goes to the library anymore, but Vera must keep working there to keep her worker's rations. Now she is on her way home from the country. She moves quickly, keeping to the shadows, with her precious bag of potatoes hidden inside her dress like an unborn baby.

She is less than a mile from the apartment when the air raid alarm goes off, blaring through the nearly empty city streets. When it stops, she can hear the planes buzzing, growing closer.

She hears a loud whistling and starts to run for one of the trenches in the park to her left. Before she is even across the street, something explodes. Dirt and debris rain down from the sky. One building after another is destroyed.

And then . . . silence.

Vera gets up slowly, her legs unsteady.

The potatoes are okay.

She crawls out of the trench. Dusting herself off, she runs for home. The city is burning and smoking around her. People are screaming and crying.

She turns the corner and sees her apartment building. It is intact.

But the building next door is demolished. Only half of it remains; the other side is a pile of smoking, pulverized rubble. As she draws near, she sees a living room in perfect shape—green flowered wallpaper still in place, a table still set for dinner, a painting on the wall. But no people. As she stands there, the chandelier above the table shudders and falls, crashing across the dishes on the table.

She finds her family in the basement, huddled alongside their neighbors. When the All-Clear sounds, they go back upstairs and put the children in bed.

It is only the beginning. The next day Vera goes with her mother and the children to the market, where they search for a burzhuika. *Without such a stove, her mother says, they will have problems come winter.*

They find one deep in the back of the market, in a stall run by the kind of people Vera normally would never see. Swarthy, drunken men and women wearing jewels they surely hadn't owned a week ago.

Vera holds her children close, trying not to make a face as the man's vodka breath washes over her.

"This is the last one," he says, leering at her, swaying.

Mama takes off her wedding ring. The gold shines dully in the morning light. "I have this gold ring," she says.

"What good is gold?" He sneers.

"The war won't last forever," Mama says. "And there's more." She opens her coat and pulls out a large jar full of white sugar.

The man stares at it; sugar is like gold dust now. Baba or Mama must have stolen it from the warehouse where they work.

The man's ham-sized fist snakes out; his fingers coil around the jar and pull it back.

Mama hardly seems to care that her ring is gone, that a man like that has possession of it.

Together, the four of them drag the stove and pipe back to their apartment, pull it up the stairs in clanging bursts. When it is up and in place, its vent going out the window, Mama clasps her hands. "That's that," she says, coughing.

The stove is a small, ugly thing, cast iron with a pair of drawers that jut out brokenly. A long metal pipe goes from the stove, up the side of the wall, and out through a newly cut hole. She finds it hard to believe that it is worth a woman's wedding ring.

"That was a lot of sugar," Vera says quietly as Mama walks past her.

"Yes," Mama says, pausing. "Baba brought it to us."

"She could get in trouble," Vera whispers, moving closer. "The Badayev warehouses are watched. Almost all of the city's food stores are there. And both of you are employees. If one of you gets in trouble—"

"Yes," Mama says, looking at her hard. "She is still there now, working late. She will be the last one to leave."

"But—"

"You do not yet know," Mama says, coughing again. It is a hacking, bubbly sound that unaccountably makes Vera think of muddy rivers and hot weather.

"Are you okay, Mama?"

"I am fine. It is just the dust in the air from the bombings."

Before Vera can answer or even think of what to say, the air-raid alarm sounds.

"Children!" she screams. "Come quickly." Vera grabs the coats from the wall and bundles her children up.

"I don't want to go to the basement," Leo whines. "It stinks down there."

"Mrs. Newsky is the one who stinks," Anya says, and her frown turns to a smile.

Leo giggles. "She smells like cabbage."

"Hush," Vera says, wondering how long this childhood will last for her babies. She buttons Leo's coat and takes his hand.

Out in the hallway, the neighbors are already lining up for the stairs. On all of their faces is the same look: a combination of fear and resignation. No one really believes that being in the basement will save them from a bomb falling on their building, but at a time like this, there is no other salvation, so they go.

Vera kisses each of her children, hugs them fiercely in turn, and then hands them over to Mama.

While her family and neighbors go down to save themselves, Vera goes up. Breathing hard, she runs up the dirty, dark staircase and emerges onto the flat, litter-strewn roof. A long pair of iron tongs and several buckets full of sand are in place along the short wall. From here, she can see across Leningrad to the south. In the distance are the planes. Not one or two as before, but dozens. At first they are tiny black dots, dodging between giant barrage balloons that hang above the city, but soon she can see their shiny propellers and the details on their tails.

Bombs fall like raindrops; in their wake, puffs of smoke and flashes of fire.

A plane is overhead. . . .

Vera looks up, sees its glistening silver belly open up. Incendiary bombs drop out. She watches in horror as one lands not more than fifteen feet from where she is standing. She runs for it, hearing its hiss. Her foot catches on a piece of wood and she falls to the ground so hard she tastes blood. Scrambling back up, she reaches for the gloves in her pocket and puts them on, shaking, trying to hurry; then she grabs up the iron tongs and tries to use them to pick up the bomb. It is an intricate task. She takes too long and fire catches on the wooden beam beneath the bomb. Smoke rises up. She positions the tongs on the bomb—the heat on her face is terrifying; she's sweating so she can hardly see. Still, she clamps the handles and lifts the long bomb, and throws it off the side of the building. It lands with a thud on the grass below, where it can do no real damage. Dropping the tongs, she runs back to the small fire started by the bomb and stomps the flames out with the soles of her shoes, then pours sand on it.

When the fire is out, she drops to her knees. Her heart is going a mile a minute and her cheeks feel singed by the heat. If she hadn't been here, that bomb would have burned its way down through the building, falling from floor to floor and leaving fire in its wake.

The basement is where it would have ended up. In that tiny room jam-packed with people. With her family . . .

She stays there, kneeling on the hard surface of the roof as night falls. The whole city seems to be on fire. Smoke rolls upward and out. Even after the airplanes are gone, the smoke remains, growing thicker and redder. Bright yellow and orange flames flicker up between the buildings, lick at the smoke's swollen underbelly.

When the All Clear finally sounds, Vera is too shaken to move. It is only the thought of her children, who are probably crying now and afraid, that makes her move. One shaking step at a time, she walks across the roof and down the stairs to her apartment, where her family is already waiting for her.

"Did you see the fires?" Anya asks, biting her lip.

"They are far away from here," Vera says, smiling as brightly as she can. "We are safe."

"Will you tell us a story, Mama?" Leo says, popping his thumb in his mouth. His eyes lower sleepily and reopen.

Vera scoops both her children into her arms, settles one on each hip. She doesn't bother to brush their teeth, just puts them to bed and climbs in with them.

At the table in the living room, Mama sits down and lights up her one cigarette for the day. The smell of it is lost in the overwhelming scent of the city burning. There is something almost sweet in the air, a smell like caramel left too long on a hot stove.

Vera tightens her hold on her children. "There is a peasant girl," she says, trying to sound calm. It is hard; her thoughts are tangled up in what could have happened, what she could have lost. And she would swear that she can still hear that bomb whistling toward her, rustling impossibly in flight, and banging down beside her.

"Her name is Vera," Anya says sleepily, snuggling close. "Right?"

"Her name is Vera," she says, thankful for the prompting. "And she is a poor peasant girl. A nobody. But she doesn't know that yet. . . ."

"It is good you tell them your story," Mama says to Vera when she comes back into the kitchen.

"I couldn't think of anything else." She sits down across from her mother at the rickety table, putting one foot on the empty chair beside her. Though the windows are closed and blacked out, she can still taste ash on her tongue, still smell that strange burned sweetness in the smoke. The world outside can only be seen in patches, in places where the newspaper droops limply away from the glass; the view is no longer red, but rather a dull orangey gold mixed with gray. "Papa used to tell me wonderful stories, remember?"

"I prefer not to remember."

"But—"

"Your baba should have been home by now," Mama says, not looking at her.

Vera feels a sharp clutch in her stomach at that. With all that has gone on tonight, she'd forgotten about her grandmother.

"I am sure she's fine," Vera says.

"Yes," Mama says dully.

But in the morning, Baba is still not back; she is one of the thousands who are never seen again. And news moves through the city as ruinously as last night's flames.

The Badayev warehouses are burned; all of the city's food stores are gone.

Leningrad is isolated now, cut off from all help. September drips into October and disappears. The belye nochi *is gone, replaced by a cold, dark winter. Vera still works in the library, but it is for show—and ration cards. Few people visit the library or the museums or theaters anymore, and those who do come are looking for heat. In these darkening weeks, when winter's icy breath is always blowing on the back of your neck, there is nothing except the search for food.*

Every day Vera is up at four o'clock in the morning, bundling up in her valenki *and woolen coat, wrapping a scarf around her neck so high only her eyes show. She gets in whatever queue for food she can find; it isn't easy just getting in line, let alone actually finding food. The strong push the weak out of the way. You have to be careful always, on guard. That nice young girl on the corner could steal from you in an instant; so might the old man standing on the stoop.*

After work, she comes home to her cold apartment and sits down to a meal at six o'clock. Only it is not much of a meal anymore. A potato if they are lucky, with some kasha that is more water than buckwheat. The children complain constantly, while Mama coughs quietly in the corner. . . .

In October, the first snow falls. Usually this is a time of laughter, when children run out to the parks with their parents and build snow angels and forts. Not in wartime, though. Now it is like tiny specks of white death falling over their ruined city. Its pretty white layer covers all their defenses—the dragon's teeth, the iron bars, the trenches. Suddenly the city is beautiful again, a wonderland of arching bridges and icy waterways and white parks. If you don't look at the crumbling buildings or burned-out heaps of brick where once a store had stood, you could almost forget . . . until seven o'clock. That is when the Germans drop the bombs. Every night, like clockwork.

And once the snow starts to fall, it never stops. Pipes freeze. Trolleys come to a stop and remain stuck in the accumulating snow. There are no tanks or trucks in the road anymore, no marching troops. There are just poor, bundled-up women like Vera, moving through the white landscape like refugees in search of anything resembling food. There is not a pet to be seen in Leningrad these days. Rations are cut almost every week.

Vera trudges forward. She is so hungry that it is difficult to keep moving, difficult sometimes even to want to keep moving. She tries not to think about the seven hours she spent in line today and focuses instead on the sunflower oil and oil cakes she was able to get. Behind her, the red sled she drags glides through the deep drifts, catching every now and then on things hidden in the snow—a twig, a rock, a frozen body.

The corpses began showing up last week: people still dressed for the weather, frozen in place on park benches or on the stoops of buildings.

You learn not to see them. Vera cannot believe that this is true, but it is. The hungrier and colder you get, the more your vision funnels to where you can't see anyone beyond your own family.

She's four blocks from her apartment and her chest aches so much that she longs to stop. She even dreams of it—she'll sit on that bench and lean back and close her eyes. Maybe someone will come by with some hot, sweet tea and offer her a cup. . . .

She draws in a ragged breath, ignoring the gnawing emptiness in her belly. Those are the kinds of dreams that get you killed. You sit down to rest and just die. That's how it happens in Leningrad now. You have a little cough . . . or an infected cut . . . or you feel sluggish and want to stay in bed for just an hour or so. And then suddenly you're dead. Every day at the library, it seems, someone fails to show up. In that absence they all know: they'll never see that person again.

She puts one foot in front of the other and slowly makes her way in the snow, dragging her sled behind her. She has come almost a mile from the Neva River, where she collected a gallon of water from a hole in the ice. At the apartment, she pauses just long enough to catch her breath and then begins the long climb to the second floor. The gallon of water she'd had on the sled feels icy cold against her chest and the cold makes her lungs hurt even more.

The apartment is warm. She notices instantly that another chair is broken. It lies on its side, two legs missing and the back hacked up. They cannot all sit at the table now, but what does it matter? There's precious little to eat.

Leo is wearing his coat and his boots. He is sprawled on the kitchen floor, playing war with a pair of metal trucks. At her entrance, he cocks his head and looks at her. For a second it is as if she's been gone a month instead of a day. She sees the way his cheeks have caved in on themselves, the way his eyes seem too big for his bony face. He doesn't look like a baby boy at all anymore.

"Did you get food?" he says.

"Did you?" Anya says, rising from her place on the bed, carrying her blanket with her.

"Oil cakes," Vera says.

Anya frowns. "Oh, no, Mama."

Vera's heart actually hurts when she hears this. What she wouldn't give to bring home potatoes or butter or even buckwheat. But oil cake is what they have now. No matter that it used to be fed to cattle, or that it tastes like sawdust or that it's so hard that only an ax will cut it. They use shavings to make pancakes that are barely edible. But none of that matters. What matters is that you have something to eat.

Vera knows that comfort will not help her children. This is a lesson she has learned since the snow began to fall on Leningrad. Her children need strength and courage now, as they all do. It does no good to cry or whine for that which cannot be had. She goes over to the fallen chair and breaks off another leg. Cracking it in two pieces, she feeds it into the burzhuika *and puts the water she brought home in a pot to boil. She will put yeast in it to fill their bellies. It won't help, of course, but they'll feel better for a while.*

She bends down, feeling the hot popping in her joints at the movement, and puts a hand on Leo's curls. His hair, like all of theirs, is stiff from dirt. Baths are luxuries these days. "I have some more of the story for tonight," she says, waiting for his enthusiasm, but he just nods a little and shrugs.

"Okay."

It is wearing all of them away, the cold and the hunger. With a sigh, she gets back to her feet, rising like an old woman. She glances across the room at her mother, who is still in bed. To Anya she says, "How is she today?"

Anya stands there, her pale, thin face so drawn that her eyes seem to protrude. "Quiet," is all she says. "I made her drink water."

Vera goes to her small, serious daughter and picks her up, hugging her tightly. Even through the bulk of her coat, she can feel Anya's boniness, and it breaks her heart. "You are my best girl," she whispers. "You are taking such good care of everyone."

"I'm trying," Anya says, and the earnestness in her voice almost makes Vera feel ill.

Vera hugs her again and then lets go.

As she crosses the room, Vera can feel her mother's eyes on her, following her movements like a hawk. Everything about Mama is pale and shrunken and colorless except for those dark eyes that hold on to Vera like a fist.

She sits down at her bedside. "I got some oil cakes today. And a little sunflower oil."

"I am not hungry. Give mine to our babies."

It is what Mama says every night. At first Vera argued, but then she started to see Anya's cheekbones, and heard the way her son cried in his sleep for food.

"I'll make you some tea."

"That would be nice," Mama says, letting her eyes drift shut.

Vera knows how hard her mother has worked to stay awake in the hours that Vera is gone. It takes every scrap of Mama's will and courage simply to lie here and watch her grandchildren during the day, though she hasn't gotten out of bed for more than a few minutes at a time in weeks.

"There will be more food next week," Vera says. "I heard they're sending a transport across Lake Ladoga as soon as the water freezes. Then we'll all be fine."

Her mother says nothing to that, but her breathing doesn't even out, either. "Do you remember how your papa used to pace when he was working, how he muttered words to himself and laughed when he found what he wanted?"

Vera reaches out to touch her mother's dry forehead, strokes it gently. "He used to read his poetry to me sometimes, when he was working. He'd say, 'Verushka, when you are old enough to write your own stories, you'll be ready. Now listen to this. . . .' "

"Sometimes I feel him in here. And Olga. I can hear them talking, moving. I think they're dancing. There's a fire in the stove when they're here, and it's warm."

Vera nods but says nothing. More and more often lately Mama sees ghosts; sometimes she talks to them. It is only when Leo starts to cry that she stops.

"I'll add a drop of honey into your tea. And you need to eat today, okay? Just today."

Mama pats Vera's hand and sighs quietly.

Every day that winter Vera wakes thinking one of two things: it will get better today or it will be over soon. She doesn't know how it is possible to believe simultaneously that her situation will improve and that she will die, but there it is. Each cold morning, she wakens with a start and reaches for her children, who are in bed with her. When she feels the slow, steady beating of their hearts, she breathes easily again.

It takes courage to get out of bed. Even wearing every piece of clothing she owns and layered beneath all their blankets she isn't warm, and once she climbs from bed, she will be freezing. While they sleep, water freezes in pots in the kitchen and their eyelashes stick to skin, sometimes so hard that blood is drawn when they open their eyes.

Still, she eases the blankets back and climbs out over her children, who moan in their sleep. Mama, on her other side, doesn't make a sound, but she shifts almost imperceptibly to the left. They all sleep together for warmth now, in the bed that had once been her grandmother's.

In stockinged feet, Vera goes to the stove. It is not far; they have moved their bed as close to the burzhuika *as possible. The remaining furniture is cluttered together, unimportant except for the wood from which it is made. She grabs an ax from the closet and hacks through the last of the bed that was once her own. Then she starts a fire in the little* burzhuika *and puts water on to boil.*

While she's waiting, she kneels in the corner of the kitchen and pries up a floorboard. There, hidden in the dark, she counts up their stores. It is something she does every day, sometimes four times a day. A nervous habit now.

A bag of onions, a half a bottle of sunflower oil, some oil cakes, a nearly empty jar of honey, two jars of pickles, three potatoes, and the last of the sugar. She carefully takes out one large yellow onion and the honey, then replaces the floorboard. She will boil half an onion for breakfast, and add a drop of honey to their tea. She has just measured out a small amount of tea when there is a knock at the door.

At first she hardly recognizes the sound, it is so foreign. There is no talking in Leningrad anymore, no neighbors stopping by. Not here, at least, where their whole family is together.

But there is danger. People who will kill for a gram of butter or a spoonful of sugar.

She reaches for the ax again, holds it to her chest as she goes to the door. Her heart is beating so fast and hard she feels dizzy. For the first time in months, she forgets that she is hungry. With a trembling hand, she reaches for the doorknob and turns it.

He stands there like a stranger.

Vera stares up at him and shakes her head. She has become like her mama, hungry enough and sick enough to see ghosts. The ax falls from her grasp, thunks on the floor at her feet.

"Verushka?" he says, frowning.

At the sound of his voice, she feels herself start to fall. Her legs are giving out on her. If this is dying, she wants to give in, and when his arms come around her and hold her up, she is sure she is dead. She can feel the warmth of his breath on her throat; he is holding her upright. No one has held her in so long.

"Verushka," he says again, and she hears the question in his voice, the worry. He doesn't know why she hasn't spoken.

She laughs. It is a cracked, papery sound, rusty from disuse. "Sasha," she says. "Am I dreaming you?"

"I'm here," he says.

She clings to him, but when he goes to kiss her, she draws back in shame. Her breath is terrible; hunger has made her smell foul.

But he won't let her pull away. He kisses her as he used to, and for a sweet, perfect moment, she is Vera again, a twenty-two-year-old girl in love with her prince. . . .

When finally she can bear to let him go, she stares up at him in awe. His hair is gone, shaved down to nothing, and his cheekbones are more pronounced, and there is something new in his eyes—a sadness, she thinks—that will now be a mark of their generation. "You didn't write," she says.

"I wrote. Every week. There is no one to deliver the letters."

"Are you done? Are you back now?"

"Oh, Vera. No." He closes the door behind him. "Christ, it's cold in here."

"And we're lucky. We have a burzhuika.*"*

He opens his ragged coat. Hidden beneath it are half a ham, six sausage links, and a jar of honey.

Vera goes almost light-headed at the sight of meat. She cannot remember the last time she tasted it.

He sets the food down on the table. Taking her hand, he walks over to the bed, stepping around the broken furniture on the floor. At the bedside, he stares down at his sleeping children.

Vera sees the tears that come to his eyes and she understands: they do not look like his babies anymore. They look like children who are starving.

Anya rolls over in bed, bringing her baby brother with her. She smacks her lips together and chews in her sleep—dreaming—and then she slowly opens her eyes. "Papa?" she says. She looks like a little fox, with her sharp nose and pointed chin and sunken cheeks. "Papa?" she says again, elbowing Leo.

Leo rolls over and opens his eyes. He doesn't seem to understand, or doesn't recognize Sasha. "Quit hitting me," he whines.

"Are these my little mushrooms?" Sasha says.

Leo sits up. "Papa?"

Sasha leans down and scoops his children into his arms as if they weigh nothing. For the first time in months, the sound of their laughter fills the apartment. They fight to get his attention, squirming like a pair of puppies in his arms. As he takes them over toward the stove, Vera can hear snippets of their conversation.

"I learned to make a fire, Papa—"

"I can cut wood—"

"Ham! You brought us ham!"

Vera sits down beside her mother, who smiles.

"He's back," Mama says.

"He brought food," Vera says.

Mama struggles to sit up. Vera helps her, repositions her pillows behind her.

Once she's upright, Mama's foul breath taints the air between them. "Go spend the day with your family, Vera. No lines. No getting water from the Neva. No war. Just go." She coughs into a gray handkerchief. They both pretend not to see the bloody spots.

Vera strokes her mother's brow. "I'll make you some sweet tea. And you will eat some ham."

Mama nods and closes her eyes again.

Vera sits there a moment longer, listening to the strange mix of Mama's troubled breathing and her children's laughter and her husband's voice. It all leaves her feeling vaguely out of place. Still she covers her mother's frail body and stands up.

"He is so proud of you," Mama says on a sigh.

"Sasha?"

"Your papa."

Vera feels an unexpected tightness in her throat. Saying nothing, she walks forward, and Leo's laughter warms her more than the burning legs of any old desk ever could. She gets out her cast-iron frying pan and fries up some of the ham in a tiny spot of sunflower oil and adds sliced onions at the last minute.

A feast.

The whole room smells of rich, sizzling ham and sweet, caramelized onions. She even adds extra honey to their tea, and when they all sit on the old mattress to eat (there are no chairs anymore), no one says anything. Even Mama is lost in the unfamiliar sensation of eating.

"Can I have more, Mama?" Leo says, wiping his finger in the empty cup, looking for any trace of honey.

"No more," Vera says quietly, knowing that as kingly as this breakfast is, it is not enough for any of them.

"I say we go to the park," Sasha says.

"It's all boarded up," Anya tells him. "Like a prison. No one plays there anymore."

"We do," Sasha says, smiling as if this is an ordinary day.

Outside, the snow is falling. A veil of white obscures the city, softens it. The dragon's teeth and trenches are just mounds of snow and hollowed-out white valleys, respectively. Every now and then a white hillock sits on a park bench or lies by the side of the road, but it is easy to miss. Vera hopes her children do not know what is beneath the cover of snow.

In the park, everything is sparkling and white. The sandbagged Bronze Horseman is only visible in pieces. The trees are frosted white and strung with icicles. It amazes Vera that not a tree has been cut down here. There are no wooden fences or benches or railings left in the city, but no tree has been cut down for firewood.

The children immediately rush forward and drop onto their backs, making snow angels and giggling.

Vera sits by Sasha on a black iron bench. A tree shivers beside them, dropping ice and snow. She takes his hand, and although she cannot feel his flesh beneath her glove, the solid feel of him is more than enough.

"They are making an ice road across Ladoga," he says at last, and she knows it is what he has come to tell her.

"I hear trucks keep falling through the ice."

"For now. But it will work. They will get food into the city. And people out of it."

"Will they?"

"It's the only evacuation route."

"Is it?" She glances sideways, deciding not to tell him about their other evacuation, how she almost lost their children.

"I will get all of you passes as soon as it's safe."

She does not want to talk about any of this. It doesn't matter. Only food matters now, and heat. She wishes he would just hold her and kiss her.

Maybe they will make love tonight, she thinks, closing her eyes. But how could she? She is too weak to sit up sometimes. . . .

"Vera," he says, making her look at him.

She blinks. It is hard sometimes to stay concentrated, even now. "What?" She stares into his bright green eyes, sharp with both fear and worry, and suddenly she is remembering the first time they met. The poetry. He said something to her, a line about roses. And later, in the library, he said he'd waited for her to grow up.

"You stay alive," he says.

She frowns, trying to listen carefully; then he starts to cry and she understands.

"I will," she says, crying now, too.

"And keep them well. I'll find you a way out. I promise. You just have to hang on a little while longer. Promise me." He shakes her. "Promise me. The three of you will make it to the end."

She licks her cracked, dry lips. "I will," she says, believing it, believing in it.

He pulls her close and kisses her. He tastes like sweet summer peaches, and when he draws back they are both done with crying.

"It's your birthday tomorrow," she says.

"Twenty-six," he says.

She leans against him; his arm comes around her. For a few hours, they are just a young family playing in the park. People hear the children laughing and come to see; they stand at the edges of the park like confused mental patients suddenly set free. It has been a long time since any of them heard a child laugh.

It is the best day of Vera's life—as impossible as that sounds. The memory of it is golden, and as she walks home, holding his hand, she can feel herself protecting it. It is a light she will need in the months to come.

But when she gets home, she knows instantly that something is wrong.

The apartment is dark and freezing. She can see her breath. On the table, a pitcher of water is frozen solid. Frost shines on the metal stove. The fire has gone out.

She hears her mother coughing in bed and she runs to her, yelling at Sasha to build a fire.

Her mother's breathing is noisy and strained. It sounds like old fruit being pushed through a sieve. Her skin is as pale as dirty snow. The flesh around her mouth is darkening, turning blue. "Verushka," she whispers.

Or did she really speak? Vera doesn't know. "Mama," she says.

"I waited for Sasha," Mama says.

Vera wants to beg with her, to plead, to say that he is not back, he is only visiting, and that she needs her mother, but she—

I *can't say anything.*

All I can do is sit there, staring down at my mother, loving her so much I don't even remember how hungry I am.

"I love you," Mama says softly. "Never forget that."

"How could I?"

"Don't try. That's what I mean." Mama struggles to lean forward and it's terrible to watch the effort it takes, so I lean forward and take her in my arms. She's like a stick doll now. Her head lolls back.

"I love you, Mama," I say. It is not enough, those three little words that suddenly mean good-bye, and I am not ready for good-bye. So I keep talking. I hold her close and say, "Remember when you taught me to make borscht, Mama? And we argued about how small to cut the onions and why to cook them first? You made a pot and put the vegetables in raw so I could taste the difference? And you smiled at me then, and touched my cheek, and said, 'Do not forget how much I know, Verushka.' I am not done learning from you. . . ."

At that, I feel my throat tighten and I can't say anything more.

She is gone.

I hear my son say, "Mama, what's wrong with Baba?" and it takes all my strength not to cry. But what good will crying do?

Tears are useless now in Leningrad.

Twenty-three

The silence that followed was so thick and gray Meredith expected to taste ash.

I can't say anything.

She looked at her mother, still in bed, with her knees drawn up and the covers pulled to her chin, as if a bit of wool could somehow protect her.

"Are you okay, Mom?" Nina said, getting up.

"How could I be?"

Meredith got up, too. Although they said nothing, didn't even make eye contact, Meredith felt for once as if they were in perfect agreement. She took her sister's hand and they walked over to the bed.

"Your mother and sister knew how hard you tried, and how much you loved them," Meredith said.

"Do not do that," Mom said.

Meredith frowned. "Don't do what?"

"Make excuses for me."

"It's not an excuse, Mom. Just an observation. They must have known how much you loved them," Meredith said as gently as she could.

Nina nodded.

"But *you* didn't," Mom said, looking at each of them in turn.

Meredith could have lied then, could have told her eighty-one-year-old mother that yes, she'd felt loved, and even a week ago she might have done it to keep the peace. Now she said, "No. I never thought you loved me."

She waited for her mother's response, imagining her saying something that would change everything, change them, though she didn't know what words those would be.

In the end, it was Nina who spoke.

"All these years we wondered what was wrong with us. Meredith and I couldn't figure out how a woman who loved her husband could hate her own children."

Mom flinched at the word *hate* and waved a hand in dismissal. "Go now."

"It wasn't us, was it, Mom?" Nina said. "You didn't hate your children. You hated yourself."

At that, Mom crumbled. There was no other word for it. "I tried not to love you girls . . . ," she said quietly. "Now go. Leave me before you say something you'll wish you hadn't."

"What would that be?" Nina asked, but they all knew.

"Just go. Please. Don't say anything to me until you've heard it all."

Meredith heard the way Mom's voice caught on *please* and shook, and she knew how close Mom was to falling apart. "Okay," she said, "we'll go." She leaned down and kissed her mother's soft, pleated cheek, smelling the rose-scented shampoo she used on her hair. It was something she hadn't known: that her mother used scented shampoo. For the first time ever, she pulled her mother into an embrace and whispered, "Good night, Mom."

All the way to the door, Meredith expected to be called back, to hear her mother say, *Wait*. But there was no last-minute revelation. Meredith and Nina went back to their own room. In a contemplative silence, they slipped past each other in the bathroom and brushed their teeth and put on their pajamas and climbed into their separate beds.

It was all connected; Meredith knew that now. Her life and her mother's. They were joined, and not only by blood. By inclination, perhaps even by temperament. She was more and more sure that whatever loss had finally broken her mother—turned Vera into Anya—would have ruined Meredith, too. And she was afraid of hearing it.

"What do you think happened to Leo and Anya?" Nina asked.

Meredith wished it wasn't a question. She would have preferred a statement she could ignore. Before this trip and all that she'd learned about the three of them, she would have gotten angry or changed the subject. Anything to obscure the pain she felt. Now she knew better. You carried your pain with you in life. There was no outrunning it. "I'm afraid to guess."

"What will happen to her when she gets to the end?" Nina asked quietly.

That had begun to worry Meredith, too. "I don't know."

According to their guidebook, Sitka was one of the most charming—and certainly among the most historic—of all Alaskan towns. Two hundred years ago, when San Francisco was barely a dot on the map of California and Seattle was a hillside of ancient evergreens, this sleepy waterfront community had had theaters and music halls and well-dressed men in beaver hats drinking Russian vodka in the warm summer nights. Built and lost to fire and rebuilt again, the new Sitka was equal parts Russian and Tlingit and American.

Shallow water prohibited the arrival of big cruise ships, so Sitka waited, like a particularly beautiful woman, for visitors to arrive in small launches. As they entered Sitka Harbor, Nina took one picture after another. This was one of the most pristine places she'd ever seen. The natural beauty was staggering on this day of blue sky and golden sunlight, the water flat and sapphire-blue. All around were forested islands, rising up from the quiet sea like a necklace of jagged jade pieces. Behind it all were the mountains, still draped in snow.

On shore, Nina capped her lens and let the camera dangle around her neck.

Mom stood with a hand tented over her eyes, gazing at the town laid out before them. From here they could see a spire rising high into the sky, its top a three-tiered Russian cross.

Nina reached instinctively for her camera. Looking through the lens, she saw her mother's sharp profile soften when she looked at the church spire. "What's it like, Mom?" she said, moving closer. "Seeing that?"

"It's been so long," Mom said, not looking away. "It makes me think . . . of all of it, I guess."

On her other side, Meredith moved closer as well. The three of them followed the small crowd who'd come from the ship. They walked up Harbor Drive and there were bits and pieces of Sitka's Russian past everywhere—street names and store names and restaurant menus. There was even a totem pole downtown that had an emblem of Czarist Russia carved into it. The double-headed eagle.

Mom said almost nothing as they passed one reminder of her homeland after another, but when they pushed through the doors of St. Michael's Church, she stumbled and would have fallen if both girls hadn't reached out to steady her.

There were glittering, golden Russian icons everywhere. Some were ancient paintings on wooden boards; others were jewel-studded masterpieces on silver or gold. White arches separated the rooms, their surfaces decorated in elaborate gold scrollwork. On display were ornately beaded wedding gowns and religious vestments.

Mom looked at everything, touching what she could. Finally, she ended up at what Nina figured was the altar—a small area draped in heavy white silk adorned with Russian crosses made of gold thread. There were candles all around, and a pair of old Bibles lay open.

"Do you want us to pray with you?" Meredith asked.

"No." Mom shook her head a little and wiped her eyes, although Nina had seen no tears. Then she walked out of the church and up a short distance. Nina could tell that her mother had studied a map of Sitka. She knew exactly where she was going. She passed a sign that advertised Russian-American history tours and turned into a cemetery. It was on a small rise, a grassy area studded with fragile-looking trees and clumps of brown bushes. A coppery dome, topped with a Russian cross, marked the hallowed ground. The grave markers were old-fashioned; many were handmade. Even the marker for Princess Matsoutoff was a simple black sign. A white picket fence delineated the princess's final resting place. The few cement markers were overgrown with moss. It looked as if no one new had been buried here in years, and yet Mom moved over the bumpy ground, looking at every grave.

Nina took a picture of her mother, who stood in front of a mossy headstone that had been knocked askew by some long-ago storm. The late spring breeze plucked at her tightly bound white hair. She looked . . . ethereal almost, too pale and slim to be real, but the sadness in her blue eyes was as honest as any emotion Nina had ever seen. She put the camera down, let it hang, and moved in beside her mother.

"Who are you looking for?"

"No one," Mom said, then added, "ghosts."

They stood there a moment longer, both staring at the grave of Dmitri Petrovich Stolichnaya, who died in 1827. Then Mom straightened her shoulders and said, "I am hungry. Let us find someplace to eat." She put her big round Jackie O–style sunglasses on and coiled a scarf around her throat.

The three of them walked back downtown, where they found a small restaurant on the water that promised *SITKA'S BEST RUSSIAN FOOD*.

Nina opened the door and a bell rang cheerily overhead. Inside the long, narrow room were a dozen or so tables; most were full of people. They didn't look like tourists, either. There were big, broad-shouldered men with beards that seemed to be made of iron shavings, women in brightly colored kerchiefs and dated floral dresses, and a few men in yellow plastic fisherman's overalls.

A woman greeted them with a bright smile. She was older than her voice sounded—maybe sixty—and pleasingly plump. Silvery curls framed an apple-cheeked face. She was the perfect portrait of a grandmother. "Hello, there. Welcome to the restaurant. I'm Stacey, and I'll be happy to serve you today." Reaching for three laminated menus, she led them to a little table by the window. Outside, the water was a sparkling expanse of blue. A fishing boat motored into shore, its passage marked by silvery ripples.

"What do you recommend?" Meredith asked.

"I guess I'd have to say the meatballs. And we make our noodles from scratch. Although the borscht is to die for, too."

"How about vodka?" Mom said.

"Is that a Russian accent?" Stacey asked.

"I have not lived there for a long time," Mom said.

"Well, you're our special guest. Don't you even look at the menu. I'll bring you something." She bustled away, whistling as she walked. Pausing briefly at a few other tables, she disappeared behind a bead-fringed curtain.

A few moments later she was back with three shot glasses, a frosted bottle of vodka, and a tray of black caviar with toast points. "Don't you dare say it's too expensive," Stacey said. "We get too many tourists and too few Russians. This is my treat. *Vashe zdorovie.*"

Mom looked up in surprise. Nina wondered how long it had been since she had heard her native language.

"*Vashe zdorovie,*" Mom said, reaching for her glass.

The three of them clinked glasses, drank down their shots, and reached immediately for the caviar.

"My daughters are becoming good Russians," Mom said. There was a softening in her voice as she said it; Nina wished she could see her mother's eyes, but the sunglasses created the perfect camouflage.

"With one drink?" Stacey scoffed. "How can that be?"

For the next twenty minutes or so, they talked about ordinary things, but when the waitress returned with the food, no one could talk about anything else. From tiny, succulent meatballs swimming in saffron broth, to mushroom soup with a bubbly gruyère crust, to a moist salmon-stuffed veal roast with caviar sauce. By the time the apple and walnut strudel showed up, everyone said they were too full. Stacey smiled at that and walked away.

Nina was the first to cut off a piece. "Oh, my God," she said, tasting the buttery walnut-filled pastry.

Mom took a bite of the strudel. "It is like my mama used to make."

"Really?" Meredith said.

"She always said the secret was to slap the dough against the pastry board. When I was a girl, we often fought about this. I said it was unnecessary. I was wrong, of course." Mom shook her head. "Later, I could never make that dough without thinking of my mother. Once, when I served it to your father, he said the strudel was too salty. This was from my tears, so I put the recipe away and tried to forget it."

"And did you?"

Mom glanced out the window. "I forgot nothing."

"You didn't want to forget," Meredith said.

"Why do you say this?" Mom asked.

"The fairy tale. It was the only way you could tell us who you were."

"Until the play," Mom said. "I am sorry for that, Meredith."

Meredith sat back in her seat. "I've waited for that apology all my life, and now that I have it, it doesn't matter. I care about you, Mom. I just want us all to keep talking."

"Why?" Mom said quietly. "How can you care? Either one of you?"

"We tried not to love you, too," Nina said.

"I would say I made it easy," Mom said.

"No," Meredith said, "never easy."

Mom reached out and poured three more vodkas. Lifting her glass, she looked at her daughters. "What shall we drink to?"

"How about family?" Stacey said, showing up just in time to pour a fourth shot. "To those who are here, those who are gone, and those who are lost." She clinked her glass against Mom's.

"Is that an old Russian toast?" Nina asked after she'd downed her vodka.

"I've never heard it before," Mom said.

"It's what we say in my house," Stacey said. "It's good, don't you think?"

"*Da*," Mom said, actually smiling. "It is very good."

On the walk back through town, Mom seemed to be standing taller. She was quick to smile or to point out a trinket in a store window.

Meredith couldn't help staring. It was like seeing a butterfly emerge from its chrysalis. And somehow, seeing her new mother, or her mother in this new light, made Meredith feel differently about herself. Like her mom, she smiled easier, laughed more often. Not once had she worried about the office, or her girls, or missing the ship. She'd been happy just to *be*, to flow on this journey with her mom and sister. For once, they felt as intertwined as strands of a rope; where one went, the other belonged.

"Look," Mom said as they came to the end of the street.

At first all Meredith saw were the quaint blue wooden shops and the distant snowy peak of Mount Edgecumbe. "What?"

"There."

Meredith followed the invisible line from her mother's pointing finger.

In a park across the street, standing beneath a streetlamp twined in bright pink flowers, there was a family, laughing together, posing for silly pictures. There was a woman with long brown hair, dressed in crisply pressed jeans and a turtleneck; a blond man whose handsome face seemed hardly able to contain the breadth of his smile; and two tow-headed little girls, giggling as they pushed each other out of the picture.

"That is how you and Jeff used to be," Mom said quietly.

Meredith felt a kind of sadness. It wasn't what she'd felt before: not disappointment that her kids didn't call, or fear that Jeff didn't love her, or even worry that she had lost too much of herself. This new feeling was the realization that she wasn't young anymore. The days of frolicking with her little girls were gone. Her children were on their own now, and Meredith needed to accept that. They would always be a family, but if she'd learned anything in the past few weeks it was that a family wasn't a static thing. There were always changes going on. Like with continents, sometimes the changes were invisible and underground, and sometimes they were explosive and deadly. The trick was to keep your balance. You couldn't control the direction of your family any more than you could stop the continental shelf from breaking apart. All you could do was hold on for the ride.

As she stood there, staring at strangers, she saw her marriage in moments. She and Jeff at the prom, dancing under a mirrored ball to "Stairway to Heaven" and French-kissing . . . her in labor, screaming at him to stay the fuck away from her with those ice chips . . . him handing her the first pages of his first novel and asking her opinion . . . and him standing beside her when Dad was dying, saying, *Who takes care of you, Mere?* and trying to hold her.

"I've been an idiot," she said to no one except herself, forgetting for a moment that she was standing in the middle of a busy sidewalk, flanked by eavesdroppers.

"It's about time," Nina said, smiling. "I'm tired of being the only screw-up in this family."

"I love Jeff," Meredith said, feeling both miserable and elated.

"Of course you do," Mom said.

Meredith turned to them. "What if it's too late?"

Mom smiled, and Meredith was struck by both the beauty and the newness of the face she'd studied for decades. "I am eighty-one years old, telling my life story to my daughters. Every year, I thought it was too late to start, that I'd waited too long. But Nina here won't take no for an answer."

"*Finally*. Being a selfish bitch pays off." Nina reached into her camera bag and pulled out a clunky cell phone, flipping it open. "Call him."

"Oh. We're having fun. It can wait."

"No," Mom said sharply. "Never wait."

"What if—"

Mom laid a hand on her forearm. "Look at me, Meredith. I am what fear makes of a woman. Do you want to end up like me?"

Meredith slowly reached out and removed her mother's sunglasses. Staring into the aqua-blue eyes that had always mesmerized her, Meredith smiled. "You know what, Mom? I'd be proud to have your strength. What you've been through—and we don't know the worst of it, I think—it would have killed an ordinary woman. Only someone extraordinary could have survived. So, yeah, I do want to end up like you."

Mom swallowed hard.

"But I don't want to be afraid. You're right about that. So give me that damn cell phone, Neener Beaner. I've got an overdue call to make."

"We'll meet you on the boat," Nina said.

"Where?"

Mom actually laughed. "The bar, of course. The one with the view."

Meredith watched her sister and mother walk down the sidewalk, away from her. Although the wind was blowing slightly, tapping a seashell chime in the eaves beside her, and somewhere a boat honked its horn, she couldn't hear anything except the lingering echo of her mother's laughter. It was a sound she'd keep forever, and pull out whenever she stopped believing in miracles.

She crossed the street, stopping traffic with a smile and an outheld palm. Passing the family still taking pictures of each other, she went to a small wooden bench that read: IN MEMORY OF MYRNA, WHO LOVED THIS VIEW.

She sat down on Myrna's bench and stared out at the gaggle of fishing and pleasure boats in the marina below. Masts cocked and swayed with every invisible movement of the water. Seabirds cawed out to tourists and dove for golden fries.

She glanced at her watch, calculated Jeff's schedule, and dialed his number.

It rang so many times she almost gave up.

Then, finally, he answered, sounding out of breath. "Hello?"

"Jeff?" she said, feeling tears rise up. It was all she could do to hold them back. "It's me."

"Meredith . . ."

She couldn't quite pinpoint the emotion in his voice, and that bothered her. Once, she'd known every nuance. "I'm in Sitka," she said, stalling.

"Is it as beautiful as they say?"

"No," she decided. She wasn't going to be afraid and she wasn't going to waste time on the kind of facile conversations that had gotten her into this mess. "I mean yes, it is beautiful here, but I don't want to talk about that. I don't want to talk about our daughters, either, or our jobs, or my mom. I want to say I'm sorry, Jeff. You asked me if I loved you, and I hit the brakes. I'm still not sure why. But I was wrong and stupid. I *do* love you. I love you and I miss you and I hope to hell I'm not too late because I want to grow old with the man I was young with. With you." She drew in a sharp breath. It felt as if she'd been talking forever, spewing really, and now it was up to him. Had she hurt him too much? Waited too long? When the silence went on—she could hear a squeaky spring as he sat down on a bad sofa, and then his sigh—she said, "Say something."

"December 1974."

"What?"

"I was in line at the CUB. Karie Dovre elbowed me and when I looked over, I saw you standing by the tetherball. You'd been avoiding me, remember? After the Christmas play? You wouldn't even look at me for two years. I tried lots of times to walk up to you, but I always lost my nerve at the last second. Until that day in December. It was snowing, and you were standing there, all by yourself, shivering. And before I could talk myself out of it, I walked over to you. Karie was yelling that I'd lose my place in the food line, but I didn't care. When you looked up at me, I remember how hard it was to breathe. I thought you'd run away, but you didn't, and I said, 'Do you like banana splits?'" He laughed. "What an idiot. It was probably twenty-five degrees outside and I ask about ice cream. But you said yes."

"I remember," she said quietly.

"We have a thousand memories like that."

"Yes."

"I've tried to fall out of love with you, Mere. I couldn't do it, but I thought sure as hell you had."

"I didn't fall out of love with you, either. I just . . . fell. Can we start over?"

"Hell, no. I don't want to start over. I *like* the middle."

Meredith laughed at that. She didn't want to go back and be young again, either, not with all the uncertainties and angst. She just wanted to *feel* young again. And she wanted to change. "I'll be naked more. I promise."

"And I'll make you laugh more. God, I've missed you, Mere. Can you come home right now? I'll warm up the bed."

"Almost." She leaned back into the sun-baked wooden bench.

For the next half hour, they talked like they used to, about anything and everything. Jeff told her he'd almost finished his novel and Meredith told him part of her mother's story. He listened in obvious awe, offering memories that suddenly made sense, times when Mom's behavior had seemed inexplicable. *All that food,* he said, *and the stuff she said . . .*

They talked about the girls and how they were doing in school and what the summer would be like with the house full again.

"Have you figured out what you want?" Jeff finally said. "Besides me, that is?"

"I'm working on it. I think I want to expand the gift shop. Maybe let Daisy run Belye Nochi. Or even sell it." She was surprised by her own words. She didn't remember ever really thinking that before, but suddenly it made sense. "And I want to go to Russia. Leningrad."

"You mean St. Petersburg, but—"

"It will always be Leningrad to me. I want to see the Summer Garden and the Neva River and the Fontanka Bridge. We never really went on a honeymoon. . . ."

He laughed. "Are you sure this is Meredith Cooper?"

"Meredith Ivanovna Cooper. That's what my name would be in Russia. And yeah. It's me. Can we go?"

She could hear the laughter in Jeff's voice, and the love, when he said, "Baby, our kids are gone. We can go anywhere."

Twenty-four

Juneau was the epitome of the Alaskan spirit—a state capital built with no roads leading in or out. The only way to get there was by boat or air. Surrounded by towering, snow-clad mountains and tucked in between ice fields larger than some states, it was a rough-and-tumble city that clung tenaciously to its pioneer and Native roots.

If they hadn't been on a quest—or it hadn't been raining so hard—Nina felt sure they would have taken an excursion to see the Mendenhall Glacier. But as it was, the three of them were standing at the entrance to the Glacier View Nursing Home instead.

"Are you afraid, Mom?" Meredith asked.

"I wasn't under the impression that he'd agreed to see me," Mom said.

"Not precisely," Nina said. "But sooner or later, everyone talks to me."

Mom actually smiled. "God knows that is true."

"So are you afraid?" Nina asked.

"No. I should have done this years ago. Perhaps if I had . . . No. I am not afraid of telling the story to this man who is collecting such memories."

"Perhaps if you had, what?" Meredith asked.

Mom turned to look at them. Her face was shadowed by the black woolen hood she wore. "I want you both to know what this trip has meant to me."

"Why do you sound like you're saying good-bye?" Nina asked.

"Today you will hear the terrible things I did," Mom said.

"We all do terrible things, Mom," Meredith said. "You don't have to worry."

"Do we? Do we all do terrible things?" Mom made a sound of disgust. "This is the talk-show babble of your generation. Here is what I want to say now, before we go in. I love both of you." Her voice cracked, turned harsh, but her gaze softened. "My Ninotchka . . . my Merushka."

Before either could even respond to the sweetness of their Russian nicknames, Mom turned on her heel and walked into the nursing home.

Nina rushed to keep up with her eighty-one-year-old mother.

At the desk, she smiled at the receptionist, a round-faced, black-haired woman in a beaded red sweater.

"We are the Whitson family," Nina said. "I wrote ahead to Dr. Adamovich and told him we'd be stopping by to see him today."

The receptionist frowned, flipping through a calendar. "Oh. Yes. His son, Max, is going to be here at noon to meet you. Would you like to have some coffee while you wait?"

"Sure," Nina said.

They followed the receptionist's directions to a waiting room filled with black and white images of Juneau's colorful past.

Nina took a place by the window in a surprisingly comfortable chair. Behind her, a large picture window looked out over a green forest threaded by falling rain.

The minutes ticked past. People came and went, some walking, others in wheelchairs, their voices floating in and out with their presence.

"I wonder what the *belye nochi* is like here," Mom said quietly, gazing out the window.

"It's better the farther north you go," Nina said. "According to my research anyway. But if you're lucky, sometimes you can see the northern lights from here."

"The northern lights," Mom said, leaning back in her orange chair. "My papa used to take me outside in the middle of the night sometimes, when everyone else was asleep. He'd whisper, 'Verushka, my little writer,' and take my hand and wrap me in a blanket and out we would go, into the streets of Leningrad, to stand and stare up at the sky. It was so beautiful. God's light show, my papa said, although he said it softly. Everything he said was dangerous then. We just didn't know it." She sighed. "I think this is the first time I've ever just talked about him. Just remembered something ordinary."

"Does it hurt?" Meredith asked.

Mom thought about that for a moment and then said, "In a good way. We were always so scared to mention him. This is what Stalin did to us. When I first came to the United States, I could not believe how free everyone was, how quick to say what was on their minds. And in the sixties and seventies . . ." She shook her head, smiling. "My father would have loved to see a sit-in or the college kids demonstrating. He was like them, like . . . Sasha and your father. Dreamers."

"Vera was a dreamer," Nina said gently.

Mom nodded. "For a time."

A man dressed in a flannel shirt and faded jeans walked into the room. With a thick black beard that covered half of his angular face, it was hard to make out his age. "Mrs. Whitson?" he said.

Mom slowly stood.

The man moved forward, his hand outstretched. "I am Maksim. My father, Vasily Adamovich, is the man you have come so far to see."

Nina and Meredith rose as one.

"It is many years since your father wrote to me," Mom said.

Maksim nodded. "And I'm sorry to say that he has suffered a stroke in the years between. He can barely speak and can't move his left side at all."

"So we are wasting your time," Mom said.

"No. Not at all. I have taken up a few of my father's projects and the siege of Leningrad is one of them. It's such important work, gathering these survivor stories. It's only in the last twenty years or so that the truth is coming to light. The Soviets were good at keeping secrets."

"Indeed," Mom said.

"So if you'd like to come into my father's room, I'll record your account for his study. He may not appear to react, but I can assure you that he is happy to finally include your story. It will be the fifty-third first-person account he has collected. Later this year I am going to St. Petersburg to petition for more records. Your story will make a difference, Mrs. Whitson. I assure you."

Mom simply nodded, and Nina couldn't help wondering what she was thinking, now that they were coming to the time when the story would end.

"Follow me, please," Maksim said. Turning, he led them down the brightly lit corridor, past hunched old women with walkers and tiny old men in wheelchairs, to a room at the very end of the hall.

There was a narrow hospital-style bed in the center of the room and a couple of chairs that had obviously been brought in for this meeting. In the bed lay a shrunken man with a bony face and toothpick arms. Tufts of white hair sprang from his bald, spotted head and his wrinkled pink ears. His nose was like a raptor's beak and his lips all but invisible. At their entrance, his right hand began to tremble and the right side of his mouth tried to smile.

Maksim leaned down close to his father, whispered something into his ear.

The man in the bed said something, but Nina couldn't understand a word.

"He says he is so glad to see you, Anya Whitson. He has waited a long time. My father is Vasily Adamovich and he welcomes you all."

Mom nodded.

"Please, sit down," Maksim said, indicating the chairs. On a table by the window were a copper samovar and several plates of pierogies and strudel and sliced cheese with crackers.

Vasily said something, his voice crackled like a dried leaf.

Maksim listened, then shook his head. "I'm sorry, Papa. I cannot understand. He is saying something about the rain, I think. I am not sure. I am going to record your story, Mrs. Whitson. Anya—may I call you Anya? Is the recording okay?"

Mom was staring at the gleaming copper samovar and the row of silver-wrapped glass teacups. "*Da*," she said softly, flicking a hand in dismissal.

Nina hadn't realized that she was the only one still standing. She went to the chair next to Meredith's and sat down.

For a moment, the room was utterly still. The only noise in it was the tapping of the rain on the roof.

Then Mom drew in a long, slow breath and released it. "I have told this story in a single way for so long, I hardly know how to start now. I hardly know how to start."

Maksim hit the record button. It made a loud clicking sound and the tape started to roll.

"I am not Anya Petrovna Whitson. This is the name I took, the woman I became." She took another deep breath. "I am Veronika Petrovna Marchenko Whitson, and Leningrad is my city. It is a part of me. Long ago, I knew those streets like I know the soles of my feet or the palms of my hands. But it is not my youth you are interested in. Not that I had much of one, when I look back on it. I started to grow up at fifteen when they took my father away, and by the end of the war, I was old. . . .

"That is the middle, though. The beginning, really, is June of 1941. I am coming home from the country, where I'd been gathering vegetables to can for the coming winter. . . ."

Nina closed her eyes and sat back, letting the words form pictures in her imagination. She heard things she'd heard before as a fairy tale; only this time they were real. There were no Black Knights or princes or goblins. There was only Vera, first as a young woman, falling in love and having her babies . . . and then as a woman afraid, digging on the Luga line and walking through bombed-out landscapes. Nina had to wipe her tears away when Olga died, and again when Vera's mother died.

"She is gone," Mom says with a terrible simplicity. "I hear my son say, '*What's wrong with Baba?*' and it takes all my strength

not to cry.

I pull the blanket up to Mama's chest, trying not to notice how bony her face has become in the last month. Should I have forced her to eat? This is a question that will haunt me for the rest of my life. If I had, I would have been pulling the blanket up on one of my children, and how could I have done that?

"Mama," Leo says again.

"Baba has gone to be with Olga," I say, and as hard as I try to be strong, my voice cracks, and then my children are crying.

It is Sasha who comforts them. I have no comfort left inside of me. I am cold to the bone, afraid that if one of them touches me I will crack apart like an egg.

I sit next to my dead mother for a long time, in our shadowy, cold room, with my head bowed in a prayer that comes too late. Then I remember a thing she said to me long ago, when I was the child who needed comfort. We will not speak of him again.

At the time, I thought it was because of his danger to us, his crimes, but as I sit next to my mother, I feel her move beside me—I swear I do—she reaches over and touches my hand and I feel warm for the first time in months, and I understand what she was saying to me then.

Go on. Forget if you can. Live.

It is not so much about who my father was, this advice; it is what life is about. What death does to you. When I look down, of course she is not moving, her skin is cold, and I know she did not really speak to me. But she did. And so I do what I must. I stand up, feeling out my new role. I am a motherless daughter now, a sisterless woman. There is no one left of the family I was born into; there is only the family I have made.

My mother is in all of us, though especially in me. Anya has my mother's solemn strength. Leo has Olga's easy laughter. And I—I have the best of both of them in me, and the dreams of my father, too, so it is my job to be all of us now.

Sasha is beside me suddenly.

He folds me into a hug and I press my face into the cold curl of his neck.

"We will be away from here someday," he promises. "We will go to Alaska, just like we talked about. It won't always be like this."

"Alaska," I say, remembering this dream of his, of ours. "Land of the Midnight Sun. Yes. . . ."

But a dream like that—any dream—is far away now and it only makes my pain worse.

I look at him, and though he says something, I see his thoughts in his green eyes, or maybe it is my own thoughts reflected. Either way, we break apart and Sasha says to our slumped, red-eyed children, "Mama and I must go take care of Baba."

Leo, sitting on the kitchen floor, starts to cry, but it is a pale imitation of my son's sadness, of his tears. I know. I have seen him burst into tears when he is healthy. Now he just . . . leaks water from his eyes and sits there, too hungry and exhausted to do more.

"We'll stay here, Papa," Anya says solemnly. "I'll take care of Leo."

"My good children," Sasha says. He keeps them busy while I wash Mama, and dress her in her best dress. I try not to notice how shrunken and thin she is . . . not really my mother at all, but . . .

It is true what they say. Children become adults who become children again. I cannot help thinking of this cycle as I gently wash my mother's body and button her buttons and pin her hair. When I am done, she looks like she is sleeping and I bend down and kiss her cold, cold cheek and whisper my good-bye.

Then it is time.

Sasha and I dress for the cold. I put on everything I own—four pairs of socks, my mother's oversized valenki, *pants, dresses, sweaters. I can barely fit into my coat, and once I have wrapped a scarf around my head, my face looks like a child's.*

Out we go, into the cold, black day. Streetlamps are on in places, their light blurred by falling snow. We tie Mama to the little red sled that once was a family toy and now is perhaps our most important possession. Sasha is strong enough to drag it through the heavy snow, thank God.

I am weak. I try to hide it from my husband, but how can I? Every step through the knee-deep snow is a torture for me. My breath comes in great, burning gasps. I want to sit down but I know better.

In front of us, a man weaves drunkenly forward, clutches a streetlamp, and bends over, breathing hard.

We walk past him. This is what we do now, what we have become. When I look back, breathing hard myself, he has fallen in the snow. I know that when we go home we will see his blue, frozen body. . . .

"Don't look," Sasha says.

"I see anyway," I say, and keep trudging forward. How can I not see? Rumors are that three thousand people a day are dying, mostly old men and young children. We women are stronger somehow.

Thankfully, Sasha is in the army, so we only have to stand in line a few hours for a death certificate. We will lose Mama's food ration, but lying about her death is more dangerous than starving.

By the time we leave the warmth of standing in line, I am beyond exhausted. The hunger is gnawing at my belly and I feel so light-headed that sometimes I cry for no reason. The tears freeze on my cheeks instantly.

There are streetlamps on at the cemetery, although I wish it were dark. In the falling snow, the bodies are hidden, coated in white, but there is no mistaking them: corpses stacked like firewood at the cemetery gates.

The ground is too frozen for burial. I should have known this. I would have known it if my mind were working, but hunger has made me stupid and slow.

Sasha looks at me. The sadness in his eyes is unbearable. I want to give in then, just slump into the snow and stop caring.

"I can't leave her here," I say, unable to even count the bodies. Neither can I bring her home again. It is what too many neighbors have done, just set aside a place for the dead in their apartments, but I cannot do it.

Sasha nods and moves forward, dragging the sled around the snowy mounds and into the dark, quiet cemetery.

We hold hands. It is the only way we can know where the other is. We find an open space beneath a tree laced with snow and frost. I hope this tree will be the protector for her I was not.

Our voices echo through the falling snow as we tell each other this is the place. I will always know this tree, recognize it, and here I will find her again someday, or at least I will stand here and remember her. From now on, I will always remember her on the fourteenth of December, wherever I am. It is not much, but it is something.

I kneel in the snow; even with gloves on, my fingers are trembling with cold as I untie the ropes and release her frozen body.

"I am sorry, Mama," I whisper, my teeth chattering. I touch her face in the darkness like a blind woman, trying to remember how she looks. "I'll come back in the spring."

"Come on," Sasha says, pulling me to my feet. I know better than to kneel, even for this, in the snow. Already my knees are colder. Soon I will not be able to feel my legs.

We leave her there. Alone.

"It is all we can do," Sasha says later as we trudge for home, our breathing ragged.

All I want to do is lie down. I am so hungry and so tired and so sad. I do not even care if I die.

"Yes," I say. I don't care. I just want to stop.

But Sasha is there, urging me forward, and when we get home, and our children climb into bed with us, I thank God my husband is there.

"Don't you give up," he whispers to me in bed that night. "I will find a way to get you out of here."

I promise.

I agree not to give up, though I don't know what it even means then.

And in the morning, he kisses my cheek, whispers that he loves me, and he leaves.

In late December, the city slowly freezes to death. It is dark almost all the time. Birds drop from the sky like stones. The crows die first; I remember that. It is impossibly cold. Twenty degrees below zero becomes normal. The streetcars stop in their tracks like children's toys that have fallen out of favor. The water mains burst.

The sleds are everywhere now. Women drag them through the streets to carry things home—wood from burned-out buildings, buckets of water from the Neva River, anything they can burn or eat.

You'd be amazed what you can eat. There are rumors that the sausage sold in the markets is made from human flesh. I don't go to the markets anymore. What is the point? I see beautiful fur coats and jewels selling for nothing and oil cakes made of warehouse sweepings and sawdust going for exorbitant prices.

We do as little as we can, my children and I. Our apartment is black all the time now—there is only the briefest spasm of daylight and very few candles are left to light the darkness. Our little burzhuika *is everything now. Heat and light. Life. We have burned most of the furniture in our apartment, but some pieces are still left.*

The three of us are wrapped tightly together all night, and in the morning we waken slowly. We lie beneath all the blankets we have, with our bed pushed close to the stove, and still we waken with frozen hair and frost on our cheeks. Leo has developed a cough that worries me. I try to get him to drink hot water, but he resists me. I cannot blame him. Even after it is boiled, the water tastes like the corpses that lie on the river's frozen surface.

I get up in the cold and take however long I must to break off a chair leg or shatter a drawer, and feed the wood into the stove. There is a ringing in my ears and a kind of vertigo that often sends me sprawling at the merest step. I know my own body by its bones now. Still, I smile when I kiss my babies awake.

Anya groans at my touch and this is better than Leo, who just lies there.

I shake him hard, yell his name; when he opens his eyes I can't help falling to my knees. "Silly boy," I say, wiping my eyes. I can't hear anything over the roaring in my ears and the hammering of my heart.

I would give anything to hear him say he is hungry.

I make us each a cup of hot water laced with yeast. It is no nutrition, but it will fill us up. Carefully, I take a piece of thick black bread—the last of this week's rations—and I cut it in thirds. I want to give it all to them, but I know better. Without me, they are lost, so I must eat.

We each cut our third of a piece of bread into tiny pieces, which we eat as slowly as possible. I put half of mine in my pocket for later. I get up and put on all of my clothes.

My children lie in the bed, snuggled close. Even from across the room, I can see how skeletal they look. When last I bathed Leo, he was a collection of sharp bones and sunken skin.

I go to them, sit by them on the bed. I touch Leo's cheeks, pull his knit cap down far enough to cover his ears.

"Don't go, Mama," he says.

"I have to."

It is the conversation we have every morning, and honestly, there is very little fight left in them. "I will find us some candy, would you like that?"

"Candy," he says dreamily, slumping back into his flattened pillow.

Anya looks up at me. Unlike her brother, she is not sick; she is just wasting, like me. "You shouldn't tell him there will be candy," she says.

"Oh, Anya," I say, pulling her into my arms and holding her as tightly as I can. I kiss her cracked lips. Our breath is terrible, but neither of us even notices anymore.

"I don't want to die, Mama," she says.

"You won't, moya dusha. We'll make sure of it."

My soul.

She is that. They both are. And because of that, I get up and get dressed and go to work.

Out in the freezing darkness of early morning, I drag my sled through the streets. In the library, I go down to the one reading room that is open. Oil lamps create pockets of light. Many of the librarians are too sick to move, so those of us who are able move books and answer research questions for the government and the army. We go in search of books, too, saving what we can from bombed buildings. When there is nothing left to do, I queue up for whatever rations I can get. Today I am lucky: there is a jar of sauerkraut and a ration of bread.

The walk home is terrible. My legs are so weak and I can't breathe and I am dizzy. There are corpses everywhere. I no longer even go around them. I don't have the energy.

Halfway home, I reach into my pocket and pull out my tiny piece of bread from the morning meal. I put it in my mouth, let it melt on my tongue.

I can feel myself swaying. That white roar of noise is back in my ears; in the past few weeks I have grown accustomed to the sound.

I see a bench up ahead.

Sit. Close your eyes for just a moment . . .

I am so tired. The gnawing in my belly is gone, replaced by exhaustion. It is a struggle just to breathe.

And then, amazingly, I see Sasha standing in the street in front of me. He looks exactly as he did on the day I met him, years ago, a lifetime; he isn't even wearing a coat and his hair is long and golden.

"Sasha," I say, hearing the crack in my voice. I want to run to him, but my legs won't work. Instead I crumple to my knees in the thick snow.

I can feel him beside me, putting his arm around me. His breath is so warm and it smells of cherries.

Cherries. Like the ones Papa used to bring us . . .

And honey.

I close my eyes, hungry for the taste of him and his sweet breath.

I can smell my mama's borscht.

"Get up, Vera."

At first it is Sasha's voice, deep and familiar, and then it is my own. Screaming.

"Get up, Vera."

I am alone. There is no one here beside me, no lover's breath that smells of honeyed cherries. There is just me, kneeling in the deep snow, slowly freezing to death.

I think of Leo's giggle and Anya's stern look and Sasha's kiss.

And I climb slowly, agonizingly, to my feet.

It takes hours to get home, although it is not far. When I fi-

nally arrive and stumble into the relative warmth of the apartment, I fall again to my knees.

Anya is there. She wraps her arms around me and holds me.

I have no idea how long we sit there, holding each other. Probably until the cold in the apartment drives us back into bed.

That night, after a dinner of hot sauerkraut and a boiled potato—heaven—we sit around the little burzhuika.

"Tell us a story, Mama," Anya says. "Don't you want a story, Leo?"

I scoop Leo into my arms and stare down at his pale face, made beautiful by firelight. I want to tell him a story, a fairy tale that will give him good dreams, but my throat is tight and my lips are so cracked it hurts to speak, so I just hold my babies instead and the frosty silence lulls us to sleep.

You think that things cannot get worse, but they can. They do.

It is the coldest winter on record in Leningrad. Rations are cut and cut again. Page by page I burn my father's beloved books for warmth. I sit in the freezing dark, holding my bony children as I tell them the stories. Anna Karenina. War and Peace. Onegin. *I tell them how Sasha and I met so often that soon I know the words by heart.*

It feels further and further away, though. Some days I cannot remember my own face, let alone my husband's. I can't recall the past, but I can see the future: it is in the stretched, tiny faces of my children, in the blue boils that have begun to blister Leo's pale skin.

Scurvy.

Lucky for me, I work in the library. Books tell me that pine needles have vitamin C, so I break off branches and drag them home on my sled. The tea I make from them is bitter, but Leo complains no more.

I wish he would.

⁂

Dark. Cold.

I can hear my babies breathing in the bed beside me. Leo's every breath is phlegmy. I feel his brow. He is not hot, thank God.

I know what has wakened me. The fire has gone out.

I want to do nothing about it.

The thought hits before I can guard against it. I could do nothing, just lie there, holding my children, and go to sleep forever.

There are worse ways to die.

Then I feel Anya's tiny legs brush up against mine. In her sleep, she murmurs, "Papa," and I remember my promise.

I take forever to get up. Everything hurts. There is a ringing in my ears and my balance is off. Halfway to the stove, I feel myself falling.

When I wake from my faint, I am disoriented. For a second, I hear my father at his desk, writing. His pen tip scratches words across the bumpy linen paper.

No.

I go to the bookcase. Only the last of the treasure is left: my father's own poetry.

I cannot burn them.

Tomorrow, perhaps, but not today. Instead, I take the ax—it is so heavy—and crack off a piece of the side of the bookcase. It is thick, old wood, hard as iron, and it burns hot.

I stand by the bed, in front of the fire, and I can feel how I am swaying.

I know suddenly that if I lie down, I will die. Did my mother tell me this? My sister? I don't know. I just remember knowing the truth of it.

"I won't die in my bed," I say to no one. So I go to the only other piece of furniture left in the room. My father's writing desk. Wrapping myself in a blanket, I sit down.

Can I smell him, or am I hallucinating again? I don't know. I pick up his pen and find that the ink in the well is frozen solid. The little metal inkwell is as cold as ice, but I carry it to the stove, where we both warm quickly. Making a cup of hot water to drink, I go back to the desk.

I light the lamp beside me. It is silly, I know. I should conserve this oil, but I can't just sit here in the icy black. I have to do *something to keep alive.*

So I will write.

It is not too late. I'm not dead yet.

I am Vera Petrovna and I am a nobody. . . .

I write and write, on paper that I know I will soon have to burn, with a hand that trembles so violently my letters look like antelopes leaping across the sheet. Still, I write and the night fades.

Some hours later, a pale gray light bleeds through the newsprint, and I know I have made it.

I am just about to put the pen down when there is a knock at the door. I force my legs to work, my feet to move.

I open the door to a stranger. A man in a big black woolen coat and a military cap.

"Vera Petrovna Marchenko?"

I hear his voice and it is familiar, but I cannot focus on his face. My vision is giving me problems.

"It is me. Dima Newsky from down the hall." He hands me a bottle of red wine, a bag of candy, and a sack of potatoes. "My mama is too ill to eat. She won't make it through the day. She asked me to give this to you. For the babies, she said."

"Dima," I say, and still I don't know who he is. I can't remember his mother, either, my neighbor.

But I take the food. I do not even pretend not to want it. I might even kill him for it. Who knows? "Thank you," I say, or think I do, or mean to.

"How is Aleksandr?"

"How are any of us? Do you want to come in? It is a little warmer—"

"No. I must get back to my mother. I am not here long. It's back to the front tomorrow."

When he is gone, I stare down at the food in awe. I am smiling when I waken Leo that morning and say, "We have candy. . . ."

In January, I strap poor Leo to the sled. He is so weak, he doesn't even struggle; his tiny body is bluish black and covered in boils. Anya is too cold to get out of bed. I tell her to stay in bed and wait for us.

It takes three hours to walk to the hospital, and when I get there . . .

People have died in line, waiting to see a doctor. There are bodies everywhere. The smell.

I lean down to Leo, who is somehow both bony and swollen. His tiny face looks like a starving cat. "I am here, my lion," I say because I can think of nothing else.

A nurse sees us.

Even though we are two among hundreds, she comes over, looks down at Leo. When she looks up at me, I see the pity in her eyes.

"Here," she says, giving me a piece of paper. "This will get him some millet soup and butter. There's aspirin at the dispensary."

"Thank you," I say.

We look at each other again, both knowing it is not enough. "He is Leo."

"My son was Yuri."

I nod in understanding. Sometimes a name is all you have left.

When I get home from the hospital, I cook everything I can find. I strip the wallpaper from the walls and boil it. The paste is made

of flour and water, and it thickens into a kind of soup. Carpenter's glue will do the same thing. These are the recipes I teach my daughter. God help us.

I boil a leather belt of Sasha's and make a jelly from it. The taste is sickening, but I get Leo to eat a little of it. . . .

In the middle of January, a friend of Sasha's arrives at our apartment. I can see that he is shocked by what he sees. He gives me a box from Sasha.

As soon as he is gone, we crowd around to look at it. Even Leo is smiling.

Inside are evacuation papers. We are to leave on the twentieth.

Beneath the papers is a coil of fresh sausage and a bag of nuts.

In utter darkness, I pack up the whole of my life, not that there is much left. Honestly, I do not know what I have taken and what I left behind. Most of our possessions have either frozen or been burned, but I remember to take my writings and my father's, and my last book of poetry by Anna Akhmatova. I take all the food we have—the sausage, half a bag of onions, four pieces of bread, some oil cakes, a quarter of a jar of sunflower oil, and the last of the sauerkraut.

I have to carry Leo. With his swollen feet and boil-covered arms, he can barely move, and I don't have it in me to waken him when he sleeps.

The three of us leave in the darkness of midmorning. Little Anya carries our only suitcase, filled with food. All our clothes we are wearing.

It is bitter cold outside and snowing hard. I hold her hand on the long walk to the train station, and once there, we are both exhausted.

In the train, we cram together. We are three of many, but no one talks. The air smells musty, of body odor and bad breath and death. It is a smell we all recognize.

I pull my babies close around me. I give Leo and Anya some wine to drink, but Leo is not happy with that. I cannot take out my food, not in this crowded train car. I could be killed for the oil cakes, let alone the sausage.

I dig deep in my coat pocket, which I have filled with dirt from the ground outside the burned Badayev food warehouses.

Leo eats the dirty, sugary particles greedily and cries for more. I do the only thing I can think of: I cut my finger and put it in his mouth. Like a newborn baby, he sucks on my finger, drinking my warm blood. It hurts, but not as much as hearing the congestion in his lungs or feeling the heat in his forehead.

In a quiet voice, I tell them stories of their father and me, of a fairy-tale love that seems so far away. Somewhere along that clackety trip, when I am so afraid and Leo is coughing terribly and Anya keeps asking when we will see Papa, I begin to call my husband a prince and Comrade Stalin the Black Knight and the Neva River takes on magical powers.

The train trip seems to last for a long time. My insides ache from being rattled around for so many hours. My fairy tale is the only thing that keeps us all sane. Without it, I think I might begin crying or screaming and never stop.

Finally, we reach the edge of Lake Ladoga. There is ice as far as I can see; there is almost no difference between my view through a clean window and one through the fog of my own breath.

We are at the start of the ice road.

Twenty-five

The army has been working for months to make a road across frozen Lake Ladoga. The road is here now, and everyone is calling it the road of life. Soon, they say, transports of food will rumble across the ice toward Leningrad. Up until now, those same trucks kept falling through into the freezing black water below. And, of course, the Germans bomb it constantly.

I check my children's clothes. Everything is in place, just as it was when we left Leningrad. Leo and Anya are wrapped in newsprint and then in all the clothes they own. We wrap scarves around our heads and necks; I try to cover everything, even Leo's small red nose.

Outside, it hurts when I take a breath. My lungs ache. Beside me, Leo starts to cough.

A full moon rises in the black sky, turning the snow blue. We stand around, all of us, matted together like cattle. Many people are coughing; somewhere a child is crying. It occurs to me to wish that it were Leo. His quiet scares me.

"What do we do, Mama?" Anya says.

"We find a truck. Here, take my hand."

My eyes water and sting as I start forward. Leo is in my arms, and as thin as he is, he weighs me down so that I can hardly move. Every step takes concentration, willpower. I have to lean into the howling wind. The only real thing in this icy blue-and-black world is my daughter's hand in mine. Somewhere far away, I hear an engine idling and then roaring. It is a convoy, I hope.

"Come," I shout into the wind, or mean to. I am so cold my knees hurt. It hurts even to bend my fingers enough to hold Anya's hand.

I walk

and walk

and walk

and there is nothing. Just ice and black sky and the distant popping of antiaircraft guns.

I think, I must hurry, *and,* My babies, *and then Sasha is beside me. I can feel the warmth of his breath. He is whispering about love and the place we will build for ourselves in Alaska and he tells me it's okay for me to rest.*

"Just for a moment," I say, falling to my knees before the words are even out of my mouth.

The world is totally quiet then. Somewhere, someone laughs and it sounds just like Olga. I will go find her as soon as I have a nap. This is the thought I have.

And I close my eyes.

"Mama."

"Mama."

"Mama."

She is screaming in my face.

I open my eyes slowly and see Anya. My daughter has pulled off her scarf and wrapped it around my neck.

"You have to get up, Mama," she says, tugging at me.

I look down. Leo is limp in my arms, his head lolled back. But I can feel his breathing.

I uncoil the scarf from around my neck and rewrap Anya's face. "Never take your scarf off again. Do not give it to anyone. Not even me."

"But I love you, Mama."

And there is my strength. Gritting my teeth against the pain that will come, I stagger to my feet and start moving again.

One step at a time, until a lorry materializes in front of me.

A man dressed in baggy white camouflage is standing beside the door, smoking a cigarette. The smell of it makes me think of my mother.

"A ride across the ice?" I say, hearing how cracked and weak my voice is.

The man's face is not drawn or gaunt. This means he is Somebody, or in the Party at least, and I feel my hope plummet.

He leans forward, looks at Leo. "Dead?"

I shake my head. "No. Just sleeping.

"Please," I say, desperate now. All around me trucks are leaving and I know we will die tonight, here, if we do not find a ride soon. I pull out the cloisonné butterfly made by my grandfather. "Here."

"No, Mama," Anya says, reaching for it.

The man just frowns. "What good is a trinket?"

I pull off my glove and give him my wedding ring instead. "It is gold. Please. . . ."

He looks me over as he takes one last drag of the cigarette and then drops it to the snow. "All right, Baba," he says, pocketing my ring. "Get in. I will take you and your grandchildren."

I am so grateful, I don't even realize what he has said to me until later, when we are all packed into the cab of his truck.

Baba.

He thinks I am an old woman. I pull the scarf off and glance in the mirror above the windshield.

My hair is as white as my skin.

It is daylight when we get across the ice. Not much light, of course, but enough. I can really see where we are now.

Endless snow. Trucks lined up, filled with food for my poor Leningrad. Soldiers dressed in white. Not far from here—three hundred yards, maybe—is the train station that is our next destination.

The bombing starts almost immediately. Our driver stops and gets out.

Honestly, I do not want to get out of the truck, even though I know how dangerous it is to sit here. There is gasoline in the tank, and no camouflage on the truck. It is a clear target from the air. But we are warm and it has been so long. . . . Then I look down at my Leo and I forget all about the danger.

He is not breathing.

I shake him hard, ripping open his coat and pulling up the newspaper. His chest is really just a brace of bones and blue skin and boils. "Wake up, Leo. Breathe. Come on, my lion." I put my mouth on his, breathing for him.

Finally, he shudders in my arms and I feel a sour little breath slip into my mouth.

He starts to cry.

I hold him to me, crying, too, and say, "Don't you leave me, Leo. I couldn't bear it."

"His hands are so hot, Mama," Anya says, and I see how scared she is by the suddenness of my yelling.

I touch Leo's forehead.

He is burning up. My hands are shaking as I reposition the newspaper and button up his sweater and coat.

We are going out into the cold again.

Anya leads the way out of the truck. I am so focused on Leo that I hardly notice the bombing and gunfire going on around me. Somewhere nearby a truck explodes.

It is like being in the eye of a hurricane. All around us trucks are rolling past, horses are clopping forward pulling wagons, soldiers are running, and we poor, starved Leningraders are looking for rides.

At last I find the infirmary. It consists of flapping, dirty white tents spread out across a snowy field.

Inside, it is no hospital. It is a place for the dying and the dead. That is all. The smell is horrible. People are lying in their own freezing filth, moaning.

I dare not put Leo down for fear he'll get worse. It seems like hours we wander around, looking for someone to help us.

Finally, I find an old man, hunched over a cane, staring at nothing. Only because he is wearing white do I approach him.

"Please," I say, reaching for him. "My son is burning up."

The man turns to me. He looks as tired as I feel. His hands are trembling slightly as he reaches for Leo. I can see the boils on his fingers.

He touches Leo's forehead and then looks at me.

It is a look I will never forget. Thank God there are no words with the look. "Get him to the hospital at Cherepovets." He shrugs. "Maybe."

I do not ask him to say more. In fact, I don't want him to.

He hands me four white pills. "Two a day," he says. "With clean water. When did he eat last?"

I shake my head. How can I say the words, tell the truth? It is impossible to get him to eat.

"Cherepovets," is all he says, and then he turns and goes away. At every step, people are reaching for him, begging for help.

"Let's go."

I take Anya's hand and we make our slow, painful way through the infirmary and across the snowy field to the train station. Our papers are in order and we climb into a car, where we are again packed in too tightly. There is no seat for me or my children, so we sit on the cold floor. I hold my Leo on my lap and Anya at my side. When it gets dark, I take out my small bag of nuts. I give Anya as many as I dare and eat a few myself. I manage to get Leo to take one of the pills with a swallow of water I've brought.

It is a long and terrible night.

I keep leaning down to see if Leo is still breathing.

I remember stopping once. The train doors opened and someone yelled out, "Any dead? Dead? Give them to us."

Hands reach for Leo, try to pull him out of my arms.

I hang on to him, screaming, "He's breathing, he's breathing."

When the door closes and it is dark again, Anya moves closer to me. I can hear her crying.

It is no better in Cherepovets. We have one day to spend here. At first I think this is a blessing, that we will have time to save Leo before we board the next train, but he is getting weaker. I try not to see this truth, but it is lying in my arms. He coughs all the time. Now there is blood in it. He is burning hot and shivering. He will neither eat nor drink.

The hospital here is an abomination. Everyone has dysentery and scurvy. You cannot stand for more than a moment or two without seeing a new Leningrader hobble in, looking for help. Every hour, trucks loaded with corpses leave the hospital, only to return empty. People are dying where they stand.

It is good that I am weak and hungry; I don't have the strength to run from place to place for help. Instead, I stand in the cold, bleak hallway, holding my son. When people pass, I whisper, "Help him. Please."

Anya is asleep on the cold floor, sucking her thumb, when a nurse stops.

"Help him," I say, handing Leo to her.

She takes him gently. I try not to notice how his head lolls back.

"He's dystrophic. Third stage. There is no fourth." At my blank look, she says, "Dying. But if we could get fluids into him . . . maybe. I could take him to the doctor. It would be a difficult few days, maybe, though."

She is so young, this nurse. As young as I was before the war began. I don't know how to believe her, or how not to. "I have evacuation papers. We are supposed to be on the train to Vologda tomorrow."

"They won't let your son on that train," the young nurse says. "Not one so sick."

"If we stay it will be impossible to get more tickets," I say. "We'll die here."

The nurse says nothing to this. Lies are a waste of time.

"We could start helping Leo now, couldn't we?" I say. "Maybe he'll be better by tomorrow."

The nurse cannot hide her pity for me. "Of course. Maybe he'll be better."

And he is.

Better.

After a night when Anya and I lay curled on the floor by Leo's dirty cot, I wake feeling bruised and cold. But when I get to my knees and look down at Leo, he is awake. For the first time in a long time, his blue eyes are clear. "Hi, Mama," he says in a scratchy, froglike voice that cuts right through my heart. "Where are we? Where's Papa?"

I waken Anya, pull her up beside me. "We are right here, baby. We are on our way to your papa. He will be waiting for us in Vologda."

I am smiling and crying as I look down at my son, my baby. Maybe it is the tears that blur my vision, or more likely it is hope. I am old enough to know better, but common sense is gone with the sound of his voice. I don't see how blue his skin is, how the boils have burst on his chest and are seeping yellow; I don't hear the thickness of his cough. I just see Leo. My lion. My baby with the bluest eyes and the purest laugh.

So when the nurse comes by to tell me that I should get on the train, I am confused.

"He's getting better," I say, looking down at him.

The silence stretches out between us, broken only by Leo's coughing and the distant rat-a-ta-tat *of gunfire. She looks pointedly at Anya.*

For the first time I see how pale Anya is, how gray her chapped lips are, the angry boils on her throat. Her hair is falling out in clumps.

How did I miss all that?

"But . . ." I look around. "You said they won't let my son on the train."

"There are too many evacuees. They won't transport the dying. You have papers for you and your daughter, yes?"

How is it that I don't understand what she is saying to me until then? And how can I explain how it feels to finally understand? A knife in the heart would hurt less.

"You're saying I should leave him here to die? Alone?"

"I'm saying he will die." The nurse looks at Anya. "You can save her." She touches my arm. "I'm sorry."

I stand there, frozen, watching her walk away. I don't know how long I stand there, but when I hear the train's whistle, I look down at the daughter I love more than my own life, and the son of mine who is dying.

"Mama?" Anya says, frowning up at me.

I take Anya's hand and walk her out of the hospital. At the train, I kneel in front of her.

She is so small, wrapped as she is in her bright red coat and wearing the valenki *that are too big for her feet.*

"Mama?"

"I can't leave Leo here," I say, hearing the break in my voice. He can't die alone *is what I want to say, but how can I say such a thing to my five-year-old? Does she know I am making a choice no mother should ever have to make? Will she someday hate me for this?*

Her face scrunches in a frown so familiar it breaks my heart. For a second, I see her as she used to be. "But—"

"You are my strong one. You will be okay alone."

She shakes her head, starts to cry. "No, Mama. I want to stay with you."

I reach into my pocket and take out a piece of paper. It still smells of sausage and my stomach churns at the scent of it. I write her name on the paper and pin it to her lapel. "P-Papa will be waiting for you in Vologda. You find him. Tell him we'll be there by Wednesday. You two can meet Leo and me."

It feels like a lie. Tastes like one. But she trusts me.

I don't let her hug me. I can see her reaching, reaching, and I push her back, into the crowd that is lining up around us.

A woman is standing close. Anya hits her and the woman stumbles sideways, cursing softly.

"Mama—"

I push my daughter at the stranger, who looks at me with glassy eyes.

"Take my daughter," I say. "She has papers. Her father will be in Vologda. Aleksandr Ivanovich Marchenko."

"No, Mama." Anya is wailing, reaching for me.

I mean to push her away so hard she stumbles, but I can't do it. At the last moment, I yank her into my arms and hold her tightly.

The train whistle blows. Someone yells, "Is she going?"

I unwrap Anya's arm from around my neck. "You be strong, Anya. I love you, moya dusha."

How can I call her my soul and then push her away? But I do. I do.

At the last minute, I hand her the butterfly. "Here. You hold this for me. I will come back for it. For you."

"No, Mama—"

"I promise," I say, lifting her up, putting her in a stranger's arms.

She is still crying, screaming my name and struggling to get free, when the train doors slam shut.

I stand there for a long time, watching the train grow smaller and smaller, until it disappears altogether. The Germans are bombing again. I can hear the explosions all around, and people shouting, and debris thumping on metal roofs.

I hardly care.

As I turn toward the hospital, it feels as if something falls out of me, but I don't look down, don't want to see whatever I've lost. Instead, I walk through the raining dirt and snow toward my son.

Loss is a dull ache in my chest, a catch in my breathing, but I tell myself I have done the right thing.

I will keep Leo alive by the sheer force of my will, and Sasha will find Anya in Vologda and the four of us will meet up on Wednesday.

It is such a beautiful dream. I keep it alive one breath at a time, like a timid candle flame in the cup of my hands.

Back at the hospital, it is dark again. The smell of the place is unbearable. And it is cold. I can feel the wind prowling outside, testing every crack and crevice, looking for a way in.

In his narrow, sagging cot, Leo is sucking in his sleep, chewing food that isn't there. He coughs almost constantly now, spasms that spew lacy blood designs across the woolen blankets.

When I can stand it no more, I crawl into the cot and pull him into my arms. He burrows against me like the baby he once was, murmuring my name in his sleep. His breathing is a terrible thing to listen to.

I stroke his hot, damp forehead. My hand is freezing, but it is worth it to touch him, to let him know I am here, beside him, all around him. I sing his favorite songs and tell him his favorite stories. Now and then he rouses, smiles sloppily at me, and asks for candy.

"No candy," I say, kissing his sunken blue cheek. I cut my finger again, let him suck on it until the pain makes me draw back.

I am singing to him, barely able to remember the words, when I realize that he is not breathing anymore.

I kiss his cheek, so cold, and his lips, and I think I hear him say, "I love you, Mama," but of course it is only my imagination. How will I ever forget how this was—how he died a little every day? How I let him. Maybe we should never have left Leningrad.

I think I will not be able to bear this pain, but I do. For all of that day and part of the next, I lie with him, holding him as he grows cold. In ordinary times perhaps this wouldn't have been allowed, but these are far from ordinary times. Finally, I ease away from his little body and get up.

As much as I want to lie with him forever, to just slowly starve to death with him, I cannot do it. I made a promise to Sasha.

Live, *he'd said, and I'd agreed.*

So with empty arms and a heart turned to stone, I leave my son there, all by himself, lying dead in a cot by the door, and once again I start to walk. I know that all I will ever have of my son now is a date on the calendar and the stuffed rabbit that is in my suitcase.

I will not tell you what I did to get a seat on the train going east. It doesn't matter anyway. I am not really me. I am this wasted,

white-haired body that cannot rest, although I long just to lie down and close my eyes and give up. The ache of loss is with me always, tempting me to close my eyes.

Anya.

Sasha.

These are the words I cling to, even though sometimes I forget of whom I am even dreaming. From my place on the train, I see the ruined countryside. Bodies in heaps. Scars on the land from falling bombs. Always there is the sound of aircraft and gunfire.

The train moves forward slowly, stopping in several small towns. At each stop, starving people fight to get on board, to be one of the glassy-eyed grimy crowd heading east. There is talk, whispered around me, of heavy fighting in front of us, but I don't listen. Don't care, really. I am too empty to care about much of anything.

And then, miraculously, we arrive at Vologda. When the train doors open, I realize that I did not expect to make it here.

I remember smiling.

Smiling.

I even tuck my hair into my kerchief more tightly so Sasha will not see how old I have become. I clutch the small valise that holds all of my belongings—our belongings—and fight through the crowd to get to the front.

Out in the cold, we disperse quickly; people going this way and that, probably looking for food or friends.

I stand there, feeling the others peel away from me. In the distance, I hear the drone of planes, and I know what it means. We all know what it means. The air-raid alarm sounds and my fellow passengers start to run for cover. I can see people flinging themselves into ditches.

But Sasha is there, not one hundred yards in front of me. I can see that he is holding Anya's hand. Her bright red coat looks like a plump, healthy cardinal against the snow.

I am crying before I take my first step. My feet are swollen and covered with boils, but I don't even notice. I just think, My family, *and run. I want Sasha's arms around me so badly that I don't think.*

Stupid.

I hear the bomb falling too late. Did I think it was my heart, that whistling sound, or my breathing?

Everything explodes at once: the train, the tree beside me, a truck off to the side of the road.

I see Sasha and Anya for a split second and then they are in the air, flying sideways with fire behind them. . . .

When I wake up, I am in a hospital tent. I lie there until my memory resurfaces and then I get up.

All around me is a sea of burned, broken bodies. People are crying and moaning.

It is a moment before I realize that I can see no colors. My hearing is muffled, as if there is cotton in my ears. The side of my face is scraped and cut and bleeding, but I hardly feel it.

The red-orange fire is the last color I will ever see.

"You should not be up," a man says to me. He has the worn look of someone who has seen too much war. His tunic is torn in places.

"My husband," I say, yelling to hear my own voice above the din. There is a ringing in my ears, too. "My daughter. A little girl in a red coat and a man. They were standing . . . the train was bombed . . . I have to find them."

"I'm sorry," he says, and my heart is pounding so hard I can't hear anything past, no survivors . . . just you . . . Here—

I push past him, stumbling from bed to bed, but all I find are strangers.

Outside, it is snowing hard and freezing cold. I do not recognize this place. It is an endless snowy field. The damage done by the blast is covered now in white, though I can see a heap that must be bodies.

Then I see it: a small, dark blot on the snow, lying folded up against the nearest tent.

I would like to say I ran toward it, but I only walk; I don't even see that my feet are bare until the burning cold sets in.

It is her coat. My Anya's coat. Or what is left of it. I cannot see the bright red anymore, but there is her name, written in my own hand, on a scrap of paper pinned to the lapel. The paper is wet and the ink blurred, but it is there. Half of the coat is missing—I do not want to imagine how that happened—one side is simply torn away.

I can see black bloodstains on the pale lining, too.

I hold it to my nose, breathing deeply. I can smell her in the fabric.

Inside the pocket, I find the photograph of her and Leo that I'd sewn into the lining. See? *I'd said to her on the day we'd hidden it—that was back when they were first evacuating the children, it feels like decades ago—*Now your brother will always be with you.

I take the tiny scrap of paper with her name on it and hold it in my hand. How long do I sit there in the snow, stroking my baby's coat, remembering her smile?

Forever.

No one will give me a gun. Every man I ask tells me to calm down, that I will feel better tomorrow.

I should have asked a woman, another mother who had killed one child by moving him and another by letting her go.

Or maybe I am the only one who . . .

Anyway, the pain is unendurable. And I do not want to get better. I deserve to be as unhappy as I am. So I return to my bed, get my boots and coat, and I start walking.

I move like a ghost through the snowy countryside. There are so many other walking dead on the road that no one tries to stop me. When I hear gunfire or bombing, I turn toward it. If my feet hurt less, I would have run.

I find what I am looking for on the eighth day.

It is the front line.

I walk past the Russians, my countrymen, who call out for me and try to stop me.

I pull away, wrenching if I need to, hitting, kicking, and I keep going.

I walk up to the Germans and stand in front of their guns.

"Shoot me," I say, and I close my eyes. I know what they see, what I look like: a crazy, half-dead old woman holding a banged-up valise and a dirty gray stuffed rabbit.

Twenty-six

But I am not a lucky woman," Mom said with a sigh.

Silence followed that last, quietly spoken sentence.

Nina wiped the tears from her eyes and stared at her mother in awe.

How could that pain have been in her all along? How could a person *survive* all that?

Mom stood up quickly. She took a step to the left and stopped; then she turned to the right and stopped. It was as if she'd suddenly awakened from a dream only to find herself in a strange room from which there was no escape. At last, with her shoulders rounded slightly downward, she went to the window and stared outside.

Nina looked at Meredith, who looked as ruined as Nina felt.

"My God," Maksim finally said, turning off the tape recorder. The click sounded harsh in the quiet room, reminded Nina that the story they'd just heard was important not only to their family.

Mom remained where she was, her splayed hand pressed to her chest, as if maybe she thought her heart would stop beating, or tumble right out of her body.

What was she seeing right then? Her once-sparkling Leningrad turned into a frozen, bombed-out wasteland where people died in the street and birds fell from the sky?

Or maybe it was Sasha's face? Or Anya's giggle? Or Leo's last heartbreaking smile?

Nina stared at the woman who had raised her and saw the truth at last.

Her mother was a lioness. A warrior. A woman who'd chosen a life of hell for herself because she wanted to give up and didn't know how.

And with that small understanding came another, bigger one. Nina suddenly saw her own life in focus. All these years, she'd been traveling the world over, looking for her own truth in other women's lives.

But it was here all along, at home, with the one woman she'd never even tried to understand. No wonder Nina had never felt finished, never wanted to publish her photographs of the women. Her quest had always been leading up to this moment, this understanding. She'd been hiding behind the camera, looking through glass, trying to find herself. But how could she? How could any woman know her own story until she knew her mother's?

"They take me prisoner instead," Mom said, still staring out the window.

Nina almost frowned. To her, it felt as if half an hour had passed since Mom's last sentence and this one, but really it had been only minutes. Minutes in which Nina had glimpsed the truth of her own life.

"Prisoner," Mom muttered, shaking her head. "I try to die. Try . . . Always I am too weak to kill myself. . . ." She turned away from the window at last, looked at them. "Your father was one of the American soldiers who liberated the work camp. We were in Germany by then. It was the end of the war. Years later. The first time he spoke to me, I was not even paying attention; I was thinking that if I'd been stronger, my children would have been with me on this day when the camp gates opened, and so when Evan asked me my name, I whispered, *Anya.* I could have taken it back later, but I liked hearing her name every time someone spoke to me. It hurt me, and I welcomed the pain. It was the least of what I deserved. I went with your father—married him—because I wanted to be gone, and he was the only way I had to leave. I never really expected to start over—I was so sick. I expected, hoped, to die. But I did not. And, well . . . how can you not love Evan? There. That is it. Now you know." She reached down for her purse and picked it up, swaying slightly, as if balance were something she had lost in the telling of her story, and started for the door.

Nina was on her feet in an instant. She and Meredith moved in tandem without a word or a look. They bookended Mom, each taking hold of one arm.

At their touch, Mom seemed to stumble harder, almost fall. "You shouldn't—"

"No more telling us what to feel, Mom," Nina said softly.

"No more pushing us away," Meredith said, touching Mom's face, caressing her cheek. "You've lost so much."

Mom made a sound, a little gulp.

"Not us, though," Nina said, feeling tears sting her eyes. "You'll never lose us."

Mom's legs gave out on her. She started to fold like a broken tent, but Nina and Meredith were there, holding her upright. They got Mom back to her chair.

Then they knelt on the floor in front of her, looking up, just as they'd done so often in their lives. But now the story was over, or mostly told, and from here on, it would be a different story anyway. From now on, it would be *their* story.

For all of her life, when Nina had looked at her mother's beautiful face, she'd seen sharp bones and hard eyes and a mouth that never smiled.

Now Nina saw past that. The hard lines were fought for, imposed; a mask over the softness that lay beneath.

"You should hate me," Mom said, shaking her head.

Meredith lifted up just enough to put her hands on Mom's. "We love you."

Mom shuddered, as if an icy wind had just blown past. Tears filled her eyes, and at the sight of them—the first tears Nina had ever seen in her mother's eyes—Nina felt her own tears welling.

"I miss them so much," Mom said, and then she was crying. How long had she held back that simple sentence by force of will, and how must it feel to finally say it?

I miss them.

A few little words.

Everything.

Nina and Meredith rose again, folding Mom into their arms, letting her cry.

Nina learned the feel of her mother then, and realized how much she'd missed by never being held by this remarkable woman.

When Mom finally drew back, her face was ravaged by tears, her hair was askew, and strands were falling across her red-rimmed watery eyes, but she had never looked more beautiful. She was smiling. She put a hand on each of their faces. "*Moya dusha*," she said quietly to each of them.

At Vasily's bedside, Maksim rose and cleared his throat, reminding them that they weren't alone.

"That is one of the most amazing accounts of the siege of Leningrad I've ever heard," he said, taking the tape from the machine. "Stalin kept the lid on it for so long that stories like yours are only lately beginning to surface. This will make a real difference to people, Mrs. Whitson."

"It was for my daughters," Mom said, straightening again.

Nina watched her mother strengthen and she wondered suddenly if all of the Leningrad survivors knew how to harden themselves like that. She supposed so.

"Numbers are difficult, of course, coming out of the government, but conservatively, over one million people died in the siege. More than seven hundred thousand starved to death. You tell their story, too.

Thank you." Maksim started to say something else, but Vasily made a croaking, chirping sound in the bed.

Maksim leaned closer to his father, frowning. "What?" He leaned even closer. "I don't understand. . . ."

"Thank you," Nina said quietly to her mother.

Mom leaned forward, kissed her cheek. "My Ninotchka," she whispered. "Thank *you*. You were the one who wouldn't let go."

Nina should have felt pride at that, especially when she saw Meredith nodding in agreement, but it hurt instead. "I was only thinking about me. As usual. I wanted your story, so I made you talk. I never once worried about how much it could hurt you."

Mom's smile lit up her still-damp eyes. "This is why you matter to the world, Ninotchka. I should have told you this long ago, but I let your father be both our voices. It is yet another of my wrong choices. You shine a light on hard times. This is what your pictures do. You do not let people look away from that which hurts. I am so, so proud of what you do. You saved us."

"You *did*," Meredith agreed. "I would have stopped her story. You got us here."

Nina didn't know until then how a word like *proud* could rock your world, but it rocked hers, and she understood love in a way she hadn't before, the all-consuming way of it.

She knew it would change her life, this understanding of love; she couldn't imagine living without it—without them—again. And she knew, too, that there was more love out there for her, waiting in Atlanta, if only she knew how to reach for it. Maybe tomorrow she would send a telegram, say, *What if I said I didn't want to go to Atlanta? What if I said I wanted a different life than that, a different life than everyone else's, but I wanted it with you? Would you follow me? Would you stay? What if I said I loved you?*

But that would be tomorrow.

"How will I go again?" she said, looking at Meredith and her mom. "How can I leave you both?"

"We don't need to be together to be together," Meredith said.

"Your work is who you are," Mom said. "Love makes room for that. You will just come home more, I hope."

While Nina was trying to figure out what to say to that, Maksim said, "I'm sorry to be rude, but my father is not feeling well."

Mom pulled away from Meredith and Nina and went to the bed.

Nina followed.

Mom stared down at Vasily, his face left lopsided by the stroke; there were tears on his temples and water stained the pillow where they'd fallen. She reached down and touched his face, saying something in Russian.

Nina saw him try to smile and before she knew it, she was thinking of her father. She closed her eyes in prayer for perhaps the first time in her life. Or maybe it wasn't a prayer. Actually, she just thought, *Thanks, Daddy*, and let it go at that. The rest of it, he knew. He'd been listening.

"Here," Maksim said, his frown deepening as he offered Mom a stack of black cassette tapes. "I'm pretty sure he wants you to deliver these to his former student. Phillip Kiselev hasn't worked on this project in years, but he has a lot of the original material. And he's not far from here. Just across the water in Sitka."

"Sitka?" Mom said. "We've already been there. The boat won't be going back."

"Actually," Meredith said, looking at her watch. "The boat left Juneau forty minutes ago. It will be at sea all day tomorrow."

Vasily made a sound. Nina could tell that he was agitated and frustrated by his inability to make himself understood.

"Can he not mail the tapes?" Mom said, and Nina wondered if her mother was afraid to touch them.

"Phillip was his right hand for years in this research. His mother and my father knew each other in Minsk."

Nina looked down at Vasily and thought again of her father and how a little thing could mean so much. "Of course we'll deliver the tapes," she said. "We'll go right now. And we'll have plenty of time to catch up with the boat in Skagway."

Meredith took the stack of tapes and the piece of paper with the address on it. "Thank you, Dr. Adamovich. And Maksim."

"No," Maksim said solemnly. "Thank *you*. I am honored to have met you, Veronika Petrovna Marchenko Whitson."

Mom nodded. She glanced briefly at the stack of black tapes in Meredith's hands and then leaned down to whisper something in Vasily's ear. When she drew back, the old man's eyes were wet. He was trying to smile.

Nina took Mom's arm and led her to the door. By the time they reached the front door, Meredith was at Mom's other side. They emerged three abreast, linked together, into the pale blue light of a late spring day. The rain had stopped, leaving in its wake a world of sparkling, glittering possibility.

They arrived in Sitka at seven-thirty.

"I could be in Los Angeles by now," Nina said as she followed Meredith out of the plane.

"For a world traveler, you complain a lot," Meredith said, leading the way up the dock.

"Remember when she was little?" Mom said to Meredith. "If her socks were wrinkled inside her shoes, she'd just sit down and scream. And if I put too much ketchup on her eggs—or not enough—out would come the lip."

"That is *so* not true," Nina said. "I was the good daughter. You're thinking of Meredith. Remember that fit she threw when you wouldn't let her go to Karie Dovre's slumber party?"

"It was nothing compared to the way you made us all pay when Mom didn't wave good-bye to you before that softball tournament," Meredith said.

Nina stopped in the middle of the dock and looked at Mom. "It was the train," she said. "You couldn't put me on a train and watch it go, could you?"

"I tried to be strong enough," Mom said quietly. "I just couldn't watch . . . that. I knew it hurt you, too. I'm sorry."

Meredith knew that there would be dozens of moments like this between them. Now that they'd begun the reparation process, memories would have to be constantly reinterpreted. Like the day she'd dug up Mom's precious winter garden. It was as if she'd pulled up headstones and thrown them aside. No wonder Mom had gone a little crazy. And no wonder winters had always been difficult.

And the play. Meredith saw it all through the prism of her new understanding. Of course Mom had stopped them from going forward. She and Jeff had been blithely acting out Mom's love story. . . . The pain of that must have been awful.

"No more apologies," Meredith said. "Let's just say it now—once—we're sorry for all the times we hurt each other because we didn't understand. Then we'll let it go. Okay?" She looked at her mom, who nodded, and then at Nina, who nodded, too.

They walked into Sitka and found rooms at a small bed-and-breakfast at the edge of town. From their decks, they could look out over the placid bay, to the green humps of the nearby islands, and all the way to the snowy peak of Mount Edgecumbe. While Nina took a shower, Meredith sat out on the deck, with her feet up on the railing. A lone eagle circled effortlessly above the water, its dark wingspan a sliver coiling around and around above the midnight-blue water.

Meredith closed her eyes and leaned back in her chair. As had been true all day, her mind was a jumble of thoughts and memories and realizations. She was reassessing her childhood, taking the pieces apart, reexamining them in light of her new understanding of her mother. Strangely, the strength she now saw in her mother was becoming a part of Meredith, too. Jeff's comment, *You're like her, you know*, took on a new significance, gave Meredith a new confidence. If there was one thing she'd learned in all of this, it was that life—and love—can be gone any second. When you had it, you needed to hang on with all your strength and savor every second.

The door behind her slid open and clicked shut. She thought at first it was Nina, here to tell her the bathroom was free, but then she smelled the sweet rose scent of Mom's shampoo.

"Hey," Meredith said, smiling. "I thought you'd gone to bed."

"I cannot sleep."

"Maybe it's the color of the night."

"I cannot sleep with the tapes in my room," Mom said, sitting down in the chair beside Meredith.

"You can put them in our room."

Mom coiled her hands together nervously. "I need to give them away tonight."

"Tonight? It's nine-fifteen, Mom."

"*Da.* I asked downstairs. This address is only three blocks away."

Meredith turned in her chair. "You mean this. What's wrong?"

"Honestly? I do not know. I am being silly and old. I know this. But I want to be done with this task."

"I'll call him."

"There is no listing. I called information from my room. We are going to have to just show up. Tonight is best. Tomorrow maybe he will be at work and we'll have to wait."

"With the tapes."

Mom looked at her. "With the tapes," she said quietly, and Meredith saw the vulnerability Mom was trying to hide. And fear; she saw that, too. After all that Mom had been through, somehow holding on to the physical evidence of her life was the thing that had finally scared her.

"Okay," Meredith said. "I'll get Nina. We'll all go." She got up from her chair and started to go back into the room. As she passed Mom, she paused just long enough to put a hand on her mother's shoulder. Through the cable-knit wool of the hand-knit sweater, she felt the angular sharpness of bone.

She couldn't walk past her mother lately without touching her. After so many barren, distant years, that was a miracle in itself. She opened the sliding glass door and went into the small room. Inside, there was a pair of twin beds, both dressed in red and green plaid, with moose-shaped black pillows. On the walls were black and white prints of Sitka's Tlingit past. Nina's bed was unmade already and piled with clothes and camera gear.

Meredith knocked on the bathroom door, got no answer, and went in.

Nina was drying her hair and singing Madonna's "Crazy for You" at the top of her lungs. With her short black hair and perfect skin, she looked about twenty years old.

Meredith tapped her on the shoulder. Nina jumped in surprise and almost dropped the hair dryer. Grinning, she clicked it off and turned. "Way to scare the crap out of me. I need a haircut. Badly. I'm starting to look like Edward Scissorhands."

"Mom wants to drop off the tapes tonight."

"Oh. Okay."

Meredith couldn't help smiling at that. There, in a nutshell, was the difference between them. Nina didn't care what time it was, or that it was rude to stop by without calling first, or that Mom had had a hard day and should be resting.

All Nina heard was a call to adventure, and she always answered that call.

It was a trait Meredith was determined to cultivate.

In less than ten minutes they were on their way, the three of them walking up the sidewalk in the direction the innkeeper had shown them. It still wasn't full-on night; the sky was a deep plum color, with stars everywhere. From here, they looked close enough to touch. A slight breeze whispered through the evergreens, the only real noise out here besides their footsteps on the cement. Somewhere in the distance a boat's foghorn sung out.

The houses on this street were old-fashioned-looking, with porches out front and peaked roofs. The yards were well tended; the smell of roses was heavy in the air, sweetening the tang of the nearby sea.

"This is the house," Meredith said. She'd taken charge of the map.

"The lights are on. That's cool," Nina said.

Mom stood there, staring at the neat white house. Its porch railing was the same ornate fretwork as they had at home, and there was more ornate decor along the eaves. The embellishments gave the place a fairy-tale appearance. "It looks like my grandfather's dacha," Mom said. "Very Russian, and yet American, too."

Nina moved in close to Mom, took her arm. "You sure you want to do this now?"

Mom's answer was to move forward resolutely.

At the door, Mom drew in a deep breath, straightened her shoulders, and knocked hard. Twice.

The door was opened by a short, heavyset man with thick black eyebrows and a gray mustache. If he was surprised to find three unknown women on his doorstep at nine-thirty, he showed no sign. "Hello there," he said.

"Phillip Kiselev?" Mom said, reaching for the bag of tapes in Nina's hand.

"There's a name I haven't heard in a while," he said.

Mom's hand drew back. "You are not Phillip Kiselev?"

"No. No. I'm Gerald Koontz. Phillip was my cousin. He's gone now."

"Oh." Mom frowned. "I am sorry to have bothered you. We have mistaken information."

Meredith looked at the piece of paper in her sister's hand. There was no error in reading. This was the address they'd been given. "Dr. Adamovich must—"

"Vasya?" Gerald's mustached lip flipped into a big, toothy smile. He turned, yelled, "They're friends of Vasya's, honey."

"Not friends, really," Mom said. "We are sorry to have bothered you. We will recheck our information."

Just then a woman came bustling toward them; she was dressed in silky black pants with a flowing tunic blouse. Her curly gray hair was drawn back in a loose ponytail.

"Stacey?" Nina said in surprise. A second later, Meredith recognized their waitress from the Russian restaurant.

"Well, well," Stacey said, smiling brightly. "If it isn't my new Russian friends. Come in, come in." To Gerald she added, "They stopped by the diner the other day. I broke out the caviar."

Gerald grinned. "She must have liked you on the spot."

Nina moved first, pulling Mom along.

"Here, here," Stacey said. "Have a seat. I'll make us some tea and you can tell me how you found me." She led them into a comfortably decorated living room, complete with an ottoman bed and a holy corner, where a trio of candles was burning. She made sure each of them was seated, and then said, "Did Gere say you are friends of Vasily's?"

"Not friends," Mom answered, sitting stiffly.

There was a crash somewhere and Gerald said, "Oops. Grandkids," and ran from the room.

"We're babysitting our son's children this week. I'd forgotten how *busy* they are at that age." Stacey smiled. "I'll be right back with tea." She hurried out of the room.

"Do you think Dr. Adamovich was confused? Or did Maksim get the address wrong?" Meredith said as soon as they were alone.

"Kind of coincidental that these people are Russian and that they knew the doctor," Nina remarked.

Mom stood up so suddenly she hit the coffee table with her shin, but she didn't seem to notice. She walked around the table and across the room, coming to a stop at the holy corner. From here, Meredith could see the usual decorations: an altarlike table, a couple of icons, a family photograph or two, and a few burning votives.

Stacey came back into the living room and set her tray down on the coffee table. She poured the tea and handed Meredith a cup. "Here you go."

"Do you know Dr. Adamovich?" Nina asked.

"I do," Stacey said. "He and my father were great friends. I helped him with a research study for years. Not academic help, of course. Typing, copying. That sort of thing."

"The siege research?" Meredith asked.

"That's right," Stacey said.

"These are tapes," Nina said, indicating the wrinkled paper sack at her feet. "Mom just told her story to Dr. Adamovich and he sent us here."

Stacey paused. "What do you mean, 'her story'?"

"She was in Leningrad then. During the war," Meredith said.

"And he sent you here?" Stacey turned to look at Mom, who stood so still and straight she seemed to be made of marble. "Why would he do that?"

Stacey went to Mom, stood beside her. Again the teacup rattled in its saucer. "Tea?" she asked, looking at Mom's stern profile.

Meredith didn't know why, but she stood up. Beside her, Nina did the same thing.

They came up behind Mom.

Meredith saw what had gotten her mother's attention. There were two framed photographs on the corner table. One was a black and white picture of a young couple. In it, the woman was tall and slim, with jet-black hair and an oversized smile. The man was blond and gorgeous. There were pale white lines that quartered the picture, as if it had been folded for many years.

"Those are my parents," Stacey said slowly. "On their wedding day. My mother was a beautiful woman. Her hair was so soft and black, and her eyes . . . I still remember her eyes. Isn't that funny? They were so blue, with gold . . ."

Mom turned slowly.

Stacey looked into Mom's eyes and the teacup she was holding fell to the hardwood floor, spilling liquid and breaking into pieces.

Stacey's plump hand was shaking as she reached for something on the table, but not once did she look away.

And then she was holding something out to Mom: a small jeweled butterfly.

Mom dropped to her knees on the floor, saying, "Oh, my God . . ."

Meredith wanted to reach out and help her, but she and Nina both stood back.

It was Stacey who knelt in front of her. "I am Anastasia Aleksovna Marchenko Koontz, from Leningrad. Mama? Is it really you?"

Mom drew in a sharp breath and started to cry. "My Anya. . . ."

Meredith's heart felt as if it were breaking apart and swelling and overflowing all at once. Tears were streaming down her face. She thought of all that these two had been through, and all the lost years, and the miracle of this reunion was almost more than she could believe. She moved over to be with Nina. They put their arms around each other and watched their mother come alive. There was no other word for it. It was as if these tears—of joy perhaps for the first time decades—watered her parched soul.

"How?" Mom asked.

"Papa and I woke up on a medical train going east. He was so hurt. . . . Anyway, by the time we got back to Vologda . . . We waited," Stacey said, wiping her eyes. "We never stopped looking."

Mom swallowed hard. Meredith could see how she steeled herself to say, "We?"

Stacey put a hand out.

Mom took it, clutched it, really, hanging on.

Stacey led her through the living room and out a set of French doors. Beyond lay a perfectly tended backyard. The scent of flowers was a sweetness in the air—lilacs and honeysuckle and jasmine. Stacey flipped a switch and a string of lights came on throughout the yard.

That was when Meredith saw the small, squared garden-within-a-garden tucked in the back of the yard. Even from here, with the inconsistent light, she could see an ornate bit of fencing.

She heard her mother say something in Russian, and then they were moving again, all of them, walking down a stone path to a garden that was almost exactly like the one Mom had created at home. A white ironwork fence with ornate curliques and pointed tips framed a patch of ground. Inside was a polished copper bench that faced three granite headstones. There were flowers blooming all around them. Overhead, the sky erupted in amazing, magical color. Darting strands of violet and pink and orange glowed amid all those stars. The northern lights.

Mom sat—collapsed, really—on the copper bench and Stacey sat beside her, holding her hand.

Meredith and Nina stood behind her; each put a hand on Mom's shoulder.

VERONIKA PETROVNA MARCHENKO
1919–
Remember our lime tree in the Summer Garden.
I will meet you there, my love.

LEO ALEKSOVICH MARCHENKO 1938–1942
Our Lion
Gone too soon

But it was the last marker that made Meredith squeeze her mother's shoulder.

ALEKSANDR ANDREYEVICH MARCHENKO
1917–2000
Beloved husband and father

"Last year?" Mom said, turning to Stacey, whose eyes filled with tears.

"He waited his whole life for you," she said. "But his heart just . . . gave out last winter."

Mom closed her eyes and bowed her head.

Meredith couldn't imagine the pain of that, how it must feel to know that the love of your life had been alive and looking for you all these years, only to miss him by months. And yet he was here somehow, in this garden that so matched the one her mother had created.

"He always said he'd be waiting for you in the Summer Garden."

Mom slowly opened her eyes. "Our tree," she said, staring at his marker for a long time. Then, slowly, she did what she always did, what she could do that so few others could: she straightened her back and lifted her chin and managed a smile, wobbly and uncertain as it was. "Come," she said in that magical voice, the one that had changed all their lives in the past weeks. "We will have tea. There is much to talk about. Anya, I would like to introduce you to your sisters. Meredith used to be the organized one and Nina is just a little bit crazy, but we're changing, all of us, and you will change us even more." Mom smiled and if there was a shadow of sadness in her eyes—a memory of the words *I'll meet you there*—it was to be expected, and it was softened by the joy in her voice. And maybe that was how it was supposed to be, how life unfolded when you lived it long enough. Joy and sadness were part of the package; the trick, perhaps, was to let yourself feel all of it, but to hold on to the joy just a little more tightly because you never knew when a strong heart could just give out.

Meredith took her new sister's hand and said, "I am so happy to meet you, Anya. We've heard so much about you. . . ."

No foreign sky protected me,
no stranger's wing shielded my face.
I stand as witness to the common lot,
survivor of that time, that place.

—Anna Akhmatova, from *Poems of Akhmatova*,
translated by Stanley Kunitz, with Max Hayward

Epilogue

2010

Her name is Vera, and she is a poor girl. A nobody.

No one in America can really understand this girl or the place in which she lives. Her beloved Leningrad—Peter's famous Window to the West—is like a dying flower, still beautiful to behold but rotting from within.

Not that Vera knows this yet. She is just a girl, full of big dreams.

Often in the summer, she wakes in the middle of the night, called by some sound she can never recall. At her window, she leans out, seeing all the way to the bridge. In June, when the air smells of limes and new flowers, and the night is as brief as the brush of a butterfly's wing, she can hardly sleep for excitement.

It is belye nochi. *The time of white summer nights when darkness never falls and the streets are never quiet. . . .*

I cannot help smiling as I close this book—my book. After all these years, I have finished my journal. Not a fairy tale, not a pretense; my story, as true as I can tell it. My father would be proud of me. I am a writer at last.

It is my gift to my daughters, although they have given so much more to me, and without them, of course, these words would still be trapped inside, poisoning me from within.

Meredith is at home with Jeff; they are preparing for Jillian's wedding and the plans are all-consuming. Maddy is still at work, managing the four gift shops her mother runs. I have never seen Meredith so happy. These days her schedule is full of things she loves to do, and she and Jeff are often traveling. They say it is to research his novels, which are so successful, but I think they simply love to be together.

Nina is upstairs with her Daniel, whom she has never married but loves more than she realizes. They have followed each other around the world on one amazing adventure after another. Supposedly they are packing now to leave again, but I suspect that they are making love. Good for them.

And Anya—I don't care that she Americanized her name; she will always be Anya to me—is at church with her family. They come down often throughout the year and fill this house with laughter. My eldest daughter and I spend hours together in the kitchen, talking to each other in Russian, remembering the ghosts in the room. In words and looks and smiles, we honor them at last.

I open the journal one last time and write, ***for my children***, in as bold a hand as I can manage at my age. Then I close it and put it aside.

I cannot help closing my eyes. Falling asleep comes easily to me these days, and the room is so warm on this late December day. . . .

I think I hear the sound of a child laughing.

Or maybe that is a leftover sound, the remainder of our Christmas dinner. We are together again this year, all of us, this new version of my family.

I am a lucky woman. I did not always know that, but I do now. With all the mistakes I have made, all the bad and terrible choices, still I am loved in my old age, and, more important perhaps, I love.

I open my eyes, startled by something. Some noise. For a moment

I am confused, uncertain of my surroundings. Then I see the familiar fireplace, the Christmas tree still up in the corner, and the picture of me that hangs above the mantel.

It hangs where once I had a painting of a troika. At first I didn't like Nina's photograph. I look so terribly, terribly sad.

But it has grown on me. It was the beginning of this new life, the time when I finally learned that with love comes forgiveness. It is a famous photograph now; people all over the world have seen it and call me a hero. Ridiculous. It is simply the image of a woman who threw too much of her life away and was lucky enough to get some of it back.

In the corner of the room, my Holy Corner still stands. The candles burn from morning to night; both of my wedding pictures stand upright, reminding me every day that I have been fortunate. Beside the photograph of Anya and Leo, a dirty gray stuffed rabbit sits slumped on his side. Comrade Floppy. His fake fur is matted and he is missing one eye, and sometimes I carry him around with me for comfort.

I stand up. My knees hurt and my feet are swollen, but I do not care. I have never cared about such things. I am a Leningrader. I walk through the quiet kitchen and into the dining room. From here I can see my winter garden, where everything is covered with snow. The sky is the color of burnished copper. Ice and frost dangle like diamond earrings from the eaves above the porch. And I think of my sweet Evan, who saved me when I needed saving and gave me so much. He is the one who so often told me that forgiveness could be mine if I would reach out. I would give anything to have listened to him earlier, but I know he hears me now.

I am barefooted and wearing only a flannel nightgown. If I go outside, Meredith and Nina will worry that I am going crazy again, that I am slipping. Only Anya will understand.

Still, I open the door. The knob turns easily in my hand and cold air hits me so hard that for a beautiful, tragic second, I am back in my beloved city on the Neva.

I walk across the new-fallen snow, feeling it burn and freeze the bottoms of my feet.

I am almost to the garden when he appears. A man, dressed all in black, with golden hair set aglow by the sunlight.

It cannot be him. I know this.

I go to the bench, hold on to its cold black frame.

He moves toward me, gliding almost, moving with an elegance that is new, or that I don't remember. When he draws near, I look up, and stare into the green eyes of the man I've loved for more than seventy years.

Green.

The color takes my breath away and makes me feel young again.

He is real. And here. I can feel his warm presence, and when he touches me, I shiver and sit down.

There are so many things to say, but I can say nothing except his name. "Sasha . . ."

"We've waited," he says, and at the sound of his voice, a shadow peels away from the blackness of his coat and takes its own shape. A smaller version of the man.

"Leo," I say, unable to say more. My arms ache to reach out for my baby boy, to hold him. He looks so healthy and robust, his cheeks pink with life. Then I see that same cheek slack and gray-blue, sheened in frost. I hear him say, *I'm hungry, Mama . . . don't leave me. . . .*

At that, pain uncoils in my chest, making me gasp out loud, but Sasha is there, taking my hand, saying, "Come, my love. To the Summer Garden . . ."

The pain is gone.

I look up into my Sasha's green, green eyes and remember the grass in which we knelt so long ago. It was there that I fell in love. Leo clings to me as he always did, and I scoop him up, laughing, forgetting how I'd once been unable to hold him in my arms.

"Come," Sasha says again, kissing me, and I follow.

I know that if I look back, I will see my body, old and withered, slumped on that bench in the snow, that if I wait, I will hear my daughters discover what has happened and begin to cry.

So I do not look back. I hold on to my Sasha and kiss my lion's throat.

I have waited so, so long for this, to see them again. To feel like this, and I know my girls will be okay now. They are sisters; a family. This is the gift from their father. This is what my story gave them, and in the past ten years, we have loved enough for a lifetime.

I think, *Good-bye, my girls. I love you. I have always loved you.*

And I go.

Acknowledgments

Writing a novel may be a solitary pursuit, but "getting it right" and publishing it well certainly are not. This book, in particular, was helped by many people. First and foremost, I'd like to thank my brilliant editor, Jennifer Enderlin, and the entire St. Martin's team, especially Matthew Shear, Sally Richardson, George Witte, Matt Baldacci, Nancy Trypuc, Anne Marie Tallberg, Lisa Senz, Sarah Goldstein, Kim Ludlum, Mike Storrings, Kathryn Parise, Alison Lazarus, Jeff Capshew, Ken Holland, Tom Siino, Martin Quinn, Steve Kleckner, Merrill Bergenfeld, Astra Berzinskas, John Edwards, Brian Heller, Christine Jaeger, Rob Renzler, the entire Broadway sales force, the entire Fifth Avenue sales force, Sara Goodman, Tahsha Hernandez, and Stephen Lee. Thanks for a great year!

Thanks to Tom Hallman for his work on my beautiful covers.

Thanks also to journalist Sally Sara for her invaluable assistance. Any mistakes are mine alone.

Thanks to Mary Moro for her help on all things related to apples and the Wenatchee Valley.

Thanks to Tom Adams for mentioning Russia one night . . .

Thanks to Megan Chance and Kim Fisk for always knowing when to laugh and when to cry, and for being so quick to tell me to try again.

Read on for an extract of *The Four Winds*
by Kristin Hannah

Available now

ONE

Elsa Wolcott had spent years in enforced solitude, reading fictional adventures and imagining other lives. In her lonely bedroom, surrounded by the novels that had become her friends, she sometimes dared to dream of an adventure of her own, but not often. Her family repeatedly told her that it was the illness she'd survived in childhood that had transformed her life and left it fragile and solitary, and on good days, she believed it.

On bad days, like today, she knew that she had always been an outsider in her own family. They had sensed the lack in her early on, seen that she didn't fit in.

There was a pain that came with constant disapproval; a sense of having lost something unnamed, unknown. Elsa had survived it by being quiet, by not demanding or seeking attention, by accepting that she was loved, but unliked. The hurt had become so commonplace, she rarely noticed it. She knew it had nothing to do with the illness to which her rejection was usually ascribed.

But now, as she sat in the parlor, in her favorite chair, she closed the book in her lap and thought about it. *The Age of Innocence* had awakened something in her, reminded her keenly of the passage of time.

Tomorrow was her birthday.

Twenty-five.

Young by most accounts. An age when men drank bathtub gin and drove recklessly and listened to ragtime music and danced with women who wore headbands and fringed dresses.

For women, it was different.

Hope began to dim for a woman when she turned twenty. By twenty-two, the whispers in town and at church would have begun, the long, sad looks. By twenty-five, the die was cast. An unmarried woman was a spinster. "On the shelf," they called her, shaking heads and *tsk*-ing at her lost opportunities. Usually people wondered *why,* what had turned a perfectly ordinary woman from a good family into a spinster. But in Elsa's case, everyone knew. They must think she was deaf, the way they talked about her. *Poor thing. Skinny as a rake handle. Not nearly as pretty as her sisters.*

Prettiness. Elsa knew that was the crux of it. She was not an attractive woman. On her best day, in her best dress, a stranger might say she was handsome, but never more. She was "too" everything—too tall, too thin, too pale, too unsure of herself.

Elsa had attended both of her sisters' weddings. Neither had asked her to stand with them at the altar, and Elsa understood. At nearly six feet, she was taller than the grooms; she would ruin the photographs, and image was everything to the Wolcotts. Her parents prized it above all else.

It didn't take a genius to look down the road of Elsa's life and see her future. She would stay here, in her parents' house on Rock Road, being cared for by Maria, the maid who'd managed the household forever. Someday, when Maria retired, Elsa would be left to care for her parents, and then, when they were gone, she would be alone.

And what would she have to show for her life? How would her time on this earth be marked? Who would remember her, and for what?

She closed her eyes and let a familiar, long-held dream tiptoe in: She imagined herself living somewhere else. In her own home. She could hear children's laughter. *Her* children.

A life, not merely an existence. That was her dream: a world in which her life and her choices were not defined by the rheumatic fever she'd contracted at fourteen, a life where she uncovered strengths heretofore unknown, where she was judged on more than her appearance.

The front door banged open and her family came stomping into the house. They moved as they always did, in a chattering, laughing knot, her portly father in the lead, red-faced from drink, her two beautiful younger sisters, Charlotte and Suzanna, fanned out like swan wings on either side of him, her elegant mother bringing up the rear, talking to her handsome sons-in-law.

Her father stopped. "Elsa," he said. "Why are you still up?"

"I wanted to talk to you."

"At this hour?" her mother said. "You look flushed. Do you have a fever?"

"I haven't had a fever in years, Mama. You know that." Elsa got to her feet, twisted her hands together, and stared at the family.

Now, she thought. She had to do it. She couldn't lose her nerve again.

"Papa." At first she said it too softly to be heard, so she tried again, actually raising her voice. "Papa."

He looked at her.

"I will be twenty-five tomorrow," Elsa said.

Her mother appeared to be irritated by the reminder. "We know that, Elsa."

"Yes, of course. I merely want to say that I've come to a decision."

That quieted the family.

"I . . . There's a college in Chicago that teaches literature and accepts women. I want to take classes—"

"Elsinore," her father said. "What need is there for you to be educated? You were too ill to finish school as it was. It's a ridiculous idea."

It was difficult to stand there, seeing her failings reflected in so many eyes. *Fight for yourself. Be brave.*

"But, Papa, I am a grown woman. I haven't been sick since I was fourteen. I believe the doctor was . . . hasty in his diagnosis. I'm fine now. Truly. I could become a teacher. Or a writer . . ."

"A writer?" Papa said. "Have you some hidden talent of which we are all unaware?"

His stare cut her down.

"It's possible," she said weakly.

Papa turned to Elsa's mother. "Mrs. Wolcott, give her something to calm her down."

"I'm hardly hysterical, Papa."

Elsa knew it was over. This was not a battle she could win. She was to stay quiet and out of sight, not to go out into the world. "I'm fine. I'll go upstairs."

She turned away from her family, none of whom was looking at her now that the moment had passed. She had vanished from the room somehow, in that way she had of dissolving in place.

She wished she'd never read *The Age of Innocence.* What good came from all this unexpressed longing? She would never fall in love, never have a child of her own.

As she climbed the stairs, she heard music coming from below. They were listening to the new Victrola.

She paused.

Go down, pull up a chair.

She closed her bedroom door sharply, shutting out the sounds from below. She wouldn't be welcomed down there.

In the mirror above her washstand, she saw her own reflection. Her pale face looked as if it had been stretched by unkind hands into a sharp chin point. Her long, corn-silk blond hair was flyaway thin and straight in a time when waves were all the rage. Her mother hadn't allowed her to cut it in the fashion of the day, saying it would look even worse short. Everything about Elsa was colorless, washed out, except for her blue eyes.

She lit her bedside lamp and withdrew one of her most treasured novels from her nightstand.

Memoirs of a Woman of Pleasure.

Elsa climbed into bed and lost herself in the scandalous story, felt a frightening, sinful need to touch herself, and almost gave in. The ache that came with the words was almost unbearable; a physical pain of yearning.

She closed the book, feeling more outcast now than when she'd begun. Restless. Unsatisfied.

If she didn't do something soon, something drastic, her future would look no different from her present. She would stay in this house for all her life, defined day and night by an illness she'd had a decade ago and an unattractiveness that couldn't be changed. She would never know the thrill of a man's touch or the comfort of sharing a bed. She would never hold her own child. Never have a home of her own.

THAT NIGHT, ELSA WAS plagued by longing. By the next morning, she knew she had to do something to change her life.

But what?

Not every woman was beautiful, or even pretty. Others had suffered childhood fevers and gone on to live full lives. The damage done to her heart was all medical conjecture as far as she could tell. Not once had it failed to beat or given her cause for real alarm. She had to believe there was grit in her, even if it had never been tested or revealed. How could anyone know for sure? She had never been allowed to run or play or dance. She'd been forced to quit school at fourteen, so she'd never had a beau. She'd spent the bulk of her life in her own room, reading fictional adventures, making up stories, finishing her education on her own.

There had to be opportunities out there, but where would she find them?

The library. Books held the answer to every question.

She made her bed and went to the washstand and combed her waist-length blond hair into a deep side part and braided it, then dressed in a plain navy-blue crepe dress, silk stockings, and black heels. A cloche, kid gloves, and a handbag completed her outfit.

She went down the stairs, grateful that her mother was still asleep at this early morning hour. Mama didn't like Elsa exerting herself except for Sunday church services, at which Mama always asked the congregation to pray for Elsa's health. Elsa drank a cup of coffee and headed out into the sunshine of a mid-May morning.

The Texas Panhandle town of Dalhart stretched out in front of her, wakening beneath a bright sun. Up and down the wooden boardwalks, doors opened, CLOSED signs were turned around. Beyond town, beneath an immense blue sky, the flat Great Plains stretched forever, a sea of prosperous farmland.

Dalhart was the county seat, and these were booming economic times. Ever since the train had been routed through here on its way from Kansas to New Mexico, Dalhart had expanded. A new water tower dominated the skyline. The Great War had turned these acres into a gold mine of wheat and corn. *Wheat will win the war!* was a phrase that still filled the farmers with pride. They had done their part.

The tractor had come along in time to make life easier, and good crop years—rain and high prices—had allowed farmers to plow more land and grow more wheat. The drought of 1908, long talked about by old-timers, had been all but forgotten. Rain had fallen steadily for years, making everyone in town rich, none more so than her father, who took both cash and notes for the farm equipment he sold.

Farmers gathered this morning outside the diner to talk about crop prices, and women herded their children to school. Only a few years ago, there had been horse-and-buggies in the streets; now automobiles chugged their way into the golden, glowing future, horns honking, smoke billowing. Dalhart was a town—fast becoming a city—of box suppers and square dances and Sunday morning services. Hard work and like-minded people creating good lives from the soil.

Elsa stepped up onto the boardwalk that ran alongside Main Street. The boards beneath her feet gave a little with each step, made her feel as if she were bouncing. A few flower boxes hung from stores' eaves, adding splashes of much-needed color. The town's Beautification League tended them with care. She passed the savings and loan and the new Ford dealership. It still amazed her that a person could go to a store, pick out an automobile, and drive it home the same day.

Beside her, the mercantile opened its doors and the proprietor, Mr. Hurst, stepped out, holding a broom. He was wearing shirtsleeves rolled up to expose his beefy forearms. A nose like a fire hydrant, squat and round, dominated his ruddy face. He was one of the richest men in town. He owned the mercantile, the diner, the ice-cream counter, and the apothecary. Only the Wolcotts had been in town longer. They, too, were third-generation Texans, and proud of it. Elsa's beloved grandfather, Walter, had called himself a Texas Ranger until the day he died.

"Hey, Miss Wolcott," the storekeeper said, pushing the few strands of hair he still had away from his florid face. "What a beautiful day it's looking to be. You headed to the library?"

"I am," she answered. "Where else?"

"I have some new red silk in. Tell your sisters. It would make a fine dress."

Elsa stopped.

Red silk.

She had never worn red silk. "Show me. Please."

"Ah! Of course. You could surprise them with it."

Mr. Hurst bustled her into the store. Everywhere Elsa looked, she saw color: boxes full of peas and strawberries, stacks of lavender soap, each bar wrapped in tissue paper, bags of flour and sugar, jars of pickles.

He led her past sets of china and silverware and folded multicolored tablecloths and aprons, to a stack of fabrics. He rifled through, pulled out a folded length of ruby-red silk.

Elsa took off her kid gloves, laid them aside, and reached for the silk. She had never touched anything so soft. And today *was* her birthday. . . .

"With Charlotte's coloring—"

"I'll take it," Elsa said. Had she put a slightly rude emphasis on *I'll*? Yes. She must have. Mr. Hurst was eyeing her strangely.

Mr. Hurst wrapped the fabric in brown paper and secured it with twine and handed it to her.

Elsa was just about to leave when she saw a beaded, glittery silver headband. It was exactly the sort of thing the Countess Olenska might wear in *The Age of Innocence.*

ELSA WALKED HOME FROM the library with the brown-paper-wrapped red silk held tightly to her chest.

She opened the ornate black scrolled gate and stepped into her mother's world—a garden that was clipped and contained and smelled of jasmine and roses. At the end of a hedged path stood the large Wolcott home, built just after the Civil War by her grandfather for the woman he loved.

Elsa still missed her grandfather every day. He had been a blustery man, given to drink and arguing, but what he'd loved, he'd loved with abandon. He'd grieved the loss of his wife for years. He'd been the only Wolcott besides Elsa who loved reading, and he'd frequently taken her side in family disagreements. *Don't worry about dying, Elsa. Worry about not living. Be brave.*

No one had said anything like that to her since his death, and she missed him all the time. His stories about the lawless early years in

Texas, in Laredo and Dallas and Austin and out on the Great Plains, were the best of her memories.

He would have told her to buy the red silk for sure.

Mama looked up from her roses, tipped her new sunbonnet back, and said, "Elsa. Where have you been?"

"Library."

"You should have let Papa drive you. The walk is too much for you."

"I'm fine, Mama."

Honestly. It sometimes seemed they wanted her to be ill.

Elsa tightened her hold on the package of silk.

"Go lie down. It's going to get hot. Ask Maria to make you some lemonade." Mama went back to cutting her flowers, dropping them into her woven basket.

Elsa walked to the front door, stepping into the home's shadowy interior. On days that promised to be hot, all the shades were drawn. In this part of the state, that meant a lot of dark-interiored days. Closing the door behind her, she heard Maria in the kitchen, singing to herself in Spanish.

Elsa slipped through the house and went up the stairs to her bedroom. There, she unwrapped the brown paper and stared down at the vibrant ruby-red silk. She couldn't help but touch it. The softness soothed her, somehow, reminded her of the ribbon she'd held as a child when she sucked her thumb.

Could she do it, do this wild thing that was suddenly in her mind? It started with her appearance. . . .

Be brave.

Elsa grabbed a handful of her waist-length hair and cut it off at the chin. She felt a little crazed but kept cutting until she stood with long strands of pale-blond hair scattered at her feet.

A knock at the door startled Elsa so badly that she dropped the scissors. They clattered onto the dresser.

The door opened. Her mother walked into the room, saw Elsa's butchered hair, and stopped. "What have you done?"

"I wanted—"

"You can't leave the house until it grows out. What would people say?"

"Young women are wearing bobs, Mother."

"Not nice young women, Elsinore. I will bring you a hat."

"I just wanted to be pretty," Elsa said.

The pity in her mother's eyes was more than Elsa could bear.

THE NIGHTINGALE

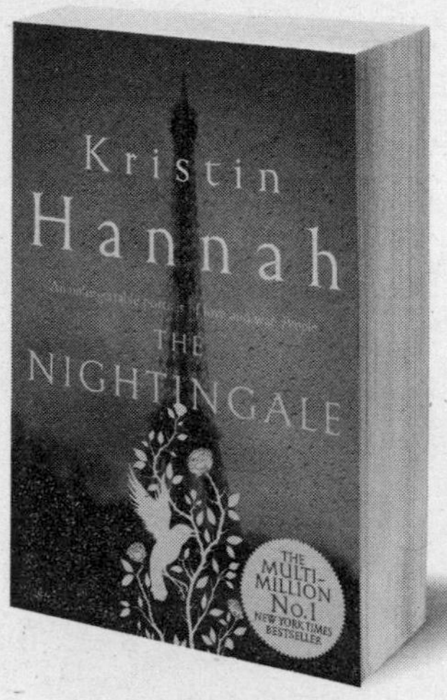

The multi-award-winning novel that has captured the hearts of millions of readers across the world – soon to be a major motion picture starring Elle and Dakota Fanning – *The Nightingale* is a heartbreakingly beautiful story that celebrates the resilience of the human spirit and the strength of women.

With courage, grace and powerful insight, Kristin Hannah captures the epic panorama of World War II and illuminates an intimate part of history seldom seen: the women's war. *The Nightingale* tells of two sisters, separated by years and experience, by ideals, passion and circumstance, each embarking on her own dangerous path toward survival, love and freedom in German-occupied, war-torn France.

The Nightingale is a novel for everyone.
A novel for a lifetime.

THE GREAT ALONE

An international number one bestseller and award winner, *The Great Alone* is a daring, beautiful, stay-up-all-night story of love, loss, the wild unpredictability of nature and the fragility of the human spirit.

With her trademark combination of elegant prose and deeply drawn characters, Kristin Hannah again celebrates the remarkable strength of women. A desperate family seeks a new beginning in the near-isolated wilderness of Alaska, only to find that their unpredictable environment is less threatening than the erratic behaviour found in human nature.

'A rich, compelling novel of love, sacrifice and survival, as epic as the Alaskan landscape it so vividly describes'
Kate Morton

'A masterclass'
Karen Swan

FIREFLY LANE

A *New York Times* number one bestseller, and now the number one Netflix series returns with season two.

A story of best friends forever and more than a coming-of-age novel, *Firefly Lane* is about a generation of women who were both blessed and cursed by choices. It's about promises and secrets and betrayals. And ultimately, about the one person who really, truly knows you – and knows what has the power to hurt you – and heal you.

For thirty years, Tully and Kate buoy each other through life, weathering the storms of friendship, jealousy, anger, hurt and resentment. They think they've survived it all until a single act of betrayal tears them apart . . . and puts their courage and friendship to the ultimate test.

Firefly Lane is a story you'll never forget . . . one you'll want to pass on to your best friend.